# Previous Praise for D.F. Bailey

*Fire Eyes*

"*Fire Eyes* is a taut psychological thriller with literary overtones, a very contemporary terrorist romance."

—*Globe and Mail.*

"To put it simply, there is some very good writing here."

—*Alberta Report*

*Healing the Dead*

"The author is not afraid to take a hard look at the darker side of human nature, at the source of fear and violence, and to explore their repercussions with unflinching honesty."

—*Monday Magazine*

D.F. Bailey writes with "unusual power ... and obvious talent." He is "becoming a player in the international arena."

—*Quill & Quire Magazine*

"You start reading *Healing the Dead* with a gasp and never get a proper chance to exhale."

—*Globe and Mail.*

Other novels by D.F. Bailey:

*Fire Eyes*
*Healing the Dead*

*To Iam*

[signature: D.F. Bailey]

# THE GOOD LIE

a novel

D.F. Bailey

TURNSTONE PRESS

The Good Lie
copyright © D.F. Bailey 2007

Turnstone Press
Artspace Building
018-100 Arthur Street
Winnipeg, MB
R3B 1H3 Canada
www.TurnstonePress.com

Turnstone Press gratefully acknowledges the assistance of the Canada
Council for the Arts, the Manitoba Arts Council, the Government of
Canada through the Book Publishing Industry Development Program, and
the Government of Manitoba through the Department of Culture, Heritage
and Tourism, Arts Branch, for our publishing activities.

Canada Council    Conseil des Arts        MANITOBA ARTS COUNCIL
for the Arts      du Canada               CONSEIL DES ARTS DU MANITOBA
                                          YEARS/ANS

Canadä

Cover design: Jamis Paulson
Interior design: Sharon Caseburg
Cover image: Larry Wells
Printed and bound in Canada by Friesens for Turnstone Press.

Library and Archives Canada Cataloguing in Publication

Bailey, D. F. (Donald Frederick), 1950-

    The good lie / D.F. Bailey.

ISBN 978-0-88801-329-3

    I. Title.

PS8553.A363G66 2007      C813'.54      C2007-905699-7

*For Adam and Lauren*

"In this profession you see everything. The thieves, the cokeheads, the pimps and prostitutes—of course they lie. Everybody expects them to lie. But sometimes, the good lie, too."

—Ben Stillwell

# THE GOOD LIE

# CHAPTER 1

A T FIRST THE KAYAK PADDLE FEELS AWKWARD IN HIS HANDS. The twin blades require a double twist for every stroke. He lifts one wrist overhand to plane the right blade through the air and plunges the opposite end under the water with a hard downward sweep. Within ten minutes Paul Wakefield has mastered the form well enough to paddle around the marina bay—although he's still doubtful about crossing the strait to Discovery Island.

"You're doin' fine," Brad calls from his kayak, a narrow-hulled custom-built boat designed for speed and maneuverability on the ocean waters.

"Yeah. Feels good," Paul calls back, suspicious that Brad's encouragement is simply intended to keep his most nervous kayaking students moving forward. But Brad Reedshaw's cheerleading appeals to the six adolescents in the class. His appeal is further established by the Patagonia rowing shirt which reveals his substantial biceps as he paddles from kayak to kayak to prompt the group of novices about their technique. His muscles expand and tighten with every stroke and his straight, red hair flags behind his ears in the light breeze. The waters cleave before him as he slices across the bay to Reg and Fran Jensen, the only other adults beside Paul in the class. Their fleet is composed of seven boats including Brad's: four single-seaters and three doubles.

Paul sets his paddle on the gunnel and lets his kayak drift toward the open water. He likes the silence of the little craft as it glides over the flat surface. A sense of timelessness envelops him. If he points the boat toward the southern tip of Discovery Island, the horizon opens into a completely natural vista. No buildings, no towers, no roads, no other watercraft are visible anywhere. It would have been like this ten thousand years ago when the first native explorers paddled out to sea to hunt the whales and sea lions. The same silence. The same slate-coloured water, the same fog leaning against the shoreline. The chalky snow peaks on the Olympic Mountains would have looked just as cold. And the raw stink of seaweed bulbs stacked against the foreshore rocks on Jimmy Chicken Island would have smelled as putrid. Yes, it would be just like this, the past and present identical. Identical except for the language in his mind—his voice assuring him, explaining the world around him. To be human without a sense of language, that would be truly primitive. The first people would have had a vocabulary of sounds and grunts, possibly a few hundred words that another person might understand. Perhaps the words for whale and fog. But they would have no word for panic, no phrase for death by drowning.

"Okay, is everybody ready?" Brad has pulled everyone together, the kayaks rafted up in pairs with the paddlers gripping one another's gunnels. "This is how you should raft up in rough water or a storm," he says facing the line of students. "Even in a rough sea you can avoid a dump if you're rafted up."

They bob and roll over the easy chop. Paul is in a single kayak braced against Reg Jensen's boat. Reg and Fran started the morning together in a double, but split up after their daughter, Jenny, decided she wanted to be with her mother on the voyage across the strait to Discovery Island. Paul could tell she was nervous despite her young bravado. Parents can read these things. Jenny was thirteen or fourteen, he decided, seven or eight years older than his own son, Eliot.

"Okay. We're goin' to paddle out to the other side of Jimmy Chicken Island," Brad says, shifting his gaze from one student to another. "Once we get out there we'll raft up like this and take a reading with the compass and establish a visual route to Tod Rock and Discovery Island." He nods with confidence. It's a simple, complete plan. "Okay, let's go."

The pairs release the gunnels and the kayaks drift a little while the paddlers establish some control. Within a minute the seven boats are moving in unison through the sea.

"Valerie couldn't make it today?" Reg Jensen asks as he gently paddles his kayak beside Paul. Reg has some canoeing experience and it's apparent that he knows how to direct his craft, at least in calm waters like this.

"She came down with the flu on Wednesday," Paul says and frowns. Granted, he would have had more fun with his wife here, but he decided to come alone. Besides, he didn't want to miss the final session of the class: the day trip across Plumper Passage, the picnic lunch and, most important, boasting rights back home with his son.

"Flu's starting the go-round." Reg pumps steadily with his paddle. He emits a sense of manic energy as though he could do this for hours without rest. "I think Jen-Jen's picked up something. This morning she was hacking and snivelling," he says with a laugh. "But we can't keep her down." He executes two quick strokes to turn his bow a few degrees right.

"I guess," Paul says and looks away. There's a hint in Reg's voice that Valerie can't tolerate a little chill and simply wimped out of the trip. More bravado. Why does he have to put up with that on a beautiful day like this?

"Mom! Stop it!"

Paul and Reg look around to Jenny and Fran Jensen in the second double kayak. Sitting in the bow, Jenny has drawn her paddle. With her free hand she brushes the drizzle of water from her shoulders. "Stop splashing me!" she orders with a snarl.

"I'm sorry," her mother apologizes and dips her paddle in the water.

"Just be more careful."

Paul turns his head to the islands and continues stroking until he's ahead of Reg and the open, untouched water fills the horizon again.

As they approach the flashing beacon on Tod Rock the sea begins to swell. Everyone realizes how different these waters are compared to the calm pool in the marina bay. During their evening classes Brad explained how the currents run up and down Baynes Channel, around the south end of Vancouver Island and through the Juan de Fuca Strait to the Pacific. When the tides and currents are in synch a vast flushing motion drags the ocean around the archipelago for hundreds of kilometres in one cycle. Since the water never settles, it always runs cold.

If you capsize, hypothermia becomes a serious hazard after five minutes. The cold leaches the heat from your arms and legs, then from your head and finally from your internal organs. You can't grip the side of your boat. You have to think to make your arms work and soon you can't think at all. Somewhere in your bones you have memorized a plan to right the kayak, hoist yourself aboard, bail the water from the cockpit, get to shore and restore the heat to your body. As soon as you tip, you have to activate the plan. If you haven't started to right the kayak within two minutes, you're in trouble. That's why everyone paddles in pairs. The buddy system ensures a helping hand is in place as the cold begins to draw the warmth from your being.

Paul tried to assimilate these possibilities as the class practised righting their kayaks in the community centre swimming pool. He dumped five or six times and by the end of the evening he could slip out of the cockpit clutching his paddle in one hand, then right the kayak and, with his buddy stabilizing the boat on the opposite side, clamber aboard and paddle to the edge of the pool. Yet despite his mastery of technique, he couldn't imagine the chill that awaited him if he capsized at sea. It would be cold, that's all you could say. Too cold.

"Okay." Brad calls everyone's attention to the distant shoreline of Discovery Island. "It doesn't look far, but you all know it's a good hour's paddle—non-stop." A rolling wave dips under the fleet of boats, lifting and dropping each in sequence. Two of the teenagers let out a cry of excitement. "So what's your call on the weather?" Brad asks as though forecasting is part of the class test.

"Fresh breeze is supposed to drop to a calm," Fran Jensen says from the rear cockpit of her double.

"With dropping barometric pressure," Paul adds. "Might even start raining."

"What's new?" Brad laughs and with the length of his paddle points to a low bank of fog south of the island. "What about that fog?"

"Ah, that's nothing," Jenny Jensen calls out and her friends cry again as another wave drops beneath them.

"No? Well, take a bearing on the island as we paddle toward it. If the fog moves our way, stay behind me and I'll take us in with the compass." He leans forward and makes a mental note of the reading from the floating compass ball that's strapped to the bow of his kayak.

Paul is impressed by Brad's array of navigational and safety equipment. In addition to the on-deck compass he has a barometer, binoculars, a portable bullhorn, several flares and flare guns, tissue-thin thermal blankets, a portable receiver tuned to the marine forecast and a cell phone. Most of these supplies are wrapped in waterproof sleeves that have double-locking seals. You can spend a lot of money on these gadgets and Brad has spared nothing to ensure his kayaking school has purchased the best. In the morning Paul felt somewhat reassured as he watched Brad load this equipment into his boat. For backup, Paul brought along his office cell phone which lies sealed in a zip-lock baggie tucked into the inside pocket of his rain jacket.

"Okay. Everybody ready?" Brad calls out.

"Charge!" one of the boys yells from the second double.

As the boats pull into the channel, Paul paddles to the north side of the fleet and begins the rhythmic stroking he'd practised in the bay. Dip, twist, dip, turn. The dream-like work comes easily and he listens to the sound of the water slipping from his paddle and thinks, this is a sound that has always been, always will be.

After an hour they cross the channel and begin to navigate the shore-line of Discovery Island. The tide is up and Brad leads them south on a course that slips above dozens of tidal pools that are stocked with star fish, crabs, anemones, and thousands of blue-shelled mussels wedged together on the sides of the black rocks.

Paul scans the basin as they float above the aquaria—the beauty of the pools almost eerie with abundance. Looking back he measures the length they have paddled, a distance difficult to gauge, he realizes, because of the low fog hovering above the water as it creeps up from the Juan de Fuca Strait. Still, he can make out a few of the urban rooftops between the budding oak and maple trees that rise above the Oak Bay shoreline. A few pleasure craft are cruising toward the marina, with their wealth of polished deck hardware gleaming even in this opaque light. Paul reassures himself that he will never purchase such a boat, even if it is within his means. Kayaking would definitely be the way to go. One hour in the open water and he's realized how perfect it is. How quiet and muscular, how completely integrated with the sea life around them.

"We'll round that next point and pull in for lunch," Brad calls out and pulls his craft to the left in two hard strokes. He carefully leads the boats in single file through the shoals and past the rock outcrops that thrust above the surface as the waves dip beneath the hulls. Paul is content to bring up the rear, stroking easily behind Jenny and her mother. By the time he rounds the point, Brad has already hauled his boat onto a grey pebble beach that stretches a hundred metres south. At the far end a stony outcrop is littered with cut timbers that have broken free from the log booms towed back and forth through the strait by the Sea Span tugboats.

Paul beaches his kayak and ties the bow to an end of driftwood. Then he sorts through his backpack, hauls out his lunch bag and wanders over to Reg and Brad, who are already halfway through their meal.

"Not bad," Paul says as he squats beside them on a flat log parallel to the shore. "Paddling like that really sets up an appetite."

"Yeah, but sitting here sets up a chill. What do you say we make a fire?" Reg rubs his hands together as if he's already warming them above the low flames.

"Can't," Brad says flatly. "Remember the fire a few years ago over on Chatham Island? Some morons burnt all the north end scrub away. After that the wild goats came down with disease and the SPCA had to shoot them. All of them."

"Right ... I forgot about that." Reg stuffs his hands in his pockets and tucks his chin into the scruff of his windbreaker. He watches his wife and daughter struggle with their boat as they tug it out of the water. "You've almost got it," he yells and turns away from them. "Yeah, I guess the Indians were a bit pissed about that fire."

"The Songhees." Brad lowers his voice. "And I don't think 'pissed' quite captures their reaction. Over fifty animals were slaughtered. Up 'til then their islands had been open to anyone who wanted to camp there. Now, forget it." He spits onto a log and bites into his sandwich.

Paul watches the tension rise between the two men, an uneven edge he hadn't noticed before. He opens his lunch bag and pours some hot tea from his Thermos. Reg pulls himself up from the log, scuffs a foot against the loose pebbles and walks toward his wife and daughter. Paul eats his sandwich in silence and listens to the seagulls cawing overhead. They've already discovered the picnickers and the prospect of scavenging a free lunch.

"How long before we get back into the kayaks?" Paul blows the steam from the top of his mug and sips at his tea.

"Maybe an hour." Brad tips his head toward the teenagers who yank Jenny's double kayak out of the water and set it next to his own. "That'll give the members of our local mosh pit a chance to run themselves ragged." He leans back on the log and weaves his fingers into the mat of red hair at the back of his head. "You may want to take a stroll around the point down there. There's an old pioneer home built by a Brit sea captain in the early 1900s. It's gone to ruin now, but worth a look to see how he laid the thing out. If you're interested," he adds, as though it's not his habit to lay on unsolicited advice.

Paul and Brad watch Reg instruct his wife and Jenny in the intricacies of tying the kayak to a beached log.

"Good lord," Brad whispers.

Paul tries to laugh but nothing more than a light moan escapes his lips. "I think I'll take that hike," he says and slips his mug, lunch bag and Thermos back into his pack. "Don't let me forget this." He cinches the pack cord and props the bag on top of a log.

"Okay." Brad keeps his eyes fixed on the group maneuvering around the double kayak. "Be back by one-thirty. I want to catch the next tide."

Of course, the tides rule all, Paul tells himself as he sets off to the south point. It's nice to have to think this way. Aligning your movements with lunar forces. He sets his track just above the tide line, across a slope of oval stones covered by a narrow strip of dried green seaweed deposited by the surf during the winter tides. His feet crunch through the nut-sized pebbles that roll under his weight. Every step is heavy and unsure, as though there's no foundation under the mass of stones blanketing the beach. This whole day is about buoyancy, he realizes. Even on dry land you've got to account for gravity and the tides.


The pioneer ruins have dissolved to little more than a few sunken timbers which mark the foundation of a four-room home that once commanded a view over the Juan de Fuca Strait. The old captain would have seen every ship moving from the Vancouver-Seattle corridor en route to San Francisco. But the past hundred years of rain and salt have dissolved most of the evidence of human habitation. The only remains of this sentry post are these rotten footings and Brad's two-sentence history of a recluse. Soon they too will disappear.

It was a fool's paradise, Paul concludes as he steps through the entryway and scans the slope down to the beach. No one could live on this flat, rocky island for long, even today. Yet he could understand the desire to anchor yourself here: the freedom found in isolation, the passing whales and sea lions, the abundance of fresh fish. But this small utopia had perished in the salty soil, the constant exposure, the madness of solitude. He walks down to the beach and finds two logs butted together and aligned with the shoreline. He settles onto the smaller log and rests his back against the larger. It's a well-designed sofa and in spite of the hard, splintered wood he swings his legs up and stretches his feet over the edge. Almost as good as his La-z-boy back home.

He checks his watch and thinks of Valerie and decides to call her. He unzips his rain jacket pocket and extracts the cell phone from the plastic baggie. She would certainly be out of bed by now, even if her flu had taken a turn for the worse. Eliot would see to that. He'd be digging through his Construx blocks, asking for lunch, wanting a story.

Valerie answers on the third ring and he can tell immediately that she's not well. "Oh hi," she says, feigning enthusiasm when she hears his voice. "How's Discovery Island?"

"Very spongy."

"Spongy?"

"Yeah. All the rocks fall underfoot when you walk along the beach. I can't imagine living here." He describes the captain's house—its disintegration in the rain and salt spray. "But it's very beautiful. Right now I'm sitting on the shore looking down the Juan de Fuca. You'd love the view."

"I'm sorry I missed it." He can hear her wiping her nose with a tissue. "Especially since it was your birthday present and everything."

"Don't worry. It's nothing." He shakes his head and considers the dreary irony: Valerie had bought them both kayaking lessons for his thirty-eighth birthday so they could get away for a few hours together.

"But I was supposed to paddle with you."

"Next time. So how's Eliot?" he asks, certain that one of them should change the subject.

"We've read chapters ten and eleven of *The Odyssey*. And he's built a tower to hold my box of Kleenex. Want to speak to him?"

"Sure." He can hear her calling to him and then her hand muffles the mouthpiece during a sneeze.

"Hi, Dad."

"What's shakin', Eliot?"

"You should see the skyscraper I built."

"I hear it's holding up Mom's Kleenex."

"How many pieces of Construx do you think it has?"

"Uhm … two hundred and fourteen."

"Nope. Three hundred and twenty-six."

"You counted?"

"Every piece." Eliot begins a detailed description of the tower, the elaborate construction method he employed to achieve its balance and extension. When he's finished he asks, "Where are you?"

"On an island. Not too far from home, but far enough away that you can't see me."

"Are there any Trojans?"

"Not that I've noticed."

"Are you a prisoner?"

"No. Just visiting." He smiles and adds, "I got a visitor's pass."

"Oh," he says and without another word hands the phone to his mother.

"He just discovered an adjustment he needs to make to the CN Tower here," she says and then pauses. "So I got a call from Mom and Dad."

"Oh yeah." Paul fixes his gaze on two freighters pushing out to the Pacific, their hulls low in the water, likely loaded with coal or wood destined for Japan.

"So they're coming down for Easter dinner."

"Think you'll feel better by then?"

"It's three weeks away—if I don't, I'm going to overdose on Tylenol."

"I hope so. That you're feeling better, I mean." It's time to hang up, he thinks. The call has reminded them both that their plan to get away together has failed and now the mention of her parents' pending visit dissolves the prospect of stolen intimacy during the holiday weekend. "So I'll see you around five, I guess."

"Okay." She pauses again. "So did you get my note?"

"What note?"

"In your lunch."

"My lunch? I didn't see any note." The two freighters slide into the approaching fog. He watches them disappear. One gone, then the other.

"In your lunch bag. Have a look," she says and lowers her voice. "It's a very hot note."

He smiles at this. "I thought you had a cold."

"The flu. But hey, come on," she begs him. "At least let me try to fake it with you. For once."

"All right. Just this once." They fall into an easy, familiar laughter—a good moment to sign off and continue the passage through their parallel worlds.

When Paul rounds the point he sees two of the kayaks already launched in the water. The other boats are being readied and everyone is engaged in preparations. He checks his watch: 1:15; he's fifteen minutes early.

"I thought we should push off a little early," Brad says as Paul approaches. "We were listening to the weather forecast. Seems like a regional low is sinking in just offshore." He holds his transceiver aloft as if to verify the forecast, then carefully seals it in its waterproof sleeve. "Besides, that fog bank keeps rolling up the strait. It'd be nice to beat it back to the marina."

"Need a hand packing up?" Paul looks around and realizes most of the gear has been stowed.

"Nope. Just get yourself into your boat and onto the bay. Once we're all afloat I'll guide us to the Chain Islets and back to the marina through the south entrance." He tosses his pack into the fore storage compartment of his kayak and seals it tight. "By the way, I put your lunch pack into your cockpit."

"Thanks." Paul walks to his boat and begins to pull on his spray skirt. Reg and Fran Jensen have just pushed off the beach in one of the two-seaters. They've switched positions with their daughter, who now floats in Reg's single in the middle of the bay, where she trades paddle splashes with one of the girls.

"Got everything?" Brad asks. He's just about to shove off the shore.

"I guess." Paul slips into his gumboots and pulls his boat from the beach. The kayak is so buoyant it floats in ankle-deep water. Perfect, Paul thinks as he straddles the cockpit with his paddle and then slides his legs into the boat. I'm actually getting good at this.

He straps the spray skirt over the combing and slips into the same feeling of immersion that he'd felt paddling across the channel in the morning. The womb-like security of the kayak: everything tucked away, sealed and dry from the surrounding ocean. All he needs now is to paddle ahead, float through the channel and home. He makes his first few strokes thinking of this—kayaking as a metaphor of birth—then realizes that it's false, that language itself is a false witness to experience. Better to paddle and simply lose yourself in the sensations of the rolling water and your muscles working into an easy, repetitive hypnosis.

The group establishes a v-formation and as the seven boats leave the bay Paul glances back to the beach. A flock of seagulls fights over a paper bag the teenagers have left behind, their squawking brash and unintelligent. The island was raw and windswept but not truly beautiful. To be beautiful a thing should nourish its beholder. The failure of the captain's pioneer home left a scar on the place. Even though that blemish had almost disappeared, the island had not healed.

As they near the Chain Islets Paul can barely make out the squirming mass of sea lions on top of the broken rockery. They are well camouflaged. Their mottled grey coats are flecked with tawny markings that blend perfectly with the granite rock face and the bits of scrub and lichen crooked into the rough fissures running down to the water. In total there are perhaps twenty small outcroppings, or islets, and three or four of them appear to be slowly writhing as the kayak flotilla approaches.

Killer whales, Brad had told them, were the only predator that concerned the sea lions. But whenever kayakers came into their limited view, their concern erupted into panic. From their myopic perspective each boat hull looks like a killer whale drifting along the surface—the paddler, a knifing dorsal fin—the mark of impending doom. The sea lions understood the hazards presented by an orca pod as it approached: likely one or two males awaited the lions on the far side of the rocks, prepared for their bellowing alarm, the flight of the young calves and mature cows—and their inevitable slaughter. Now, as the boats ease closer to the rocks the unmistakable sight of seven killer whales moving up from Hecate Passage inspires near pandemonium.

"Don't get too close," Brad calls when they draw near enough to see one of the male lions dashing back and forth across the highest rock, pushing the cows and calves off the far edge into the water. "That bull will come straight at us if you frighten him enough."

"Let's try it!" one of the boys calls and splashes his paddle toward them. He turns and smiles, his mouth riveted with metal braces.

"Try it and you'll have me to deal with!" Brad yells and in five strokes he pulls next to the boy and grips his paddle.

"Okay," the boy cries and turns his face away.

The bull fakes a series of charges toward them. He's careful to hold his ground at the shore, but his black eyes are full of blind fury. Paul has never seen an animal in such extreme panic. It's clear his next instinct will be to throw himself at the kayaks. The huge bulk of the lion is on full display as he charges up and down the rock face. In an instant his bellowing lifts a flock of birds on the surrounding islets. The air fills with their screaming.

Brad locks the boy's paddle in his fist. "Reg, head up to the north side of the rocks," he calls.

"You bet." Reg and his wife begin to paddle to the right. "Jenny, let's go," he says to his daughter in order to establish some authority over the teenagers.

Slowly the boats regroup. Once the other craft begin to follow Reg, Brad releases the boy's paddle without a word and the two boats fix a course around the islets. Paul trails behind them, reluctant to leave the sea lions so quickly. But when he looks back he can see no trace of the animals. All that remains of the drama are the barren rocks and the hundreds of birds whirling silently overhead, their sharp cries now forgotten. These are separate worlds, he realizes, one in the air and the other immersed and invisible beneath him. And he inhabits a third sphere, one out of place here, a world in transit.

They paddle the next twenty minutes in silence, Paul trailing the group, happy to linger and maintain the slow, crawling pace of a long-distance swimmer. The fog has become a thick, low wall sliding along the southeast shore of Vancouver Island. Every few minutes another yacht cruises toward the marina, slipping into the mist and then disappearing quite suddenly, as if a grey curtain has fallen over the boat and extinguished its existence. Brad was right to hurry them along. In an hour the whole coast will be shrouded in fog. Their pace picks up a little, faster but without urgency and noticeable only in the shoulders. Minutes later, the sea eases to a low, rolling swell and the boats slide onto a blanket of floating seaweed: thick cords knotted together in a ten-metre patch buoyed above the sea.

"Let's raft up," Brad says and the kayakers quickly align themselves in a parallel formation and lock their paddles together. "If you find yourself in a rough sea, you can raft up and weather almost any condition. Especially if you can find a kelp bed like this to set under your kayaks."

Everyone is amazed by the sturdy seaweed platform. It looks thick enough to walk across. Jenny begins jabbing at it with her paddle, testing its buoyancy.

Reg and Fran seem pleased that Brad has re-established his control over the teenagers and Fran passes a bag of trail mix along the row of kayaks. The paddlers scoop a handful into their mouths and quietly chew on the raisins and nuts while Brad continues his lesson.

"Looks like we may have to navigate by instrument," he says as they gaze at the shoreline. The entrance to the marina is invisible now and the fog has obscured the foreshore of Jimmy Chicken Island. "Once we get into the mist it'll be really important to stay in visual contact with the boat directly ahead of you. I'll be in the front. Then Allison, Aaron and Jess, okay?" he waits for the boys to acknowledge the plan. "Then Reg, you and Fran follow next and then Laura, Mark and Jen-Jen. Jess and Jen: are you all right paddling on your own?" They look at one another and nod silently. "Paul, are you okay bringing up the rear?"

"Love the rear," Paul says and winks at Brad.

"Just make sure nobody falls behind you." He tags Paul with a serious look.

"No problem."

"All right. Now if you lose visual contact, then stay in voice contact. If you need to, just blow on your whistle." He lifts the whistle pinned to his life vest and gives it a half-blast. "But before it comes to that I'll get you all singing—and you don't want hear me do that," he laughs. "Okay, let's go while I can still see my deck compass."

After a moment of confusion the boaters release their hold on their gunnels and struggle over the kelp bed onto the open water. Within minutes they form a single line behind Brad, a half metre apart in unbroken sequence.

Paul dutifully takes up his position as rear admiral, fascinated by the group's unseasoned discipline. Perhaps a taste of fear has inspired their new morale. They had the sea lions to thank for that. But no one is ever grateful for fear until it passes, and Paul wonders if the lions knew how lucky they were or if they'd already forgotten their terror and returned to the rocks to sleep out the rest of this grey day.


As they paddle toward the marina another yacht cruises past them and slips into the fog. He's going pretty fast, Paul thinks and then he hears the engine throttle back to a near idle in the distance.

"Okay, here we go," Brad calls out as they penetrate the sheets of fog. Within ten strokes they enter a new world, this one blind, silent, claustrophobic. "Can everybody see the boat ahead of them?"

"Yup."

"No problem." The confirmations echo up the line.

"All right, let me hear you sing it: *Row, row, row your boat ...*"

Within a few bars everyone is singing. After two verses, someone breaks into a round. Then another round breaks away and suddenly they are all singing in overlapping harmonies. Paul is impressed. They actually sound pretty good and their voices cast a dull echo in the fog. For a moment he thinks about the acoustics of mist and realizes that something is wrong with what he hears: the fog should dampen their voices, not reflect them. As he puzzles with this problem the red stern of Jenny's kayak disappears, then appears and disappears again. It's a gentle fading of perception, a cinematic effect.

The singing falters and Brad calls out across the fleet. "All right, close up so you're right on the kayak ahead of you. Don't worry if you're touching. Just take her steady as she goes."

The stern of Jenny's kayak glides back into view. "Is that you, Jen-Jen?" Paul asks.

"Yeah. It's thick, isn't it?" Her voice is much softer than Paul expected, soft and tremulous. Then she adds, "I don't see Laura and Mark's kayak."

"Are you sure?" Paul paddles two hard strokes and pulls beside Jenny. Indeed, there's no sign of the double kayak anywhere. He realizes that Jenny may have been paddling blind for some time now and leading the two of them away from the others. "When did you last see them?"

She shakes her head without speaking. A band of fog moves between them and for a moment Paul cannot see the bow of his own boat. "Where's everybody else?" she asks softly.

"Just ahead of us," Paul reassures her and then calls out. "Brad? Give us a voice check. Jenny and I need to regroup."

"Right over here." Brad's voice is clear, but farther away than Paul would like. "We're going to raft up and wait for you right here."

"Jen-Jen?" Reg calls through the fog to his daughter. "Are you with Paul?"

"Yes, Daddy."

"You just stay with him, okay?"

Jenny lifts her paddle in the air. Her posture freezes and then loosens slightly. "Okay," she says and dips one end of the paddle into the water.

"We're fine, Reg," Paul says. "We're rafted up here. No troubles."

"Paul, just stay with Jenny and begin paddling toward the sound of our voices. Mark, Aaron, give us a verse—*row, row, row your boat.*" The singing begins again and immediately breaks into two rounds. "Okay, I've also got a flashlight going. Paul, can you see it?"

Paul can see nothing. But he's sure their voices are coming from his starboard bow. With a little concentration, they should be able to paddle alongside the others in a minute or two.

"I can see the light," Jenny says.

"Where?"

"Back there." She points past her stern with the paddle tip; the exact opposite direction from the singers.

A dim orb is apparent behind them. Paul considers this new mystery: how can the voices call from starboard, yet the flashlight beckon from port? He stares at the light. After a moment he realizes the intensity of the beam is growing as the light approaches them. When he hears the low drone of an engine chugging forward, the light fades into the mist.

"A powerboat," he whispers under his breath.

The boys continue their singing. "*Merrily, merrily, merrily ...*"

"What?" Jenny's voice is high, alert.

"Brad, I think there's a powerboat coming through." Paul can hear an edge in his own voice. "Coming this way," he adds with forced calm when he's certain of the engine's position.

"Raft up and stay together." Brad's words become part of the fog: vapourous and disembodied.

The boat engine throttles back and Paul can see the lamp, or more likely a searchlight, scanning back and forth in a narrow sweep ahead of the boat.

" ... *Life is but a dream* ... "

Paul grips the combing on Jenny's kayak. "Just hold on." He cannot see her face; she's turned toward the sound and light of the approaching ship. It's coming in very slowly. Paul imagines it has some kind of radar that has already detected them.

"They're going to hit us!" she cries.

"No, they won't." Paul tries to establish the vector of the boat as the light sweeps toward them. If it continues in a straight line, the cruiser might just glance off Jenny's kayak. In that case, he'll grab her and pull her onto the hull of his own kayak. That should work, he tells himself. Just don't say anything to her until the time comes. She might get wet, but she'll be okay.

As they wait in the shroud of fog, the search lamp seems to lift in the air as it approaches. When the yacht is finally visible, Paul can barely breathe; the bridge rises at least three metres above him. He gasps as the kayaks disappear under the shadow of the ship's hull and they spill into the ocean.

As he breaks the surface, the water seems to freeze on his face and around his ears. He sucks in a lungful of air and paws the salt from his eyes.

"Help!" he screams and some sea water gutters down his throat. He spits it out and calls again. "Brad!"

He hears the boat engine moving away, the sound of water lapping his ears, and Jenny calling frantically.

"Help!" she cries.

She's right beside him; her flailing arms shake Paul's body. He realizes he's still holding his paddle. This was part of the survival training. He remembers he must find the kayak. He reaches out and there it is, the hull overturned, almost within reach. He kicks with both feet. One, two, three and he is there. He's at the boat and the frozen fingers of his free hand grip the thin keel and establish a hold.

"Jenny," he calls and swallows another mouthful of water.

"Help. Help me!"

She swims behind him and wraps both arms over his life jacket and around his neck.

"Stop." His head dips under the water as she climbs onto his shoulders and he inhales the sea water through his nose. There's a moment when he thinks he will die. Then he forces his head back to the surface and vomits the water from this throat. "Back off!" he yells when she straddles his back again.

"Help!"

Paul still holds the paddle in his right hand. His fingers release the kayak and he butts her shoulder with his forearm. Jenny falls beside him. Her face dips into the water and her arms begin flailing back toward him.

"Jenny, grab the kayak," he tells her. His voice is firm and he knows now he's thinking straight. "Just work with me and we'll right the boat and climb in."

His voice seems to calm her, but when he looks into her eyes they appear inhuman. In one move she climbs onto his back once more and he can feel her tugging at his life jacket. He releases the boat again and tries to shove her away but her fingers claw at his face in panic. Paul turns his chest away from the boat and lifts the paddle from the water. In one heave he swings it over his shoulder and feels the wood smack into the side of her skull. The impact makes no noise at all, at least nothing he can hear. At first he thinks he must have missed her, but at the same time, Jenny's fingers relax and she slumps into the water and drifts behind him.

"Oh God," he moans. He drops the paddle and swims toward her. He reaches her in two strokes and cradles her head against his chest. The kayak drifts away. He grips her life jacket ring in his fist and swims with one hand toward the boat. Five, seven, ten strokes, yet he cannot pull them any closer. The cold begins to enter his chest. He releases Jenny's life vest and kicks towards the kayak. He cannot hear the boat engine any more. He cannot hear Brad calling his name or the sound of the others' voices muffled in the fog. Only the icy voice of the water is speaking. It whispers a secret chant, murmurs a prayer from the ocean's heart, a message that fades into silence.

# CHAPTER 2

AUL WAKEFIELD RESTS COMFORTABLY IN HIS BROWN LEATHER LA-Z-
BOY, HIS HEAD CUSHIONED BY THE HEADREST. He opens his eyes
and stares through the window past the crabapple tree to the
white stucco bungalow on the other side of Transit Road.

Two unfamiliar cars are parked next to the Meekers' house but
they are dated models, and too small to serve as unmarked squad
cars. Besides, there'll be no need for secrecy during the arrest. More
likely the television crews will be on hand to witness his apprehen-
sion. His public humiliation will be a necessary part of the procedure: he must be seen to be a criminal. So will begin the first install-
ment of his punishment, a down payment on the long mortgage of
his redemption.

The arrival of a single cop at his door would signify that Paul has
merely been summoned to the station; perhaps an appointment will
be set for sometime next week. But the appearance of two officers
certainly implies that he must immediately accompany them to some
hidden interrogation room. Negotiation would be unthinkable; he'd
be cuffed and dunked into the back seat of their car. Maybe he'd

have time to scratch a note to Valerie: "Police taking me down to the station. Get a lawyer."

He listens for the sound of car tires crunching the gravel in his driveway, but he hears nothing other than the slight ringing in his ears, the buzz of his consciousness alert to its own being. This alone has become his companion in the past few days, a muse feeding the anxieties that fill his stomach. But the greatest, most gnawing anxiety centres on the timing of his arrest. Will the police come today? Tomorrow? Next week? The moments slip from his mind like drops of water spilling into a chasm. None returns a sound or echo. Their existence is lost the instant they appear and slide from his being.


A steady knocking at the front door rouses Paul from his nap. His dread returns instantly. He moans softly, leans toward the window from his chair and pulls the office drape to one side to check for police cruisers. Only one car remains parked on the roadside, a red Dodge 500. He checks his watch: 11:30. Typical of his pattern lately, a night-long bout of insomnia followed by a fitful morning snooze. In another half-hour he'll drive to the school and pick up Eliot from his grade one class, escort him home and prepare two peanut butter and banana sandwiches—Eliot's favourite.

The knocking comes firmly again, without hesitation. Paul makes his way to the front door and pauses. There's no other noise, no hint that anyone attends him on the other side. He's beginning to suspect that some of the sounds he's heard in the past few days have been imaginary. Especially the faint noises that pass in and out of his auditory range, submerged or uncovered by the surf ringing in his ears. He stands uneasily, listening to the pattern of his own breathing. After another inhalation, two knocks strike the wood door.

Paul opens it at once. In front of him, his face turned to one side, stands Reg Jensen. Paul steps backward and then his head dips forward as though he's been struck in the chin. "Reg?" He smiles as if to suggest his memory of their acquaintance is very dim, perhaps many years old.

"Yes." Reg tilts one hand slightly and shrugs. "So. You are here," he says as though he were answering a question.

"Yes. Of course I'm here." Paul steps forward again, reclaiming his lost ground. He has a sense that he should invite Reg inside, but he decides to stall and encourage the possibility that this visit will be momentary, a polite exchange concluded with a handshake.

"I've been sitting out in my car there for a little while," Reg says and points to his Dodge. He plants his hands in his pockets as though this statement is a kind of conclusion, a final analysis of their common tragedy.

"I didn't know...."

"Since about 11:00 or so," he adds. He pulls a hand from his pocket and draws it forward from the bald patch on the crown of his head and across his eyes. "I.... " He shrugs and turns his face away. "I was just thinking about Jenny. Fran and I were talking about Jenny and what must have happened out there last week. Fact is, we can't talk about anything else."

"Is Fran in the car?" Paul cranes his neck to look at the Dodge. If they're going to talk he would sooner speak to Reg alone.

"No. No, I just came by myself." Reg shuffles one foot ahead of the other and then back into position. "Look, I just drove over without even knowing if I would knock on your door."

Paul nods.

"Without even knowing ... if you'd be home."

"Well—guess you lucked out," Paul says and attempts to smile. "We both are, I mean."

Reg stares along the front porch with a vacancy that nearly overwhelms Paul. Any talk of Reg's "luck" is caustic. Paul can sense the word burning through Reg Jensen's belly. "Look, can I invite you in for a coffee?" He realizes their talk has already grown painful. "I've got to pick up my son from school in twenty minutes. But that's time enough for some coffee, right?"

"Sure." Reg follows Paul into the house. They walk down the hallway, a corridor lined with paintings and illuminated by a row of skylights. Paul and Valerie think of the hallway as their personal art gallery. It was the most extravagant aspect of the renovation they'd finished two years ago. They both loved art and they wanted to display their fondness for beautiful objects. Everyone who entered the home walked through the gallery to the kitchen or down the stairs to the living room. Valerie called it "the art-way," a wonderful passage she'd designed to please their friends, old and new.

"So you've got the one son?" Reg settles into a chair in the breakfast nook and watches Paul nurse the boiling kettle, then pour two cups of coffee.

"Yes. He's six years old. Just started grade one this year." Paul considers asking if Jenny is also an only child but he decides to keep the focus on Eliot. "He goes to Monterey Elementary. Just a few blocks over." He crooks his thumb in the direction of the school and pours the coffee.

"I've heard of it." Reg adds some milk and sugar to his mug and gives it a half stir. "Jenny goes to Shoreline Secondary."

Paul is heartened by this news. At least he's thinking in the present tense. "I hear it's a good school."

"Got its good points and bad, just like everything else." Reg cocks his chin to dismiss the idea and when he does, Paul can make out a scar cut along the underside of his jaw. It looks like someone ran a corkscrew into his throat, then gave it a good twist. He'd noticed it before—during their Wednesday evening kayak lessons—but never had it appeared so vivid as it did now.

"I guess," he says and averts his eyes from Reg. He realizes that it was a mistake to bring him into his home. The uneasy silence is broken only by their sipping at the coffees.

"Look," Reg says and cups his palm over his eyes as though he's shading them from the sun. "Fran and I've just been sick—"

"I'm sure—"

"Just ... just let me finish." He moves his hand as though he's bringing a line of traffic to a halt and lifts his head slightly. "We're sitting by Jenny's bed almost every waking hour. Fran does nothing but pray she'll come out of that coma."

Paul looks at him and waits. Just let him get it all out and then maybe they can talk. Like parents. Like two fathers who have found the same pleasure in raising their children.

"The doctors are giving us some hope but both of us know the longer she's under the less likely it is she'll come out."

Paul nods and gazes at the floor. Every day when he called the ward nurse to inquire if Jenny had snapped out of the coma, he'd worried that the delay could prove fatal. God, what a mess—somehow it was worse than death. If he'd had the strength to hit the girl harder neither of them would be here now trying to talk through the lingering pain of the accident. The only conceivable blessing in this horror was that no one except Paul knew exactly what he'd done.


Reg struggles through the next ten minutes describing their lives over the past few days. The ambulance speeding from the marina through the city to the hospital. The contained panic in the emergency ward. The rush to provide her with life support systems, the efficiency of the respiratory team, the consultations with the pediatric specialists. Finally, when she was deemed "stable," the following days were consumed with the vigil at Jenny's side, testing the warmth in her hand, trying to detect a shift in her condition and what it might portend. When Reg concludes his monologue he looks at Paul and says now they're faced with only two questions: how did this all happen and when will it end?

"Wish I knew," Paul says. "I haven't slept one night this week. All I can ask myself is what went wrong."

"Can you tell me," Reg asks, holding Paul with his eyes, "what you remember after we went into that fog?"

"I don't know." Paul stares past the kitchen at one of the paintings on the hallway wall, one of Jack Wise's mandalas. "Since I came out of the water I haven't been able to think very clearly about it."

Reg nods his head. For the first time he's the person shouldering the empathy between them. Paul is surprised that Reg has any sympathetic capacity at all; it adds a little more substance to his assessment of the man. "It's going to take me a bit more time to sort it out."

"But do you think you could?"

"What?"

"Sort it all out. It would mean a lot to Fran and me." Reg pauses and then gazes at Paul in a way that holds him with his eyes. "Look

... we're just sitting in that hospital and we don't know what ... really happened."

Paul rubs his fist against his chin. "It was the other boat. It was the yacht that capsized us, right?" And then what I did, he thinks.

"Yeah." Reg leans back in his chair and tilts his head. The scar under his chin is the colour of a ripe plum. "I heard the police are trying to track it down through the marina records."

"I guess they are." Paul glances at his wristwatch. It's near time to get Eliot. "Look, I've got to pick up my son." He stands up and clutches both coffee cups in one hand and sets them in the sink.

"I suppose you do," Reg says and follows him through the kitchen. He pauses a moment in the hallway to examine the mandala. "There's a lot of detail there that you don't notice from a distance."

"That's a Jack Wise: his *Rainbow Mandala*. He gave it to me." Paul is always pleased to tell people about his brief relationship with Wise. This time, however, he's more pleased to see Reg break the obsession with his daughter. "It's the only mandala he ever painted that isn't bordered by a ring of fire." He's fascinated by this painting, the way the concentric circles float above the aquamarine surface, then thrust inward to their own internal physics.

"Mmm." Reg considers the painting another moment, walks down the hallway to the front door and then turns back to Paul. "So can we count on you to see both of us?"

"Sorry?"

"To meet with Fran and me."

Paul nods and opens the door. "Of course." He owes them that much. Even though he knows it could push him over the edge, he'll find the strength to tell them something they can live with. Or something they can let their daughter die with.


"Too bad we have to meet them in the hospital of all places." Valerie wipes her nose with a tissue; she's suffering from another bout of sneezing, the remnants of her recent illness. "They'd be a lot more comfortable if they could come to our house." She checks the vanity mirror under the Volvo's sun visor and tries to dab away some of the weariness in her eyes.

"I guess one of them stays here all the time," Paul says and he sets the emergency brake with a short tug. They're parked on a slight incline and he doesn't want the car to roll away as it once did during their first trip to San Francisco. No more accidents, he tells himself.

"Well." She presses her lips together and looks at him. "Are you going to be okay?"

"I don't know." He stares through the window at the Victoria General Hospital parking lot and tries to decide if it is half-full or half-empty. "I really don't."

Valerie leans over and pulls his hand into her own. "Ah, sweetie. You tried so hard to save her. I'm sure they know that."

"I don't know that they do."

Valerie sighs and glances away. "Well, we'll give them a half hour. After that I'll say we have to go back and relieve the babysitter."

They make their way into the hospital, up the elevator to the third floor and along the corridor leading to the nursing station. Valerie asks where they can find the Jensens and they're guided to a small day room with well-worn furniture and a view overlooking the woods on the west side of the building. Apart from two sofas, three chairs and a TV, the room is vacant. A bank of fluorescent lights illuminates the room and casts a bright glow on the linoleum tiles. Everything appears—smells—freshly scrubbed. Paul stands next to the window and looks for signs of the scores of rabbits that are said to wander freely about the property. After a minute he realizes it's too dark to see anything, let alone rabbits. In fact, he can barely make out the trees a few metres away. He takes this as a danger signal, a tip that his expectations and reality are not aligned. "Best to beware," he whispers to himself and he sits next to Valerie in one of the sofas opposite the TV.

"What'd you say?"

Paul closes his eyes. "Nothing." He would like to cancel this meeting, to leave with a brief apology and go home to Eliot. As he rehearses a few words of regret there's a knock at the door. It eases open and the Jensens walk into the room towing a third person behind them.

"This is my cousin, Sam Watson. He just dropped by to see Jenny," Fran says and she sits on the sofa opposite Valerie.

Although the women met at the kayaking school they'd exchanged no more than a few words over the month-long course. Valerie claimed she felt no chemistry with Fran. "I can't figure out who she thinks she is," she told Paul after the first class. "And somehow who she thinks she is, is more important than who she is." Looking at Fran now, Valerie can say nothing—or think of anything that might change the past.

Paul stumbles forward through the silence. "I'm Paul," he says and shakes Sam's hand and everyone settles onto the two sofas. "So how's Jenny doing today?" He casts a glance at Reg who turns his head away.

After a pause in which neither Reg nor Fran can form a response, Sam perches both arms on his knees and says, "I guess the same. Have you seen her?"

"No. We came to visit once but the duty nurse said we didn't have any privileges. Not being family members," Paul adds and tries to ease his shoulders against the sofa. This is starting badly. Here he is trying to offer them some kind of comfort, yet they can barely tolerate him mentioning Jenny's name. "I've been calling in every day. All they'll tell me is there's no change."

"I'd like you all to know that in spite of what's happened to Jenny," Valerie says, "and we can imagine it's been ... well, just horrible—that this hasn't been easy on Paul, either."

Paul feels his back compressing against the sofa. He's reached a point where he can either sit here immobile, and say nothing—simply let Valerie provide a series of excusable maladies that will rationalize his silence—or dive straight into their formal agenda. As he ponders this choice he can feel a bitterness bubbling through his stomach and his sense of caution dissipates. All of this happened to him, too. They had to fish him out of the ocean too, damn it. He realizes this idea, this small footnote to their tragedy, might make a good starting point. They should understand that—before they condemn him simply because he survived.

"They got Jenny out before me," he says. He's surprised by the weakness in his voice and pauses to clear his throat. "Before I could even tell who was pulling us out of the water."

"That was Brad," Reg says. Paul looks at him and for the first time they briefly establish eye contact. "Brad left us all rafted up and paddled over to you on his own."

Paul nods. Maybe that was how it happened: Brad was alone and pulled both of them from the water. "First, he got Jenny out and onto the bow of his boat. Then he slung me up behind the cockpit."

"Other way around," Fran says. "You were on the front. She was on the back."

Paul casts his eyes to the floor and his certainty dissolves.

"No, I think Paul's right on that point," Reg says in a low voice that carries a note of condescension.

For a moment Paul suspects the Jensens could start into an argument. In some ways that would be better than having to review the events leading up to the rescue. Perhaps the rescue itself is all that's important. "You have to understand I was in the water for a long time," he continues. "I'm really not sure what happened once we dumped."

"I think Reg and Fran were wanting to know what happened before that; what precipitated the accident," Sam says. His voice is dispassionate. Weathered, like his greying hair.

*Precipitated.* Paul steeples his fingers together over the bridge of his nose and considers the implications of this word: rain, snow, sleet, hail—all of it spat out of the sky. "Even that's pretty foggy," he says as if he's answering a question posed long ago.

Valerie slips her hand onto Paul's knee and gently squeezes. "He hasn't even been able to tell me," she says and daubs her nose with a Kleenex.

There's another pause in which everyone studies Paul's fingers braced against his forehead. "Anything ... would be a help," Sam says.

"There was the boat," Paul says and drops his hands into his lap. "It came through the fog right at us. Up along Jenny's side. God, it must have been six metres above us." His voice is free of anxiety now and he feels like he can tell them something—what, he has no

31

idea. "It had a search light sweeping ahead of it, but I guess it didn't pick us out. Did you see it?"

"No. But we could hear it." Reg looks to Fran for confirmation. She nods once and stares at Paul.

He assumed everyone knew about the search light. Their mutual denial of this small detail reveals how isolated he and Jenny were. He alone can tell this story and any *facts* are conjectural, deniable, fictive—whatever he wants to make them. Knowing this he feels more confident. Yes, he should tell them what they want to hear. What he'd practised and recited over the past two days.

"There was nothing to suggest we were in trouble at all," he begins. "Not at first, anyway. When I realized that Jenny had lost track of the boat ahead of her I had some concern. But we could hear you singing, so we knew you were up ahead even if we couldn't see you."

"What do you mean by 'Jenny lost track of the boat'?" Again, Sam is the chief inquisitor. Apparently he's a seasoned collector of facts. Fran and Reg sit beside him, their eyes cast to the floor as Paul continues.

"That's the way Brad had us navigate through the fog. Each boat tagging behind him and so on down the line. He had me bring up the rear behind Jenny." Paul remembers Brad's exact instructions now and feels heartened to have this small assurance in his grasp.

"Yeah, that's how it was," Reg says. "It made a lot of sense."

"At the time," his wife adds with some doubt. "Maybe."

Sam Watson waves his hand; a slight, dismissive signal intended to shut down comments from the Jensens. He returns his gaze to Paul and in a low voice encourages him to continue: "Please, go on."

Paul settles his back into the sofa. Valerie rests her hand on his knee again and tips her head slightly, a gesture suggesting that he can continue now. This is the time that everyone will listen and perhaps hear the truth about what happened. But as he speaks, Paul realizes how false his words are to their shared experience. Worse still is the gnawing conviction that his memory is unable to capture the events of that day, that ten-minute episode in which everything in their lives flipped upside down. He is left with words alone, a story that explains how they've come to sit together in this room, a testament that their daughter was not at fault, or better still, how she discovered an inner strength in her last few minutes of consciousness.

He decides to alter things slightly. He tells them that once they were in the water, Paul began to flounder badly and it was Jenny who pulled him by his life jacket toward the kayak. God knows how, but she found the strength to drag them both to the overturned boat. Then as they clung to the hull, he realized that Jenny had stopped shivering; somehow she'd lost her grip and slipped away from the kayak. He could see her floating a few feet away, her eyes half-open, staring blankly ahead. Paul called to her and when she didn't respond, he called to Brad again and again. Then he remembered the whistle and pulled it between his teeth and began blowing with every breath he possessed. He felt so cold. He could feel parts of his body hardening, as though his internal organs were lumping together. He was certain his lungs and stomach were turning to ice.

Apart from the memory of being hauled onto Brad's kayak, he had no idea of what else happened to them in the water. His next recollections were of the ambulance racing to the hospital, the hypothermia treatments, then Valerie and Eliot hugging him, crying and laughing together. But in his narrative to the Jensens he omits the details of his reunion and celebration with his family. His last words recall his simple dread: "I was so cold." He stares at the floor, amazed that he's survived to describe it. "I'd never felt cold like that. Never."

The room is quiet except for Fran's light sobbing. She has a tissue pressed to her eyes and Reg examines her and frowns. "Thank you," Fran murmurs but she cannot look at Paul.

"Tell me something," Sam says and he leans forward slightly. "You say that Jenny pulled you from the open water to the kayak."

Paul looks at Sam and nods. "Yes, I think so."

"Can you tell me what might have caused the heavy bruising on her temple?" His hand traces a path between his right eye and ear.

Paul looks at the wall. All of his talking seems useless at this point; Sam, the fact-collector, is less interested in his story than detailed conjecture. He can feel Valerie's hand squeeze his thigh and then release as she pulls it away. What can he say that will confirm his innocence—yet explain the blow to her skull?

"The doctors are suggesting that the concussion is the cause of her coma," Sam adds.

"It must have been when the boat hit us," Paul says with a shrug. "The boat came at us from her side."

"If the boat hit her as you capsized, Mr. Wakeman," he continues, "hit her hard enough to cause a concussion and likely sent her into a coma, then how—how can you explain her ability to rescue both of you?"

There is a brief silence, then Valerie turns to face Sam. "Excuse me," she says and narrows her eyes, "but ... are you a lawyer?"

Sam eases back into the sofa. After a moment he says, "I'm here as a member of the family."

Valerie purses her lips and inches forward. "I asked you a question: are you a lawyer?"

Another pause. "No. I'm a forensic accountant."

"Well you're bloody well behaving like a lawyer. I can't believe this." Valerie stands and shoves her purse under one arm. "Come on, Paul," she says and wheels around to address Fran and Reg. "This is disgusting. We came here to help you. Not to submit to a third-degree interrogation."

Paul pulls himself out of the chair. It's taken a moment to understand what Valerie is talking about.

"If you think you'll get another word from us, then think again," she says and leads Paul to the door.

As they leave the room, Paul can hear Sam Watson offering a piece of advice: "I suggest you talk to your lawyer. We'll likely be filing a suit."

Unable to contain herself, Valerie wheels back into the dayroom. "Yeah, well after this episode, maybe *you'll* need one!" Then feeling an unbearable itching that runs the length of her nasal passage, she takes a deep breath and sneezes.

"It's entrapment, pure and simple." Although she's plumped her pillow and nestled herself into her customary place in their bed, Valerie is still angry. Furious. "Do they have any idea what this accident has done to *us*? What it takes to relive *their* tragedy?"

Paul is staring at the ceiling, at the moonlight cast through the semi-circular window above their bed. The window was his idea, along with the cathedral ceiling in their redesigned bedroom. The entire home renovation, including the front hallway (their glorious gallery), Eliot's bedroom addition, the marble-and-maplewood kitchen update, the aggregate stone patio and yard landscaping—all were delivered six months late, twenty-five thousand dollars over budget and somewhat sub-standard in construction. Still, Paul liked what they'd done to their house and often he'd stand at a strategic location, the kitchen entry, for instance, and look at his surroundings. It pleased him. As did this cloudless night view through the elevated window during the fullest phase of the moon.

"Don't you think you should phone Ben?" She props herself on an elbow and looks at Paul's face.

"Yes, I told you I will in the morning." His voice is desultory; the thought of bringing Ben Stillwell and his team of lawyers into his growing nightmare is almost more troubling than the nightmare itself. Nonetheless, he can understand Valerie's concern. He's been sinking into the possibilities of his legal problems for several days now, whereas Valerie's just awakening to the disaster rising around them. It's as though she's finally been dumped into the water, too. "Don't worry. It'll all work out."

"Don't worry?" She stares at him as though she's penetrating his being. "How can you lie there after what they did to us tonight?"

"What am I supposed to do?" He looks at her eyes, then back at the ceiling. "I was trying to comfort them. You know that. How was I supposed to know Watson's a forensic accountant?"

She purses her lips. "He's probably given court testimony a hundred times. I don't think they can use what you said against you. Not in those circumstances. Not without him coming forward and saying, 'I know how these things work and everything you say can and will be used against you.' " She smiles weakly, dismayed by this feeble cliché.

Paul glances away from the window and then turns his head on the pillow to face her. He looks at her breasts, lovely and full under her nightie. He sighs. "Why should we think anything can be used against me? What incriminating statements did I make?"

She eases her head back into the pillow and slips her arm under Paul's neck. "I don't know," she admits. "Maybe I'm just paranoid." Her voice is resigned; as though she's finally releasing her fear and suspicion.

"Yeah." He breathes in the comfort of her presence and places a hand on her breast. "Yeah, that's how I've been feeling, too."

"It's just the way it all came out as this surprise." She presses her thigh against his and opens her legs slightly. "You're right. Let's just forget it."

He nods and rolls his belly next to hers. His hand drops from her breast and finds its way around her waist to her back. He likes this place, the soft familiarity of it, a place no one would consider intimate or a source of secret pleasure.

She relaxes under the weight of his hand and sighs again. "I just don't want anything to stop this," she says, "to wreck the life we've made together."

"Me neither." They have not made love since the accident and now Paul thinks there may be a chance for it, a possibility that his exhaustion and her anger can be dismissed for a moment at least, or even transformed from exhaustion into depletion, and from anger into charity.

"So," she whispers, "you never told me if you read my little note to you."

"What little note?"

"The one I put in your pack."

"I must have lost it," he murmurs and moves his hand back to her breast. "What did it say?"

"Mmm ... I'll tell you later." She draws her leg over his thigh and they kiss briefly and she pulls away. "Oops. You don't want to catch my flu."

"Don't tell me you're still infectious."

"Maybe not," she whispers and kisses him again. "But I'm affectionate." They hear a footstep on the staircase leading down from

Eliot's attic loft, then a deep moan followed by the bleating sound of his crying.

"Eliot?" Valerie pulls the covers aside as she calls to him. She walks to the bedroom door and up the few steps to where her son sits with his face pressed between two staircase spindles. "What's wrong, sweetie?"

"I dreamt someone was taking me away," he bawls.

Paul pulls his bathrobe around his waist and looks up at his wife and son. She perches Eliot on her lap and pulls his head to her shoulder. "No one's going to take you anywhere. Mom and Dad are right here with you."

But her assurance offers little comfort and Eliot begins a long sob that he cannot control. Valerie leads him down the rest of the stairs and into their bedroom.

"You come into bed with us." She sighs and looks at Paul with a frown. In one move she lifts Eliot onto the mattress, slides beside him and drapes the covers over them both.

Paul climbs onto his side of the bed and wraps his hand over Eliot's shoulder. The boy squirms between his parents and soon finds the assurance needed to quell his crying. Yes, now it's Eliot's turn, Paul thinks; he needs to purge his terror, too. If the three of them could bind their flesh and minds together, then maybe they would find some safety, the protection offered by unity and love. Maybe that's all it would take.

Again, sleep fails him. For an hour he's been listening to the light wheezing of his wife and child, watching the gradual shifting of the moonlight as it tracks across the wall and the mirrored closet doors. When he realizes that sleep is truly unreachable, he lifts the covers, steps into his slippers, pulls the bathrobe over his shoulders and makes his way down the gallery to his office at the front of the house.

This is his favourite room, his personal world. He sinks into his leather chair and lifts his feet onto the ottoman and considers his options. He could fire up the computer and surf the Internet, reviewing case law in the public-access legal sites. He's already spent several hours researching on-line files to assess how his situation might play out in the courts. Trouble was, there were no cases identical to his own. He found two that had some parallels and they both resulted in convictions for criminal negligence causing bodily harm. At the very least, Paul thought he might be guilty of some lesser form of negligence. On the other hand, if Jenny died, the prosecutors might be able to build a credible manslaughter case against him.

His head slumps forward into his hands. No matter how he imagines the many permutations of his case, he arrives at the same conclusion day after day: if he can maintain his denial of the truth, then he will maintain his freedom, his life with Valerie and Eliot, his job at the Ministry of Advanced Education. Yet his legal success will condemn him to harbouring the secret lie forever. How many nights will he sit here, in this same chair, unable to sleep as he dissects the cadavers of truth and duplicity?

This is a question he cannot objectively answer. At the age of thirty-eight he still does not know if he possesses a soul. Not in the old-fashioned, Christian sense of the word. Sure, he's a good man. A good father and husband. Never had an affair with another woman—has rarely even been tempted, so satisfied is he in his marriage with Valerie. He works hard, promptly pays his taxes and bills, has been issued but one traffic warning (an illegal left turn) in over twenty years of driving. Yet despite all these assets, when he honestly tries to assess his moral worth, he cannot say whether his good life is the result of consciously choosing virtue over sin—or merely the outcome of life-long social programming.

Even if he did choose to live a virtuous life, did it mean an independent conscience existed within him with its own freedom to question and doubt the choices he'd made? Was this how freedom worked—with multiple internal identities struggling against one another in a moral stalemate?

His lips blubber together as he exhales a long, penitent sigh. He is too exhausted to deal with these questions. They always seem to plague him when the beacon of sleep becomes hopelessly distant. At least he's growing used to that, to the routine of insomnia. He sits back in his chair and pulls a caftan over his bare shins to warm them. His ears ring and he listens to their steady alarm, tries to convince himself that the noise is a mantra and all he need do is listen and let the buzz of his senses escape into the night sounds: the odd passing car, the light surf knocking against the rocky shore at the end of the street, the flag flapping on the neighbour's balcony next door.

He places a hand over his chest and feels his heart beating. It's steady, reassuring. As long as you can feel that you'll be okay, he tells himself. Then he begins to wonder what it would be like to feel nothing at all.

# CHAPTER 3

Each day over the next week Paul escorts Valerie through her morning ritual. First, they drop Eliot off at Monterey School, then make their way into the Oak Bay village and settle onto the stools next to the window bar at the local Starbucks outlet. Paul usually orders an Americano. Valerie tends to drink a specialty coffee that suits her mood: a non-fat cappuccino if she feels zesty, a double latte if she needs a boost. Usually they share a muffin and then—since the accident—Paul drives home, reads the paper, struggles with a mid-morning catnap, picks Eliot up for lunch, then returns him to school for the afternoon session. From Starbucks Valerie walks down the avenue to her store, the Sky Light, an art gallery and framing shop she bought after Eliot started pre-school and which has developed into a thriving business.

But today they plan to alter the routine. Valerie intends to work a half day and Julie, her only employee, will carry the load while Paul visits his director, Andy Betz, at the Ministry. Since he's been off work more than a week, Paul has to complete the bureaucratic procedures with Andy in order to secure his medical leave. He's also set up a lunch meeting with his lawyer, Ben Stillwell, the brother of one of Valerie's old boyfriends, Rory Stillwell. Having an amorous connection to his lawyer (once-removed, so to speak) has always given Paul reason to pause. Since the kayaking episode, he can imagine the brothers discussing Paul's fall from grace and the pity that would be assigned to the beautiful Valerie for her sorry decision to marry outside the family. Ben himself was a credible lawyer: dedicated to his clients, discreet, intelligent. Still, Paul has decided to approach Ben with caution, to tiptoe his way through the legal dynamics of his case.

With their amended routine in place, the Wakefields leave the coffee bar and head toward town in their Volvo. Paul parks the car in front of Valerie's gallery and she climbs out, her hands weighed down with art catalogues.

"I hope it goes well," Valerie says and leans through the car window and blows a kiss toward Paul's cheek. "Say hi to Andy for me."

"I will." Paul notes the omission of a salutation to Ben—and by extension, to Rory. Rory the rival. He considers mentioning this subtle nuance, then dismisses the thought and drives into the traffic after he flashes a smile to his wife.

She is beautiful, he thinks. Right down to her soul. Although Paul has never asked him about it, he suspects Rory Stillwell deeply regrets suspending his romance with Valerie in order to tour around Europe and sort out his feelings about their relationship. That was nine years ago. Then on July 6th that summer, three weeks after Rory had departed, Paul met Valerie at an art show in the Open Space gallery. Four months later they married. That Christmas, when Rory returned to Victoria, he realized he'd lost Valerie forever.


Andy Betz's office is located on the third floor of St. Anne's Academy, a heritage building located on some of the most prized real estate in downtown Victoria. Once a nineteenth-century Catholic Convent, St. Anne's had been abandoned, neglected and dismissed as a derelict relic. Charmed by its prime location, the city's ever-watchful tourist entrepreneurs proposed its demolition and in its place, construction of an international playground the corporate visionaries dubbed "Disneyland North." But the government of the day, wise and socialist, insisted on a program of heritage preservation and transformed the interior of the stone structure into a bureaucratic hive. Only the chapel, a small annex on the building's south side constructed in the manner of a rural Quebecois church, was restored to its original glory. It was once a beautiful retreat, one certainly worth saving. From time to time Paul has sat out his lunch hour in the back pews contemplating the spiritual world embodied by the revived enclave.

As you approach St. Anne's north entrance from Humboldt Street it's easy to pretend that you are about to endure the rigours of a British colonial education administered by a group of dedicated nuns pledged to serve their ordained mission on the farthest shores of the Empire. Except for the chapel, however, the building's interior has been transformed into one more government-run cubicle-land: a warren of two-metre-high, fabric-lined baffles that separate scores of work pods, each equipped with a desk, chair, telephone and computer terminal. The entire maze could be reconfigured in less than a day. Likely few would notice.

Andy Betz's office is one of a dozen fixed units located in the building's corners. It possesses a real door as well as floor-to-ceiling walls. More important, it overlooks the front lawns of the site. As he approaches the Director's open doorway, Paul finds his boss standing at the window examining a compact circle of Japanese tourists who are wandering the grounds below.

Andy's body is tightly packed and he carries himself like a retired rugby player, careful not to rouse old injuries. His face is round and his forehead thick above his eyebrows. On first meeting him, Paul wrongly assumed that Andy was "not the brightest light in the heavens." (Actually, this was Valerie's description, made after observing Andy spilling his red wine onto a plush, white carpet at a staff Christmas party.) On the contrary, he proved to be remarkably astute at navigating the Ministry's inter-office politics. In three years Andy scored two promotions and became Director of Personnel in the Ministry. Furthermore, since Paul is the Ministry's Manager of Professional Development, he reports directly to Andy.

"Lovely day to admire the bleeding flowers," Paul says, imagining the same thought running through Andy's mind.

"Paul!" Andy turns from the window and checks his wristwatch. "Geez. That time already?" Then gesturing to the tourists, he adds, "Yeah. Well, at least they keep shelling out enough coin to fill the government coffers. Ha-ha!"

Paul sits in one of the two chairs facing Andy's desk while Andy discreetly closes the door, settles into his own chair and plops his feet onto an open drawer. His unspoken message is: we are alone, my friend, and we can speak frankly. The whole truth and nothing but the truth will pass between us.

"So. You all right?" He steeples his hands and raises his eyebrows into the heavy mass of his forehead.

Paul shrugs. "Well, I lost the office cell phone."

"What?" Andy presses his lips downward in a puzzled frown.

"I had it with me in the kayak. You know, in case of emergency." This is not so much a confession as a diversion, a way to ease into the difficult talk ahead. Besides, Paul knows Andy doesn't give a damn about cell phones, computers, Palm Pilots—all the electronic fetishes that have become indispensable to government managers. "When we rolled and the spray skirt ripped away, everything in the kayak was dumped. Including the phone."

Andy waves a hand and shakes his head. "Big deal. I'll get Shirley to file a report on it; I'd be surprised if we didn't have it replaced by this afternoon. But getting Moynihan to deliver our budget—that'll take another two months." He laughs again, a brief staccato intended as a bridge to more sober conversation. "But how are you, Paul?" He drops his feet from the drawer and leans forward. "Really, are you all right?"

Paul skips his eyes away to the window and exhales a long breath through his nostrils. If he says yes to that question, Andy will have him back to work in a day.

"It was that bad, huh?"

Another shrug. "Jenny's still in the hospital."

"Brad told me." Andy's voice flattens. "Still comatose?"

"Yes. At least she was yesterday when I called." Paul nods and looks back to the window. A wave of guilt washes through him and he clenches his fists to steady himself.

"Geez." Andy sets both hands on his desk and clasps them together. He's genuinely distressed to hear this. "How're Valerie and Eliot?"

"They're fine."

"Good." Andy seems relieved to have finally struck some positive news. "And what about you, Paul? Please. Be honest. What can we do to help?"

The royal *we*. Paul stands up and walks to the window. He slips his hands into his pockets and rolls a lump of change in one fist. "I don't know," he says. "I can't say things are any better. Sometimes I think they're getting worse. There's talk of a lawsuit." This is the first time he's spoken openly about his prospects. He realizes it's a good thing he's looking out the window when he makes this confession. A good thing no one can see the sense of anguish in his face.

Andy sits at his desk a moment and when the silence becomes uncomfortable, he stands and walks to the opposite side of the window-casing from Paul. "I guess ... I mean, I'm sure ... it's been hard," he murmurs. "Really, I can't imagine what it was like at all."

Paul hears the awkwardness in his voice. He knows Andy is very uncomfortable with this, but he likes the idea of him struggling, just a little, with someone else's pain. When Andy heard the news about the accident, he called Paul at home and told him to take the next week off. But now one week has rolled into two and procedural issues have to be resolved. Andy gazes briefly at the ceiling, then back to Paul. "If you need more time off, you can have it. But you'll need your doctor to sign off on it."

Paul looks at him and then shuffles back to the desk and sits down. "I'd like that, Andy. There's talk of lawyers getting involved now." He wipes his face with one hand. "I just don't know where this is going."

Andy nods his head in sympathy as he walks around the desk and back to his chair. "As long as you have a medical justification, you can make a case. Last year Jim Sneddon managed to book stress leave when his wife came down with breast cancer."

Paul studies Andy's face. For the first time their eyes hold in mutual sympathy. They are reaching an agreement, a tacit, open arrangement whose end-point doesn't need to be settled today.

"I imagine you've got as much justification as Sneddon did." Andy wraps his arms across his chest. "Maybe more."

Paul takes a deep breath. He's worked for Andy for two years, but never really known him, or rather, known if he could trust him. "I'll see my doctor and ask him to send you a letter. That'd be all you need?"

"Yeah. I'll fax your doctor an Approval for Medical Leave form, get him to sign it, fax it back, then I'll forward it to Jerry and get your status amended for an extended leave." Then with a hint of restraint, he adds, "After three months, there'll be a review."

"Well ... I hope I'll know where I stand before then."

"Me too." Andy shifts ground, happy to move on now that their formal agenda has been dispensed. "Brad's kept me up to date about the search for the yacht that clipped you. Of course no one's stepping forward. The marina manager has no log of anyone mooring their boat in the half hour after you were hit."

"I know." Paul hasn't thought much about Brad since the accident. "It's as though it simply vanished."

"That's exactly what Brad said." It was Andy Betz who had recommended Brad's kayaking company, Island Ocean Adventures, last Christmas. Andy was once legally related to Brad (a nephew via his ex-wife) who'd started a winter sea kayaking school to balance the off-season against his summer ocean guiding business. Andy himself had never been on the open water with Brad, but he'd assured Paul that he was "a worthy guy," someone trying to find a toe-hold in the wilderness tourism business.

Paul looks at Andy as though he's living in two overlapping spheres: the conversation he's having now, and the one he had months ago in which Brad—and the events that led to the kayaking accident—was introduced to him. The feeling is so immediate, he decides to test the overlap on Andy: "That Brad," he says, "he's a worthy guy."

Andy glances away, then back again. "Yes, I'd say so."

"You did say so."

"What?"

"Never mind," Paul says and makes his way to the door. "Really, it's nothing." But what he wants to say, what is on his lips and he has to bite away before he screams it aloud is this: Three months ago. That's how you described Brad. That's why I decided to go out on the water with him!

"All right then," Andy says. "Good to see you." He joins Paul at the office door and shakes his hand.

"Thanks." Paul walks down the corridor to the elevator without glancing at his old cubicle space. He has the sense he'll never see it again. Perhaps this is what retirement is like: you simply walk away and leave your desk and chair for someone else. Then the phone rings, the new man answers and your past life disappears forever.

The early morning promise of good weather is in full flower when Paul emerges from the office building. He decides to leave his car parked on Humboldt Street and walk to his lunch meeting with Ben Stillwell. He checks his watch, allows twenty minutes for the stroll to Chinatown and sets a course for the harbour causeway.

The salt air in Victoria on a sunny day in March is buffered with the perfume of blossoms and fresh tree sap. When he first moved here, Paul developed a theory that the air-borne floral pheromones were infectious; that simply breathing them in inspired renewal. Perhaps the regenerative airs were responsible for the city's popularity as a retirement haven and as a hotbed of newly-wed bliss. They certainly invigorated Paul's sexual impulses—and Valerie loved to tease him about the beneficial effects. In fact, they'd conceived Eliot on a particularly fecund St. Patrick's Day seven years ago, a glorious celebration of their love that left their eyes shining well into the late-night darkness.

Now, as he walks toward the waterfront, Paul hopes to rediscover this springtime cure. The fact that he and Valerie have not made love since the accident has created nagging uncertainties. First, there was his hospitalization (two nights), then the effects of hypothermia that left him shaking (psychologically at least; his flesh was still, but in his mind he trembled for days), and finally (following that bizarre visit with the Jensens in the hospital), the coitus interruptus brought on by Eliot's nightmare. These impediments were further troubled by his bout of insomnia, a waking exhaustion that completely depleted Paul's stamina.

With these doubts percolating in his mind, he steers himself through the back entrance to the Empress Hotel. Normally, a five-minute tour of the Empress is sufficient to cure anyone of over-blown self-consciousness. The guiding architectural concept of the building is that of BIG (British Imperial Glory) and as you stroll through the lobby and corridors your personal identity shrinks in awe. Everything from the ornate Persian carpeting to the hand-carved ceiling beams is designed to communicate the reach of Empire wealth, power and prestige. The shrubs and lawns outside the building are flanked by similar icons of the era: the Parliament Buildings, the Union Club, the Crystal Gardens. Upon these metaphors of nineteenth-century stability and grace the city has built its identity: from the Victorian mansions along Rockland Avenue to the mock-Tudor dwellings that dot Oak Bay and Fairfield—from its very name—Victoria has fostered a gentile, English atmosphere that is ingrained in its affluent citizens. It's no surprise that when Rudyard Kipling washed up on the island during one of his world tours he was reported (falsely) to announce that the city was "more English than the English." Still, this nugget of apocrypha gleams in the minds of residents and visitors alike. And at the centre of this nostalgia—on a drained swamp-bed opposite a small Songhees Indian village long ago eradicated by smallpox—stands the Empress Hotel.

Each day the hotel lobby is set for high tea, an elaborate, forty-dollar-a-cup ritual dismissed by the locals but patronized by the hundreds of tour groups floating into the city on two-day junkets from the mainland. In addition, scores of American couples (most from Seattle, Spokane and Portland) snuggle into the Empress for weekend getaways. For them, the idea of properly steeped tea (let alone *high* tea) is a delightful novelty and they can be seen sipping from the ornate china teacups with awkward enthusiasm.

Despite the Empress's blatant pandering to Yankee tourists, Paul has spent many good evenings in the Bengal Lounge, a large, south-facing sun room with a grand piano stationed in one corner. On the nights when Morry Stearns or Louise Rose hit their groove in the old jazz standards, he enjoyed some of the best solo piano he'd heard on the west coast. And years ago, the Empress maintained a small bar tucked into a corner of the building, The Library, that he and Valerie would occasionally stumble into on their way home after a night on the town. But that was gone now, replaced by a First Nations' gallery that specialized in high-priced paintings and soapstone sculpture.

As Paul leaves the building and steps onto Government Street he considers the irony of the Empress's pretensions. Every reputable seismologist has prophesied that the Empress will sink in a bog of liquefaction when the cycle of cataclysmic earthquakes rolls through the region again. Indeed, the five-hundred-year rhythm is already past due for a good shake-out, a fact that inspired Paul and Valerie to anchor the wood plating of their house to its concrete foundation with twenty-centimetre bolts. This minor renovation eased Paul into a smug sense of calm when he considered the probable aftermath of the quake: the Empress ruined beyond possibility of restoration, while his own modest wood-framed home remained solid and upright.

Although he's often felt a mild disdain for BIG architecture in the downtown core, Paul has a real affection for the city. The buildings represent the essence of Canadian social aspirations: peace, order, good government. Yes, he thinks, as he crosses the road to the harbour causeway, even with the *faux-antique* cuteness of the place, it feels good to live here. And he realizes this is the first feeling of satisfaction he's had since the accident. He inhales deeply and fixes a smile on his lips.

Navigating around the bunches of tourists that amble along the brick-faced sidewalks, Paul climbs the gentle incline up Government Street into Victoria's retail zone. In the past few years, this five-block promenade has become one of the priciest retail corridors in the nation. The independent stores have carved out an upscale niche that ensures a steady flow of cash into their tills. W&J Wilson, Murchie's Tea & Coffee, Rogers' Chocolates and Munro's Books are flanked

by the mid-size clothing chains and coffee shops. All of it follows a
150-year-old tradition of merchandizing anchored on the corner of
Fort and Government Streets.

Paul stops at the intersection; for a moment the passing crowds
disappear and he dreams of the 1840s when the Hudson's Bay
Company fort stood here: eight log cabins surrounded by a post
stockade with a west-facing gate. Only a few sketches document
its size and orientation. Any remnants of the fort have dissolved
or been destroyed. He loves this facet of the local history: the utter
disappearance of an era.

Paul walks a few more blocks, turns left onto Pandora, crosses
the street and enters Fan Tan Alley. This metre-wide corridor into
Chinatown is the entry into the maze of secret, brick-lined passage-
ways typical of nineteenth-century Chinatown. The first Asian im-
migrants had a reputation for extracting millions of dollars in trea-
sure from gold claims abandoned by whites. They also laboured,
at a reduced wage, in the coal mines and later in the fishery. Their
denigrated status was further injured by immigration and entitle-
ment laws: whereas the Europeans were encouraged to purchase
vast tracks of land, Asians were prohibited from property owner-
ship. As a result, they congregated in the cities and developed a
thriving urban subculture. Until the opium factories were banned
in the early nineteen hundreds, Chinatown was the centre of an
expanding drug trade into the United States. It also provided access to a warren of opium dens and bawdy houses known as the
"forbidden zone" just north of the district's main artery, Fisgard
Street.

What remains is now the legitimate home of the Chinese community, a busy place populated by restaurants and grocery stores,
furniture shops and tourist outlets. Foo Hong's, Paul's favourite
Chinese restaurant, stands on the north side of the street, one door
up from the Gate of Harmonious Interest, an ornate arch straddling
the width of the road. This is where he is due to meet Ben Stillwell
for lunch, and the place where he used to meet with Jack Wise to
discuss Jack's *curriculum vitae*.

He enters the restaurant and realizes it is empty. Daylight streams
through the south-facing windows and fills the restaurant with

the shadows of the passing pedestrians and street merchants. The brightness of the room has always attracted Paul to this restaurant. He checks his watch (11:40) and settles at table number six, next to the window. The place has about a dozen tables on the main floor, each with a number imprinted on a brass plate. A set of stairs climbs up to a second-storey loft, where another ten tables are laid out, reserved for an overflow of clients.

"Ready to order?" The waiter brings him a pot of green tea and a menu.

"We'll start with Chinese tea. For two," he adds with a shrug. "I'm waiting for a friend."

Years ago that friend was Jack Wise. They met at Foo Hong's for the first time soon after Paul had arrived on the west coast following his five-year walkabout in Africa and India. A few weeks after he found an apartment in Victoria, he decided to start a résumé service, build up a stable of job seekers, then broker their talents to employers. He placed an advertisement in *Monday* magazine; Jack answered the ad and they arranged to meet at Foo Hong's.

As he entered the restaurant, Jack had both arms wrapped around a three-by-four-foot art portfolio. He navigated through the doorway, back to the staircase, then returned to the front of the room, taking great care not to brush the portfolio case against any of the customers. He sauntered over to Paul and set the portfolio on the chair beside him.

Paul watched this event with curiosity. Jack simply landed beside him as though they'd been old friends with no need for introductions. After a moment's hesitation, Paul extended his hand and said, "I'm Paul Wakefield."

"Yes, I know." Jack shook his hand and smiled. A dozen deeply etched lines extended from his eyes across his high, delicate cheekbones. His skin appeared to be bleached, almost sickly in its pallor. His hair, a thick crop of blond and grey strands, was swept behind his ears.

Paul looked at him. "Nice to meet you," he said. "But how did you know me?"

"I spent years in Asia and learned to spot westerners at a thousand paces," he said and glanced around the room. "You're the only Caucasian here. The only possible Paul Wakefield in this time and space." He laughed and tapped his index fingernail on the table as if to designate their precise location in Einstein's space-time matrix.

The gesture was entirely charming. For a moment Paul felt like a child taking instruction from a distant relative, a great uncle passing through town for a few days. "The only Caucasian," he repeated, "excepting yourself."

"Careful—I'm always excepting myself. Once I start doing that I start to form ideas for everybody but myself." Jack's eyes widened with a hint of self-amusement. "So I try to remember that I'm merely a transient consciousness. One of uncounted billions. An energy pulse attempting to record a few images of The Mind." His emphasis was clearly upper case, as though The Mind was a universally revered entity.

The waiter filled their teacups with green tea and Jack moved to the business at hand.

"I'm trying to land a job with the art school at the university in Nelson," he explained and began to unzip his portfolio. The worn leather case had a broken handle, and the zipper snagged as he moved it around the corner seams. "I need a little help putting the things I've done in some kind of order. Some kind of chronological organization they can understand at the art school."

His long fingers pulled sheaves of papers onto the table. Itineraries, letters of reference, announcements of gallery showings, documents written in Asian pictographs, scores of art posters, critical reviews of his work, news clippings announcing his awards and accolades, letters from the Canada Council. Dozens of photographs of his paintings, all of them mandalas, were bound together by a wide felt ribbon. Paul flipped through the pictures and began to recognize the detailed artwork he had read about in the press. *Of course, this is Jack Wise,* he thought. The guy who introduced the traditional Buddhist mandala as an art form to the western world in the 1960s. Within a few months, the media had transformed the mandala into a drugged-up pop icon. But Jack had brought it over from the Far East in its purest form, then made it his own—an orb of The Universal Mind, a visual metaphor for the then-new utopia of transcendental consciousness.

Jack emptied the portfolio and stacked the papers into eight or nine piles: references, gallery openings, travel papers, critical reviews, teaching assessments and so on. He seemed bewildered by it all, nostalgic for certain past triumphs, forgetful of most of the reviews. Worst of all, he felt incapable of organizing this mass, the paper trail of his career, into a *curriculum vitae*. Furthermore, he needed to assemble the materials within two weeks in order to meet the university's application deadline. Yet he felt a calling, a sense that this job had "emerged from the realm of possibility" and that it merely awaited his response. He asked Paul if he could handle the project. Could he summarize everything in four or five pages? Was it realistic to ask him to reduce "thirty years of artistic self-apprenticeship" to a few pages and still express a sense of accomplishment—within fourteen days?

"Perhaps," Paul said as he flipped through the reams of paper and clippings. Though he was unsure what it all meant—and how all this material could be properly *sequenced*. Yes, that was a key term to apply to the situation, to convey a parallel to primary archival research. "Though I have to say, you've got a lot of material here, Jack. Just sequencing it is going to take some time."

"I know," Jack covered his eyes for a moment. His voice was despondent. He shook his head. "It's a very messy sequence. I'm sorry."

"Don't worry." Paul held a hand aloft. "I can do this. But I may need your help. Just to clarify things as I go."

Jack leaned forward and smiled. "Thank you." He had a lovely smile. There was nothing beautiful about his mouth or teeth, but he conveyed a sense of hope, a righteous optimism that the providence of The Mind would steer events. Hence, worry was pointless. Moot. And his smile conveyed that notion of careless ease.

"How much will this cost me?" He sipped at his tea as he asked this, as though the question had no significance and money was not a barrier.

Paul considered this a moment. The longer they talked, the more he remembered what he'd read about Jack Wise. His work was already being collected. One day his paintings could fetch some real money. "Tell you what," he said. "How about if we trade my work for some of your art?"

"I like that." Jack nodded and his face developed a warm glow. It was the first time Paul detected a healthy colour in Jack's skin. "I'm very pleased that's how you'd like to do it. Really. I'm delighted!"

"Good." Paul felt a bond enveloping them. Perhaps The Mind had embraced him, too.

"Which painting would you like?"

Paul shrugged. "I don't have a clue."

"Okay." Jack held a finger in the air. "Let me decide then. I have something I think you'll like." His head ticked to one side, as though a special insight had just come to him. He sipped his tea and smiled and began to talk about his travels in Asia and his discovery of Buddhism.

Paul suspected that Jack had many women who took intimate comfort in this smile. Needy women, probably. It was just a guess. As the years unfolded, he never met anybody associated with Jack. In fact, they only met together three times. Always in Foo Hong's. Always to drink green tea and discuss Jack's artistic sequence and his theories of art. He believed that art could transform human consciousness and in that way, change the world. In spite of his illness, he maintained an idealistic view of his life and welcomed any debate about what he called "our human purpose." Years later, when he read Jack's obituaries, Paul was pleased to have Jack's paintings hanging on the wall of his home. They formed a link to his memory, a set of mental fragments located in Paul's zone of space-time, a place where he still maintained a bond with the most dedicated artist he'd ever met.

"Paul. Good to see you."

Paul turns his eyes from the pedestrians passing along the sidewalk in front of Foo Hong's window. "Ben?—sorry! I didn't see you come in."

Ben Stillwell shakes Paul's hand and sits opposite him. "You must have sailed in early to get the prized window table." He folds his suit jacket over his briefcase and sets them both on the nearest chair.

"Yes. A little," Paul glances out the window again. Now that Ben has arrived a sense of foreboding washes over him. The memory of Jack's voice dissolves in the clatter of the small restaurant; he can smell the red heat of chaos burning in the kitchen skillets with the scent of curry. He shakes his head and tries to focus.

"Listen, I don't mean to sound abrupt, but I've got to be in court in less than an hour." Ben fixes Paul in his eyes. "I understand there was an accident." The intensity in his face is unnerving, as though Ben has the ability to contain a life within his gaze, yet know absolutely nothing about it, nor care.

"Yes." Paul presses two fingers against his mouth. "How much do you already know?"

"Only what was in the papers."

Paul drops his hands to his lap and takes a deep breath. In an instant he realizes that if Ben is going to help him, he must confess everything to him. Everything except perhaps the small portion of truth which he will reserve for himself. Yes, that would be best. "Well ... it was a *simple* accident," he begins, "only ... now it's taken a turn for the worse. The young girl, Jenny Jensen, will probably get a lawyer—I mean her parents will—and there's talk of a lawsuit."

Ben leans forward. "It's standard procedure. There probably will be a lawsuit. Their lawyer will want to bring everyone into the suit who's linked to the accident. The kayaking school, the school owner, the kayak manufacturer. And you. What they want is money to care for the girl. So they'll go after your insurance. If your house insurance has a rider providing you with public liability coverage—and most do these days—then they'll go after your insurance. But don't panic. It's not really about you. It's about your money, or more precisely, your insurance company's money. Besides, from what I read, you're as much a victim as the girl."

"True." Paul eyes his teacup. "Except Valerie and I met with her parents. I told them about the accident. Or rather ... a variation of what actually happened—just to make them feel better about their daughter. I didn't know it, but the guy with them was a forensic accountant. You could tell he'd given testimony a dozen times."

Ben nods his head as though he expected this little wrinkle. "Let's order," he says as he flags the waiter. "Then tell me what happened—then what you said happened."

They order curried jumbo prawns, mushroom chow mein and steamed rice. Within minutes—typical of the efficiency at Foo Hong's—the food arrives at their table along with a fresh pot of green tea. Ben spoons the food onto his plate and begins to eat. Paul absently scrapes his share of the meal onto his plate and continues to relate his tale.

"It was our last kayaking lesson, the wrap-up trip when we were supposed to paddle to Discovery Island and back. Everything was going well until we returned to the marina. That's when we entered the fog and everything went wrong." In fact, he thinks, they entered the fog before they reached the marina. He remembered watching the grey vapour from the shore of Discovery Island, draped above the water like a curtain. He remembers the seven kayaks rafting up as they floated atop the heaving kelp beds. Isn't that when Brad explained the plan to move ahead in single file? Or perhaps that had been somewhat later. Brad had the compass strapped to the deck of his boat and would take the lead. He asked Paul to bring up the rear, to make sure no one slipped behind him. And he'd done that. He'd done the one thing he'd been asked to do. He'd even made a half joke about bringing up the rear, but he can't remember how it went. He tries to tell the joke to Ben, but gives it up in mid-sentence with a bleak frown. Perhaps there had been no joke; maybe it was just a feeling of amusement. Then he explains how he and Jenny realized they were separated from the other paddlers, how they called out for help as they heard the sound of the approaching yacht. He recalls the feeling in his stomach when the impending collision became a certainty. As Paul recounts the events leading up to the accident he's surprised to realize how fluid the details have become. He describes his plan, how he would lift Jenny from her kayak onto his own. Then came the shock of capsizing into the ocean. At this point, he realizes there are no more facts to relate. Only speculation, intentions and broken memories.

When his story falters, Ben gathers Paul up in his eyes again and leans forward. "Was Valerie with you?"

"No. She had the flu that day."

"Umm." Ben checks his watch, slips his chop sticks onto his plate and cleans his plate with a fork. "And how do the facts differ from what you told the Jensens?"

Paul picks at his food with the chop sticks. He realizes he's eaten almost nothing. "I told them that once we were in the water, she saved me."

"Did she?"

"No. It was exactly opposite." As he says this Paul hesitates. Now is the point at which he must decide to tell the truth—or not. Does he mention clubbing Jenny with his paddle? Should he describe her concussion and the subsequent coma? Or does he let this detail slip into the void of omission?

"What do you mean?"

"She was climbing all over my back. She completely panicked. That's when I went under ... when I almost lost it." He can feel a wedge of anger in his voice. It was her fault, damn it. Everything that happened, happened because she panicked.

Ben raises his head slightly and smiles. "When the time comes, Paul, remember what you just said. And remember how you said it. Remember your feeling of outrage."

Paul begins to express how utterly guilty he feels but stops himself. He didn't realize he'd also felt ... *outrage*. But, yes, that's what it is: blind anger. And the strange part of the anger is how good it feels now that he knows it.

"Did their friend, the accountant, say anything?"

"Yes." Paul sighs and looks across the room. Every table is full. People are eating, talking, laughing. A cell phone buzzes. "He wondered how Jenny was injured and then still able to save me. She got a concussion, just above her temple." He touches the skin along his hairline. "The doctors are saying it caused the coma. He implied that I was lying—maybe covering something up."

"You *were* lying. And you were covering up the lie you told them." Ben slips the last few grains of rice into his mouth and wipes his lips with a paper napkin. "In this profession you see everything. The thieves, the cokeheads, the pimps and prostitutes—of course they lie. Everybody expects them to lie. But sometimes, the good lie, too. And the lie you told was to make them think better about her panic, right?"

Paul nods abstractly. He could be agreeing with anything.

"Look, I've got to run." Ben pulls himself from the chair and gathers his jacket and briefcase in one arm. "Two things: one, don't talk to anyone about this, especially the Jensens or their lawyer—and especially not the police. Second, when they call you in for the examination for discovery—that's the first time you'll need to say anything about what happened—call my secretary, Ginny, and get her to schedule your testimony so I can be there with you." He pulls a business card from his pocket and sets it on the table.

Paul feels relieved, almost energized. For a moment, he suspects his revival is due to contacting his buried anger, a break-through he wasn't expecting. He looks up at Ben, intending to say good-bye, but instead he asks, "How's your brother, Rory?"

Ben's face slackens and he absorbs the image of Paul the way he did when he came into the restaurant: with a clinical, distant embrace. "Rory's quite ill. I thought Valerie might have heard."

"No." Paul shakes his head. Damn it. Why did he ask this question, this one huge, blundering, asinine question? "No, I didn't hear anything about it." Then, as if to make up for his ignorance, he adds, "I'll get Valerie to call him."

Ben tilts his head to one side, a gesture of remorse, a terse signal that this might have been a good idea if Rory wasn't still devastated by Valerie's betrayal so many years ago. With another formal glance, Ben opens the door and disappears into the passing crowds on Fisgard Street.

# CHAPTER 4

T HE SMALL PAIN IN PAUL'S LEFT LEG BEGINS TO BEG FOR ATTENTION. For awhile he's been able to ignore it. But now he can feel the wound opening, a chunk of flesh torn from the meat of his calf. Looking into the water, down the length of his body, he can see the beast rising beneath him, its primitive anger about to devour him limb by limb. The black mass swirls and cuts, probing him for the right moment—the right intersection of place and time—to slice him in half. When Paul realizes the instant of death is *now*, the sea lion surfaces. His round, vacant eyes widen as he bellows in vengeance, a cry meant to revenge his doomed children, the generations lost to unending predation.

Paul's leg twitches violently. He throws a hand in front of his face to save himself from the vision of his own death. Finally he stumbles into the space, the nebulous half-time between sleep and the shock of awareness, where he realizes that he is not drowning. He sucks a draft of air into his lungs and grips the armrests of his chair. His fingers clutch the metal frame and he tries to heave himself into his

kayak. Then he discovers there is no boat. No sea lion. No ocean
waiting to swallow his body.

Despite the reprieve, his terror lingers. His face oozes perspiration. He turns his head to the clock; it is 4:20. He has managed to
capture fifteen minutes of sleep.

He pulls his legs together on top of the ottoman and wraps his
housecoat around his calves. The La-z-boy has become his night
refuge now, a habitual retreat in the small office at the front of his
house. Down the hallway he can hear Valerie's quiet wheezing, the
last, lingering symptom of her recent illness. It is the only noise in
the night. As he listens for other sounds he hears the emptiness fill
with the light ringing in his ears. Not ringing precisely, more an
electrical sixty-cycle hum. But he can mask it, he's discovered, by
filling his attention with other sounds. For a few minutes he listens
to the even rhythm of Valerie inhaling and exhaling. He tries to live
there, vaporized in the air as she absorbs it into her body, the invisible molecules travelling through her lungs and blood, lost but full
of vital purpose.

Then he thinks of loving her, of finding his way back into her
warm, inviting flesh and how that would purge his memory and
mind. That's the gift of sexual love, to provide an exit from the
incessant grind of time.

Paul's new midnight routine is to sit in front of the computer and
surf the Internet. Yesterday's morning paper mentioned a site worth
investigating: sleepers.net. He clicks their home page, scans it a moment, and answers their forty-two-question "Sleep Test." Do his legs
twitch in the night? Yes. Is his mouth often dry when he awakes?
Yes. Does he have trouble falling asleep? Two points there. He completes all the test items and clicks the score button. Up comes the
near-certain diagnosis: "It's possible you have insomnia. You are
advised to discuss your symptoms with a competent physician ..."
Competent? In an instant the credibility of the website dissolves,
sunk on this single word. Why would anyone seek the opinion of an
incompetent physician?

Next he begins the diligent phase of his insomniac surfing, the quest to uncover legal precedents related to his case. He clicks through several law sites and then onto some of the related news archives. During his nights sitting in front of the screen he has found little related to the accident. But now he discovers a new headline: DROWNED CHILD VICTIM OF "DEPRAVED HEART"—MANSLAUGHTER SENTENCE TO FOLLOW.

He clicks on the story link and the following text fills his screen:

Jefferson City, Missouri — The jury of eight men and four women took two days to return a guilty verdict against John Ribbenstahl in the case of an eight-year-old girl, Joanna Bentsen, drowned in Lake of the Ozarks last summer.

The unusual "depraved heart" clause—added to the indictment of manslaughter to denote the degree of extreme negligence in the case—created a media stir throughout the state and required the presiding judge, Murray Frammen, to enforce strict control of the proceedings from the outset of the trial.

Ribbenstahl and his neighbor, Jackson Bentsen, were fishing on the lake with two of Bentsen's daughters in an eight-foot aluminum boat when a squall came up on the water from the west shore. As they tried to adjust to the chop, the boat tipped and all four passengers toppled into the lake.

According to testimony from Bentsen and his surviving daughter, Meredith Bentsen, the two girls were wearing life jackets. Ribbenstahl and Bentsen, however, had used their jackets for seat cushions and lost sight of their floats after they were immersed. When it was clear they would not

be able to right the craft, Ribbenstahl
insisted that they swim for shore. Bentsen
urged them to stay with the boat and wait
for help.

In the shouting match that followed,
Ribbenstahl determined that he would strip
the life jacket from the deceased, Joanna
Bentsen, swim to shore with the young girl
in tow, then return to the boat and rescue
the father and his older daughter. Halfway
to the Raeside dock, Ribbenstahl lost his
grip on the child. Her body was found two
days later after an intensive search-and-
rescue operation discovered the corpse
three miles east of the accident site.

Following the investigation of the accident, Ribbenstahl revealed that he'd panicked and felt remorse for taking the girl's
life vest in order to save his own life.
Police Chief Warren Strafford testified that
Ribbenstahl "volunteered his confession two
weeks after we formally interrogated him."
In a news interview after his testimony,
Strafford observed that "without his confession, I don't know that we'd have this
conviction to hang our hats on."

Under the depraved heart clause, Ribbenstahl
faces the possibility of life in prison
without parole. The sentence hearing is set
for the third week of March.

Paul rereads the story until his eyes can no longer focus on the screen.
The parallels to his own situation are inexact, but there are motiva-
tional similarities. Indeed, if Ribbenstahl had taken the girl's life vest
only to save himself, then certainly he was guilty—even depraved.

But what if Ribbenstahl's first instincts were correct? What if the lake currents were about to sweep the girl away, just as it had carried his own life jacket out of reach? In that case, Ribbenstahl had correctly assessed the dangers and knew he had to swim with the girl to shore. And the only way to do that was to take the vest and Joanna Bentsen together and swim to safety. In that case, it was all a horrible accident. And a legal catastrophe.

If the court misjudged the facts, how had Ribbenstahl so badly ensnared himself in the law? In two ways, from what Paul could see: First, he'd hesitated with some critical information (admitting he'd taken Joanna's jacket)—which made it appear he was trying to hide the fact. In Paul's situation, the parallel issue was his lie to the Jensens about their daughter's efforts to save him. But he'd set the record straight when he spoke to Ben Stillwell. He knew he'd have to go on record with that statement again at the examination for discovery. That's why Ben encouraged him to remember his anger about it—his anger about the truth of what had happened.

Second, Ribbenstahl had talked to the police. Of course, if you refuse to talk to the police, their suspicions deepen. But in his case, Paul's lawyer instructed him to say nothing—especially to the police. His defense against undue suspicion then becomes a simple declaration: "My lawyer instructed me to refuse to speak to you." The cops were pros at weeding confessions from people, even the innocent. Ben knew that and warned him to beware of entrapment.

Paul leans back from the computer and stares at the wall. If he keeps his wits about him, he might get through this ordeal without injury. Ben would be his guide and ally. He imagines Ben's unmoving face, the way he absorbs the details of the lives around him without emotion or attachment. For the first time Paul can understand that attitude. How essential it is to survival.

After breakfast Paul eases down the front staircase toward his driveway and walks toward the car, prepared to warm up the engine while Valerie prepares Eliot for school. As he pads along the gravel path his neighbour, Jerry Sampson, calls out from his front porch.

"Morning, Jerry," Paul says and waves an arm in the air. "How's Chester keeping?" Chester is Jerry and Bettina Sampson's yellow Lab. Since Bettina fell and broke her hip in January they haven't been able to devote much time to Chester's daily walk. Once or twice a week Paul has taken the dog up to Anderson Hill Park, just behind their houses. It's a neighbourly gesture and provides Paul with an excuse to wander around the hill overlooking the sea.

"The old mutt could use a good run," Jerry says and frowns. It's obvious he hates to concede his independence. On the other hand, he's got a bad leg and since her accident, Bettina has become more than a handful for him.

"No doubt."

"Then again, I could use a good run, too!" Jerry laughs a little too hard and Paul waves a hand dismissively, a gesture intended to spare them both the embarrassment of Jerry openly asking for assistance.

Valerie and Eliot appear on the front step and she locks the house door. "How's Bettina?" she asks when she sees Jerry braced against his doorway.

Jerry tips his head to one side. "Doing great. Doctor says another month and she'll be dancing jigs at the Legion Hall."

"Hi Jerry!" Eliot waves a hand and climbs into the car. "Come on, Dad—beam us up!"

"How 'bout I come by later today and walk Chester up the hill?" Paul says and closes the door beside Eliot.

Jerry nods: indeed, a walk would be very helpful. "That boy of yours sure is a smart kid," Jerry says and saunters back into his house.

Valerie and Paul settle into the Volvo. He drives along Central Avenue to Oliver Street and turns right, then idles the engine as the car pulls them up the half-block to Monterey School. So far Eliot has adapted pretty well to grade one and the rigours of a six-hour day followed by a little homework. There were a few tears in the fall, when he felt too tired to stick it out, but just as it looked like they were headed for a crisis, Eliot found his pace and cruised all the way to the Christmas holiday without missing a day. Valerie was delighted.

She leans over the seat and unzips his backpack to ensure everything's in place. "Okay, honey. Got your lunch?"

"Yes, Commander." Eliot unbuckles his seat belt and waits for Paul to open the back door. The right rear door latch has broken. The outside door lever still works but the interior spring mechanism has disconnected, another annoyance Paul has indexed on his list of pending car repairs.

Paul pulls himself out of his seat and walks behind the car, ducking his head under his jacket hood to avoid the light rain. Although it's almost 9:00, he still feels as though he hasn't woken up. A natural outcome, he tells himself, of running on twenty minutes' sleep. He opens the door and Eliot scrambles to the sidewalk. "I'll pick you up after three," he calls after him.

"Make it so!" Eliot yells and he runs to the queue of children waiting to cross the street with the crossing guard.

Paul watches him jog along with the others, musing on Eliot's recent fascination with *Star Trek* reruns. *Make it so.* Perhaps that's how these kids adapt to the school system: the Yankee can-do spirit is infused into their minds before they know how to spell.

He watches Eliot pick up a conversation with Jason Banks, a slight kid from the next block who is already learning to play the violin. He watches Eliot walk toward the crosswalk, the looping way he moves his shoulders under the weight of his backpack, a brief hand movement to adjust his ball cap so the rain doesn't strike his face. His son becomes infinitely observable, and he knows this is one of the great pleasures of fatherhood, one of the moments of pride in seeing a part of himself walking up the sidewalk independently, the details of his future unknown yet the general themes completely predictable. Many lessons still to be learned, of course, but—

"Paul?"

He glances at the car. Valerie inches the window down.

"Okay, I'm coming."

"Who's that?" she asks and points across the street.

He pulls his jacket hood behind his neck and darts around the Volvo and slides onto the driver's seat. "Who do you mean?" he asks.

"There. In that car. Isn't that Reg Jensen?"

Paul turns his head and sees the back of an old Dodge 500 accelerating down the road. "I don't know." He thinks of Reg's visit to the house. He had a red Dodge.

"What the hell is Reg Jensen doing here?" Valerie asks. "Especially at this time of day?"


"Tell me I'm not paranoid." Valerie is halfway through her double latte and still obsessed with Reg. "I mean, his kid sits comatose in the intensive care unit and he's cruising the schoolyard—not his own kid's schoolyard, I might add—looking for ... well, for what?"

"I really don't think it was Jensen," Paul says. Although he's sure she's right, he doesn't need Valerie to lose her equanimity. Not now. Not with the insomnia pressing him into such a funk. Not with John Ribbenstahl—the depraved heart—starting his first month of life without parole. And certainly not with the news of Rory the rival's illness in the air. Except for brief updates about his ongoing insomnia, he has not told Valerie any of this. Though it's possible she knows about Rory, and may already be consoling him without mentioning it to Paul.

"But what if it was?" she says pressing her head forward. "If it was, then he's stalking us. And if he's stalking us, what does that say about his stability?"

"Not much, I guess." Paul looks away. The steady queue of Starbucks' patrons saunters forward to place their orders with the baristas. The enterprise is an unrelenting cash cow.

"You guess? Doesn't this matter to you?"

"Yes, it matters to me." His voice steps up a notch. He takes a breath. "It's just that I can't take on anything more. With the lawsuit coming up and this damn sleeplessness...."

Valerie presses a knuckle against her lip and looks at her husband's face. "I know," she says with a sigh. "But you have to realize this is all part of that."

"Yeah, I know."

There's a pause and then she adds, "I've told you before, I'm not going to let anything take what we've made for ourselves."

"I know." He reaches out and takes her hand in his own. "And neither will I, okay?"

"Okay." Valerie holds him in her eyes and for a moment nothing else exists in the world except the intimacy of their connection.

Paul knows that if they were at home, if Valerie didn't have to open her shop, if he didn't have to meet his doctor in twenty minutes—they would tumble into bed and make the long-overdue connection that has eluded them. "Look," he says, giving her hand a last squeeze. "Can we remember this minute—right now—and bring it up again tonight?"

"Bet on it," she says and she props her chin in her free hand. She smiles and leans forward. "You can bring it up again any time you want."

As he sits in Dr. Edward Biggs' waiting room, Paul considers the individual privacy that he and his wife maintain. Certainly he knows the tally of the many things he has not shared with her. Within the past few weeks, since the accident, there have been several acts of secretive discretion. His failure to reveal the truth of his struggle with Jenny Jensen in the water off the marina, Ben Stillwell's injunction to remember his anger, his undisclosed knowledge of the trial of John Ribbenstahl. And there are other, nagging—yet unproved—worries that he harbours: about the duration of his current impotence, or his fear that indeed, Reg Jensen is stalking them. And what of Valerie's own secret life? Is it possible that she knows of Rory Stillwell's illness, whatever it might be? And if she does, has she covertly been tending to him in his time of want and need?

There is no way of knowing the answers to these questions, to be sure. Besides, who could possibly live a completely disclosed life? Even the most intimate confession must cover some aspect of the truth. Or is it possible to live a truly open life? It's an ideal, but—

"Mr. Wakefield." The medical receptionist, Shelley Gardner, stands at the entrance to the hallway, a manila file propped in one hand.

"Hi." Paul stands and follows her down the corridor, happy to dismiss the guilt that's been prying open his conscience since he awoke in a panic this morning.

"The doctor will be with you in a minute." Shelley parks his file in a wall-mounted Plexiglas holder, opens the door to a small white room and points to the lone chair in the corner next to the examination table. "Just slip out of your clothes and pull on the paper drape when you have a minute." She nods toward the neatly folded gown with a wink and closes the door.

Paul edges over to the table, pulls off his clothes and tugs the paper sheet around his shoulders. He ties the waistband string, then lifts himself onto the examination table and scans the room. The walls are decorated with cutaway posters of the human skeleton, muscular structure and organs. Detailed diagrams of veins and arteries adorn the back of the closed door. Opposite the table stands a four-legged footstool and a weigh scale; behind them is a sink and above it a cabinet containing various surgical appliances. A small window (draped) overlooks the parking lot. A box of rubber gloves sits poised on the sink countertop.

Dr. Ed Biggs knocks on the door and enters the examination room with a mock grin on his face. He's just heard a weak joke from another physician in the corridor and he wears the look of comic compliance: that wasn't so funny, but ain't it a laugh you felt the need to share it with me. He has a stethoscope slung around his neck and sports a fresh haircut, a two-centimetre trim that stands the bristles of his hair on end.

Paul discovered Ed after a four-year search in which he tried on a doctor a year until he found one who truly attended to his health. Ed himself is a model of health and fitness. He bicycles to his office, runs marathons, eats vegetables both raw and steamed, and keeps his body fat to less than 10 percent of his weight. Or something like that; Paul cannot remember the exact weight-to-fat ratio, but he does recall Ed assuring him it was "in the zone."

Ed shakes Paul's hand and assumes a position on the stool at the foot of the examination table. His mood changes and in a few seconds he has turned all other concerns aside so he can focus on Paul.

"I hear you had quite a tumble into the ocean." He says this with a sympathetic look.

"Yeah." Paul nods and shrugs his shoulder. He's surprised to find himself in the middle of this conversation already.

"Happened to me last year," Ed says and opens Paul's file. "We were practising Eskimo rolls off Willows Beach. Trouble was, I went over but failed to come up the other side. In my case, I just ripped off the spray skirt, stood up and walked to the shore," he adds. "Still, it was ice cold."

"I guess I was in the water for fifteen minutes or so."

"I see they treated you for hypothermia." Ed scans the hospital report. "Looks like you had a pretty bad dose."

"Enough to pass out."

"You're lucky," Ed says with finality, as if to suggest a few minutes more and he would have died. "Anyway, live to fight another day, right? To which end, your director at the ministry, Andy Betz, faxed this Approval for Medical Leave to the office last week." Ed Biggs lifts the fax from Paul's file.

"Yes." Paul presses his lips together. "I need more time away."

"I can imagine." Ed looks at Paul without blinking. "Tell you what: you tell me what's going on. Then we'll do a physical. Then I'll fill out the form for your boss. Okay?"

Yes. He thinks the word *yes*, but doesn't say it. He's nearing the same point he's navigated around several times now. The same breach he's faced with Valerie, the Jensens, Andy Betz, Ben Stillwell—the demarcation point where he must re-approach the accident from the perspective of his survival and Jenny's collapse. But this time he's not reliving the crisis they faced in the water. This time, it's about his insomnia, his impotence, the constant humming in his ears, the dreaded sea lion swallowing him whole.

At first he explains his circumstances in short, punchy statements ("I just can't sleep," "the buzzing in my ears won't stop," "I get five minutes sleep—maybe—then the nightmare comes back"). Ed sits and listens, makes a few notes in his file and asks Paul to go on. Paul describes the collapse of his motivation without mention of his temporary impotence with Valerie. Then, though he knows it's not a medical issue, he tells the story of Reg Jensen's visit, how he and Valerie drove to the hospital to offer the Jensens some reassurance. He stops short of revealing the lie he told them, remembering Ben Stillwell's injunction against repeating the details of the accident. But he does reveal the pending lawsuit and his counsel with his lawyer.

When Paul finishes, Ed lifts himself from the stool and draws his stethoscope from his neck. "Sounds like common procedure," he says. "Especially if she's still in a coma. But it could be worse. Roll up your sleeve."

Paul pulls his sleeve up and Ed wraps the blood pressure cuff around his right biceps and gives it four brisk pumps. "How could it be worse?"

Ed concentrates òn the stethoscope reading. He checks the gauge on the pump, re-inflates the cuff and takes a second measure. He pens another note in Paul's file. "Okay, lie down and let's have a look at your ears."

Paul levels himself on the table and takes a deep breath. He is now required to render himself an object of. examination: bones, brains, blood, bladder—all of it reducible to a diagnosis followed by the benefit of prognosis and treatment. Such is the ritual that yields the miracle of modern medicine.

Ed inspects Paul's ears, feels the lymph nodes above his neck, then prods the flesh around his ankles. Through the entire examination he is silent, then he murmurs, "I'd like to feel your liver and belly, then your groin." His hands work expertly across Paul's flesh and Paul draws some comfort from the formality of his routine; it sets the rules about how they ought to behave and respond. Ed taps and listens, pushes deeper until he contacts the organs in Paul's body and tests their vitality. His fingers probe the lymph nodes in his groin and a thumb rolls over the spheres of his testicles. "Okay, sit up and let's listen to your chest." Paul eases forward, certain now that the most intimate probing is behind them. Ed applies the stethoscope to his chest, front and back, instructs Paul to cough. He enters a few more notes in his file then wraps the blood pressure cuff around his arm once more. "This time lie down while I take a reading. But first relax. Forget about the stock market. Forget about the accident. Think of a beach somewhere. There you are with your wife. What do you see?"

"A whole lot of white sand."

"Good." Ed inflates the cuff and makes a third assessment.

Paul closes his eyes and settles onto the sand with Valerie. They are alone on the island. She slips out of her top. The long blister of her scar has faded into her tanned skin and she rolls her breasts onto his chest....

"All right, you can get back into your clothes." Ed squats on his stool and studies his notes while Paul dresses. After a moment, he closes the file and says to Paul, "So, I'm going to recommend a three-month leave for you."

Paul nods. Mission accomplished.

"But it's not just out of sympathy. Your blood pressure is elevated, Paul." He pinches his lips together then continues, "It's currently 185 over 105. Your reading over the last three years has been a rock-steady 120 over 80."

Paul takes a shallow breath. His spine stiffens slightly and he leans back to release the tension around his shoulders.

"Because it's been so consistently normal, we can assume that the new reading is related to the accident and the stress you're feeling."

"I guess." Paul looks at him with a sense of relief. Suddenly his angst has concrete substance and meaning. It's real: he is ill.

"So, we want to get it back to what it was as soon as possible. I'm going to prescribe some hydrochlorothiazide and I want to you to take one a day, starting today." Ed pauses to write the prescription on a pad. "I want you to monitor your blood pressure every day. You can buy one of these"—he lifts the tail end of his stethoscope—"or test it in the recreation centre; they've got a public monitor in the hallway. Or if you like, they've got one near the pre-scription counter in almost every pharmacy. In any case, each day write down your score. If it starts to elevate, book an appointment with me immediately. Understand?" Ed tears off the prescription and passes it to Paul.

"Yes."

"Now, once we get it down to about 165 over 100"—he writes this on another slip of paper—"I want you to come in and we'll modify the medication. Okay?"

"All right."

"Now look: at this dose this medication is quite powerful." Ed turns to establish complete eye contact. "There are side effects. You may feel like you're in a fog, especially as the blood pressure drops. That's normal. So don't get confused—by the confusion—okay?" He laughs a little and Paul tries to laugh, too.

"Okay." He shifts his position to indicate a change of topic. "Now, I suspect your insomnia is also directly related to the stress. So, we'll deal with the stress to solve the sleeplessness. In my view, the best thing you can do is get some daily aerobic exercise. An hour's brisk walk is perfect. Do you have a dog?"

"No. But sometimes I drag the neighbours' Lab up the hill."

"Perfect. Do yourselves both a favour and walk the pooch every day. There are a few other tips." He opens a cupboard door above the sink and tears another sheet from a pre-printed letter-size pad. "Here's the seven-step solution to insomnia. We have it printed in bulk. I don't want to sound dismissive, but insomnia's the third most common syndrome doctors treat."

Paul takes the sheet and scans the SEVEN-STEP SOLUTION: *Avoid alcohol or caffeine two hours before bed. Don't read in bed. If you can't sleep, get out of bed until you're ready to sleep....* Then he asks, "So what's the most common thing you treat?"

"First, high blood pressure. Welcome to the club." Ed wraps his hands over his lap and frowns. "That's followed by depression. Doctors treat one in three North Americans for depression at some point in their lives."

Of course. He'd just read a similar statistic on the Internet. The whole phenomenon sounded like the Dow Jones Average of Mental Health: down thirty-three and a third.

"As for the ringing in your ears," Ed says as he sets the file folder on the countertop, "there's no sign of infection or damage at all. The sad fact is a substantial minority of the people in our age group report episodes of tinnitus. You probably have your share of rock concerts to blame."

"Worse. As a teenager I was the bassist in a rock band."

Ed tilts his head forward as if to ask: So what did you expect? "If it becomes chronic, we'll work on it after we get these other issues under control." He smiles and checks his watch. "Anything else?"

"One thing. Earlier on we were talking about Jenny's coma." Paul shakes his head slightly. "You said it could be worse. What could be worse?"

Ed rolls his shoulders and frowns. "She could die. The longer she's comatose, the more likely her prognosis will deteriorate. There are exceptions, of course. Those are the cases that make it into the papers." He smiles again and shakes Paul's hand. "We can hope for that," he adds, then opens the door and walks down the hallway.

Paul glances away. So far he hasn't fully considered this possibility; he'd turned away from this option more out of fear than logical analysis. Yet the future probabilities are clear: if Jenny dies, the examination for discovery would lead to an inquest and, most likely, a manslaughter investigation. Then the full resources of the state will be brought to bear on his case. The legal precedents of people like John Ribbenstahl could be invoked. Despite Ben Stillwell's expert maneuvering, Paul could be indicted by the prosecution and portrayed in the courts as another depraved heart.

# CHAPTER 5

P AUL STANDS NEXT TO THE SINK IN HIS KITCHEN AND EXAMINES THE SMALL WHITE PILL IN HIS PALM. In the other hand he holds a plastic vial of tablets. He rereads the label: *50 mg hydrochlorothiazide, take one per day.* The medication appears so innocent, so inert, yet he knows it possesses transformative powers. Shrugging off the last suspicion of doubt, he places the pill on his tongue and washes it down with a swig of tap water. There. You gotta feel better already, right?

His intention is to wait a short while, say half an hour, to assess the onset of any side effects: the funk of depression or a hint of psychosis. These were the two potential side effects that he read about on the Internet and he decided he would call Ed Biggs if he felt anything unusual coming on.

When he was twenty-one, during the era of his Montreal rock 'n' roll band, Forged Destiny, he'd swallowed a miniscule opaque square of window-pane acid—LSD—and within ten minutes he felt the gradual ebb of psychosis unmooring his ties to reality. An hour later the effect was that of a psychedelic hydro-plane ripping up his spine and through the top of his head until it gained a level altitude. By the time he settled into a cruising speed he'd lost sense of his identity. He spent over an hour flicking through the contents of his wallet, trying to assemble a notion of who he was and what to do with the ribbons of energy that streamed from his fingertips. The effect was so powerful that he was certain he'd scrambled his DNA. Years later, when Valerie became pregnant with Eliot, he worried that the baby would arrive horribly deformed or demented (another secret he'd withheld from his wife: Valerie never knew of his psychotropic experiment until Eliot's first birthday). But Eliot appeared to be perfect in every way and Paul finally purged this nagging concern. In retrospect, he learned nothing meaningful from his experience with drugs except to respect the power of pharmaceuticals of every kind. Hence his caution with the recently ingested medication.

After a few minutes of self-analysis he begins to roam the house aimlessly. First, to his bedroom, where he adjusts the bedcovers and plumps the pillows, then to the family room over-looking the backyard. There he sees Chester, the Sampsons' yellow Lab, stretched out in a narrow shaft of sunlight next to the garden shed on the rain-drenched lawn. Paul makes a mental note to walk the dog up Anderson Hill. In fact, it'll be his first order of duty once he's waited out the self-imposed half-hour, drug-side-effect assessment. Yes, let's walk the dog every day, he tells himself as he wanders down the hallway gallery to his office. It is there that he notices the *message waiting* indicator flashing on the telephone answering machine.

"Hi. This is a message for Valerie. Valerie, it's Rory Stillwell. Give me a call ... 602-2458—in case you've forgotten."

Paul sits at his desk and listens to the message again. The words, the phrasing, the sarcastic edge in Rory's cynical tone run through his mind. Rory Stillwell—"in case you've forgotten"—was a good-looking, narcissistic, stay-at-home remittance man who realized far too late that Valerie was the best thing that ever happened to him.

76

And *in case you've forgotten* weeks after he left Valerie, she met Paul and began to live her life happily ever after.

Paul narrows his eyes and considers what to do with this piece of lovelorn history. His first inclination is to delete it from the digital memory of the answering machine and say nothing about it to his wife. Then he considers the malice of that, the insecurity that it reveals. No need to let this message turn you toward the dark side. In fact, it could well be a test of your resistance to any ill effects from the hydrochlorothiazide. Indeed, let's make a point of leaving the message for Valerie to pick up and respond to as she sees fit. No need to comment or even question her about whatever comforts Rory might be seeking in his time of illness. If you can maintain that kind of self-assured composure, then there's no question of losing a grasp on reality.

He moves to the window and gazes onto Transit Road for a moment. A car pauses in front of his house and then moves past the Sampsons' yard and down the road toward Shoal Bay. He thinks of the neighbours' dog, Chester, and Ed Biggs's instructions to take a walk every day. He takes a deep breath, pulls on his jacket and walking shoes and leaves the house. The entire procedure is managed without reconsidering the decision about the answering machine—a triumph of reason over passion.


Chester leads the way up the trail to Anderson Hill Park. It's an easy five-minute hike along the well-worn path behind his house and along the ridge to the wide, rolling meadow that overlooks the ocean. There's no wind and the afternoon sun warms the rain-soaked grasses, the clumps of broom and heather. The air is fresh with the dewy fragrance of early blossoms and tree sap. As Chester noses from bush to bush, Paul stands atop the hill and closes his eyes. He breathes in the zest of spring air and feels it entering his blood. For a moment he recalls his childhood, the mornings he would get up and lie on the back lawn of his parents' home and fill his lungs with the energies in the air. (He remembers his mother calling to him from the back porch. "What are you doing, Paul?" "Just lying here." "But what are you thinking?" she asked. "Nothing." "You must

be thinking something!" "No," he replied, "I'm just pretending."
When she asked no further questions, he realized that pretending
was a justifiable end-point. Acts of imagination required no further
explanation.)

He opens his eyes, looks across Enterprise Channel to Trial Island
and scans the barren ground surrounding the lighthouse there. Not
a soul in sight. He turns to the left and wanders up the hill toward
the rocks overlooking Discovery Island. Since the accident he hasn't
troubled himself with a visit to the marina or the kayak school.
Hasn't once glanced across the open water toward the Chain Islets.
But today it will be okay, he assures himself. Today he'll be able to
look across the channel and see where everything went so wrong,
yet see it for what it really is: a place of extraordinary beauty that
bears no memory of the past.

As he reaches the top of the hill, Chester darts ahead of him to a
dish of water that has been set out by Mrs. Wentworth, a local resident whose beagle, Ella, passed away last year. Every day she walks
to the hilltop and sets out a bowl for the dogs who run through the
park. Chester slops up a little water in two quick licks; he doesn't
drink from thirst, but as a ritual to honour Saint Ella.

"Good boy," Paul says and he sets his feet on the highest rock
and fixes his eyes on the islands below. He's pleased to confirm how
beautiful it is. Mount Baker rides the eastern horizon; its snow-
packed, volcanic peak glows in the sunlight—a weathered triangle
suspended above a thin strip of clouds and, far below, the forested
archipelago scattered in the stretch of slate-coloured water. A few
freighters ease into the Georgia Strait toward Vancouver, others
trace a path down the Puget Sound to Seattle. Closer in, two yachts
press out of the marina and up the bay where a dozen sailboats
drag the air for whatever winds they can find. There is no panic, no
disaster evident anywhere.

When he told Jack Wise that he'd considered moving somewhere
near this ridge, Jack said that the hill had long been revered by the
Songhees Indians. They tended their camas plants just below the
meadow and from the summit they maintained a lookout for raid-
ing parties of Haida who clipped down the strait in their war canoes.
When the Europeans made contact and smallpox began to decimate

their number, the Songhees laid down two power circles on the hill. It was a way to preserve the dynamic energy inherent in the place, he said. A way to ensure the sacred spirit of life could survive the period of darkness that had descended on their nation.

Paul wanders a few metres back down the slope to a park bench and scans the field for some sign of the power circles. He settles on the wooden slats and unbuttons his jacket. Chester hunkers onto the grass beside him and slips his muzzle onto his front paws. "What do think Jack meant by 'power circles,' Chester?" Paul scratches his chin and props his elbow on the back of the bench. "What do you think Jack meant by most of what he said?"

Like all their sessions together, their second meeting was convened at Foo Hong's. Paul had catalogued Jack's career in a *curriculum vitae* that required almost twenty pages to summarize his gallery showings, awards, publications, and so on. It was impressive, no doubt, and Jack seemed somewhat flabbergasted by the extent of his own accomplishments.

"Well, yes, uh-uh," he said, as he flipped through the pages, reading some passages very carefully and casting past others without a second glance. "You got most of this right the first time." He pencilled in a few edits here and there. "There's the odd change, but not"—he made another note, and yet another—"so many as I thought we'd need. I mean that was a total mess that I handed you." He looked at Paul as if to apologize, and to applaud him for organizing his *curriculum vitae*, a task that clearly challenged his organizational abilities.

"Just make whatever changes you like and I'll get you a final copy in a few days."

Paul drank his tea and watched Jack work through the document.

After about ten minutes he seemed satisfied and passed the text back to Paul. Then he reached into his battered portfolio and pulled out a sheaf of loose photographs he'd taken over the years. There were at least a hundred pictures of mandalas, circles of every size and ornamentation. Some were painted on rock faces, others on fine parchment. Still more adorned clay pots and vases.

"What I discovered in Asia is the archetypal nature of the mandala." He leaned forward slightly and took a sip of his tea. "It's not a regional art form; the mandala shows up in ancient Egypt, India of course, Tibet, Greece. Even in pre-Columbian America."

Paul had never considered the universal extent of the form. "But why does that make it an archetype?" he asked. "Isn't the circle one of the first things to enter a child's mind when he begins to draw?"

Jack smiled and tilted his chin to the table. "Perhaps. It started that way, I suppose. But in every culture, the mandala evolved to become a sphere of consciousness. And there are always some artists who are able to infuse their intelligence within the structure of consciousness." He lifted his eyes and with the thin smile still on his lips he said, "And where there's intelligence, there is always power."

Jack Wise began an extended lecture on the nature and potency of the eastern mandala. "The best way to understand it is through a simple analogy." He poured more tea into their cups. His long thin fingers appeared as fragile as they had the first day Paul met him. His face retained its drawn look, yet beneath his gaunt pallor he conveyed considerable vitality, as though his body had become a passing nuisance that he would endure but not indulge. "Think of the water passing through this teapot. It rests in the cup, then we drink it and it nourishes us. Then it passes from us into the earth and from there into the ocean."

Paul nodded. He thought Jack would be a very good art professor. He loved talking and he spoke with conviction and certainty. It was enough simply to listen to him without worrying about the niceties of truth, proof, facts or conjecture. As he listened, he found himself agreeing with the analogies and the clever paradoxes that Jack assigned to the Buddhist mysteries.

His key analogy linked the water cycle with the mandala archetype. Paul accepted it as a completely original idea. Jack began by drawing a parallel between consciousness and the ocean: a great pool of awareness that surrounds Earth. This vast, ever-changing sea connects all knowledge of things past or to come. It was similar to Carl Jung's idea of a collective unconscious, the primal repository of knowledge all humans share across time and culture. But Jack believed this awareness was more vital than a passive reservoir. His concept embraced the total mind—not mere memory. He referred to it as The Mind, assigning it an upper-case status because it affected events throughout the planet just as the tides constantly shaped the global shoreline.

From the ocean surface, Jack lectured, vapours rise into the air. This nearly invisible process reveals the intimate connection of the ocean to the masses of clouds that surround the earth. Their parallel is a ghost consciousness: spirits rising through the air casting glimpses of a half-remembered world. Jack suggested that it's difficult to assign any clear meaning to the vapours since they are in the most distant arc of the cycle, a sector opposite to our own position of individuated consciousness.

In the upper atmosphere the vapours drift and separate, clustering into clouds and then dissipating again. The clouds possess the same aspects of The Mind as the ocean, the same universal consciousness.

From the clouds are born tiny droplets: snow and rain, sometimes hail—and at this point The Mind becomes individuated consciousness. This is the portion of the cycle we inhabit. Sadly, our materialistic culture turns most of us into what he called "meat puppets."

"Taken together," he said, circling a finger in the air, "they all form a full cycle moving through four quadrants: universal consciousness, ghost awareness, pre-destiny, individuation, then the return to universal consciousness." He flipped through a few photographs again, tracing a fingernail over specific design elements within various mandalas. "Look carefully at each image. They all testify in one way or another to the cycle of The Mind. Therein lies your archetype.

"Death, you see, is the doorway to unimaginable bliss," Jack concluded and his eyes embraced Paul as though their meeting was, unquestionably, a contrivance of the gods.

Paul enters the Sampsons' basement door and walks across the cracked concrete floor to his neighbours' mud room. He knows Bettina likes to wipe Chester's paws before he waddles up the steps onto the main floor carpeting. Once he has cleaned the dog, Paul calls up the staircase: "Chester's home."

There's a brief silence, then Jerry's head peers around the doorway at the top of the stairs. "You're back," he announces. "Come on up, Paul. I've got something for you."

Paul climbs the flight of steps and wonders how Bettina, laid low with her broken hip, has navigated the staircase for the past few months.

"Come on." Jerry wags a finger and leads Paul into the living room where his wife sits in a wing-back chair, her legs mounted on a low ottoman. She smiles delicately yet her fingers don't miss a beat as they knit a long skein of wool into what appears to be a doggy sweater for Chester. "I have to keep count," she says apologetically, tallying the knots of wool on one of the needles. She writes a number on a slip of paper, then points to a chair. "Please sit down. You've been so good to walk that mutt. I just can't thank you enough."

"I've always liked Labs," Paul says.

"At least they're real dogs." Jerry scratches an ear lobe. "Shih Tzus and cockapoos—they've been concocted by quack breeders. Even their names sound like something yanked out of an unflushed toilet." Jerry laughs heartily, pleased with his joke.

"Jerry...." Bettina's knitting needles slap together with a firm clacking sound.

"Sorry, Tina." Jerry snickers and he waves a hefty snifter in one hand. "Scotch or brandy?"

"Gee. I don't know—"

"Brandy it is, then." Jerry pours two snifters and leads Paul to a chair next to the fireplace. Chester has settled onto a mat next to the hearth. A newspaper lies scattered on the floor.

Paul studies the scene. He guesses that the two old folks had been sitting here before he called up the stairs, Bettina tending her knitting and Jerry dozing with his newspaper. They haven't always been so comfortably retired. A month after Paul and Valerie moved into their house, the Sampsons invited them in for drinks and revealed their life histories. As soon as he turned eighteen, in 1943, Jerry volunteered to join the Glengarry Highlanders and was attached to the Third Canadian Infantry Division. A year later he found himself gunning the Germans out of Holland. It had been tough sledding, he confessed with a weary look that betrayed some unspeakable horrors. At one point he found himself cut off from his own men and scrambled into a root cellar. He hid behind a sack of turnips. When calm—and his common sense—returned, he looked around and saw Bettina huddled next to him. "We were both nineteen," she'd said with just a hint of Dutch accent. "But I knew just looking in his face that I could trust Jerry. Since that day, I always have." After the war they married and Jerry joined the RCMP and moved up the ranks until he secured the position of staff sergeant. When he retired he became a fishing guide in Campbell River. He fondly revealed that each summer he made more money yachting Yankees through the Johnston Strait than he did from a year's police pension. "Those were good years," Bettina confirmed. "Even though he was out on that ocean, I knew he was safe. But I never once thought he was safe when he was with the RCMP." When they were in their seventies Jerry sold his fleet of guide boats and, like so many other senior citizens, the Sampsons settled in Victoria.

It is Jerry's police experience that intrigues Paul now. As they sip their brandy, he wonders how to place a question that has been percolating in his mind over the past week: If you were to commit a crime—any crime—and you were suspected by the police, what's the best way to avoid conviction? He decides to ease into that conversation through the back door. It would take some manipulation, a deft turn of phrase or two, but Paul feels compelled to pry an answer from an authority on the topic and Jerry is his only resource. "So Jerry," he begins, "tell me about your years with the RCMP."

Jerry cocks his head and looks at the ceiling. "Let's see. It seemed like a long haul at the time: from 1948—that's when I became a paid officer—to 1980. They force you out at fifty-five."

"You were ready to go," Bettina murmurs without looking up from her wool.

"I guess," Jerry sighs and takes a pull on his brandy.

"What were some of the toughest situations you had to face?" Paul leans back in the chair, worried that he's asked this question too soon.

"I guess it would be in the early 1970s." He brushes aside the newspaper with one foot and stretches his legs toward the fireplace. "That would have been when we lived in Penticton."

Paul had never been there, but had heard of it often. "In the Okanagan?"

"Yup." Jerry coughs, and then continues. "Every summer in those years we'd get the bikers coming up from the States."

"You mean Hell's Angels?" Paul asks.

"Or wannabes." Jerry rolls his head in disgust and takes a nip of brandy from his snifter. "The James Deans and Marlon Brandos raising hell on their bikes."

"There might be hundreds of them at a time." Bettina looks at Jerry, shakes her head once and returns to her knitting.

"And every time you knew it would end bad." Jerry pulls the palm of one hand over the crest of his balding scalp. "We'd get a call in from another town down the road. 'They're headed your way.' *Headed our way*—we knew what that meant."

Jerry pauses and both men sip their brandy in contemplation. After a moment, Paul pries for a little more detail. "So what did it mean?"

"It meant one way or the other we'd be in a bloody fist fight. It was terrible. We'd have all the officers in the valley patrolling the town. You'd think these creeps would see what lay ahead if they pushed too hard. But no. By God, within a few days, maybe a week sometimes—but no matter how long they stayed—it would always come to having to beat them down."

Bettina pinches her lips together and draws a deep breath. "Pass me my juice, will you," she says.

Paul realizes neither of them wants to relive these memories. He feels guilty for pressing the story this far and decides to shift gears.

"I bet some of the most fascinating stories you heard in the force weren't the violent ones, though." Paul leans forward and pets

Chester's head. "What about the guy who got away with the big one? Did you run into a situation like that? A perfect crime?"

Jerry cocks his head again, an evasive gesture implying there were some pretty foxy capers. "Oh yes, there were a few of them, too."

"That fraud with William Burston," Bettina says, quite pleased that the conversation has moved into white-collar territory.

"You can't say it was fraud, Tina," Jerry says. "There was never proof of it. Apart from the missing six hundred-odd thousand from the local Northwest Bank."

"And their closure the next month," Bettina adds. "Following the disappearance of the manager and all their records for the time in question."

"That, too. See, that was the problem. The absence of proof."

With both Bettina and Jerry engaged in telling the story, an elaborate web of public deceit and fraud unravels over the next half hour. It's quite a tale, Paul decides, not so much because of its scale, but because Bettina and Jerry personally knew all of the characters in it, especially William Burston, the bank's comptroller.

"So what saved him?" Paul asks. "With all fingers pointing at Burston, what was it he did that saved his skin?"

Jerry finishes his brandy and examines the empty snifter. "I guess it comes down to him not saying a peep."

"What do you mean?"

"Since there was no concrete evidence linking him to fraud and the only possible witness disappeared, the only way to convict him was by means of his own confession. But he didn't say a word." Jerry smiles despite himself. "We had him grilled on and off for six months by the boys from Vancouver. But Bill Burston had one thing and one thing only to say for himself: 'My lawyer has instructed me to say nothing to you.' He didn't expose so much as a dirty fingernail. Without his statement there was no hope we could take him to court. And as I understand it, you still can't convict a man in this country without giving him his day in court. Thank God."

Paul ducks through the drizzle as he sprints across the Sampsons' lawn to his house. He's feeling better, he realizes, and imagines the medication has already achieved a salutary effect. Or it could be the double dose of brandy, a medicinal concoction that usually causes the skin on his face to feel thicker and somewhat duller. No matter, he decides, his chat with Jerry revealed all he needed to know about the police interrogations that may come his way. To quote Jerry: don't say a peep. Ben Stillwell would concur, of course, and braced by the congruence of these expert opinions, Paul feels secure for the first time since he read the news story about John Ribbenstahl's depraved heart.

"Hey-ho," he calls as he eyes the front hallway, his signature greeting upon entering his house—one he hasn't employed since the accident. There's no response, but in the back rooms, a murmur of voices. He hangs his jacket on the coat rack and enters the kitchen. Valerie is on the phone. Eliot huddles above a mass of Lego which has cascaded across the linoleum in the eating nook.

"Okay, Mom." Valerie makes a knife-cut motion below her throat. Apparently she's been trying to wind up the call, yet Jeanine, ever full of advice (all of it freely, and generously, dispensed) presses on with new tips and household hints. "Yes. Of course. We'll wait on the Easter egg hunt until you arrive." She rolls her eyes and pushes her face toward Paul, her expression full of desperation: please *spare* me. "Oh, guess what?" she says interrupting her mother, "Paul's home. Gotta go now—"

There's a pause and Valerie turns away to face the stove as she's dragged into another dimension of her mother's on-going monologue. "Yes, I know he does …. "

Paul smiles and spots her glass of wine next to the sink. She's been into at least one glass, a necessary brace to support her spirits during conversations with her parents. With her free hand Valerie stirs a pot of pasta sauce on the stove-top, Eliot's current favourite, mushrooms and green pepper.

He settles on a chair next to Eliot and examines the oblong construction which occupies his son's hands.

"It's a kayak, Dad." He holds it aloft, but the rising motion breaks an end piece onto the floor where it shatters into twenty-odd blocks.

Paul expects a minor fit of frustrated anger. But it doesn't come. Instead Eliot utters something Paul considers quite mature; perhaps it marks a new step forward: "I didn't need that part, anyway. A kayak doesn't have an engine, does it, Dad?"

"Nope. Not the good ones." Paul smiles. He realizes he's been smiling since he came through the door. The gesture is so simple, yet generates such relief. "Do you want to see a picture of one? Maybe that would help you build your own."

"Yeah. That'd be good." Eliot brushes away the stray pieces of kayak engine, takes his father's hand and follows him along the gallery to his office. The room harbours numerous treasures, secrets from Paul's catalogue of experience that he reveals one at a time. The home-run baseball he hit in Little League, a pressed four-leaf clover, the varnished shell of a long-dead snapping turtle. Each artifact offers a glimpse into Paul's past, a life so wise and full that it gives meaning to the phrase he whispers to the child every night: "Now off to bed and slide into sleep, safe and sound."

Paul digs through his four-tier filing cabinet until he unearths the file he'd kept from his kayaking lessons. It's a thin folder containing a few letter-sized sheets on safety tips, weather patterns, tide and current charts. Among these he finds the schematic diagram of a standard kayak, a cutaway revealing the construction of the cockpit, gunnels, storage ports, rudder, and the like. He passes it to Eliot, who seizes it in his hands and studies it intently.

"I can make this," he announces after a moment. " I can really make this!"

"I'm sure you can."

His son darts back to the mass of Lego in the kitchen and Paul closes the filing cabinet drawer. As he leaves the room he notices the telephone answering machine. The blinking message light has changed to a steady glow. That can only mean the message from Rory Stillwell has been erased, that Valerie has listened to his call.

Paul tries to determine if he'd actually forgotten about the message during his walk with Chester. If he had, it would be a positive sign: he'd been untouched by a passing moment of jealousy. Certainly in his conversation with the Sampsons he'd put it out of his mind. Yet now a new hesitation develops. What if Valerie says nothing about Rory? After all, he said nothing to her about Ben's closing comments in Foo Hong's and the revelation that Rory was ill. He decides to wait and see. Wait for Valerie to reveal her reconnection with her old flame, or maintain her silence about this renewed link to her past.

Paul walks back to the kitchen and pours himself a glass of white wine from Valerie's bottle. She is still on the phone with Jeanine: "Yes, Mom, everything will be ready for your arrival on Easter weekend." She signals to him to pour her another glass, then slowly stirs the pasta sauce. The kettle bubbles over and she drops the pasta into the boiling water. "Ten minutes 'til supper," she whispers over her mother's voice.

"Okay," he says and settles in the chair next to Eliot. He slips into this quiet moment of domesticity, one in which he can observe himself from a distance, in a time and space not so different from the world of his own childhood. Yet in spite of this constancy, this ongoing atmosphere of nourishment and contentment in both his past and present life, somehow he never anticipated the world he now occupies from the perspective of his past. He couldn't see how the path from one life would lead to the other. There were too many chance interventions between them. Too many lucky turns and fateful diversions.

Like Eliot, Paul was an only child. Like Eliot, he was adored by his parents, John and Doreen Wakefield. They were an upper-middle-class couple living in the anglophone community of Montreal West. His father had established a successful one-man enterprise, Wakefield Fabrics, in the textile import-export business. "It can be a tricky game," his father confessed. "You have to judge which way the wind blows and know when to shift from the import to the export side six months ahead of the trend." Although John maintained

a comfortable life for his family, Paul had no interest in the opportunity John offered to expand the business as a father-and-son
venture.

Paul obtained a degree in psychology from McGill University and
began to troop around the maritime provinces with his rock band,
Forged Destiny, playing gigs in high schools, bars and legion halls.
After six months in which they barely covered the cost of buses,
hotels and the ongoing "festival of beer" (as Mickey Schwartz, their
now-deceased drummer, once put it) Paul returned to Montreal and
took on a nine-to-five job in the personnel department of Alcan's
head office in the Place Ville Marie tower. To his great surprise he
enjoyed it. He administered aptitude tests to the steady stream of
job applicants seeking employment in the company. Once the tests
were scored, he assessed recruitment objectives with management,
filled any vacant positions, then ran the orientation and training
programs for the new hires.

Within two years he'd found a niche as a corporate trainer and
ran all the in-house executive development programs for Alcan's
head office and regional centres. He surveyed the company's di-
rectors and vice-presidents, identified their key training priorities,
found the right mix of consultants who could deliver the training
packages and scheduled it all in a biannual course rotation that
came to be called Alcan-u by the vp of Personnel, Maurice LaRose.
Paul was twenty-four and realized that he'd found a career-track.
He sold his bass guitar and amplifier, moved out of his grotty Lorne
Avenue apartment in the McGill ghetto and rented a one-bedroom,
fifteenth-floor condo in LaCité on Avenue du Parc. Weeks later, another surprise: his dating life improved to the point where it achieved
complications. The greatest hazards he now faced arose from dou-
ble-bookings in his tightly scheduled dating game. But within six
months he met Michelle LaBaie and his romantic life became more
focussed and the game took a serious turn.

His new groove came to a halt on October 17<sup>th</sup>. He'd spent the previous evening with John and Doreen, a Thanksgiving turkey feast more elaborate than most because Doreen wanted to impress Michelle LaBaie, Paul's new girlfriend from the office.

"She's very pretty," Doreen whispered when Michelle absented herself from the dining table and closed the bathroom door. "With much more personality...." Compared to Marnie and Giselle and what-was-her-name?—but Doreen was too gracious to speak this aloud even to her family.

"Honey, you're shameless," John said and laughed as though he was well used to it. Then he added more seriously, "But she does know a little something about business."

"True." Paul nodded, intending this one word to respond to both parents' comments. His parents always liked any woman he brought home; the more the merrier. They'd sooner see his harem than see him barren. But when he'd joked about this over the telephone, Doreen became embarrassed.

Michelle returned to the table and smiled. "So, Paul tells me you're seeking a little place in the Laurentians." She spoke with a very slight French accent and a tendency to fumble the odd bit of vernacular.

"We're going to drive up to St. Sauveur tomorrow," John said.

"We've got our hearts set on a place near one of the lakes. It doesn't have to be waterfront," Doreen submitted, "but a place with water views would be just lovely in the summer."

"St. Sauveur?" Michelle tilted her head. "You should meet my uncle, Guy Benoit."

"Oh?"

"He's been doing real estate there for years. It's his back of the woods," she added.

There was a pause.

"It's either his neck of the woods," Paul said with a laugh, "or the back of his hand,"

"Yes. Of course!" Michelle started laughing too. "Maybe I should have said the town is the back of his neck—or is it his pain in the butt?"

"Got that one right!" John snorted, and soon Doreen began

laughing too. Michelle had a lovely, self-effacing way of brushing away her malapropisms that endeared her to everyone. Before she departed for the evening she dug through her address book for Uncle Guy's phone number, pencilled the information onto a slip of paper and pressed it into John's hand.

"She's adorable," Doreen whispered into her son's ear as he left their home with Michelle. These were the last words she spoke to him. Of course, no one knew that at the time.

Twenty minutes after the children departed, John and Doreen climbed the stairs to their bedroom and made love for the first time in two months. Back at his condo at LaCité, Paul and Michelle renewed their intimacy for the second time that day.

On the evening of the 17th Paul sat alone in his condo reading the *Montreal Gazette*. Michelle had gone shopping with her sister and called to say they would be having a light supper in a local café and she would drop by on her way home.

When his buzzer sounded at 7:35, he assumed it was Michelle and simply rang her up without checking the intercom to ensure that indeed, it was Michelle at the building entry, or more likely, Michelle with her sister and a bundle of parcels.

But then he opened the door and was confronted by two police officers. He soon lost track of the details of their conversation. Later he could only assemble phrases, snippets of dialogue—none of it exact or memorable. He was asked if he was John and Doreen Wakefield's son. Yes. Did they drive a blue '84 Buick LeSabre? Yes, why are you asking? We're sorry to tell you ... but we have bad news. They died today in a traffic accident in St. Sauveur-des-Monts....

A bread truck had collided with them head-on. The driver, André Landry, two weeks short of his retirement day, had suffered a heart attack en route from the bakery to the local dépanneur. He was found slumped over the steering wheel, unmarked by the accident. Paul's parents were less fortunate, but the police conceded that "it was over in a minute." Those were the only words he remembered with precision. They were the words he used to try to calm Michelle.

When he revealed the news to her, Michelle collapsed. She wasn't hysterical—but she dropped onto the sofa unable to move over the next four hours. "*C'est ma faute,*" she whispered over and over. "No, it isn't," Paul insisted, in an effort to shift her mood. But Michelle claimed that since the accident had occurred on Route de L'Eglise, two blocks from her uncle's real estate office, John and Doreen were dispatched to their fate because of her intervention. Paul couldn't change her opinion and soon he realized that her despair had overpowered his own sense of grief.

Her demeanour failed to improve after the funeral. Days later, when Paul sorted through his parents' possessions, he came across Guy Benoit's business card in his father's wallet. As he held the card in his fingers he wondered what to do with it. His instinct was to destroy it and never mention its existence to Michelle. Then he decided that interpersonal honesty required him to disclose this detail to Michelle. Although his parents had died coming from her uncle's office, Paul said he attached no blame to her. "They could as easily have been killed twenty kilometres away."

When she became inconsolable he left her. He lost the emotional stamina to deal with his own pain and Michelle's dissolution. He found himself brooding alone in his condo for days at a time. After a brief leave of absence from his job, he returned to work but found he could barely tolerate the routine activities. He was late for meetings. His hours became erratic. To purge his misery he indulged in a quick and dirty affair—which he revealed to Michelle to ensure the break in their relationship would be complete. He spent the last of his vacation days meeting with lawyers over the probate of his parents' wills, assessing the value of their real estate and his father's business operations, sorting through their possessions and discarding all but a few items he guessed he might want somewhere, sometime down the road.

When it became apparent that he would inherit a little more than five hundred thousand dollars, he decided to quit his job, sublet his condo and travel for a while. He had no plans, no itinerary, simply a curiosity to see the world. After a few months in Europe, he hopped a freighter along the west coast of Africa. After half a year there, he wandered through India, then Japan. He travelled for almost five years before he returned to Canada and settled in Victoria. A few months later he met Valerie. Within another four months they married. For years afterward they joked about their cliché relationship. Their child, their jobs, their house and home. All of it perfect, newly-wed bliss.

Valerie settles Eliot into his bed and walks down the flight of stairs to Paul's office. Paul can tell she's suffering from the end-of-day exhaustion that strikes them both around 8:00. But tonight Valerie's mood carries a little more edge than the usual evening ennui. "I need to talk to you," she says with a tone reserved for substantial issues.

Paul folds the newspaper over his lap and looks at her. Perhaps she wants to talk about Rory Stillwell. The illness Ben had mentioned. Maybe he'd come down with something terminal and she needs to say good-bye, to reveal that her warmth for him is fully extinguished.

Valerie paces over to the window. "I saw Reg Jensen this afternoon—"

"Again?" Paul presses a hand to his forehead. His newspaper drops to the floor.

"Yes. At the school." Valerie turns and faces her husband. She holds a finger to her lower lip. "I was picking up Eliot and there he was. Sitting in that beat-up car of his."

"Was he looking at you?"

"Yes. I'm sure of it." She sits opposite Paul and clutches her hands. Her head tilts to one side and he can see she's worried. "He was just sitting there. Waiting for something."

Paul shakes his head. How can this make sense? What the hell does Reg think he's doing—stalking Valerie? "Are you sure it was him?"

"I went over to him. But when I got close to his car he pulled away from the school without even glancing back at me." Valerie pauses as though she has more to add, but instead of continuing she wipes a single tear from her eye. "Bastard," she adds in a whisper.

Paul glances away. She seldom cries, a strength he's always appreciated. "All right," he says after she's re-established her composure. "I'll talk to him."

"You mean telephone him?"

Paul thinks about the options. The steady ringing in his ears distracts his attention. If he could wish anything away if would be this constant irritation. But now he needs to eliminate a new threat: the strange obsession that has seized Reg Jensen. "It'd be better to talk to him in person. Maybe I should call and set up a meeting. Just the two of us. I worry about setting him off if I do anything *official*."

Valerie leans forward. "Maybe you should have Ben Stillwell with you."

Paul nods his head and glances into his wife's eyes. "Good idea. I'll arrange it through Ben."

A silence lingers between them as each considers what lies ahead. "I just feel so threatened by all this," Valerie says.

"I know." Paul eases over to her chair and wraps an arm around her. It feels so good to comfort her. He realizes he hasn't consoled anyone since the accident; everyone's been tending to him. Maybe that will change now. Maybe facing up to Reg and all his other problems is all he needs to do. Become proactive. A take-charge guy.


"Do you remember this morning?" Valerie asks as they climb into bed. The moon pours a wide stream of light through the window onto the bed and across her shoulders.

Paul tries to reconstruct the earliest part of what feels like a very long day. The morning is a vague memory drifting in a week-old fog. "Yes," he says. He remembers parts of the morning at least. Dropping Eliot at school. The first sighting of Reg in his Dodge. Coffee at Starbucks. Holding Valerie's hand there and pledging to rekindle the spark of intimacy they'd both felt. "I remember looking at you," he says and turns his face to her.

"Look again." Valerie inches her head a little closer to him. She is at her most beautiful like this: offering him complete access to her—through her eyes. She opens an inner world of tenderness and a capacity to absorb all his cares and unspent energy.

"You're so lovely," he whispers.

She smiles. "Think so?" she asks and with one hand she unbuttons the top of her nightie, rolls on her back and exposes both breasts and the eight-inch scar that runs between them.

"Yes." The light from the moon and her breasts merge in his eyes. He could worship here, at this church made of flesh and luminescence. He kisses her and lingers on the sensations pouring into his body through his mouth.

"Tell me what's so lovely." She wraps an arm around him and abandons herself to his lips.

"All of you," he murmurs and his hands work along her waist and over her thighs. Now everything finds its centre once again. Paul and Valerie fit their love together like twin arcs of a circle looping back to their beginnings. When the closure is complete their senses roll in a still, dreamless pool and for a few hours at least, in the fragile vessel of their love, they establish a perfect harbour there.

# CHAPTER 6

THE WEEK BEFORE EASTER, DR. EDWARD BIGGS CHANGES PAUL'S MEDICATION. His blood pressure has fallen to 166 over 98, but until his hypertension completely abates, the new drug of choice is metoprolol; two pills a day. While the medication is relatively high tech, the side effects can be disorienting.

"You may find yourself in a bit of a fog," Ed says as he signs the new prescription slip. "In fact, it can feel quite pronounced. But don't worry. It's a sign your blood pressure is falling according to plan. Just step out of whatever situation you're in until the feeling passes. You'll find the episodes come and go, but if one lasts more than a day, don't hesitate to call me."

Paul takes the warning to heart. On Tuesday he begins to feel the first impressions of the fog wavering above him. He decides to compensate by keeping an edge to his routine. Rather than simply scan the newspaper, he carefully studies it. As he listens to Valerie and Eliot he tries to read their lips. When he drives the car he tunes his ears to the hum of the tires on the road.

As they drive along Oak Bay Avenue he explains all of this to his wife. She's understanding—even sympathetic—and suggests he postpone any confrontation with Reg Jensen, especially when she begins to examine the paranoia underlying her fears. "I just feel so crazy even thinking that he could be stalking us. I mean, what reason would he have to do something so outrageous?"

"I can't imagine," Paul says.

"But what if there's another episode?"

"Then I'll call Ben Stillwell and we'll have a talk." He looks through the Volvo windshield and feels he's achieved a reprieve from an uncomfortable confrontation. Destiny has been shunted aside—at least for the moment.

"Promise?"

"Of course." A contingent promise. One easy to make because it depends on circumstance. And no one, he knows, could ever be blamed for conditions beyond his control.


On Tuesday afternoon as Paul steps through the doorway into his house he can hear Valerie and Eliot arguing.

"So you don't know anything about this?"

"I told you already," Eliot whimpers, "I don't know anything."

Paul pulls on his slippers and stares through the kitchen doorway. Eliot sits at the breakfast nook, his eyes cast to the floor. Valerie paces across the linoleum floor in front of him, the fingers of both hands knotted together. "I'm not accusing you," she says to her son. "It's just that I need to know you didn't do it."

"Well, I told you that already."

"And you don't know who did."

Eliot locks his wrists with his hands and buries his face in the crook of one arm.

"What happened?" Paul says and walks into the middle of the room. Until now he's been ignored.

"Look downstairs," Valerie says without glancing at him. She embraces Eliot in her arms. "I'm sorry, sweetie. I didn't mean to make you feel so bad. I just need to know how this happened."

Paul walks down the flight of stairs to the living room and through the passageway into the family room. As his feet touch the carpet he sees the spray of glass cast across the floor from the window. In the middle of the room lies a rock the size of a football.

"What the hell is this?" he calls up the stairs. Nobody responds. He can hear Eliot lost in a soft jag of crying and Valerie's murmurs of comfort. Paul carefully crosses the family room to look at the shattered window. A jagged ring of glass spikes clings to the window casing. A light breeze wafts past his face. He lifts the rock with both hands and dusts off a clump of soil. It's one of the rocks from the back garden next to the compost bin. No doubt about it, someone meant to do this.

He carefully treads over the glass to the telephone and calls a window repair specialist. Better to get this fixed right away, he tells himself. As the phone rings against this ear, he considers the malice intended by this vandalism. The premeditated anger. Next he'll get Valerie to call the police. Better to let her make the call. That way there will be no chance for him to fall into an entrapment related to the accident.

An hour later, in the privacy of his small, cluttered office, he makes another phone call. It's become habitual, he now realizes, a routine he's built into this day. For reasons he cannot fathom, he always ensures he's alone when he places this call and that Eliot and Valerie are occupied elsewhere in the house, or better still, busy with an errand in town.

He dials the number from memory and waits three, four rings.

"Peds, June Hallett speaking." The voice is officious, but not rushed.

"Hello, this is Paul Wakefield. I'm calling about one of your patients, Jenny Jensen."

"Ah, yes, Jen-Jen," she says as if the girl were a friend of her own daughter, a neighbourhood kid who dropped by every few days. "Well ... she's resting comfortably."

"Any sign of change?" Paul's voice sinks a half tone and then he adds, "I was with her during the accident, so I was hoping...."

"Yes, I know," she says. "I'm the head nurse. I've heard that you've been calling. We have your number and believe me, we'll call you as soon as there's a change."

Paul thinks about this. "So you think there will be a change?"

"We all hope for it." Then in a voice that reveals she does not want to create false hope, she says, "But there are no guarantees. No one can forecast the outcome."

"I know." He shifts the handset to his left ear. "Look, I don't want to be any trouble. But do you mind if I call again?"

She pauses to consider this. "Of course. Any time you want."

After he hangs up, Paul stares out the window, at the trees across the road. He understands now why he must be alone to make this call. So that when there's a change, when Jenny finally comes around, he'll have a moment to himself, a small space in which he can release the gathering madness.

The next morning, Wednesday, the side effects of the new medication have intensified enough to induce Paul to walk—rather than drive—Eliot to school. No point in jeopardizing anyone on the road, he advises himself as he heads out the door in the morning. He is also aware that he has begun an internal dialogue, a steady patter between the drugged, hypertensive insomniac that he has become and another being, a cautious, benevolent caretaker who attempts to manage his skewed perceptions and impulses. He likes to think of the latter as *the real me* and the former as someone named Nark. "Face it," he instructs Nark, "the car wheels are a little out of your control."

"What's that, Dad?"

Paul looks at his son with surprise. "Nothing," he says. "I'm just wondering if I should take old Chester out for a stroll. After I drop you off at school."

"Okay. There he is." Eliot has virtually adopted Chester in the past week, especially now that Paul is exercising him every day. "I'll get his leash," he says and hitches his backpack around his shoulders and sprints over to the Sampsons' lawn.

Paul watches his son clip the leash to Chester's collar and drag him across the open yard. It's a typical pattern for the dog: initial reticence, followed by easy compliance and finally an urge to lead his pack into unknown adventures. Within a minute Chester begins to strain at the leash and Eliot passes the lead to his father and they head up Transit Road and turn onto Central Avenue.

"You know how you can tell it's spring, Dad?" Eliot kicks at a rock and sends it flying across the road. "I mean, tell by signs that you can't see."

"Signs that you can't see?" Paul thinks a moment. "You mean like the air's a bit warmer in the morning."

"Yup. Know what else?"

"The sun rises earlier each day and a little more to the north." Paul loves this, trading facts with his son as though they are pieces of currency—nickels and dimes to be saved then cashed in when Eliot's bank of accumulated knowledge begins to burst. Then Eliot can give his parents or grandparents a formal presentation about the weather or space travel or the dissection of worms. "He's going to be a lawyer!" Jeanine would announce. Everyone would nod, thinking, yeah, maybe....

"The way I can tell it's spring using a sign you can't see," Eliot continues, "is when you can't see the eagles' nest any more." He points to the high trees behind the lots on the south side of the street.

"Gee." Paul gazes up to the tree line. "You're right." True enough. In mid-winter when the leaves are down you can see the bald eagles' nest atop the big alder just below Anderson Hill. It's the size of a washtub. It amazes Paul when he considers the labour required to patch the nest together.

"I heard the eaglets crying yesterday; you know in their little screech. Yeet-yeet." Eliot puckers his lips and with an open hand set like a bull-horn to his mouth he broadcasts the harsh cry of the baby birds.

Not a bad imitation, Paul thinks and he tries it but immediately feels self-conscious as they turn the corner on Oliver and the school draws into view. He yanks on Chester's lead to keep the dog in heel as they approach a cluster of children clotting next to the crosswalk.

"There's Barry," Eliot says as they cross the road. "I'm going to show him my eagle call, okay?"

"Sure. See you at lunch."

.F. BAILEY

"All right," Eliot yells over his shoulder as he runs off with his bull-horn pushed against his lips.

Paul stands at the link fence surrounding the schoolyard. God, I love you, he whispers to himself. I never thought I could love anyone like I love you. "Thank you," he says aloud—with no idea who he is addressing. With this delicate sense of gratitude filling his mind he looks across the block and sees Reg Jensen sitting in his red Dodge 500.

As Paul reaches the car, Reg guns the engine and tries to pull away from the curb. Paul flags him with one hand, a gesture of friendship intended to pull him aside for a bit of chat. But Reg cranks his head around to check for oncoming traffic, tags the accelerator again—only to have the car lurch forward, and then stall a metre from the curb.

Paul smirks inwardly and mumbles Valerie's word: *bastard*. "Surprised to see you here, Reg," he says and peers through the half-open window.

Reg rolls his eyes away, clearly embarrassed to be seen stalling his car and—after two more tries—unable to start the engine.

"I didn't know you knew anyone at Monterey School." Paul inches forward. He's not sure how to begin what must be said. He feels a quiet anger in his belly and the sense that he can control it.

"I guess you wouldn't," Reg says through the glass.

"What's that?" He stands just far enough away from the car to reduce any sign of aggressive posturing. On the other hand, he only wants to talk to Reg Jensen once. Make no mistake, he says to himself, and be crystal clear with this creep.

Reg rolls the window down a little more, enough to be heard and seen, but little enough to prevent anyone from pulling him through the opening. "Nice dog," he says after a moment.

"What?" Paul can hardly believe what he's hearing.

"That your dog?"

The school buzzer sounds in the yard. At once hundreds of children run screaming toward the building and begin to flood through the doors.

"Yeah, she's my dog." Paul presses closer to make room for a passing car. He realizes subtleties are not going to work with this guy. He narrows his eyes and leans forward. "Listen, Reg, Valerie has seen you here a couple of times now." He lets this sentence hang in the air to see what Reg says.

"Yeah." He scratches the stubble that's come up on his face. "Well, she might have."

"So ... what's happening?" The closer he gets to the car, the more clearly Paul detects the extent of Reg Jensen's growing disintegration. His eyes are bloodshot, his dirty shirt lies unbuttoned over his belly, his lips, flakey and dry, purse together with each breath he takes. It's obvious he's had some kind of lapse. Paul decides to probe a different angle. "How's Fran?" he asks.

Reg shakes his head and looks away.

Great. Paul assumes they've had some kind of split. Fran is probably bunked out in the hospital next to his comatose daughter while Reg nurses a bottle of Scotch back home.

"You walking that dog back to your place?" Reg asks.

Paul glances at the roadway. Another car brushes past him and his patience begins to ebb. "Yeah," he says with a shrug. "I'm walking the dog back home. Look, Reg, are you getting any sleep? Are you eating right?"

"Up yours," he blurts out.

"All right." Paul steps back, then forward as another car bleeps the horn and slides behind him. "Look, I can't talk here, but I want to tell you: back off from my wife and kid." He narrows his eyes and studies Reg's face. It feels good to have that out. Good enough that he decides to say it again. "Just keep away from them and stop stalking them here at the school."

"I'm not stalking anyone." Reg's jaw hinges open exposing a line of perfect teeth. With one stiff crank of his arm he lowers the window another turn.

"All right." Paul feels the anger in his belly turn to water. "I'm just saying to give us some space." He holds a hand in front of his chest and makes a slight pushing motion. "Valerie had nothing to do with what happened," he adds, "and she and Eliot don't need this."

"Eliot? That's his name then." He tips his head toward the schoolyard.

Paul curses himself for letting this out. He tugs on the leash and begins to walk away. When Paul reaches the sidewalk, Reg opens the car door and steps onto the road. "I'm not stalking anybody. I want you to know that."

Two mothers push a pair of baby strollers along the sidewalk and glance away when they hear the despair in Reg Jensen's voice.

"All right," Paul says. He's standing on the sidewalk next to the schoolyard fence. "But what about my back window? Tell me who broke that."

A blank look falls across Jensen's face. For a moment the two men stand staring at one another with a sense of mutual confusion.

"You tell me," Reg says as if he's responding to a half-forgotten question. His voice lowers but it's still sharp and full of bereavement. "Just tell me how come my kid's lying in the hospital right now. Why is she there and you get to walk your kid into·school every day with your Goddamn dog?"

Paul can listen to no more. The bitterness pouring through Reg is too much to bear. He yanks on the dog leash again and starts to quick-step down the block with Chester in tow.

"You tell me that—you dumb fuck—tell me that one thing and then you'll see the last of me!" Reg calls after him and slams the car door shut.

When he reaches the end of the block, Paul turns around and watches Reg pull the Dodge through a tight u-turn in the road and drive up the far end of the street. Bastard, he says to himself and a shudder runs through him.


Paul walks Chester another block to the foot of Oliver Street, across Beach Drive and onto the rocky shore of Shoal Bay. For a moment he considers jogging straight back to his house and calling the police. He'd been threatened, no doubt about that. Threatened by a certifiable nutbar. But instead of making a rash move, first he decides to think through his situation. He unclips Chester from the lead and follows the dog to the water's edge. As his feet crunch over the loose gravel, his mind fills with two possible scenarios: one, smashing Reg Jensen in the face and the other, Reg Jensen kidnapping his son.

He considers a physical fight. It could be brutal. Paul recalls the swell of Reg's arms, how the years labouring in his butcher shop had bulked them into massive knots. Fuelled by his blind fury, he would be primitive in taking his revenge—crazy as the idea was that revenge might be his due. Or was it so lunatic? After all, Paul had beaten Jenny into unconsciousness—a fact he had almost buried in the ongoing struggle to maintain his own equilibrium. Indeed, some people would argue that Reg had a right to inflict the same damage on Paul. That it would be fitting for Paul to take his punishment, to absorb Reg's anger until it was spent and Reg could find some measure of his own redemption. That's what Gandhi had done: he'd accepted the beatings of the world. How could he have done that? How did Gandhi look into the face of such rage and consume such terrible anger?

The other option—a kidnapping—was more difficult to envision. How would it unfold? Enticing Eliot into the Dodge 500 seemed improbable. Reg was a train wreck; no one, certainly not Eliot, would fall for the inducements from such a broken soul. But Reg was street-wise, tough. When the time was right, within a few seconds he could muscle the child into his car. On the walk home from school—or right in front of their home. An easy snatch-and-grab without witnesses to confirm the fact that Eliot had been taken.

Worse were the unknowns that would follow. Where would he take the boy? And what would be his end-game? Perhaps Fran Jensen maintained some kind of rational intention, but could she influence her husband? Would she even know about the abduction? An entire day could pass without anyone but Paul and Valerie believing that a crime had been committed. In that time Reg's madness could run its course to its disastrous conclusion.

Paul gazes at the lighthouse on Trial Island and scans the length of the beach. Chester roams the driftwood sniffing out shellfish in the flotsam dumped at the top of the tide-line. He realizes this is the first time he has been to the waterfront since the accident. I guess that part is over, he says to himself. The fear of what happened is gone—or has been replaced—he adds as a minor correction. He stands near the light surf thinking about the passage of time, how it alters things without any physical intervention at all. It's a force of change that you cannot see. That's how Eliot would describe it.

He returns Chester to the Sampsons' basement, then shuffles over to his own house, exhausted by the episode with Reg. The torpid effects of insomnia sweep through him as he settles into his La-z-boy and stares through his office window onto the street.

He eyes the telephone directory. In a few minutes he will make a call, either to Ben Stillwell or to the police. There's a question of urgency to be considered: if Reg now makes a decisive move against Eliot or Valerie, it has to be met with direct force. That would have to involve the police. He's certain he's no match against Reg unless he has some kind of weapon—and the skill to use it.

Ben Stillwell was very clear about speaking to the police. Under no circumstances was he to say a word to them without Ben present. That's why Valerie called the police about the broken window. Ben's warning was restricted to the kayaking accident, of course, but Reg's threat was tied to the accident and therefore Ben would want to be party to the discussion. On the other hand, if he waits to speak to Ben about Reg's threats, given Ben's packed schedule it could take days before he reaches him.

Finally there is Valerie to consider. Reg's behaviour this morning would only heighten her sense of peril. Sure, she's tough-minded, but beneath her willingness to speak up about a cause lies a hidden vulnerability. She is terrified of violence.

One option is to tell Valerie nothing. He has learned too many times that honest, open disclosure can lead to disaster. That's what had happened when he revealed to Michelle LaBaie that his parents had met with her uncle just before they died. He could have hidden that. He could have called her uncle and sworn him to secrecy. As time passed he would have revealed his duplicity when she was able to bear it.

And face it, he says to himself with a shrug: there are already several secrets between us. Valerie has yet to unveil the news about Rory Stillwell's telephone call. Likely she's just hiding news of her reconnection to spare Paul any unnecessary jealousy. Her fling with Rory is history. Meaningless. Perhaps she's already seen him and wished him well with a final, parting kiss. Even if she is seeing him right now, does it matter?...

Despite this logic, he feels himself falling into a web of arguments—all of it spinning wildly from his own mind and woven from the threads of anxiety, medication, insomnia and guilt. He exhales a long breath of air. His confusion is so deep and wide that he can no longer tell the shoreline from the sea. Enough, he tells himself. Rory Stillwell is an adolescent distraction. Until now, you've been thinking things out quite logically—for a guy pumped up with metoprolol. He scratches his head a moment. Did he swallow his morning dose? Yes, of course, with your juice, and then—

The telephone rings.

Paul eyes widen as though he's just discovered that the telephone is a life form. An entity with consciousness. Intention.

It rings again.

He pulls himself from his chair and answers on the fourth ring. "Hello?"

"Is Paul Wakefield there, please?" A woman's voice. Professional, agenda-oriented.

"Speaking."

"This is Corporal Marianne Woodford calling from the city police. I'm following up on a vandalism complaint. Your wife reported a broken window. Is that right?"


When he first hears Woodford's voice Paul's hand begins to shake. Despite his shock from this phone call he has the presence of mind to find a little breathing space.

"Listen," he says after Corporal Woodford has spoken a few sentences about the window. "I don't have a pencil and paper at this phone. Give me a minute to switch, okay?"

"Well ... I just need a few facts, then we'll canvass your neighbours to see if anyone—"

"Look," Paul interrupts, "I really have to switch phones here."

"Do you want me to call back?" she offers.

"No. Not necessary," he says, thinking that this pause will create even more suspicion. "Just give me a sec."

He sets the handset next to his computer and walks a few steps backward. What to do? His left hand cradles his face and he stares at the telephone. Then he thinks of the business card that Ben Stillwell passed to him. Make all appointments through his secretary, he had said. Yes, that is what you must do now. Get your wallet, find the card and tell Woodford to contact Ginny Steiner. Now you're thinking straight again. You'll be okay. But another voice tells him otherwise and he knows he is trading illusions for reality.

He picks up the phone and says, "Sorry, I'll just be another sec," then rests it on the desk without waiting for her response. He finds his wallet on his bedroom dresser and jogs back to the telephone, worried that this is all taking too long. In another moment Woodford will hang up, drive over to the house and cuff him.

"Hello?" He can hear her calling through the handset as he returns.

"Hi. Okay, I'd like you to make the arrangements through my lawyer's secretary, Ginny Steiner."

There's a pause. "You know ... that's not really necessary. We just need to get a few facts from you. What time was the window broken? Did anyone see what happened?"

A ploy. But one poorly disguised. "I'd rather do it my way," he says firmly.

"All right." She's curt now and dutifully copies down Stillwell's office number.

Her shift in tone is unsettling and Paul decides it's wise to break off the call as soon as possible. But before he hangs up, he wants to open the possibility of discussing Reg Jensen. "Listen," he says tentatively, "there's something else I'd like to talk about ... do you mind if I call you back?"

"Any time," she offers, but hangs up before he can say more.


Paul pushes out the foot kick on his La-z-boy and considers what he should say to Corporal Woodford about Jensen. He has a link with the police now. They know him and they know about the accident in the marina. Ben Stillwell can navigate whatever rough waters might emerge from the accident. But this new trouble with Reg Jensen, they knew nothing about it. And if there is a pressing issue, it has to do with Jensen and his threats. He decides to limit his contact to Corporal Woodford and to discuss only the confrontations with Jensen. That will be all—absolutely no overlap with the accident itself. He presses the fingers of both hands to his temples and paces about the room. The pressure in his head throbs and he feels as though he's about to slip under the weight of his own being. Focus, he tells himself. *Focus.*

Then he hears the sound of water flowing from the tap in the kitchen. *My God, soon it will be drowning the house.* He sprints through the gallery and stands before the sink. An intermittent drip clicks against the stainless steel shell. "You can't tell me you heard that from the office," he says aloud. He tightens the tap and waits for another drop to fall. Nothing.

Paul sighs deeply and wanders into the bathroom, relieves himself and walks back into the kitchen to double-check the tap. "You see—it's fine," he declares. "You're not losing your mind." But a part of him recoils in doubt. He has crossed an unmarked zone, a narrow band that separates what is certain from an elaborate dream world.

He finds himself holding the telephone in one hand, but is unsure how it came to be there. Moments later he hears himself addressing Woodford again.

"Listen," he says pressing his elbows to the desktop and staring at the chipped wall plaster near the door casing. "There's something related to the accident that I want to report."

He pauses, unsure of the sound of his own voice. Are you really speaking or?... He checks himself, quickly determines what to say first, and then proceeds.

"Yes. The girl's father—the girl in the coma—Jenny's father, Reg Jensen. He's been stalking my wife and son."

Within seconds Paul's mood shifts. He feels in control now, proactive in dealing with the menace that has confronted him. Once he begins to describe the crime plotted against him, against his wife and child, then he feels focussed and certain and his old energy returns. He flexes his fingers as he speaks.

"The most recent episode was this morning," he continues, "about three hours ago." He describes Valerie spotting Reg around the school. Not once, but twice. As he speaks he pauses for her to absorb the details, and clarifies specific facts, times, dates. She's taking it all very seriously, he assures himself. Finally someone is dealing with this menace.

"There were several witnesses to his threats today," he says, trying to remember the names of the parents milling about the schoolyard and the two women pushing their strollers along the sidewalk during Reg's final outburst. He curses his inability to remember names. Was it Wendy Palmer and Barb Peters?

As this memory lapse rises in his awareness, it evokes some doubt about what actually occurred. Then he senses the medicinal fog emanating from the floor and enshrouding him. He hesitates. Why was he on the phone again? He realizes now he needs to memorize everything he said and did and report it to Valerie this evening.

*And what exactly did Reg Jensen threaten to do?*

Paul thinks a moment. "A general threat. He said, 'I'm gonna get you and your kid.' He got out of his car and started shouting that at me."

*Did he say that?*

"What?"

*That he was going to get you. You and your kid.*

Paul detects a note of skepticism. He suspects that Woodford is now less diligent about recording each fact as he lays them out for her. "Look. He got out of his car screaming at me. That it was unfair that I'm alive and his daughter's in the hospital."

*Why would he think that, Mr. Wakefield?*

"Why? Because she could be dying and I'm not."

*I'm sorry ... I missed that.*

"Because I beat her into a coma!"

Paul covers his mouth with one hand. He was doing it. He was doing what Ben Stillwell and Jerry Sampson had explicitly told him to avoid: talking to the cops—with his confession of all things....

*Mr. Wakefield?*

Paul switches the handset to his left ear. "Listen, I'm sorry. I'm on medication. Everything that's happened since the accident has been very stressful."

There is a pause.

"Who am I speaking to?" he demands. He pulls the handset from his ear and examines it as though it might be planted with a bug that can pick up his thoughts. A wireless connection to his brain.

He sets the phone onto the cradle and a dull shudder rolls through his chest. "Who was I speaking to?" he cries, his voice filling the empty room.

Oh God, he whispers to himself. This is no longer a joke, some prank from a comic personality—the deranged part of himself—named Nark. That was supposed to be funny. A bit of self-mockery. This was something much worse. And the only word he can think of is *disaster*.

When Valerie returns home she detects his distress at once. She enters the office where Paul dozes half-asleep, barely able to acknowledge her presence. "I spoke to the police," he says as if it were a confession of guilt. "They called about the broken window and I asked them to call Ben Stillwell."

"Ben?"

He nods and thinks what he should say next. "And I saw Reg Jensen at the school this morning."

Valerie drops her purse and art portfolio on the desk and walks around the chair so she can see her husband clearly. "Did you speak to Jensen, too?"

"Yes." Paul glances at her and then looks away. "But it was a mistake. Everything I did today was a mistake." His lips quiver and he gasps for air. "Sorry. It's this medicine Biggs gave me. I can't … think straight."

"Paul, don't worry." Valerie leans over and kisses his forehead. "You're going to be okay. Remember, he said this could happen."

"Not like this. I didn't think it would get like this." I've had a psychotic break *and I beat that little girl into a coma*, he wants to tell her. Instead he looks into her eyes and prays that she can just see it in him. So that she knows what happened without him having to say the words.

Valerie studies his face.

For a moment Paul thinks he can read her mind: *You look so weathered, so beaten.*

"I'll call him for you," she says. "I'll get you in to see him tomorrow."

"Okay." He closes his eyes. She did see it. She knows something's broken loose inside him.

"Then I'll call Ben Stillwell and the police. Just to make sure everything's clear."

Paul considers this—considers arguing the merits of calling the police again, then decides he cannot fight any more and that Valerie should carry some of the burden now. "Okay," he repeats after enough time has passed that he has forgotten the thread of their conversation. He closes his eyes. He must sleep now.

"We'll talk later."

"Yes," he murmurs.

Valerie closes the door and walks into the kitchen. In the daze of his half-consciousness, he can hear her pacing the hallway, then she picks up the telephone and begins a series of calls.

That evening after Eliot settles into bed, Paul feels somewhat relieved, as though he's finally touched the bottom of the abyss into which he's fallen. Now that he's secured a toehold of stability, he can navigate along the narrow path ahead of him—if he can maintain his balance.

As they sit at the kitchen table drinking herbal tea, he tries to explain to Valerie his version of the day's events. It's tricky, he decides, because of the powerful side effects from the drugs, effects more pronounced than Dr. Biggs suggested. Biggs' notion of a fog that might envelop him has manifested itself as a shroud that turned his thinking into a psychotic fantasy. Worse, he finds himself doubting simple facts. His imaginary conversation with Corporal Woodford proved that.

On the other hand, by disclosing almost everything to Valerie he feels unburdened. He describes the details of the confrontation with Jensen, the first—real—conversation with Woodford about the broken window, and his second—crazy—monologue driven by his pervading sense of guilt. Was he truly blameless? he asks. Or was there something he'd done to deserve all this?

"Of course not." Valerie shakes her head once and smiles a little, a mere curve of the upper lip.

"I mean, he has been stalking you. And then these threats today. At least ten people witnessed it."

"I know. I talked to Wendy Palmer. She called and told me all about it. She and Barb described exactly what you told me."

Her voice is so soft. Paul would like to ease her into his arms. "You see?" he asks. "You see how bad this has become?"

She sips her tea quietly, waits for Paul to continue, to say whatever he needs to confess.

"I'm glad this is all out," Paul concludes. He's truly feeling better now. "For a while I wondered if it was best not to tell you what was going on."

"Why would you do that?"

"To protect you, I guess."

"Not if it involves Eliot." She wraps her hands around her mug to warm her fingers. "If it involves him, you have to tell me. Wouldn't you want the same thing?"

Paul nods. Of course; it's obvious. "It's this medication. Everything seems like a mirage ... I'm starting to doubt even the simplest perceptions."

Valerie narrows her eyes and scans his face. "I've got you lined up to see Dr. Biggs at 9:00 tomorrow morning."

"Right." Paul remembers that she was going to call him. Yes, that was the tail end of their conversation this afternoon before he drifted off.

"Tell me again about the conversation you had with the police, Paul." She turns her head, a slight adjustment to bring him into better perspective. "What was her name again?"

"Corporal Woodward." He frowns, then tries again: "Woodford. She was asking about the broken window. But I got mixed up. I told her to phone Ben Stillwell. Then I called her back—or I thought I did—and told her about all this crap with Jensen. About him stalking you and the threats he made today." He pauses and holds a hand next to his ear. "I actually had the phone in my hand ... thinking I was talking to her." His arms slide to the edges of the table and his fingers curl over the wood trim. Hold on to something, he tells himself.

"It's all right." Valerie's shoulders dip forward. "It happens when people go through this."

When people go through this. He can tell she's forcing her empathy. She must be much more worried than she's letting on. He frowns and then continues, "I gave her the direct line to Ben Stillwell's secretary. Did she make the call?"

" ... Yes." Valerie tilts her head again and glances away.

She's leading up to something, Paul thinks. There's a subtle shift in the ground underfoot. " ... And?"

"And it looks like Ben is busy in court most of this week and—"

"I knew he would be," Paul interrupts. "You cannot count on that guy in an emergency situation."

Valerie shrugs. "In any case, Ginny says the examination for discovery will be on the seventeenth. She says you should be there at ten o'clock. At the court reporter's office," she adds. "I've got the address."

"So. It's set." He tries to count the days. "Another ten days."

"Twelve," she whispers. "If you include the weekend."

They look away from one another and consider the challenge ahead. Now that the court proceedings are fixed in time and place, they have become a physical reality.

"Better later than sooner, don't you think? It'll give Dr. Biggs time to help you settle down."

Yes, he needs that. Paul nods in agreement. More time will help change things.


Unburdened. That's the feeling he has as he lies in bed that night listening to Valerie's light breathing. He possesses the sense of being emptied; yet it's not a feeling exactly, but the memory of it: when he told Valerie what had happened today, his relief was palpable. As though the burden he bore was vacated and as a result he rose unimpeded through the mass of his own body, like a bubble rising to the surface of the sea. For an instant, then, he felt almost normal. This terrible guilt had slipped its leash on him and he was free. And what was the price of this freedom? To simply say—in plain English—what had happened. To tell the truth. Could it be so easy?

Valerie turns on her side and pulls the covers over her shoulder with one hand. Her fingers clutch at the edge of the sheet and hold it in place. She sighs deeply and falls into unconsciousness. Paul studies her in the darkness, how easily her form merges with the emptiness of the room surrounding them. He must tell her, he decides. He must share this burden and let her decide what part of it she wants to reveal. He leans on an elbow and peers into her face. So calm. So effortless in her comfort.

"Valerie." His lips utter her name without a sound. He draws a breath and whispers to her. "Valerie. I have to tell you something."

He waits for her to respond but she says nothing. He studies her face for a sign of consciousness. Her mouth slips open and closes again.

He turns his face to the window and he says, "There is something I haven't told you. Something I should have said but didn't. I was too frightened. Too ashamed," he adds, admitting that this is the better word. He thinks a moment and decides to simply state what he has buried so deeply inside: "When we were in the water I hit Jenny. I hit her with my paddle when she climbed on top of me in panic. I panicked, too. I … I couldn't help myself."

He stops his mouth with the back of his hand and takes a deep breath. Again he looks into his wife's sleeping face. He has now told her everything. But has she heard it? Yes, of course; in some way she would understand his desperate panic and the terrible guilt he bears. And now that she knows all, he can hope for that feeling again. The unburdening that should now be released through his body to free him.

How long will he have to wait?

# CHAPTER 7

"GOOD MORNING. THIS PAUL WAKEFIELD CALLING."

"Hello, Mr. Wakefield. How are you today?"

"Fine, thanks. Any news about Jenny Jensen?"

"She's resting comfortably."

"Any change?"

In the waiting room outside Dr. Biggs' office several rows of chairs face the glass kiosks where three medical secretaries maintain their stations, each attending to the physicians who share the clinic. A children's play area, equipped with a fire station, a box of plastic horses and a collection of picture books, occupies one corner of the room. A small boy runs a fire truck up and down the carpet as he hacks away with what sounds like chronic whooping cough. Six other patients await their appointments, each separated from the others by a distance of three or four chairs.

Paul checks in with Biggs' receptionist, then randomly selects a magazine from an aluminum rack that holds a collection of

*Maclean's* magazines. He sits as far away from the child as possible and begins to flick through a six-month-old edition. Although none of the articles catches his interest, the action of flipping his fingers over each page is soothing. The studied monotony provides a lull that enables him to calculate what he must say to Biggs. What he must say and what he must omit.

He feels comfortable now in admitting to himself that indeed, he had not actually spoken to Corporal Woodford about Reg Jensen's tirade. He'd told the story aloud, of course. That was the best part about it. Getting it off his chest. Purging his anger. The fact that he'd used the telephone as a prop made the whole experience more tangible. And because he didn't say anything to the police about Jensen, he'd kept his conversation within his lawyer's strict boundaries. Looking at the episode objectively, at one level, he'd employed a thoroughly therapeutic method of dealing with the problem. That was your good self doing that, Paul assures himself, and nods his head in quiet agreement. The one who's looking after you through all of this.

On the other hand, you did experience a kind of psychotic break, he adds cautiously, just to modify any over-enthusiasm. He knows a little about psychosis from his undergrad days at McGill University. The psychology courses and the weeks he spent in observation on the psychiatric wards in Montreal taught him what can happen when you have a break from reality.

There was a lot of medical jargon and speculative theory used to explain psychosis. But Paul's understanding of the illness was basic and pragmatic. He thought of consciousness as a running stream that mediates an outer reality and an inner adjudicative mind. Indeed, consciousness likely pertained to dogs, mice, even ants—but that was another debate. Fully attuned human consciousness can always be oriented to three dynamics: person, place and time. Simply put, you know who you are, where you are and what day it is. If you know these facts, you can pinpoint where you are in the continuity of your life and world events. And with this knowledge you can function, often quite productively.

From what Paul could see, most psychiatrists considered these principles as a foundation of mental health. Some of their patients had neurotic ailments (obsessions, compulsions, eating disorders) that were best treated with behaviour modification. Many others presented various forms of depression. Their symptoms were most often treated with drugs—and a wish and prayer that the underlying causes would evaporate. Paul suspected that most depression resulted from individual isolation within modern culture. The annihilation of natural society—tribal culture—also destroyed the links to an extended family. But this, too, was another debate.

Unless they were chronically ill, many of the depressed and neurotic patients were treatable. With drugs, talking therapy and behaviourism, each could be reoriented to his or her individual person, place and time. Most could hold down a job and try to keep their families together. But they would surely struggle. Many of them would spend two or three days a month fighting just to get out of bed. Yet with a little help, perhaps the occasional adjustment to their meds, they could adapt and carry on their lives as tax-paying citizens.

The psychotic patients were another case. The worst were schizophrenic and liable to harm themselves—or, rarely, harm others. They heard voices. They believed other people (or cats—even aliens) were controlling them. The CIA had implanted microchips in their cerebral cortices. Bugs crawled the walls. They lived in a world painted by Hieronymus Bosch and in that world, they could not orient themselves to person, place or time. Their existence was a visceral hell and when Paul spoke with these patients he was frightened down to his bones. Usually they were given a course of drug therapy that flattened their hallucinations. Once they were medicated, Paul noticed that every one of them, without exception, lost a part of his or her humanity. They became drones.

After his practicum on the psychiatric wards Paul's curiosity about whether he possessed the internal stamina to deal with the patients' trauma was exhausted. He knew he would not have a career working with the mentally ill. The realization led to a period of disorientation. He turned away from psychology, yet he did not turn to another calling. Since his first year at university he'd focussed on the single objective of obtaining a degree in psychology and once he abandoned it, nothing took its place. He finished his degree at McGill, then spent weeks noodling away on his bass guitar, picked up with a tribe of like-minded musicians and formed Forged Destiny.


"So, you're in for a tune-up." Ed Biggs studies Paul's file and after a moment of contemplation, looks up at his patient.

Paul tips his head to one side and presses his hands together. "I guess you could call it that," he confesses. "But I don't feel much like a car. Though at times I wish I did."

"Then you'd feel nothing at all. I guess that's your point, huh?"

Paul nods in the affirmative as Biggs approaches the examining table, slips his stethoscope from his neck and makes a gesture to roll up the sleeve.

Paul dutifully submits to the procedures that unfold: three separate evaluations of his blood pressure, prodding of his flesh (emphasis on the liver area) and a cursory study of his ears, nose and throat.

"Still hear the ringing?"

"Only when I listen for it. Trouble is, once I start listening, the garage band plays for hours without intermission."

Biggs frowns as if to say, I know; too bad there's nothing we can do for it.

"What about your sleep patterns?"

"I've had a few good nights." An exaggeration. He considers the single occasion in which he collapsed into blissful sleep next to Valerie. Expired from love.

"Just a few?"

"I get a nap almost every day. I fade into it sometime after noon."

Ed Biggs walks back to his chair and sits facing Paul. There is a pause. He smiles. "I see a note here," his hand dips to the file folder, "that your wife said you'd been threatened."

Another pause. "Yesterday," Paul says when the silence becomes protracted. "By the girl's father."

Biggs uncrosses his legs and yields his full attention to Paul. "Tell me what happened."

Paul expected something like this. He didn't anticipate this specific entrée, but he knew he would be invited to explain things.

He begins with the stalking episodes and Valerie's fears. Then he describes Reg Jensen's outburst. To his surprise his voice is calm, as though he's contained this bit of personal history in a closed chapter, one safe to recount to his doctor and lawyer. Soon he'll be relating the adventure to friends at parties. Intuitively he knows this is his protective self at work again. Managing investigative conversations. Assembling facts and revealing them for what they are.

"Paul, I'm speculating here," Biggs says once the story runs through Reg's shouting episode, "but there's a good chance that Reg Jensen is under considerable stress himself."

Paul ponders this a moment.

"And if that's the case, I'm sure his doctor is trying to deal with it." Biggs leans forward and in a low tone intended to reveal his reverence for doctor-patient privilege, he says, "It's possible that Jensen is on a similar medication. In which case, the same disorientation you're experiencing—could be hitting him."

"… At the same time it hits me.… "

Biggs closes his eyes and nods. "It could be that simple."

"Could be."

"Yes."

"Could be something else, though, right?"

"Perhaps." Biggs shrugs. "But does he have a history of stalking or violence?"

Paul stares at the linoleum floor tiles. He has no answers. "I don't know."

"Ask your lawyer. Have you told him what happened?"

"Valerie called him yesterday. We haven't heard back from him yet."

"Get him to assess whether you're facing a real danger here." Biggs levels his hand in the air between them. "But the real danger that concerns me is your inability to relax. Getting your blood pressure under control and getting you back to healthy living."

Paul takes a deep breath. Yes, that's why we're here, after all. "So what is the blood pressure reading?" He points to the file folder, the docket of information that holds his vital statistics between its plain brown sleeves.

"142 over 92."

"Still pretty high."

"The trend is down. But you're in the window where you'll feel the full effects of falling blood pressure. You can feel faint, like your body's falling through your legs. Some people report broken sleep patterns."

"Like insomnia. I've got it in spades."

Biggs shrugs, yes, and Paul glances away. He's telling you that it will get worse before it gets better, Paul says to himself. "Is there another pill I should take?"

"The metoprolol is deflating the hypertension the way it's supposed to. I'd like to stick with it another week or so."

Paul thinks a moment. He realizes that he has to create islands within the flow of time in which he can think clearly. Then he swims through the surrounding waters until another island appears. Now that's he's on shore for a minute, he has to tell Biggs about the bogus call to Corporal Woodford. About his incipient psychosis. How the metoprolol is causing this ... breakdown.

"Did Valerie say anything about my telephone call with the police?" He forces his eyes to look at Dr. Biggs. Be direct. Just tell this the way it happened. "How she called about a broken window and then I called her back to lodge a complaint about Jensen?"

"No." Biggs leans forward again.

"Except I didn't call her back. I just thought I did." He lets this statement settle in as though the implications are self-evident.

"And you're worried that the stress has created the fantasy." Biggs raises his eyebrows and lets them fall. "I'm not surprised. Stress alone can do that. Mix in the—"

"Fantasy? You don't think it's a little bit ... psychotic?"

Biggs draws a deep breath. "No. Not truly psychotic. Not with all the stress you're under. The accident. The medication. The trouble with Jensen, the pending legal inquiry. No psychiatrist would treat you for psychosis without dealing with all the underlying circumstances first."

It's true. Paul shakes his head. Yes, it's absolutely true that none of this would have come up on him without all these other factors. "Thank you," he says once he realizes that he is not—given the array of underlying circumstances—definitely not psychotic.

Biggs smiles again. "You're going to be okay. Haven't I told you that?"

"I don't remember."

"Well, you are. Just keep taking those meds. Don't drive your car until you're past this. If you need to get downtown, take the bus. If the effects start to weigh in on you, stay home. Talk to Valerie. Just 'be here now'—that old '60s mantra. Remember that?"

"Yeah."

"And enjoy the Easter weekend." He stands and clasps the file folder to his chest. "Buddy up with the in-laws and all that."

Paul sits back in the chair. How could Biggs know about his mother- and father-in-laws' pending visit? "Did Valerie tell you they were coming?"

"No." His lips press together in a deep pout. "But mine are. I just guessed that you'd be sharing the pain." He winks and steps into the corridor, then walks down the hall to another waiting patient.


Paul met Wallace and Jeanine Burbank following his first vacation with Valerie, a meandering road trip along Highway 1 down the Washington, Oregon and California coastlines to San Francisco that concluded with a two-day return trip to Vancouver on the US Interstate-5. They indulged in a month-long love-fest and still radiated the full glow of their romance when they pulled into the driveway to the Burbanks' Point Grey home in Vancouver.

Holding a watering can in one hand as she doused a box of geraniums outside her front door, Jeanine Burbank took one look at Paul and Valerie strolling hand-in-hand toward her and called through the open doorway to her husband: "Wally, the lovebirds have arrived. Put on the steak."

"Mom, you don't have to be so blatant," Valerie said. Her cheeks flushed and she wrapped her arms around her mother in a light embrace.

"So. This must be Mr. Right." Jeanine cocked her head to one side to examine Paul.

"You can just call me Paul," he said and held out a hand to her. And within three months I'll be your son-in-law, he almost added, but instead he deferred to Valerie's request to reveal their engagement only when the time was right.

"None of that!" Jeanine brushed past his hand and kissed his cheek. He could feel a drizzle of water spill onto his leg from her water can.

"Hey-ho!" Wally appeared at the door with a newspaper in his hands. "You're a day late—but hell, it's good to see you!"

"It's lucky we're only a day past due," Valerie said. She led the way into her parents' home and set her suitcase on the tile floor. "We had a minor problem in 'Frisco."

"San Francisco," her mother corrected. "People in California hate anyone calling it 'Frisco."

"Jeanine." Wally gave her a distant look and turned to Paul. "Thank you for bringing her back safely," he said.

"Pleased to be back safely myself." Paul flashed Valerie a subtle wink as he shook Wally's hand.

"Did you take Highway 1 all the way?"

"On the way down, yes." Paul breathed in the sea air as it drifted across the lawn from English Bay. It felt good to be back in Canada.

"It's a long road. I've driven it two or three times. There's a few good curves in it."

"Yes, there are." Paul realized that he might get along with this man. With a little manoeuvring, they could reach agreement about most things.

But his wife was another case. Jeanine had her own ways.


Despite her claim to know the minds of Californians, Jeanine had visited San Francisco only twice. She was a native of New York City (or rather, Westchester, one of its suburbs) and loved to boast of the city's wealth, culture, energy, restaurants, galleries ... anything the rest of the world appeared to lack in the proportions assigned to New York.

Wally was a son of Toronto. Apart from his often repeated observations about the world-class height of the CN Tower, he couldn't one-up any other claims Jeanine attached to New York. Instead, he would wax eloquent about Vancouver. The beaches, the clean air, the green spaces, the mountains, the view of English Bay from their bedroom window. Jeanine would find herself in agreement with her husband on each point, a not-too-reluctant enthusiast for their jointly adopted city. Nonetheless, when she needed to, Jeanine would play her New York card and claim incisive knowledge about some cultural point at hand. Hence, the dig at her daughter's use of the diminutive, 'Frisco. Yet the assertion was not intended to correct her. Indeed, it was meant to slam her for parading her sexual wantonness with a strange man before her parents.

Not that Jeanine and Wally were models of the Puritan ethic. In fact, two months after Jeanine and Wally met, they eloped and set up house in Vancouver where Wally, a recent graduate of pharmacy school, landed his first job. (About a year following Paul and Valerie's marriage, Wally revealed—after a rainy evening fortified with multiple nips of Glenlivet—that he and Jeanine at one time enjoyed a "very happy sex life." Jeanine whispered his name in a steely tone—"Wallace!" and darted off to the guest room in Paul and Valerie's new house. Wally then enjoyed another dose of Scotch, as a wide smile stretched across his ample face.)

Five years after they eloped, Wally established his own pharmacy in the upscale Kerrisdale area and over thirty years built it into a chain of five outlets. The day he turned sixty he sold the whole lot to a national syndicate and took up sailing around the shores of Vancouver Island in his twenty-five-foot ketch—alone. Valerie never explained to Paul why her parents had eloped because she was never told. It was a secret. Perhaps Jeanine's parents disapproved of their child marrying an un-moneyed Canuck. But once Valerie was born, the chill thawed. The grandparents were elated by the beautiful blond baby. Without knowing it, Valerie renewed the bonds across the generations. Like Paul, she was an only child and became the centrepiece of her long-established New York family.

Jeanine built a life in Vancouver that consisted of goodwill adventures. She tended the needs of widows in the neighbourhood. She visited hospitals to buoy the spirits of friends and relatives afflicted with one ailment or another. Sometimes she accompanied people to various agencies to ease them through the paperwork required to access their lawful benefits. It was as though she'd established a personal charity service. When Paul asked, "What do you do?" she bluntly replied, "I help people who need it." And she performed her mission in her own way. She would tell doctors and social workers that she was their clients' niece, daughter, sister—whatever tale would provide the entry she needed to assist her chosen flock. "I do it my way," she explained, "because of the government. With all their rules and regulations, they simply don't know what they've done to the people. They've made the hospitals into a socialist gulag and the patient service groups—who are sincerely trying to help—into unwitting KGB franchises."

KGB franchises? Better not fight her about this one, he thought. Or any other matter. And over the years, there were many other matters.

As Paul pulls the Volvo into the driveway on Transit Road he spots the Burbanks' Mercedes-Benz parked under the garry oak tree at the side of his garage. His in-laws have a well-established travel routine. Once they've driven onto the ferry they settle into the upper deck buffet as they sail across the Georgia Strait and through the Gulf Islands to Victoria. But as soon as they arrive at Paul and Valerie's home, they become passive recipients of their daughter's hospitality. In Paul's mind his in-laws' attitude is perfectly captured by their black Mercedes-Benz SL 450 that sits almost out of sight (but never out of mind) during their stay. That way, whenever they decide to dine out or run Eliot off to a ball game, everyone piles into Paul's car. "Gee, we could have taken the 'Benz," Wally notes as they ease out the driveway.

"I hope Valerie's home," Paul mutters aloud as he walks up the steps to his front door. He scans the Sampsons' yard for signs of life. Chester lies on the grass, his yellow coat full of lawn clippings. Obviously Jerry Sampson has managed to limp about his property pushing his lawn mower over the thick spring grass. Paul makes a mental note that if he needs a break from the Burbanks over the next three days he'll simply announce that he must trim his own grass—and escape outside for an hour by himself.

The door is unlocked. Voices percolate from the kitchen at the back of the house. There is mock laughter—Valerie's. Good, he thinks, and slips into his office, where he carefully stores his car keys, wallet and loose change. At least this small part of his world is still well ordered. Yes, he commands himself, and be sure to keep it that way.

"Paul, we're in the kitchen!" Valerie calls with the unmistakable plea in her voice reserved for those times when her parents are at hand. It's as though she's calling for divine intervention: If you don't get in here and spare me from my parents, I shall sacrifice them on the shattered remains of Moses' sacred tablets!

When Paul enters the kitchen he notices Jeanine's new hairstyle. It's still bouffant, but more blond than ever before—impossibly blond except for the labours of some stylist she's recently discovered in the hundred-dollar-an-hour spas of Vancouver. "Mom—good to see you," he chirps and pecks her on the cheek where she sits at the wrap-around breakfast nook. "New hair," he adds and shakes Wally's hand as it rises towards him. "Hi, Dad."

"Do you like it?" Jeanine cocks her chin to one side—a false gesture requesting a dishonest assessment, Paul decides. A typical double bind. He withholds comment and Jeanine continues, "I got a new stylist last week. I'm just not sure.... "

"It's great, Mom," Valerie says when she sees Paul hesitate.

"It's incredibly blond," he says at last. "How do they get it so blond?"

"Spray it with gold dust," Wally chuckles with a snort. "Least you'd think so for the cost of it!" Then, with a quick switch of focus intended to bury the topic of hair and money, he adds, "Hey, let's have a drink. I brought you an Easter present: a fifth of Glenfiddich." His hand points to the bottle gleaming on the counter next to the refrigerator.

Paul prepares four glasses of Scotch, two neat (for the men), two with ice and soda. They settle into the living room and when the Scotch begins to loosen the social fibres constricting them, the conversation finds its way to Paul's kayaking expedition, the accident and the growing troubles that have ensued. But as always, Paul steers the talk around the obvious shoals. He's become accomplished at this easy navigation simply by keeping a focus on elementary facts. Yes, the accident was terrible—indeed, traumatic—and Jenny Jensen still lies in a coma. Paul himself will be off work for another month or two and is being treated for hypertension. But there's no mention of Paul and Valerie's visit to the hospital and the confrontation with the Jensens, no talk of the pending lawsuit, the broken window, the call to the police, and certainly not a hint of Reg Jensen's outburst at the school.

In fact, the extent of their vulnerability isn't revealed until breakfast the following morning when Eliot lets slip a few words.

"Say Granny, what games did you play when you were a girl?" Eliot scoops the last spoonful of sugared flakes into his mouth and studies Jeanine as she rinses the dishes at the sink.

"Lots of games." Her shoulders droop a little as she considers this question. Like everything Eliot asks, she believes it requires a serious answer. "Hopscotch. Blind man's bluff. Hide-and-seek, of course."

"What's hopscotch?" He slides a hand under his chin as he watches her wipe the plates with a J-cloth.

"You don't know what hopscotch is?" She casts an eye at her daughter who raises the pages of the newspaper a few centimetres to cover her face. "Valerie, have you not taught Eliot how to play hopscotch?"

"How do you play it?" Eliot ignores this diversion and stands next to his grandmother.

"You draw a bunch of squares on the pavement, then—"

"How do you do that?'

"With chalk. A bunch of squares, all connected in a line and about as long as that wall." She points to the wall running from the doorway to the south window. "Then you throw a stone from the starting point and see if you can hop on one foot to the box where your stone lands, pick it up and hop back. Like this."

Paul glances over his section of the paper as Jeanine hops the length of the room, bends over on one foot and bounces back to the sink. You've got to admit, he thinks, she'll give anything to that boy.

And she'll do it without any mind games. Not one double-entendre, never a sarcastic comment or a raised eyebrow. Eliot is the boy she never had and she's determined to bind him to her forever.

"There. That's how you play it." She gulps a bit of air to cover her panting.

"Don't wind yourself, old girl," Wally says without looking up. He turns a page in the business section and sips his coffee.

Jeanine narrows her eyes, glares at her husband and continues. "Surely you can't tell me that you haven't seen anyone play hop-scotch before."

"Well ... yes, I guess I have," Eliot confesses.

Valerie leans forward and stares at her son. "Then why did you tell Granny you'd never heard of it?"

"Because," Eliot says and raises his eyebrows, "I wanted to see if I could get Granny to hop around the room."

There is a brief pause, then Wally begins to laugh aloud. "Gotcha there, kiddo," he exclaims and jabs a finger toward his wife.

Jeanine plumps her hands on her hips and, for a moment, looks slightly betrayed. "Wallace, please," she says when Wally's last gasp of laughter sounds just a little forced.

"Don't scold the child for that one," Wally says and turns his nose back to his paper. "He's cut from your cloth, darling."

Valerie giggles at this last statement. Paul feels free to display his own amusement. "And a lovely tweed cloth it is," he says tactfully.

"Surely you play hide-and-seek." Jeanine engages her grandson again as though his last deception had not occurred. "Hide-and-seek is played the world over. I can't imagine a time when children didn't play hide-and-seek."

"We used to," Eliot confesses again. He has decided to reveal the truth in all things—at least to his grandmother. "Until about two days ago."

"What happened two days ago?"

"Rat-face Jensen found us."

Paul and Valerie look at Eliot.

"Who's he?" Jeanine asks.

"Where'd you see him?" Valerie asks.

"Outside the school. Just across the street in the cross-path." He pauses and then adds, "He's been there every day this week. One place or another. Everyone thinks he's spooky. That's why we don't go hiding around there any more."

Paul flattens his newspaper on the table and looks at his son. "Eliot," he asks, "how do you know it was Mr. Jensen?"

"Because," Eliot says and casts his eyes to the floor. "He's the same guy who was yelling at you last week."

"Yelling at you?" Jeanine's voice rises like a wave about to hit the shore. "Who was yelling at you?"

"Rat-face Jensen. Jenny's dad." Eliot rubs his chin with his fingers. "The girl in the coma."

That evening after Eliot is settled into bed, Paul pours another round of four Scotches and prepares for Jeanine's inquisition. He knows she'll employ her full range of skills to extract the truth. Hours earlier Paul and Valerie quietly conferred about how much to reveal to her parents. Valerie convinced him that they should hear it all. In fact, they could have no better ally than her mother if she could be brought on-side. "Besides," Valerie whispered, "once Jeanine has a goal in her mind ... resistance is futile."

They congregate in the living room overlooking the back garden and lawn, none of it yet trimmed and pruned. Paul and Valerie sit on the sofa, Jeanine and Wally each take up one of the matching chairs on the opposite side of the coffee table.

"Time for me to get the lawn mower out there." Paul deploys this notion strategically; maybe tomorrow he can escape outside and push the mower around for an hour or two—if he can stretch it.

"There's no end to it," Wally says. "How 'bout those apple trees, did you prune them back in January?"

"Didn't have the time," Paul says. Wally nods in sympathy and for a moment they share the suburban working-man's lament.

"It's hard enough just to keep my yard clean," Wally says. "And I've got all week to tend to it."

Tomorrow morning Eliot will be running around out there, Paul thinks, grabbing the foil-wrapped chocolate eggs that Valerie and Jeanine intend to hide in the most obvious places. Jeanine has prepared her video camera for the event and her spirits bubbled as she triple-checked the tape speed and recording mechanism. But now, the mood is heavy with its unspoken questions. Diversionary small talk consumes them: discussion of the evening's Italian desserts that Wally purchased at Ottavio's in the village. Mixed praise for Eliot's school teacher. Paul takes a deep breath and waits. At last, and most mercifully, Jeanine weighs in with a direct opening.

"Paul," she says, "I know you would like to protect us from some things.... But really, you have to understand that this—whoever he is—this Rat-man is beginning to affect us too."

Paul closes his eyes and takes another sip of Scotch. It's Rat-face, he thinks. Not Rat-man. Perhaps he should remind her of that. But no, he cannot start down that path with Jeanine. "I'm sure it is affecting you," he admits with a tone of capitulation. He realizes now that she won't have to drag anything from him. He'll gladly assign her as much of the burden as she can handle. "It looks like Jensen has been broken by this tragedy over his daughter."

"What's he done, Paul?" Wally leans forward. His voice fills the room with genuine concern.

"Following us," Valerie says. "Like he's stalking us. Or Eliot, anyway. I've seen him at the school a couple of times. Just hanging there. In a mist, as though he's distracted."

"He's at distraction's end," Paul adds, as though it could be a physical place, a zone beneath the equator where the heat of your own life causes a total meltdown.

"Well, if Eliot's safety is at risk, then we need to act." Jeanine's voice is certain, steely.

"Just hold on," Wally says. "Let's first get the kids to spell out everything that's happened." He lifts his hand in the air and lets it sink, palm down, to his knee. "Take us through each day. From the time you got out of the hospital after the accident."

After the accident. Paul considers this phrase and he realizes that while everything has stemmed from the accident, there is now a time that begins *after the accident*. He no longer needs to obsess over his culpability—his depraved heart. He has entered a new period with its own discrete causes and effects that hinge around Rat-face Jensen's madness. But instead of affecting Paul alone, as the accident had done, the new phase has encompassed his entire family. The task at hand, then, is to extract themselves from Jensen's influence and rise from the centre of his disintegrating spiral.

This is clear reasoning, he thinks. Your good self looking after you. For a moment he worries about the little compartments he has constructed to deal with his life. What if they collide? What if they forget to keep two car-lengths' separation as they all hurtle along the highway?

"Tell them, honey," Valerie says and she lifts his hand into her own.

"Right after the accident," he begins, "there's really nothing to report. I was in shock. The cold—from the hypothermia—seemed to last days. Then I heard about the girl. That Jenny was in a coma. At first the news was another shock but I thought, she'll get over it, these things happen in the cold like that. You realize that. Once you're in the ocean you realize that death is just seconds from you. Coming out alive, even in a coma, is a victory—just because you've survived. But then the weeks passed and Jenny wasn't moving to the next step. That's why I call the hospital every day. To see if she's made it to the next step. It was like her coma was a long, slow dump back into the ocean and there was no way to climb out." He stops to consider this. "You see, if she were to snap out of it today, all this trouble with Jensen would just stop. He could call us right now"—he points to the telephone—"and say 'she's back.' And that would probably end it. In fact, we'd probably be the first people he called." He looks at Valerie and realizes she's still holding his hand. "That would end it, don't you think?"

"Probably," she says. "I'm sure it would."

But her voice holds no conviction and Paul immediately wonders if indeed, Jensen can pull out of his tailspin. There's no certainty about any of it, he admits to himself. He swallows another hit of Scotch and narrows his eyes to digest this notion.

"Tell us specifically what Jensen has done," Wally continues. "What are his behaviours? Has he—"

"Val, tell me," Jeanine interrupts, "has he touched Eliot?"

Valerie releases Paul's hand and eases back into the sofa. "I don't think he's like that. It's more like this background thing. Like he's lurking. Nothing overt, except it's so creepy because you get the sense that he's not even thinking about what he's doing."

"Do you think he's a threat?" Jeanine asks.

Valerie sips her Scotch and thinks about this. "He worries me," she admits.

Paul can see she's trying to minimize the impact on her parents. A careful selection of words is needed to balance the perception of danger and a paranoid response to it.

"What about this episode in front of the school," Wally asks. "How serious was that?"

Paul tilts his head to one side. He can feel the heat rising in his ears, the chorus of electricity humming through his eardrums. Over the past day he has been able to maintain some equilibrium with his in-laws, but now the inevitable weariness is bleeding energy from his body. He shrugs. He sips at his Scotch and glances at Val: tell them. And get them to back off.

"I heard about it from Wendy Palmer, a friend who'd just dropped her oldest daughter off at the school and saw the whole thing, " Valerie says, as though this new perspective should provide an unbiased view. "Paul approached Jensen when he saw him sitting in his car and asked him what he was doing there. That's when Jensen reacted."

"Reacted?"

"Yeah." She glances at Paul but when it's clear he has little to add, she continues, "He got out of the car and began screaming. He simply lost control. Like a breakdown."

"Well." Jeanine squares her shoulders and looks at her husband. "I can see why you're worried. He's obviously unable to control himself. The fact that he's become obsessed with Eliot puts the child in direct danger."

Valerie nods in agreement. Her eyes sweep across the floor.

"Have you called the police?"

Paul cringes when he hears this. Soon they'll be pressing him to reveal the details of his calls with Corporal Woodford. The real call and his phantom dialogue.

"There's an examination for discovery. It's the first step in a law-suit against us. Or against me, anyway."

Valerie pulls a strand of hair over her shoulder. "It's been sched-uled for next week."

"That's standard." Wally frowns and glances at his wife. "They go after anyone with money in these cases. They have to find the money to pay for her care."

"Exactly what our lawyer says."

"All right. That's for the accident." Jeanine's voice hardens. "But have you called the police about Jensen's threats?"

"I called our lawyer and left a message," Valerie says. "But ... he hasn't called back"

"Hasn't called back? Why not?"

"Jeanine, slow down." Wally lifts his hand in the air again but his wife is quick to dismiss him.

"I will not slow down. We are talking about our grandson." She turns and examines her daughter. "I cannot believe what I am hear-ing. Eliot is your only child!" Then she tilts her head to bring Paul into her gaze. "Paul, what is going on that you will not call the police to protect that little boy"—she points with one finger to his bedroom upstairs—"from this deranged man?"

Paul returns her look and then glances away. It's all black and white to her. But maybe it really is. Maybe there are no greys at all. Someone should lock Jensen up until he's sane. Or maybe lock him away forever. "I don't know," he whispers at last.

"What was that?"

"I ... don't know."

"Then let's get the police over here right now. We want to file a complaint and ensure that man—and Eliot—are being watched."

"Mom, it's Easter Sunday tomorrow. Let's give it another day. We're all here to look after him this weekend. Nothing will happen today or tomorrow."

Jeanine pauses for a moment. She's been building a rising tempo and her daughter's calm logic has deflated her momentum. Paul takes a last sip of Scotch while she re-orients herself.

"All right," she agrees. "But on Monday morning if you don't call the police about this, I will. And if they cannot protect that child, we will take him to Vancouver with us. Ratman Jensen can't touch him there."

The conversation doesn't end at that point; nonetheless, Paul decides he has to take a break.

"I'm sorry," he explains, "but I haven't been sleeping. I need to take a break. My doctor said I should take a good hour's walk each day. And I haven't been following orders," he adds as a closing point when he leaves the room.

The words echo in his mind as he laces up his shoes. Yes, you should walk the dog down to the beach and if the night's clear enough, head up to Anderson Hill. That'll clear your head.

As he pulls his jacket over his shoulders he hears Wally's heavy footfalls on the staircase. There's a pause, then his father-in-law walks into the kitchen, turns about and heads through the gallery to Paul's office. He holds an empty glass in one hand. He leans against the doorframe and makes a broad pout with his mouth, as if to say, believe me: you'll never get your way with Jeanine, but the old girl means well.

Paul ignores the body language. "I put the Scotch on the kitchen counter. Next to the stove."

"Thanks, I'll get some a little later." Wally settles his body in place.

He is quite huge, Paul decides. In his college days he might have been a football player, one now long past his prime. Instead he followed his course of studies in microbiology and pharmacology. A wise choice, certainly. In any event, Paul cannot pass through the doorway without dealing with him. "Yes. Well, it's good Scotch." Paul zips his jacket.

"You mentioned your doctor had suggested a walk each day." He blinks and turns his head to examine Paul. "That's not Dr. Freedman, is it?"

"No. Biggs. Ed Biggs."

"Biggs? No, I don't know him. I know three or four of the GPS over here. But not Biggs." He lets this hang. It's clear he wants to chat a bit more, something in the spirit of a man-to-man discussion. Discreet. Honest.

"From your days in the pharmacy business," Paul says.

"Yeah." The conversation is engaged and Wally smiles. His face is broad and worn with the benign lines of success. It's hard not to like him. "So has he got you on a course of medication?"

"He's just moved me onto metoprolol. I started out with hydrochlorothiazide."

Wally nods. "Hypertension. Don't worry, metoprolol will do the trick."

Paul glances away and shrugs. "Yeah. Then there's the insomnia and this damn ringing in my ears."

They settle into a brief silence. There's no point in pursuing details of the diagnosis. Besides, Paul has revealed enough for the moment; to say more would be a breach of family etiquette.

"Do you mind if I sit?"

"Of course." Paul flags the La-z-boy with one hand.

Wally moves from the doorway and eases into the chair. He sets his glass next to the computer and fumbles as he unhitches the top button of his golf shirt. "I know that Jeanine can be difficult to take some days," he says.

"I guess you would." This is not an extension of sympathy, but a quick jab. Paul drops onto another chair and leans forward. He doesn't want to imply their talk should run more than a few minutes.

"Especially," Wally continues, blithely ignoring his son-in-law's tone, "when someone close to her heart is threatened."

"Well, let's not suppose that Eliot is not close to our hearts, too," Paul cautions. He's tired of being outflanked on the concerned-parent front. "But frankly, Wally, I can't talk about this any more. Not right now."

"I understand." Wally raises his hand again, a bit of a personal tic, Paul figures, from years of trying to keep a tight rein on Jeanine. "I just want you to know our bottom line."

"All right." Paul eases back in the chair. A wave of exhaustion drags through his bones. It feels like he's tried to leave this conversation for the last half-hour. But the force of it, the questions, the necessary explanations are unavoidable.

"I want you to know," he says, his voice calm, genuine, authentic, "I want you both to know that Jeanine and I will do anything we can within our power to help you. I know that you've been hurt. That

136

you're still suffering from that hurt. I know the medication you're taking probably makes the situation seem worse than it is. Hell, it happens quite a bit. Especially in post-traumatic disorders."

Paul startles as these last words wash over him. "Post-traumatic disorder?" He envisions soldiers deranged by exploding shells. "You think I have that?"

"Maybe. It's not for me to say. What is for me to say is that I love Valerie. And I love Eliot and you, too." Wally shrugs. "Don't think it strange. You're the only connection we have to the future. Jeanine would never tell you this, but she loves you as well. She says it to herself, anyway," he adds, as though to confess he's never heard her say it to him either.

Paul considers this. Maybe Wally has to believe that about her. Probably he has to believe many things about her—and their relationship. Otherwise, why would he still be married to her?

"And one last thing. It's up to you to tell us what you need. Don't wait for us to offer. If it's money, lawyers, doctors—even hired protection. We've got all that." He lifts the empty glass, turns it a half-rotation and sets it back down. "And it's yours if you need it."

Paul weaves his fingers together and squeezes them until the joints hurt. He wonders if he should tell Wally that he loves him, too, but he dismisses the idea. He could say that he knows Eliot and Valerie love him—but that would imply that he did not. After a moment he looks at his father-in-law, grasps his thick hand, gives it a firm shake and says, "Thank you."

# CHAPTER 8

PAUL STEPS OUTSIDE ONTO HIS FRONT PORCH. A HINT OF SALT AND
BRINE DRIFTS IN THE WIND AS IT FUNNELS UP THE ROAD FROM THE
BEACH. He imagines the ribbons of seaweed on the shore and
their fetid stink lifting from the rocks and driftwood. No, it's not the
salt he smells, but the rotting flotsam thrown on the land from the
daily churn of the sea.

He crosses the yard and works his way over to the Sampsons'
house. The door to the mud room is closed but unlocked. He enters
and peers up the stairs to the kitchen landing. A triangle of pale light
illuminates the staircase walls. Chester barks once and waddles over
to the open door. Jerry Sampson follows close behind, hitching his
suspenders over his shoulders.

"Just me," Paul calls up the narrow stairway, wondering—yet
again—how his aging neighbours manage to navigate the steep incline without tumbling to the concrete below. "Thought I'd take
Chester for his walk."

"Go right ahead," Jerry whispers. "Bettina's sleeping," he adds.
He waves a hand and coaxes Chester down the first three steps.

Once the dog recognizes Paul he thunders down the rest of the stairs and brushes his wet nose on Paul's pant leg. "Take your time," Jerry says with another wave and eases the landing door closed.

Paul leashes the dog and heads down Transit Road toward the ocean. He needs a good walk, he decides, something that will clear his mind of all the talk from Jeanine and Wally. When he reaches Beach Drive, the setting is exactly as he imagined it: low tide, the sand and rocks sopping with streams of waxy seaweed, the massive driftwood logs heaved onto the shore awaiting the next tide to bear them aloft. He leans on the green iron guardrail that runs above the seawall and examines the length of the beach. There is no one in sight. Four blocks down, at the far end of the road, a car flicks on its high beams as it cruises toward him. The street lights are on. The full moon is barely visible above the Olympic Mountains. The smoke rising from the pulp mills in Port Angeles fades into the dusky blue slope of the hills. The world maintains its order—this confluence of nature and machinery—and Paul wonders if it's only natural for humans to overrun the planet. Success breeds excess. And human excess is merely the latest cause of global warming. One day the ice caps will melt (once again), the sea levels will rise (once again), and wash away the nasty mess we've made. The geological survey shows that in the cycle of planetary warming and cooling over millions of years the high water mark on Vancouver Island reached ninety metres. The height of a thirty-storey building. Next time 'round, all of Victoria will be submerged. Wolf eels will lurk in the corridors of his office building. Sea lions will dive for herring in his living room.

He considers walking the dog along the shore. He sees himself at the water's edge tossing a stick into the waves for Chester. His foot could slip, wedge between a rock and one of the logs. He attempts to free it—only to fix himself deeper into the trap that locks his leg in place. The tide begins to rise. How long will it take for the ocean to inch above his legs and shoulders? Next he'll be choking on the seawater—vomiting it through his nose. He had done that. That had happened. He shudders and turns away from the railing.

"Come on, Chester," he says flatly. "Let's head up the hill."

Paul and Valerie dubbed the stretch of six or eight properties along Beach Drive from the Victoria Golf Club to the Oak Bay Beach Hotel "Millionaire's Row." The name was derived not from the home owners' wealth (which was considerable), but from their exclusive location. Every property looks onto the junction of the Juan de Fuca and Georgia Straits, the southeast corner of Vancouver Island—and the southernmost point in western Canada. Most of the homeowners had a boat launch hidden in the rocky foreshore, some had a private beach. The most exclusive homes were set down the slope, behind the stone walls, shrubs and trees that blocked the tourists' view of the private world of West Coast old money. For example, the Rosses (owners of the Butchart Gardens), maintained their family home here through several decades. Next to the sidewalk they kept a border garden that always contained the freshest blooms in town. Chester especially enjoyed sniffing out the buds, and when the mood was right, he liked to pause and release his urine into the perfectly weeded soil.

As Paul strolls along the sidewalk he can feel the effects of the Scotch whiskey in his legs. Woozy. That's the Scotch combined with the new meds, he tells himself. Wally certainly understood its side effects. Had he once endured a bout of medication for hypertension? Not likely; his alertness to Paul's symptoms probably stemmed from his pharmaceutical career. In so many ways Wally was the perfect father-in-law. Distant, never quick to interfere—nor to utter a wayward comment even slightly salted with sarcasm. Furthermore, he was a successful businessman generous with his money. And a saint for maintaining his loyalty to Jeanine.

Paul's parents would have liked Wally. Sometimes he fantasizes about hosting a dinner party with John and Doreen, Wally and Jeanine, and Valerie, Eliot and himself. Christmas dinner. He once described it all to Valerie. They would start with a round of cocktails during which the fathers would espouse their congruent views on the merits of the small business entrepreneur. Over dinner and desserts, the mothers, despite the vast differences in their personalities, would make allowances for one another. By the end of the night Doreen would quietly confess to Paul that she "really, honestly did like Jeanine." She couldn't understand Paul's reservations.

Overhearing this aside, Valerie would smile at Paul. Later in bed, discussing the evening, they would laugh out loud.

But when Paul told all this to Valerie she did not laugh. A tear slowly worked its way down her face. "It's a might-have-been," she said. "One I wish we could-have-seen." When he saw her reaction, he decided not to discuss it further. He had long ago finished mourning his parents. But he realized that Valerie felt a deep emptiness because John and Doreen would never be more than phantoms to her. The effect was heightened after Eliot's birth. The senselessness of their deaths affected her when she grasped that they would never see their beautiful grandson.

And he was beautiful. Eliot was more beautiful than anything Paul had ever known. Everyone thought so. That's why Jeanine was so eager to fight for him. To fight the Ratman—that would be something to behold: Jeanine in full witch-mode—besieging the Ratman's paranoid world until he withdrew in humiliation. But did Jensen possess enough blind anger to smash an aging woman with his fists? Possibly. It could be that Jensen was so gripped by his despair that he would break anything that blocked his mission. But what was this crusade he'd devised? What could it possibly be? His child lay comatose—only her revival could save him. Didn't he see that?

Twenty minutes pass before he reaches the gate to Anderson Hill Park. He could have taken the path behind his house on Transit Road and climbed to the summit in five minutes, but over the past week, his walk around Beach Drive and Newport Road had become habitual. His daily constitutional prescribed by Dr. Biggs.

This evening, however, his legs feel the weight of a much longer walk. They're heavy with the traction of insomnia. That and the effort required to cheer along his in-laws over the past two days has drained his already low reserve of energy. Take away the lethargy caused by the drugs and the Scotch, and you're running on nothing but fumes, he murmurs to himself. He calculates each negative as though he's performing a grade-school subtraction problem, bending a finger into his fist as he ticks off each component of the problem.

"Yup, nothing but fumes," he says to Chester and bends over to unleash the dog once they start to climb the chip trail leading up to the bluff. Chester immediately romps around the bushes, takes a quick pee, dashes up the hill, then back to Paul.

"You always come back to me, don'tcha?" He pets the scruff around Chester's throat and the dog canters back up the path, careful to keep Paul in sight. "You don't wander too far now. It's already dark."

Beyond the ridge they reach the green bank that overlooks the houses strung along both sides of Beach Drive and the ocean below. He'd walked that same stretch fifteen minutes ago. From here he scans the Juan de Fuca Strait and the Olympic Mountains in Washington State. The full moon hovers above them in the cloudless air. It will be warm tonight. The smoke pouring from the mills is no longer visible in the dusk above Port Angeles, but the city lights illuminate the entire bay where the port sits snug beneath the melting glaciers. It must be twenty kilometres away, he thinks, maybe thirty—yet from here it looks like a stone's throw. He recalls sailing across the water on the ferry, the Coho, when he departed for San Francisco with Valerie. Neither of them paid much attention to the distance they were travelling—just the time they had together.

And how time slips away. "*Time is a river without banks*," Jack Wise said toward the end of their second meeting at Foo Hong's. "It's a title of a painting by Marc Chagall—this surrealist picture of a grandfather clock and a fish and violin flying above a river in the night. But that doesn't matter; the key thing is the idea of it. A river without banks floods everywhere. It lifts and carries everything with it." He lifted both hands in the air as if the water were carrying his arms aloft. "Everything that it doesn't drown," he added, as though it was understood that ultimately everything would drown anyway—all in good time.

Paul considered this a moment and leaned forward. "If it floods everywhere, then time has no direction."

Jack smiled. "That's one of the three most important things I've discovered," he said. His smile was still lovely: broad and full of even, square teeth. "Time can flow sideways, backwards, it can sit still as a deep pool." He took a long, even breath. "And you can't control it. You can't hurry time. If you want to govern your life—to control your actions—you have to wait for a favourable moment to arrive before you initiate anything. Hence the importance of discipline and patience. A sailor stands ready to launch his boat, waiting for the right combination of wind, current and tides. As a painter I do the same. Each day I keep a pact with my brushes and paper. That's my discipline. And my patience is to forgive the muse her many late arrivals."

He chuckles at this, his nose lifting slightly, stretching the skin beneath the pea-sized mole next to his nostril. "My own little joke," he says when Paul fails to laugh with him.

"What are the other two?"

"The other two?"

Paul sits back in the chair and glances about the restaurant. People stand at the door waiting for free tables so that they can sit and order their lunches. Two rounds of patrons have been served since he arrived at Foo Hong's but he is in no rush to leave. Nor is Jack. "What are the other two most important things you've learned?"

Jack frowns a little and turns his head away, then dips his chin forward again. "The second is a corollary of the first. If time flows without direction, then to achieve anything you must set your own course. No one else can do this for you. You must set your direction on the horizon and focus on it to the exclusion of everything else. Like our sailor, you await a favourable combination of currents and tides, then initiate your course of action. Everything else dissolves into nothingness. That's the wisdom of the great Buddhist masters. Hence it is important to pick a goal that matters."

The Buddhist masters. They were the essence of obscurity as far as Paul could determine. Before they parted ways, Jack recommended that Paul buy a copy of the two-volume *Buddhist Logic*, by Stcherbatsky. In good faith to the memory of his friend, Paul ordered the books and began to study them. But after reading a few chapters he became totally lost in the language, the syllogisms, the threadbare connections among words, meaning and reality.

Years later, scanning the titles in his bookshelf, he came across the books and realized that he neither understood Buddhism as a system of thought, nor had he ever established any direction for his own life. He had tried things. His efforts to start a business in personnel recruitment faded soon after its launch in large part because he bartered away his labour with clients like Jack Wise. His job with the Ministry was never more than a Plan B stuck in a rut. There was his marriage to Valerie. He'd wanted that and so had she. But marriage wasn't really a direction. It was a process—a furnace that transformed fuel into heat. And to keep it burning, you're constantly on the lookout for new kindling.

"And the third thing?"

"Ah-h-h." Jack looked through the window onto Fisgard Street and sipped his tea. "My third discovery is about prayer." He let the thought linger a moment to test Paul's reaction. Not everyone wants to talk about prayer or God and eternal life—or is it eternal death?

Paul appreciated the respect within this gesture but he wanted to know everything that Jack could impart. He was the best painter Paul had ever known personally and Jack possessed a sense of certainty about the world that was extraordinary. He believed that Jack had discovered something about how to master life itself. "Go on," he said.

"It's not about praying to God," he began. "It's about contacting The Mind."

"This kind of ... universal spirit that governs the earth?" Paul cycled his right hand in a tight circle as he tried to recall a few words to capture what Jack had said earlier about the spiritual cycles of life.

Jack nodded doubtfully, suggesting that this was only partially correct, but as a basis to understand his system of prayer, it would do. "Yes. But you'll understand it more not by talking about it, but by practising the method."

"The method of prayer."

"Right." Jack held his left hand to his chest and pressed the palm over his heart. "You begin by lying flat on a bed. Be sure you're comfortable and when you're relaxed, close your eyes. Then place your left palm over your heart and let it rest against your skin. Slip into the feeling of it. It's like a meditation at first. All your senses collapse into awareness of your inner world. But pay attention to your heart. Eventually you want to feel nothing but your heart beating in your palm as it connects the rhythm of life to your consciousness."

Jack tried to illustrate the posture sitting in his chair. His voice tone dropped. His eyes closed and the flesh of his eyelids became smooth and clear.

"When you can feel the heat of your heart in your hand, at the point where it is beating directly into your flesh—then set your right hand on the mattress with the palm facing up." He extended his right hand, palm up, and placed it on the table. He opened his eyes and looked at Paul. The demonstration was over and he blinked—a faint suggestion that he could reveal little more; the rest would depend upon Paul's own efforts with prayer.

"This all sounds odd, I know." He took a final sip of tea and pushed the cup away. "But your right palm facing upward is like an antenna receiving and transmitting energy to The Mind."

Paul nodded and glanced away. Yes, it was odd. Odd enough that he began to doubt Jack's overall wisdom.

"It's a bad analogy—plagued by associations with engineering and electricity. But I cannot think of any other image that comes closer than the idea of antennae." He stopped and wove together the fingers of both hands. "And that's how I pray," he concluded.

Paul finished his tea. He realized he didn't want to hear any more about prayer or antennae or The Mind. On the other hand, they'd reached a point that called for some kind of denouement. "What do you pray for?" he asked and immediately suspected this question was far too personal. Too invasive of Jack's inner life.

But Jack seemed pleased to answer. "I pray that I may be a channel for the creative energies of the world. That they can find expression through me and guide my brush on the canvas. It's a faith I keep. And it works best when my mind is open; fed by the life force in my pulse and attuned to the messages of the universe."

"Come on, Chester. Let's head up to the top."

Paul has lost sight of the dog but in a few seconds the Lab is at his side again. They pick their way through the moonlit darkness along the rocky path to the top of Anderson Hill. After a few minutes they are overlooking the world below, a 360-degree view of the ocean, the clipped greens of the Victoria Golf Club, the curving roadway of Beach Drive, and on the American side of the strait, the Olympic Mountains.

The best light is provided by the moon. Its clarity is refracted by the choppy water in a long beam that widens as it approaches the shore. In the centre of the beam stands the lighthouse on Trial Island. On the five or six rocky islets in front of the lighthouse, he can make out the shapes of sea lions camped amid the driftwood. They are quiet for now, but at any time they can rouse and begin a chorus of barking that might last for hours and be heard for several kilometres up and down the coast.

The vast illumination provides a feeling of warmth and Paul wraps his arms across his chest and considers the universe before him. The moon was like this the night he and Valerie made love the first time. It was their third date; they'd finished dinner at Café Brio and planned to catch a movie at the Capitol Six. A few weeks later, neither of them could recall the name of the movie. In fact, they never saw it.

"I'm not really in the mood for a flick," Valerie said.

"No?" Paul shrugged slightly. He didn't care. As long as they could spend more time together, who cared what they did? "Me neither," he added to reinforce her mood.

"So what would you like to do?" She leaned forward, the tips of her blond hair brushing against her bare forearms. Paul could smell her. The aroma entered his lungs and he could think of little else but burying his face in the long strands of her hair.

But he could not say that. At the same time, he guessed that she knew this. Somehow she had discovered the password to his libido. She had opened the door to everything that he desired, and she stood there patiently, waiting for him to lead her through the passage. He started to laugh at the thought of this.

"What are you laughing about?"

"Nothing." He waved a hand and smirked.

"No, really." She leaned forward and placed her hand on his forearm. "Tell me what you're laughing about." She began to laugh, too—a sign that she'd go along with the joke no matter what.

"I just had this crazy thought," he confessed. "That somehow you'd figured out how to read my mind." He looked at her without laughing.

She smiled and held his eyes. "Maybe I have."

"Oh?" He realized that he held a small edge in the conversation. "And so what am I thinking, my swami?"

"Mmmm. Lots of things." Her face seemed radiant now. He loved to look at her. She had brilliant green eyes. But the best part of her eyes was the way she invited him into her soul. "Oh yes, I can think of a thing or two."

"Like what?"

She waited a moment. "Like you tell me and I'll tell you if I'm getting it right."

He leaned forward. Their faces were inches apart. "Like maybe going back to my condo," he whispered.

"Yes. I read that. You see? I do have this special talent. Now ... what else?"

He laughed again. It was working. It was all going to work out between them—he knew this for certain now. "Like maybe having a little dessert."

She giggled and moved her hand up his arm, just above his wrist. "Oh, I do like a gentleman who offers desserts to a lady."

"Desserts? But I have only a single treat to offer the charming lady."

She smiled. "Now this is getting a little difficult to read. You are becoming somewhat opaque."

"Opaque?"

"Yes. You need to be more specific. Put the thought in the front of your mind and dwell on it. Maybe then I can contact your innermost secrets." She lifted her face and gazed at the restaurant ceiling. "Ah—I think I'm getting a clearer picture. Tell me what it is and I'll confirm."

"You'll confirm it if you're right?" He laughed again. The game was coy. "This is too easy for you."

148

"So? Make it easy for me. Tell me what you're thinking."

"What dessert I'm thinking about."

"Yes. What single, treat-a-licious dessert you have in mind. For your lady," she added.

He leaned back in his chair and looked at her face. Her skin had the sheen of clear honey. "All right," he said, "I'm thinking of a piece of pie."

"Pie?" She started laughing.

"Yes. Pie. Did you read that?"

"What kind of pie?"

"What kind?" He leaned forward again and said: "Cherry pie."

She began to laugh louder and held her napkin over her mouth. Her face reddened with laughter. The waiter walked past to determine if she was choking. She held her hand up to him. "I'm fine," she managed to say as she forced her laughter under control.

Paul waited a moment. It was fun to watch her, this array of emotions washing over her face. "So you didn't think of cherry pie, eh?" Paul cocked an eyebrow at her.

She looked at him and folded her napkin on the table. "Come on," she said. She was back to whispering again. "Let's pay the bill and see if we can find our way back to your condo without any mentalist contortions."


Paul's condo occupied the top floor of a three-storey heritage house that had been converted into a strata-title property by a now-bankrupt developer. Fortunately, Paul had not been financially damaged by the owner's ruin. He'd spent half of the money from his parents' estate on the condo, thinking it would be a solid, live-in investment. He was right. Six months after he married Valerie, he sold the condo for 20 percent more than he'd paid and bought their house on Transit Road. The real estate deals made him feel shrewd. Like his father and Wally.

The south view from the top floor looked down the hill into Fairfield. It was a few blocks from the Lieutenant-Governor's mansion just off Rockland Avenue. When he and Valerie stood together gazing over the balcony railing, he could feel the electricity building between them. He wanted two things: to inhabit this one moment forever frozen in time, and to rush through it as quickly as possible.

"Would you like brandy?" he asked her.

"Sure. The moon's pretty tonight. Do you think it's full?"

"Yes. It's better if it's full, isn't it?" He poured the brandy and returned to where she stood.

"Better than what?"

"Better than if it's not."

"Of course." They clinked glasses and tasted the brandy. It burned as it descended their throats. Fuel for their fire.

He pressed closer to her and their arms brushed together. They held steady. He put his free arm around her waist. His hand fit perfectly over her hip. She purred a little and sipped her brandy. "That's nice," she said.

"E & J blue label, from California."

"I'd like to go there one day and see how they make it."

"Yes, let's," he said and his hand travelled over her dress. Her skin was soft beneath the cotton and he wondered exactly how they would get from the balcony to the bed.

"I didn't mean just that," she said and sighed.

"Just what?"

"When I said it was nice. I didn't mean that just the brandy was nice."

"No?" he pressed his face to her hair, just above her ear. He breathed deeply, carried her scent into his lungs. "And what else was so nice?"

"The way you held me just then."

"Just then?"

"Then," she murmured, considering this as his hand slipped under her breast, "and now."

Every word she spoke was an invitation. She held open the door to his desire. He wanted to stay in this moment yet rush through it. He tightened his arm around her. "Would you like dessert now?" he asked. "Or then?"

She turned, careful to remain in his embrace. "Now ... and then," she said and settled her arms over his shoulders. Her embrace was very light but she did not release it. Clinging together like this, their arms wrapped around one another, they walked from the balcony to the bed, each holding a snifter of brandy—careful not to spill a drop.

Yes, that moon was much like tonight's, Paul assures himself and he tugs up the collar of his jacket. It was warmer then, but the moon was just as clear. He can feel the exhaustion of the day sink through his arms and legs as he stands atop the highest rock on the hill. It's time to pick his way home through the park paths. If he were lucky, within twenty minutes he would be lying in bed and maybe two or three hours of sleep would embrace him before the insomnia roused him once again. Perhaps he'd drift into a little more sleep; he had gone a long stretch without a nap, and the Scotch and medication were bringing on the old fog again. He can sense it like the heavy dew welling from the blue camas plants around him.

"Come on, Chester," he calls and steps off the summit onto the surrounding rock. After a few minutes he has made his way along the path leading back to the meadow on the ridge. In the night air the yellow Lab appears golden against the mass of blue flowers. "Let's look at the pits," he whispers to the dog and veers away to the right.

Anderson Hill, like Beacon Hill, is known for its camas growth. For thousands of years the Songhees natives gathered the bulbs from the soil each spring. They washed and prepared the vegetables on the meadow slope in open pits, rounded half-spheres dug into the soil and lined with rocks. The rocks were super-heated in open fires, then sprayed with sea water. The camas was steamed above the rocks in multiple layers of fern and cooked like potatoes. The bulbs were a tasty carbohydrate staple traded up and down the coast, as far south as Panama. Each year after the harvest the band members would light the meadow's lowest edge and a shallow fire would creep up the hills, burning off the scrub and setting down a fresh layer of carbon to nurture the next year's crop. All that remains of this age-old industry are a few pits. Although they're overgrown, the pits are deep enough to step into and hide from passersby. They looked like war-zone shell-holes and Eliot and his friends often dropped into them to act out imaginary battle-front dramas.

"Look at this, Chester." Paul stands at the edge of one of the pits. He's surprised to see it lined with cedar bows and fern fronds. Someone had taken the trouble to turn the pit into a circular bed, a soft mattress of fresh-cut greens. "Doesn't that look inviting, boy?"

He sets a foot onto the edge and is pleased to feel it support his weight. "What happened to all the rock that was in there?"

Chester steps onto the pit without sinking through the web of greenery. He stands in the middle, turns to Paul and wags his tail. A slow wag of the tail: comfortable, but tentative.

"Is that going to hold me, too?"

The dog walks to the far side, then back to the middle. He stretches his front legs forward and hunkers down in the centre of the bed, lays his chin on his forepaws.

"Don't be so selfish." Paul takes another step. His weight is fully supported. He can feel the round surface of the boulders beneath the matting but the cedar limbs have been interwoven to cushion the rocks underfoot.

"Amazing. All right, Chester, make room for Dad." He gently slides a foot under the dog's flank. Chester stands and examines Paul, who then squats in the middle of the bed. The Lab hunkers down again and slips his chin on Paul's thigh.

"Good boy," Paul murmurs and pets the dog's head. What a lovely creature. His hand works over the dog's neck and he settles into the pleasure of stroking the thick hair. He eases back on the mat and tests the support of the cedar and ferns under his back and shoulders. Good. He pulls up his legs, bending at the knees so his feet don't creep up the far wall of the pit. The dog moves between his thighs and sighs. It's like camping.

He recalls the summer nights with his parents in Quebec, his father's two-week annual holiday passed most years in the Laurentian Mountains north of Montreal. There was one night, completely cloudless, when the moon was down and the stars filled his eyes as he lay on a blanket beside his mother in front of their cabin. He was four or five years old. The vibrant presence of the universe entered him somehow, in a way he couldn't anticipate. It wasn't so much the vastness of the universe that enthralled him, but its jewelled surprise.

Now when he looks up from the ancient fire pit he can see nothing but the sky. He lies just beneath ground level, beneath the gentle sweep of the wind and with Chester wedged between his legs, he feels warm. None of the surrounding shrubs and trees is visible. None of the camas or broom. There is only the night sky and in the centre of it, the full moon. A few stars are visible, but he suspects they may be planets. He gazes at them to determine if they twinkle. Planets don't twinkle, his mother told him, they cast a solid, continuous light. But he cannot discern any differences; except for the moon, everything in the sky is shimmering.

He turns his attention to the moon. This must be the night when it is truly full—perhaps the exact minute of the hour of its fulfillment. Jack would appreciate this, a mandala moon, perfectly reflecting the light. Indeed, lying in this ancient spherical pit—another mandala—was *so* Jack. Had he ever tried this? He'd mentioned that the natives had sanctified some power circles on this hill to preserve the spirit of the place during the European occupation, but that no one had disclosed where they might be. Jack himself confessed that he could not find them.

Paul decides to make a tribute to his deceased friend. He slips his hand under his jacket and shirt and places his left palm over his heart. He has never tried this before. In the years since Jack described his method of prayer, Paul had always dismissed it. Not that prayer was some kind of nonsense. Until now prayer was simply unnecessary.

He can feel his heart beating. The pulse is steady as it warms his hand. He stretches out his right arm beside his thigh and turns the palm up. His antenna. The air is quiet and still. The dog advances his muzzle along Paul's leg. For the first time in many weeks he feels completely at rest. He sets his eyes on the moon and closes his eyelids. He can feel his heart—almost hot—in his hand. A thin tissue of flesh separates his fingers from the pulse of his blood. The rest of his body unravels into thin fibres that flow into the grasses, the meadow and the air itself. His mind clears and he feels elevated, as though he's floating a few metres above the earth. The shock of surprise is so sudden that he gasps and as he gasps the sensations of flying diminish. No—go back, he tells himself. Hold on to this.

He focuses on the moon again. It is a beacon to guide him through this flight, wherever it might go. Yet it goes nowhere. He hangs suspended between earth and moon, in the middle kingdom of consciousness. In the minutes of his levitation, he realizes that he is engaged in a state of mind, not travel. This is prayer, he reminds himself. Remember that.

And if this is prayer, what should you pray for?

He cannot think of an answer. He can feel himself descending and his body becoming visceral again. Pray for something. Ask for it.

What could you possibly want? Or need? Forgiveness—a personal amnesty.

"Please forgive me," he whispers. "Forgive me for hitting that young girl. Please forgive my ... depraved heart." He closes his eyes again and imagines his heart floating, drifting higher until it fades into the darkness. When it disappears he sighs in relief and slips into an easy sleep.

The morning air is crisp and damp on his skin. He brushes a hand over his face. No. *No,* it's impossible—could he have slept here all night?

His shoulders quake. He stumbles to his feet and out of the camas pit.

"Chester?"

There's no sign of the Lab. No wagging tail, no muzzle pressing against his hand. "Where the hell did you go without waking me?"

Paul walks around the pit. He crosses back to the ridge where he can see the sun nudging above the eastern horizon. A bank of clouds has blown up against the Coast Mountains. In a few minutes the sun will lift above them—and he will be missed at home. The Easter egg hunt. Eliot will rouse Valerie, Jeanine and Wally to witness his discovery of chocolates hidden around the back yard.

He starts to run along the path through the woods. He dips under the garry oak limbs and over the root-entangled rocks to where the path is groomed with cedar chips and gravel. He jogs around the corner, through the wire mesh gate and jumps down the steps to Transit Road hitting them two at a time. On the last stair he trips and rolls once, a perfect somersault. *Hell.* He dropped and rolled like this when he played football as a kid. But back then he expected tackles and the misery of mud. This time, he drops, rolls and recovers only to hear the back of his jacket rip open as it snags on a tree root.

"Damn it," he moans and brushes himself off. He stands and tries to jog again but realizes his left knee is shmucked. There's no tear in his pants, no blood oozing through the denim, but a whacking great pain hammers through his knee cap. "Jeezus," he cries and sucks a long breath of air into his lungs.

He stumbles onto Transit Road, turns left and limps up to his lawn. Chester saunters over from the Sampsons' front porch.

"Why the hell didn't you wake me?" he asks and narrows his eyes. "Look what happened to my bloody jacket 'cuz of you!" An image of his foot stomping the dog's face flashes through him. "All right," he says as the dog brushes against his good leg. "It's okay. You didn't do anything wrong. I'm the crazy one. Go on home and just let me get into my house."


Running water. It's the only noise he can make out as he eases the front door closed behind him. There's no sign yet of his in-laws or Eliot. He slips off his shoes and jacket. The shoes are soiled with mud, the jacket ruined. He tosses them behind the La-z-boy in his office and slinks through the gallery to his bedroom.

The sound of splashing water sizzles from the shower stall in their en-suite bathroom. That means Valerie is up. He will need to explain his absence—his all-night pit-snooze—and maybe now is the best opportunity. She'll be naked, in the shower, the curtain drawn. Perfect.

He slides into the bathroom. The showerhead is set to PULSE and thumps away at his wife with its steady rhythm. "Valerie?"

"Oh-my-God—is that you?" Her head appears from behind the shower curtain.

"Yes." He leans against the vanity counter top and frowns. "Sorry." He shrugs as if to suggest an excuse: the car broke down and I was hours from a phone. Otherwise, you know for sure, I would've called.

"Are you okay?" She pulls a few strands of wet hair from her face. The skin around her eyes is blotchy. Tired. "I was so worried."

"I'm sorry."

"Sorry? What happened?" Her voice raises. Sorry isn't good enough. She lets the plastic curtain fall, leans forward and kicks the shower knob with her foot.

"I fell asleep," he says while she's still behind the curtain. He doesn't want to see her face as he says this. It sounds too dysfunctional. How can anyone fall asleep when you're walking the dog? Especially in a camas pit. "I fell asleep on Anderson Hill," he adds hoping an exact location will lend credibility to his explanation.

She pulls the curtain. The scar between her breasts has turned pink from the heat of the shower. She tugs a towel from the rack, wraps it over her chest, tucks a corner tight under her armpit.

"You fell asleep? Do you know how many times I almost called the police last night?" She wipes her eyes. She's been crying. "I thought that God-damned Jensen had done something." She stands in the tub and glances away. "That he'd done something to you." A tear emerges from her left eye and she quickly wipes it away.

"No." He shakes his head. He is truly sorry for this. He approaches her and wraps his arms around her.

"Stop!" she whispers—but it's a firm command. "You're filthy. What happened to you?"

"I tripped on the stairs just now. I was running down the stairs on the path and bam—I went down on the last step." The hammering in his knee starts up again and he squats on the toilet seat. He doesn't want to discuss it any more. "Do your parents know?"

"Know what?" She steps out of the tub onto the mat.

"Know that I was out all night."

"I don't know." She begins to brush out her hair, vigorously yanking at the knots. "When you weren't back by ten o'clock I told them you'd probably stopped in for a nightcap with Jerry and Bettina. You know Mom and Dad. It was tennsies, and off they went."

Tennsies was bedtime for Wally and Jeanine. Occasionally, especially when they were visiting, they'd also take two-twos, a post-lunch nap in the basement guest suite. Their room was beneath the dining room, away from the main corridors of the house. Paul rubs his face with one hand and tries to assess the damage control required to manage this new situation. He assumes that if they dropped off promptly at ten, they don't suspect his absence.

"You better take a shower yourself." Valerie examines him coldly through the mirror. "The Easter egg hunt starts pretty soon. And it would be good of you try to stay awake for Eliot's sake ... don't you think?"

# CHAPTER 9

FOLLOWING A HALF-HOUR-LONG SHOWER, PAUL MANAGES TO RE-MAIN ALERT THROUGH BREAKFAST, THE EASTER EGG HUNT AND THE ROUNDS OF COFFEE AND TEA THAT VALERIE SERVES THE REST OF THE MORNING. If Wally and Jeanine know about Paul's absence during the night, they do not let on. Jeanine would certainly let Paul know her view of his waywardness if she suspected it. Because she says nothing, he assumes all is well. But by the time Valerie ladles out the luncheon soup, Jeanine has said so very little to Paul about anything that he believes she is furious with him. Wally must have persuaded her to button up, he thinks. That would be a first.

After lunch, his in-laws pack the Mercedes and prepare for the trip back to Vancouver. Though it's not a great distance, on long weekends you can always count on an hour-long ferry lineup and the hour-and-a-half sailing across the Georgia Strait. With the drive time, door-to-door, the entire trip can take four hours. Six, if you miss the ferry connection.

"It'll be good to be home before dark," Wally says, hefting Jeanine's suitcase into the cavernous trunk of the Benz.

"Always good to get home to your own bed, isn't it?" Paul says and hands him her second bag. Over the past hour his conversation with Wally has reverted to little more than social niceties. There has been a shift in tone between Jeanine and Wally that has thrown Paul off balance. Whereas Wally's upright demeanour is usually diminished by Jeanine's constant instructions and admonitions, this time Jeanine's silence has become too much to bear.

Paul glances up to the porch where Jeanine is offering her daughter some last-minute advice. Eliot appears at the door and passes a chocolate egg to her. She bends over and hugs her grandson, then the three of them walk down the steps and approach the car.

"It's been lovely," she says with a gush and embraces Paul and briefly presses her brittle blond hair against his cheek.

"You remember what I said," Wally whispers and shakes Paul's hand. "If you need anything.... "

Paul nods as Eliot grips his hand with his chocolate-stained fingers. Valerie kisses her parents again, and another series of hugs is bestowed on Eliot before the grandparents climb into the Mercedes. The windows glide down as the car backs out the driveway. There is a round of waves and blown kisses and then they are gone.

"That was funny watching Granny hopscotch," Eliot says.

"You were the funny one," Valerie says, her voice releasing an air of exhaustion. "Why did you make her bounce up and down the hall like that?"

"Because I missed getting her on April Fool's Day and I wanted her to bounce like a rabbit."

"I think she liked it." Paul turns and walks toward the house. "I know I did."


"I think my mother's changing." Valerie is propped against the bed pillows. She holds a copy of *Art World* magazine in her lap and flicks through it as she speaks. "I mean it's hard to believe anyone could change at her age. Especially my mother. But she said something to me today that she's never said before."

Paul turns his head away from the glare of her bedside lamp. Building on his sleepover in the park last night, he's hoping to start a new trend: a routine sleep pattern. Nod off at eleven and sleep straight through without interruptions. The clock reads 11:17. Already he is seventeen minutes behind the new target.

"I don't know if you saw her speaking to me this morning. After breakfast and then just before she left. When we were standing on the porch."

Eighteen minutes off target.

She flicks a few more pages. "She said something to make me think she actually has regrets."

Paul turns and faces his wife. She continues to stare into the magazine. "Really? What regrets?"

"About when I was kid." She folds the magazine on her lap.

"You mean your fever?"

"She said she was sorry."

"She never said she was sorry before?"

"Nope." Valerie frowns and flops the magazine onto the night table. " 'Sorry' has never had a place in her vocabulary…. As if you hadn't noticed."

Paul considers this a moment. The tenderness in his wife's voice suggests a new perception of her mother. "So what did she say exactly?"

Valerie takes a deep breath and clicks off the lamp. She pulls the covers around her shoulders and snuggles next to Paul. "That when I was sick she was sorry she lost the antibiotics. That she was in such a panic to get me some help that she dropped it."

"You mean when she dropped the first aid kit overboard?"

Valerie nods and with little see-saw motions of her head, slides her cheek against Paul's shoulder. "And that she was sorry so much trouble came afterwards."

"Yeah. I bet."

"At least she's said so now."

"You're right. Maybe she has changed." Paul pushes his arm under her shoulder and his hand eases over the small cove in her back.

"Mmm, that feels good."

"I know." Paul glances at the clock again and realizes his new sleep pattern could be delayed by another twenty minutes or so. If he's lucky.

After they finished their desserts on their second dinner-date, Valerie told Paul the story of the voyage with her mother and father in Wally's new boat, *The Miss Tandy*. During the August before she started grade four, her parents decided to sail the yacht from Vancouver through the Malaspina Strait to Desolation Sound, then up to the end of Toba Inlet.

"I was nine years old," Valerie said as she toyed with the straw in her Spanish coffee. "It was the first big trip—like an expedition—we ever took together."

"Same with me," Paul interrupted. "I was nine the summer we drove all the way to Banff and the Rockies. You see, we're twins; we have all these parallels," he added in an effort to convince her that their destinies were about to converge.

They'd decided to eat at Spinnakers, a brew-pub overlooking the Inner Harbour. During their dinner they'd discovered several other compatibilities: their love of the Group of Seven, especially the paintings of Lawren Harris, their fondness for seafood, a shared obsession with Miles Davis jazz recordings from the 1950s, the fact they were "only" children, that they had both loved and lost—and that they did not want to lose at love again. This last point went unstated, yet it was understood. They both knew that love held real risks. That was why Valerie decided to tell Paul about her illness—and the scar that cut across her chest—before they took steps she might regret.

She ticked her straw against the coffee glass. He could tell she wanted to reveal something important and he sat back and listened. "Sorry," he said. "I interrupted."

"No problem." She looked at him and then glanced away. "The day after we left the marina in Vancouver, I could tell I was getting sick. But I didn't say anything. I really wanted to go up the channel so badly. My dad and I both loved that boat. It was a thirty-four-foot Albin with a double cabin. When he was looking for a boat to buy he always took me along with him. I was the one who first spotted *The Miss Tandy* in the Steveston Harbour. 'Yes, she's just perfect,' he said. It was as if he was saying the same thing about me. That I was perfect because I'd found *The Miss Tandy* for him."

"I've never really been out on a boat," Paul confessed. "Not for days at one time, I mean." Although this marked a difference between them, he wanted to reveal his ignorance about boats so Valerie didn't interpret the look on his face for lack of interest or boredom.

"Well, this was going to be our big trip. My mother didn't really want to go. She wouldn't say it directly, of course; everything was revealed in nuances. But she wasn't enthusiastic. Believe me, when she's not enthusiastic about something, it means she actually hates it."

Paul tried to imagine Valerie's parents. They were nothing more than names to him. But when Valerie finished her story, he understood that they'd all been wounded. And that they all learned to hide it well.


Valerie felt the onset of strep throat one day after they boarded *The Miss Tandy*. By the time the lump in her throat began to swell and harden they were well up the coast and into Desolation Sound. But she didn't want to say anything. The look on her father's face as he steered the boat from the flying bridge, the sound of her mother belting out Broadway tunes as she racked the dishes in the galley, and the rhythm of the yacht cutting over the waves in the sound—all of it made her think they'd entered a paradise. She didn't want to destroy that. Not with it still so fresh and new.

The fifth night on the boat the fever took her in its grip and she could no longer hide her misery from her parents. At the same time her throat constricted around the growing infection. It was like a big peach stone, she told her father. It was hard and rutted and it gouged the centre of her throat. Her bed was in the fore cabin, squeezed into the v of the bow, a little nook that she filled with stuffed toys, drawing tablets, crayons and a stack of Nancy Drew mystery novels. She lay with her head on the pillow thinking she'd never been this sick before. So sick that she wanted out of her body.

"Let's have a look," Wally said. He opened his mouth and pointed

at her lips. She dutifully opened her mouth. She could barely extend
her tongue over her lips, but he held it down with the handle of a
spoon and pointed his pen flashlight at her tonsils. He peered down
her throat and said nothing. She gagged but when she recovered and
sipped some water, he said, "Let me have another look."

He examined her again and went to consult with Jeanine. They
walked out of the main cabin into the cockpit. She could hear their
voices discussing her condition at some length. That's when she
knew that something was wrong. Then she noticed that time began
to stretch. That was her fever, she thought. The fever had somehow
melted time so that it stretched in disconnected threads like a bar of
warmed toffee pulling apart in strands so she couldn't tell minutes
from days. The passing hours were marked by the rough chop that
pitched the overhead lamp by its swag. Back and forth it swayed, a
metronome beating out the distended passage of time.

The rest of the night Wally treated her with regular doses of acet-
aminophen and her mother bathed her with a cool washcloth until
Valerie broke into heat shivers and begged her mother to stop. The
next morning the fever failed to break. Her throat constricted to the
point where she could barely speak.

"Maybe she has tonsillitis ... or maybe strep throat," Wally said
as he peered into this daughter's throat.

"Tonsillitis?" A dark look crossed Jeanine's face. "We've got to
go back if she's got tonsillitis."

"We're heading back no matter what she's got. Let's give her
some penicillin first and see if she can keep it down. I put it in one of
the pill bottles in the first-aid kit. It's under my side of our bed."

Valerie remembered her mother stumbling out the cabin door and
slipping on the cockpit deck as a swell of water lifted the boat. But
she couldn't remember much else. She concentrated on the rhythmic
swinging motion of the overhead lamp. That, and the calm look on
her father's face, which betrayed no worries or fears.

Valerie's story of the return voyage was not based on her own memories, but on the tales told by her mother over the years following

the trip. Compared to her mother, her father had very little to say about it, other than to confirm Jeanine's version of events.

Jeanine had turned her ankle as she stepped into the cockpit that separated the two cabins. The deck was wet and as she made her way toward the stern cabin, she cursed the sills around all the doors on the boat. "If it wasn't for those damned step-overs," she said later, "you would have been just fine."

She found the first-aid kit under the bed. It was an old tin lunch box, stencilled in red tartan, with a metal clip closure. Wally had stocked it with bandages, disinfectant, scissors and various un-marked bottles of pills. As she sorted through the box looking for the bottle of penicillin pills, a shock of pain drummed through her ankle. She sat down and cursed again. She decided to take the entire first-aid kit to her husband. Let him dig out the right pills rather than make a mistake and have to stumble back to the stern cabin if she'd selected the wrong medication. She waited for another wave to roll under *The Miss Tandy,* then walked to the cabin door. She braced herself against the door frame, took a breath and stepped over the sill. At the same time, a bigger wave lurched beneath her and she fell onto the cockpit deck.

"I fell twice within two minutes," she confessed. In some versions of the story she would state this with a stark laugh, as if Fate had conspired against their lives. Other times she said it with a slight gasp, as though she was falling all over again and she was bracing herself for the pain. In yet another telling of the tale, her voice swelled with bitterness, an unrelenting regret that she'd agreed to join their expedition at all.

But it wasn't the fall that hurt so much. As she hit the deck, she released the first-aid box. But she never saw it slip overboard. She spent another five minutes hunting for it, certain it must have fallen under a tarp, or some rope, or back into the stern cabin.

Finally, she leaned into the main cabin and asked Wally if it had fallen into the galley.

"What? I told you it's in our cabin," he said.

"No," she mumbled. "I dropped it. I just wondered if it fell in here."

"That's when I knew it was lost," Wally said. He always said this

D.F. BAILEY

the same way. No matter how many variations of her story Jeanine provided, his conclusion was always delivered with the same tone of resignation.

When Jeanine saw the look on his face—that's when the deepest pain hit her, the pain that stayed through the years. "Like a spike had fallen through the sky and lodged in my stomach," she said with a sigh.


Valerie's fever broke after the voyage home, five days spent fighting the storm that blasted the length of the Georgia Strait. Although Valerie had won the battle she was exhausted and recovered slowly. Once she was home, her doctor swabbed her throat and diagnosed streptococcus, and a course of penicillin was prescribed even though the worst effects of the infection had passed, or so everyone thought.

About a month later, shortly after she'd started back to school, the backs of her knees began to swell and she complained of aching joints. The fever and exhaustion returned, but this time, when she lay in bed, her heart beat uncontrollably.

"It turned out to be rheumatic fever," she told Paul as they sat in the restaurant. They'd finished their Spanish coffees and the waiter hovered about the table, eager to clear it for the foursome standing at the door, eyeing their table with an air of impatience.

Paul looked at her. He didn't recall the symptoms and progress of rheumatic fever but he knew the implications were serious. "Isn't it a disease that attacks your heart?"

"The heart valves, sometimes," she said. "Especially after an untreated bout of strep. It can come back a little later like it did with me. In fact, I'm a textbook case."

"Meaning it didn't attack your valves."

"No." She glanced at the waiter, poised to take her coffee mug. "Meaning it did."

Valerie studied the bank of windows overlooking the Victoria harbour. Perhaps she shouldn't have told this story so soon.

"It did.... " Paul wonders how to carry the conversation forward.

Where does talk like this lead? "So what happened to the heart valves? Your heart valves, I mean."

"Surgery." She looked at his face and turned her chin to one side. "Last year, I had the surgery and a valve was replaced.... With a pig's heart valve, of all things!" She smiled, hoping this would provide enough novelty to lighten the mood.

"You're kidding?"

"No." She decided not to tell him (not then) that eventually the pig's valve would degrade and she would need another surgery in another ten years. At that time the surgeons would install a plastic valve that would last the rest of her life. But following this second procedure she would require a daily dose of beta-blockers—also for the rest of her life. If she wanted children, her doctor warned, it would have to be before the second surgery.

"One outcome of the story," she said leaning forward and embracing him with her eyes, "is that I have this scar." Her index finger touched the top of her blouse and traced a path to the bottom of her rib cage.

Paul was absorbed by her gaze. It provided a completely open, honest revelation of who she was. He had never experienced such a feeling, such willing self-disclosure. "It doesn't matter," he said after a moment and wiped his mouth with his napkin.

"No?"

He pressed his lips together and shook his head. "No."

"Well ... you needed to know," Valerie said and took a deep breath. "Or at least, I had to tell you."

She hadn't told Rory Stillwell. She'd let him discover the scar for himself and the outcome was ... distressing. No, the silent approach hadn't worked at all. It didn't work because she never had a chance to assess Rory's reaction to what happened to her. Instead, she could only witness his reaction to what happened to him—when his fingers discovered the dark, blistered incision that cut between her breasts. It was as though he was the sudden victim of disease and the surgery had sliced open the palm of his hand.

The night after Wally and Jeanine return to Vancouver Paul sleeps eight hours without waking. Maybe without moving. He awakes with a renewed sense of vigour and tells Valerie that he wants to make love to her each night for the rest of the week.

"Sure," she says and laughs. "Let's see if you can make it to Wednesday."

"Do I detect a skeptical note?" He likes to see her laugh like this. If he can do nothing else, he will find the stamina to carry the joke on for a few minutes.

"Of course not." She buttons her blouse and calls up the stairs to Eliot's room to ensure he's getting ready for his visit with Jeremy Bowles and his family, who have invited Eliot on an outing to Salt Spring Island. "How could I possibly be skeptical of my stud-muffin?"

"Your stud-muffin has been on a slow bake for a month now. Time to chow down!"

Valerie laughs again, walks into the hallway and calls up to Eliot once more. "Come on—you're going to be late!"

Paul pulls the duvet up to his chin. There's been a change, he says to himself. Sleep—deep, REM-type unconsciousness—has achieved magical effects. But it's more than that; a new spark has been lit within him. Maybe the medication has finally stabilized his blood pressure. Perhaps he doesn't need to follow the prescription anymore.

Eliot rumbles down the stairs. Paul can hear Valerie checking his backpack. He needs supplies for the Bowles' annual Easter Monday trip to their cottage. It's a school holiday and Eliot has been invited as the guest worker. On the way to the ferry they'll stop in at McDonald's for breakfast, then he and Jeremy are going to help—or pretend to help—his parents build a new deck on their cottage.

When the doorbell rings, Paul calls into the hallway, "Give me a hug, Eliot!"

Eliot races into the bedroom and gives his father a squeeze around the neck.

"Have fun!"

"Yup!" Eliot runs back into the hallway and the door slams behind him.

Paul's good mood continues through breakfast. "You know," he says to Valerie after explaining how much better he feels, "maybe I should give Andy Betz a call. Tell him that I might be able to come back to work soon."

"Really?" Valerie pours another cup of coffee. "You're feeling that good?"

"Almost."

She thinks about this a minute. "Let's wait until we get through your day in court. And see what happens with Jensen."

"Yes." Paul glances away. He hadn't forgotten about it, of course. But he wants some distraction. The pending lawsuit is like a freighter coming toward him from the distance. It is certain that the ship will arrive within an hour or two. But it is equally certain that no one can steadily focus on the ship every minute of its approach. Nonetheless, Valerie is right. Vigilance is essential—especially now that he possesses the energy to remain on guard. "You're right," he concurs. "I'll wait before I phone Andy."

"It's just a few days until the examination for discovery starts."

"I guess I didn't want to think about it." He realizes that's exactly the case; his urge to get back to the office is an avoidance strategy.

There is a sound at the front steps, then the doorbell rings. Valerie lurches from her chair. "I bet Eliot forgot his jacket," she says and hurries to the front door.

But it's neither Mrs. Bowles nor Eliot. From his chair in the kitchen Paul listens to the quiet conversation at the front door. Valerie is talking in hushed tones with someone. Another woman? The door closes. The sound of two people walking toward him sends a shiver of dread through his stomach.

Valerie enters the room with a police officer at her side.

She's dressed in navy blue, her hat tucked under one arm, her blond hair pulled into a bun behind her head. She's thirty-something and smiles when Valerie introduces her. "This is Corporal Woodford," she says. "I think you spoke to her last week on the phone."

Paul blinks. "Oh yeah. Of course."

"It seems that Mom called the police about Reg Jensen. She's here to investigate a complaint." Valerie rolls her eyes and offers Woodford a chair. "Would you like a coffee?"

"Only if you have it ready," she says and smiles.

"Let me get it," Paul says and pulls himself from his chair just as Woodford sits opposite him. With his back to her he flashes a warning look to Valerie: get her out of here!

The two women engage in some preliminary chat: the unusually warm weather, the Easter weekend. In the meantime Paul carefully selects the coffee mugs, pours the cream into a creamer, removes the breakfast dishes from the table. All this provides breathing room, the pause he needs to determine what to say, and—more important—what not to say about Jensen.

"Just black for me," Woodford says and opens a spiral-bound notebook.

Paul sets a mug before her and sits on the other side of the table, opposite Valerie. Woodford is between them. If the need arises, Paul intends to direct attention back across the table to Valerie. The ping-pong strategy.

"So Mrs. Jeanine Burbank is Eliot's grandmother, is that right?"
Paul nods.

"And she's a resident here?"

"No. She lives in Vancouver." He takes a deep breath and looks at Valerie as he continues. "But she was here this weekend. Until yesterday. I take it she called about our son, Eliot. Am I right?"

"This morning."

"Wow." Paul is genuinely surprised. "You got here fast."

"We take threats against children very seriously these days." She tests the warmth of the coffee with her lip, blows across the brim then takes a sip. "Is Eliot here right now?"

"No." Valerie's voice carries a note of concern. "He's off with family friends for the day. Is there a reason we should be worried? Is Eliot vulnerable on Salt Spring Island?"

"I don't know that he's vulnerable at all." Corporal Woodford frowns slightly, a look that suggests half of the complaints she hears are the result of rampant paranoia. "Your mother said your son was threatened. By a Mr. Jensen. She has some concern that he's been stalking members of your family. That he is"—she checks her notes for a direct quote—" 'a certifiable lunatic.' "

Valerie and Paul exchange a look of disbelief. Jeanine had gone right over their heads.

Woodford looks from Valerie to Paul. "Is there legitimate cause for concern here?"

Paul takes a deep breath. What can he say? As he mulls this over, the answer comes to him: Nothing. His lawyer's strict instruction was to say not a word to anyone about the case, especially to the police.

"There may be," Valerie says and braces her fist under her chin. "We've noticed Jensen at the school. The boys have seen him lurking around the playground. Then Paul had a shouting match with him last week. And you know about the broken window at the back of the house. We don't know if he had anything to do with that, of course. But someone intentionally smashed in that window." Her voice rises on the last few words, as though the inductive logic alone is enough to indict Jensen. "You can go look at it yourself, if you want," she adds.

"How about when we're finished with this." Woodford continues to fill in her report. She then looks up at Paul. "You had a shouting match with him?"

Paul leans back in his chair. "Listen, I have to explain something here."

Woodford sets her pen on the table and takes another drink of the coffee. "That's good," she says and smiles. With these two words she has complimented her host on the quality of his coffee and encouraged his confession. "Please. Continue."

Paul glances at Valerie, a look that says: here goes nothing. "You may or may not know that Reg Jensen is the father of Jenny Jensen." He searches for a look of acknowledgement from Woodford. "The young girl in the kayaking accident last month. She's still in the hospital. Recovering."

"Oh yes. I remember." Woodford studies Paul's face. "You were there too, weren't you?"

Paul can feel his heart thudding. She's trying to associate him with the accident itself. Trying to uncover his culpability. "Yes. But in another kayak," he adds.

"Paul was dumped into the ocean with the girl," Valerie says. "He was hurt by this, too."

Paul holds a hand aloft. "Listen, here's my point. I don't mean to be rude, but I can't say anything about this. About Jensen or about what my mother-in-law has told you. It's my lawyer's orders. See, the Jensens have included us in a lawsuit against the kayak school. It's not that we've done anything wrong," he explains, "it's our home owner's insurance they're after. If things don't go well, then it could cost millions to look after their daughter."

Paul leans forward and looks at Valerie for confirmation. That's his final position and he wants her to support it.

"I understand," Woodford says and turns to Valerie. "Are you named in the lawsuit, too—or just your husband?"

"Just Paul," she says and wraps both hands around her coffee mug.

"Then maybe you can explain a few more things for me." She smiles again and finishes her coffee. When Valerie offers her another cup she pauses and with a coy look says, "Just a freshener, please." She could easily have added, Good police work is all about patience.

As the dialogue between Woodford and Valerie continues, Paul's discomfort begins to ease. Valerie proves to be quite capable of handling even the most subtle questions. Despite the fact Woodford has no first-hand knowledge of any threats from Jensen, she keeps the focus on the reports of Jensen's bizarre behaviours.

"You can speak with Jeremy Bowles, the boy Eliot is visiting right now. They'll be back in town tonight." She leans forward to ensure Woodford is copying the name into her report. "He was with Eliot after school when they ran into Jensen hiding in the bushes."

"What bushes?"

"On the road home. Just off St. Patrick Street." She lays her palms flat on the table with a light thud. "He was lurking in the bushes!"

"What about this shouting episode with your husband? Did you witness it?" Woodford has her attention exclusively focused on

172

Valerie. Paul's right to remain silent seems to have rendered him invisible to her.

"No, but you can speak to a friend of ours, Wendy Palmer." Valerie presses her hands together and takes a moment to recall what she'd heard. "She was passing the school as the morning bell rang. She saw the whole thing. In fact, Paul didn't want to tell me about it," she adds to emphasize his protective instincts. "Wendy reported the entire episode just the way Paul said it happened."

Woodford dutifully copies this down without a glance at Paul.

"I'd like to add that Eliot has been having nightmares since all this began. He's just six years old. The little boy has been affected." She glances away then adds, "and so have I."

"And by 'since all this began' you mean?"

"Since the kayaking accident."

"So it began before Mr. Jensen appeared at Eliot's school?" Woodford scans Valerie's face.

"No. It began with Jensen's bizarre reactions to the accident. He started it all. On his own."

Valerie's voice is firm, her phrasing enough like Jeanine's to make Paul relax in his chair. If there were ever a time you'd want to be like Jeanine, he decides, this is it.


After promising that she'd follow up her inquiry with the neighbours Valerie identified, Woodford closes her notebook and stands. Valerie escorts her down the steps to the family room, to examine the newly replaced thermopane glass in the vandalized window. They'd rushed the repair job so they could avoid explaining the episode to Wally and Jeanine. Of all the tactics they'd planned prior to her parents' visit, this was the only one that worked.

Standing at the kitchen sink overlooking the sunken living room, Paul listens to their speculations about what might have caused the attack. Valerie displays the rock that was found on the floor after it had been pitched through the window. Woodford tests its heft, is surprised by its weight. "Wow. No doubt someone meant to break that in," she says flatly.

Yes, no doubt, Paul thinks. Now do something about it.

Once they return to the main floor, he joins them in the hallway, in the gallery of paintings leading to the front door. Woodford pays no attention to their collection, a forced disregard that annoys Paul just enough to press her.

"So will you be putting some kind of restraining order on Jensen?" These are the first words he's spoken to her in the past twenty minutes.

"That's up to a judge, not me." She looks at him distantly. "I'll continue my investigation, though. At some point I'll be talking to Mr. Jensen. That alone is often enough to settle these things down."

As she leaves the house and descends the front stairs, Paul feels like he's survived a long-dreaded event. He leans against the wall as Valerie closes the door.

"Thank God, that's over," he says.

"I know." She steps forward and wraps her arms around him. "I didn't know that was going to happen. Even though Mom said she'd call the police if we didn't. Honestly, I didn't believe she'd do it."

"Nobody would."

"I should have guessed she'd do something like this after what she said yesterday."

"You mean saying she was sorry for when you were so sick?"

"Yeah." Valerie pulls away and wipes the back of one hand over her eyes. "I guess she can't stand the thought of Eliot's vulnerability. Or the idea that she can't stop it."

Paul looks at her face. "You know something," he says. "I think she's right. I think she was right to call the police and get something going against Jensen. I thought we couldn't because of the lawsuit. That's what Ben Stillwell said. But now that's it's opened up, it's better."

"Is it?" She sets her jaw and looks away. "What if Woodford goes to Jensen now and then he goes ballistic?" Her face is pale, almost bloodless. Paul wonders if this is how she looked as a child. When she realized that all her mother's good intentions had only made things worse.

# CHAPTER 10

"M AY I SPEAK TO JUNE HALLETT, PLEASE." Paul holds the telephone handset to his ear and stares through his office window onto the street. The air is grey, misty—but it's not raining.

"I'm sorry, she's not on shift today. She called in sick."

Paul hesitates. He's not used to a break in this routine. "Is someone taking over for her as head nurse?"

"Probably Sandra. Hang on."

Paul inhales deeply and waits. It's like he's sinking beneath the surface once again. Every day he must make this call. Someday, someone will speak the words that will finally retrieve him from his despair: "She's awake!"

"Hello, Sandra Ward speaking."

"Hello Sandra. I'm calling about one of your patients, Jenny Jensen." His forehead slips into the palm of his free hand. "To see if there's been a change."

"Is this Paul Wakefield?" she asks.

He realizes they all know him. Everybody right down to the

janitorial staff is expecting his daily call for salvation. "Yes," he says in a whisper, then again to ensure she will hear him: "Yes, it's me."

Although Jenny's condition remains unchanged, Paul begins to notice more improvements in his own health. The most important is the restoration of his normal sleeping pattern. He can barely believe his good fortune when he sleeps through five successive nights. Each morning as he awakens, he utters a silent prayer: Thank you for letting me sleep. He has also benefited from the hypertension medication and Dr. Biggs has pared back his drug therapy to one half pill per day. With this reduction, he no longer suffers from the vapours that seemed to arise from the ground and consume him. Each day Paul walks Chester into the Oak Bay village, ties the dog leash to a lamppost and enters the Pharmasave where he takes the free blood pressure test. His systolic-diastolic readings, while not quite ideal, are not far off, and clearly within the normal range. Most mercifully, his impotence has vanished and thanks to Valerie's tolerance of his sometimes bizarre behaviour during the month of his recovery, they have completely restored their love life—and then some. "Just to make up for lost time," he says to himself.

In fact, the only symptom that persists from the days following the accident is the ringing in his ears, an annoyance that he has learned to tolerate. Only when he sits in his La-z-boy, in the silence of his empty house, does the ringing overwhelm him—like a hum buzzed through the electrical outlets and plugged directly into his ears. His Internet research has convinced him there is no available cure. A few of the alternate therapy sites suggest the best he can hope for is the calm that comes from meditation. Since he's never learned a formal meditation technique, he usually lies on his bed with his left hand placed over his heart and his right palm turned upward, an antenna homing in on whatever silence he can detect. He does not pray or ask for forgiveness for hitting Jenny Jensen. He simply lies in solitude for about a half-hour in the mid-afternoon. On two or three occasions, if he's lucky, the buzzing tunes down to a barely perceptible hum. A slow leak in the vast electrical grid surrounding the world.

As the day of the examination for discovery approaches, Paul finally sets a date to meet Ben Stillwell. Paul's impatience is mixed with his dismay that Ben never returned Valerie's call about Jensen. The office manager apologized for the mix-up; apparently the new receptionist had deleted several clients' messages when she was learning how to use the voice mail system.

Despite his misgivings, Paul feels attentive and calm as he begins their discovery preparation meeting in Ben's Broughton Street office. Settling into the upholstered chair opposite Ben's vast oak desk, he tells himself, this will all work out; everything will be fine.

"Before we get into the discovery hearings I've got to ask you about this trouble we've been having with Jensen," Paul says when he finally has Ben's attention. "Did your secretary tell you that Valerie called last week? I had to explain it to her again. We were hoping to hear from you, and I guess her message was deleted somehow."

"I know. Please let me apologize. I just found out about this today." He tilts his head away in embarrassment. "I understand Valerie thought Jensen might be dangerous." He waves a hand as though he's grasping for details. "I'm sorry ... please, fill me in."

"We've had several events—threats, really—from Reg Jensen." Paul studies Ben's face for the effect this statement might make. But Ben provides so little visible reaction that it's difficult to judge how seriously he takes their concerns.

"Tell me what happened." Ben steeples his fingers and presses them over his mouth as Paul recounts the episodes that mark Reg Jensen's growing obsession. His story culminates with his description of the Corporal Woodford's visit to the house to investigate Jeanine's complaint.

"Did you say anything to Woodford about Jensen?"

"No. But Valerie did."

Ben Stillwell considers this a moment. "Good. And you must remain silent about him. Remember our primary goal: to immediately sever you from the civil suit and absolve you from any blame. Next best would be to settle the case out of court with a proviso that the details of the entire case are sealed. In other words, completely removed from the public and legal domain."

"Right." Paul nods. Although they had discussed this at their first meeting at Foo Hong's, somehow he'd never identified it as a probable outcome. He could be completely absolved. If he keeps the pact of silence with himself, no one—ever—will know what truly happened to Jenny out on the water.

"If a criminal case emerges against Jensen for harassment relating to you or your family, we want to keep it entirely separate from the civil case. Do you understand?"

"Yes." Paul takes a deep breath. Ben's explanation is not the answer he's looking for. He presses his back against the chair and considers the key question. "Look, Ben—what I want to know is this: is Reg Jensen a threat? I mean, should I be trying to protect Eliot and Valerie from this maniac?"

Ben casts his eyes away. "I don't know." He turns back to his client and adds, "But I can find out if he has a record of violence. If not, then it's a reasonably safe bet that he's not a real threat. Usually these things are pretty much ingrained by our age." He smiles; an attempt to provide reassurance. "I mean, you're not about to take up a life of crime any time soon, are you? In any case, I'll do a criminal records check and get back to you." He makes a note in a large day scheduler under a heading marked TO DO.

"In the meantime, let's focus on the issues immediately before us. Now, if it were somehow to emerge that someone—not something—struck Jenny Jensen and caused her coma," Ben explains as he moves piles of folders from his desk onto the adjacent credenza, "then this would become a criminal case instead of a civil suit. We wouldn't be going to court for examination for discovery. Instead we'd be looking at a coroner's inquest."

"But someone did strike her," Paul says. He waits for this to sink in and divert Ben's attention from clearing his desk.

"They did?" He stops his busy-work and looks at Paul.

"Yes. The captain of the yacht."

"He's never been found," Ben says and frowns. "There's no record of the boat mooring in the marina. It's possible the captain became aware of what happened and just motored through the bay and anchored somewhere up the peninsula for a day or two. Until the coast was clear."

"The marine equivalent to a hit-and-run."

"You could think of it that way." Ben shrugs off the analogy and clears the last folder from his desk blotter. "More specifically, this is a classic personal injury case and the Jensens' lawyer, Bonnie Emerson, is proceeding exactly as I would. It's all about money. Somehow they've got to amass enough money to care for the girl for the rest of her life. My guess is they need six to ten million."

Paul sits in silence. He can't imagine how this money will materialize.

"That's why Emerson is joining every conceivable party to the suit. The kayak school, the school owner, the kayak manufacturer, and every adult who was party to the accident—and that means you. Just remember," he adds to boost Paul's spirits, "the only reason you're included in the suit is because you have homeowner's insurance. They're not after you, or your money or your house. They're seeking a personal liability payout from your insurance."

Ten million. Paul takes a deep breath. "And if she doesn't make it?"

"If she dies before the suit is settled, the costs incurred will be less. The most expensive scenario is if she recovers—and if she recognizes the limitations of her recovery. The more she recovers her faculties, the more expensive it can get. Unless, of course, she has a full recovery, which—months after the accident—would be considered extremely unlikely."

"How does it work?" Paul juggles his hands as he tries to sort out the inverse relationship of money and damage.

"Assume she remains comatose. The costs will be mostly fees related to her long-term care. In a bed. In a room. A rotating series of attendant nurses." Ben plants his hands on his desk. "Now assume she recovers but is unable to walk. She's confined to a wheelchair for life. She can attend school yet her intellectual faculties are damaged to the point where she cannot earn a living. It's unlikely she'd marry. The costs associated with her care multiply enormously. Furthermore, if she recovers to the point where she realizes the extent of her loss, we can expect another half-million award to compensate for her pain and suffering."

Paul shakes his head in disbelief. Although these kinds of awards are reported in the press every week, the real dollar costs come as a shock. "I don't know what to say. I thought it would be better if she recovered."

Ben shakes his head doubtfully. "I've seen people come out of comas like Jenny's, but they usually suffer from pre- and post-traumatic memory disorder."

"Meaning?"

"Meaning she won't remember anything about events leading up to, or immediately after, the accident."

Paul gazes through the window. He would be the only one to know what happened. It was one part miracle, one part eternal damnation.

Ben examines his client with an absorbing look that seems to penetrate Paul's thoughts. "It's not so bad. In the States it would be ten, maybe fifteen times that amount. Remember, they're after your insurance money. Even if they win the case—which is debatable in the claim against you—it's likely your annual premium will bump up just a few dollars, if at all."

Paul nods and turns his head back to the window. The view looks onto the south side of Broughton Street; a few businessmen are striding along the block in the direction of the courthouse.

"The bottom line is this: once you start to testify, simply tell your story. Bonnie Emerson will question you in minute detail about the events leading up to the accident and what happened afterward. You must answer everything she asks—there's no US fifth-amendment clause in Canadian civil law. On the other hand, don't answer anything she doesn't ask. I've had more than one client destroyed because he offered information that wasn't called for. That opens the door for further questions. Then the contradictions emerge and the lies are out."

Ben lets this last statement weigh in. Nothing in his tone implies a suspicion that Paul may be harbouring a lie. It is simply a warning: there is danger in giving legal testimony of any kind.

Paul senses their meeting is coming to an end. The next time they meet will be in the court reporter's office for the discovery hearings. "Tell me something," he asks. "Do I need to worry about what I said in front of the Jensens' cousin, Sam Watson?"

"What did you say?" Ben asks with a shrug.

180

"When I lied about their daughter." What a fool he'd been. First to lie, then to be so naïve about the Jensens' plot.

"Yes, I remember you told me about that. It's likely to come up. But what you did is only human. When you're asked about it, you'll confess to that lie. Tell me what you'll say." Ben leans forward and his eyes sweep across Paul's face.

Paul glances away. He frowns, wondering what to say. "I'll say, it was a mistake."

"A mistake?"

"Yes. A mistake to try to cheer up the girl's parents."

"A mistake to try to cheer them up—or a mistake to lie?" Ben twists this question on him without blinking.

Paul sets his jaw. He can feel his heart racing again and his stomach tightens. "It was intended to make them feel better. And to cover the fact that their daughter panicked. It was lucky she didn't drown," he says emphatically. "She could have—"

"Stop." Ben holds a hand aloft. "Do you hear yourself? Don't start to speculate about anything. Before the last two sentences you sounded very solid and certain. That's critical. Just be firm."

"All right." Paul eases back into the chair. His palms are sweating. He slides them into his pockets and clenches the fabric in his fists.

"Don't open any doors by answering questions you aren't asked." Ben raises his eyebrows and waits for Paul to acknowledge his warning.

"All right," he says and pulls his hands into his lap. "The doors are shut. Nailed tight," he adds and tries to smile. He thinks a moment and asks, "So ... do you think I'm going to be okay?"

"Don't worry. For a case like this you need a specialist. Only the best," Ben says and then winks. "Someone like me."

Ben escorts Paul along the corridor to the office reception area. The office supports six lawyers, the manager, a staff of eight secretaries and the new receptionist stationed at a desk overlooking the lobby. A half-dozen framed parchments are mounted like paintings on the walls. Paul examines them briefly and realizes they are antique legal documents. One is a duplicate of the Magna Carta. Legal text as art.

"All right, we'll see you tomorrow at the discovery," Ben says and shakes Paul's hand.

Paul nods and walks from the office to the elevator bay. Once he's outside the building, he strolls up to Johnson Street and waits for the number two bus. Valerie has the Volvo today and Paul is happy to embrace the public anonymity provided by the city bus system. It will give him another chance to sit and think. The bus arrives a few seconds later and he finds a seat near the back, on one of the elevated benches littered with candy wrappers and discarded newspapers.

After his conversations with Ben and the long counsels with his own conscience, he has decided to stick with his story. It is a lie, yes, but a lie calculated to achieve the most benefits for everyone. It is a complicated problem, but after he's reviewed all the possible solutions, he determines that his math is correct.

First, Paul assumes that if he reveals the truth, that he assaulted Jenny, the case would automatically change from a civil suit against Brad's kayaking school, Paul and the kayak manufacturer, to a criminal case against Paul alone. Would his honesty in any way affect Jenny's medical condition? No. Would it alter the vast fortune required to nurture her care for the rest of her life? Yes, it would substantially diminish Jenny's award. Paul would likely lose his house, his mutual funds, his pension plan and most of his personal assets in order to pay for Jenny's care. At best, this would yield nine hundred thousand dollars—less than a tenth of what she would be awarded otherwise. Furthermore, Brad's liability and that of the kayak manufacturer would be reduced or even eliminated. Thus, the substantial financial resources available to Jenny would evaporate once their lawyers hung criminal responsibility for the accident around Paul's neck. Even Ben Stillwell would have trouble fending them off.

A second impact of telling the truth: Valerie and Eliot would be forced out of their home. Her parents might intervene, of course, but a renewed dependence on them would be debilitating. Furthermore, if the legal precedent of John Ribbenstahl's depraved heart case carried any weight, Paul would likely be imprisoned. A public disgrace, he would certainly lose his job and possibly his wife and child. No, he could not let that happen. That was Valerie's one goal. She'd articulated it very clearly: "I don't want to lose what we have." Neither did Paul.

Now in balance consider the outcomes if he maintains the secret of his lie, the secret that no one has yet imagined. The Jensens win their civil suit against Brad, his kayaking school, the kayak manufacturer and Paul. They are found to have been negligent in their supervision of the child, Jenny Jensen. Damages are assessed at ten million dollars. The individual portions of the assessment against the defendants are say, one million against Brad, one against Paul, seven against the school and one against the manufacturer. When the inevitable becomes apparent to everyone, the parties agree to settle out of court. The award outcome and legal records are sealed and everyone is sworn to silence.

This way, Jenny's care is assured. No criminal blame is attached to anyone. The insurance companies fulfill their role: to provide the resources needed to mitigate exceptional, unforeseen loss. Brad will abandon his dream of becoming an outdoor adventure entrepreneur. The kayak company will reassess its boat design to ensure greater stability. Paul and his family will get on with their lives. And Paul alone will bear the secret to his grave.

This last point is the only one that sticks. In the examination for discovery he will be required to swear an oath to tell the truth. When he tells his lie—when he repeats it five or six times to Bonnie Emerson—some part of him, a part of his identity outside the lawsuit, may be condemned. But he cannot assess the true importance of this. He is unsure if he possesses a soul. Maybe he has a conscience about the impact of what he does and fails to do. But if he has a conscience, does it mean he has a soul? And if he has a soul, is it eternal?

Paul stares out the window as the number two bus crawls through the Oak Bay village. Life would be much easier if Jack Wise's theology—or whatever he called it—governed the universe. When he died, his soul would merge with The Mind. He would be a drop of spit absorbed by a vast ocean that would cleanse him completely and wash away the memory of his sins in the renewal of universal consciousness.

On the other hand, if his soul survived as an individuated entity, then he would bear the sin of his lie and his crime through eternity. Indeed, that would be Hell. That would be the price he would pay to ensure Jenny received the care she needed. To ensure that Valerie and Eliot could lead a normal life.

This, he decided, was the aftermath of his moral calculations, the equations that proved the right thing to do—was to lie. And to lie with absolute conviction.


The telephone is ringing as he enters the house. He sprints the few steps into his office and picks up the receiver just before the answering machine cuts in. "Hello?"

"Mr. Wakefield? It's Corporal Woodford calling. From the police department."

He takes a breath. He wasn't expecting to hear from her again.

"Is Mrs. Wakefield there?"

"No. She's at her gallery. The Sky Light." This must be about Jensen, he decides. "Can I take a message?"

"No need. I've got the number for the gallery right here." She hesitates a moment and Paul tries to think of how to extract whatever information he can from her.

"Is this about Reg Jensen?"

"I'd rather talk to your wife if I could."

Paul presses his lips together. "Well, I understand that. But in case you don't get through to Valerie, could you just let me know if you talked with Jensen?"

She hesitates. "Yes. I did."

"And?"

Another pause. "I'll call her right now at her office. If you check with her in ten minutes, I'm sure we'll have covered everything by then."

Paul can feel the blood flooding his heart. He sits in his chair and decides to wait ten minutes, then call Valerie, distressed as she is—unless she calls him first.

The phone rings precisely five minutes after Paul hangs up the line with Woodford. He lifts the handset, and assuming the call is from Valerie, immediately asks the key question: "So what did Woodford tell you?"

There is a pause, a deep sigh, then a cough—followed by the soft click of the line going dead.

Paul stands next to his office desk holding the handset in dismay. How could this be—a crank call in the middle of the day? More important, who could it be from?

He sets the telephone back in its stand and walks to the window. There is a 50 percent chance the call is a genuine misdialled number. But there's a good chance the caller is Jensen. Jensen assessing if anyone is home so that he can continue his lunatic vandalism. He gazes out the window to the street. No cars are visible. The air is bright with sunshine filtered through the moist green leaves on the crabapple tree. There is also an outside chance the caller is Rory Stillwell. Rory-still-on-the-prowl-for-Valerie. Paul has yet to speak to Valerie about Rory's telephone messages. They're her secret; one that he doesn't want to breach. Whatever its nature, their liaison was complicated by the fact that Rory and Ben were brothers and that in some ways, Paul's fate was governed by Ben's skill and good-will. No, there was no benefit in lifting the veil on whatever distant relationship Valerie maintained with Rory. If any, he assures himself. He knows that jealousy is the most poisonous of emotions, an adder that crawls through the veins. To defeat it, you must spit out the venom before it enters the heart. No, there is nothing concerning Valerie to fret about, he tells himself as he dwells on their renewed sexual harmony. Nothing to worry about at all.

He turns from the window and calls Valerie at the gallery. She answers on the first ring.

"I was just about to call you." Her voice carries a hint of surprise at their synchronicity. She's always enjoyed the cosmic threads that weave them together—a sign they were meant-to-be.

"So did you hear from Woodford?"

"Yes, just now."

"And?"

"And she talked to Jensen," she says and her tone shifts to a serious monotone. "She couldn't tell me too much. Or wouldn't, maybe. You never know how much the police will reveal."

"That's crazy." Paul expels a long, uneven breath. Absurd that the police would call and then say nothing. "So what exactly did she say?"

"Well." Paul can hear her settling into the wicker chair next to the cash register at the front of the gallery. "She went to Jensen's house. Somewhere over in Esquimalt. She talked to him on the doorstep. Apparently he wouldn't let her in. So I guess they spoke for maybe five minutes."

"Great. Compared to the half hour she spent with us. Who the hell is she investigating here?" As soon as he asks this, the question sticks in his mind.

"You wonder, eh? Anyway, she brought up the times we'd seen him around here. The argument he had with you in front of the school. The window smashed in at the back of the house. And guess what?"

"What?"

"He denied it."

"Denied it? But Wendy Palmer saw him coming at me on the street. She's an eye witness. Barb saw him, too."

"She saw someone coming at you. But can she identify who it was?" Valerie sighs and shifts her weight on the chair. "Woodford said that when it comes to criminal harassment—things like stalking, or making threats—all the stuff Jensen's doing—the police can't lay charges without the Crown Counsel's approval. One of the things they consider is independent evidence of harassment. Woodford said that when she talked to Wendy Palmer, Wendy claimed she only saw the back of Jensen's head when he was yelling at you. In fact, she and Barb were so frightened by his outburst that they immediately turned away and jogged to the end of the block. If neither of them can positively i.d. Jensen it's unlikely a charge can be brought against him."

Paul closes his eyes. Jensen's covering up. He's doing exactly what his neighbour, Jerry Sampson, advised: denying everything. "Did Woodford tell you anything about Jensen himself?"

"Like?"

"Like his background. Does he have a record?" More important, is he dangerous?—but Paul doesn't want to suggest that; Valerie is worried enough about the damage he might cause.

"No. She didn't say."

There's a pause. Paul could probe further, ask if Valerie had pushed Woodford for an answer on this. But he senses she couldn't bring herself to ask about Jensen's record—if he had one. "So that was it?" he asks.

"Pretty much." Paul can hear the bell ringer above Valerie's door. Someone has come into the gallery. The visitor, apparently an acquaintance, exchanges greetings with her. "She said they'd be watching him," she says in a hushed tone.

"That's an assurance." But he doesn't believe it. If anything, Woodford's visit will sharpen Jensen's wits.

"You think so? Look, I've got to go."

"Sure. Let's sort it out tonight."

"Okay. I love you."

"I know. I love you, too." That much is true, he thinks after he hangs up. Loving you and Eliot may be the only true thing I know.


Over the rest of the afternoon and evening Valerie and Paul come no closer to discovering anything more about Reg Jensen. Not a word from either their lawyer or the police. Then, from a source Paul would never have suspected, he learns more about Jensen than he wanted to know.

Brad Reedshaw is sitting outside the court reporter's office the morning of the examination for discovery. At first Paul fails to recognize Brad, who is dressed in a blue suit, his hair cut and trimmed, the ponytail shorn, his face lean and worried. Paul has never seen him anywhere other than the kayak school and has barely given him a passing thought since the accident. Yet as he sits in the chair beside him and senses Brad's bleak funk, he's immediately sympathetic to the mutual concerns they face.

"You're looking well turned out," he says to lighten the mood, and then he fingers the lapel on his own suit jacket.

"My one and only suit," Brad says and shakes Paul's hand. "I assume you're here to testify?"

"Yes." Paul glances away. He wasn't expecting to see anyone other than the Jensens here. Discovery hearings are not open to the public but any party to the inquiry can sit in on the testimony. It's a pleasant surprise to find Brad, a co-defendant and ally, at his side.

"I just finished an hour's go-round. They're grilling the rep from the marina now. That ought to be short; he doesn't know a damned thing about the yacht that rammed you guys. That's why I thought I'd take a break from the inquisition."

"What about the Jensens?" Paul leans forward and braces his elbows on his knees. "Have they talked to him yet?"

"Yeah. I only heard Reg's story. The bastard hasn't changed in twenty years," Brad says with a snarl. "With that guy, everything is always someone else's fault."

Paul leans back in the chair and looks squarely at Brad. "What do you mean? You knew him before the accident?"

"My Uncle Ned did," he says and sucks in a long draught of air. "After the accident Uncle Ned told me everything. They were buddies in high school together. Until Reg dropped out. I guess it was about six months before graduation."

Paul scans Brad's face, looking for an explanation. "Couldn't finish the race, huh?"

"Not quite. He got his girlfriend pregnant," Brad says with a frown. "Instead of doing something about it, he bailed out. Joined the navy and became a ship's cook."

Paul considers this, calculates the years to determine if Reg's mistake turned out to be Jenny Jensen. "So was it with his wife, Fran?"

"Nope. She probably doesn't even know about it."

Paul and Brad sit quietly for a minute. A woman walks down the hallway carrying an armload of folders and disappears into another office. Paul studies the heavy oak door to the court reporter's room. It would be impossible to guess what is being said on the other side of the door. He could have sat in on all the testimony, of course, but he decided that his ongoing appearance would lend the perception of neediness, or worse: desperation.

"What else do you know about Jensen?" Paul asks this in an easy, conversational tone, as though Brad's answer is unimportant, and all their talk is meant to pass the time and nothing more.

"He's a bastard." Brad shakes his head as though he should have known what was coming the day the Jensens registered for lessons in his kayaking school. "I guess it was a year or two after he signed up for the navy that he was charged with assault for knocking the lights out of some kid who wandered into his neighbourhood. It was a big story in the papers. I remember my brother reading it to me at the time. This guy from Halifax was visiting town. He'd been here only a few short days—didn't know a soul—and stumbled onto the road sometime after the bars closed. That's when Jensen came across him. Beat him into a coma. No one even knew the guy's name. It took a week before his relatives showed up and flew him back home."

A coma. Paul considers the dark irony of the situation. Jensen was travelling a karmic loop of sorts, his daughter's tragedy made worse by his sense of guilt. "What happened after that?"

"In the end? Nothing. There were no witnesses to the beating. I guess the circumstantial evidence couldn't force the conviction when Jensen denied everything."

"So he got off?"

"Yes. But—who knows if it's related—a few months following the trial he was discharged from the navy. Or maybe that was a gift, too," he says with disbelief. "After that he opened Jensen's Meats. Not much later he married Fran. If anything started to bring him around it was her. She's fairly religious. A bit of a seeker, I've heard. I guess when Jenny was born he finally settled into the straight and narrow." Brad flattens his hand and points to the end of the hallway. "The kayak lessons were a present for his daughter's thirteenth birthday. Believe it or not, I gave him a discount."

A moment later Ben Stillwell arrives, his arm weighed down by a briefcase, his face sombre and distracted. "Sorry I'm late," he says and shakes Paul's hand. "I was here for Brad's testimony but I had to rush out for a minute. Obviously they haven't started without

D.F. BAILEY

us." He forces a smile onto his lips, checks his watch and glances down the hallway. "Are they still in there with Mr. Peters?"

As soon as he asks this, the door swings open and Jake Peters, the representative from the marine club, emerges from the room with a look of exhaustion on his face. He spots Brad and saunters over to him. "Lawyers," he says and shakes his head. "In my entire life I never felt so boxed in by words."

"I know what you mean," Brad says and stands up. Paul has forgotten how tall and fit he looks. His athletic physique is apparent even under the layers of the three-piece suit.

Jake dips his head and eyes Paul. "You next?"

"I guess." He glances at Ben, who has passed through the doorway and waves at Paul to follow him.

"Good luck." Jake dips his head again, a trait that seems more of a nervous tic than a gesture of friendship.

Brad trails Paul into the court reporter's room and settles into a chair against the far wall. Beside him sits Reg Jensen.

# CHAPTER 11

THE COURT REPORTER'S OFFICE IS NOT MUCH LARGER THAN THE DINING ROOM IN PAUL'S HOME. One long wall is lined with a collection of case-bound legal texts, neatly stacked in an oak bookcase. Opposite the wall of books is a row of five floor-to-ceiling windows that looks onto the mid-morning traffic of Douglas Street. The first window has been opened to admit some fresh air. At the far end of the office, between the windows and bookcase, is a row of chairs where Brad and Jensen sit side by side. Brad whispers something to him, stands and walks to the far end of the row where he settles into a chair and stares out the window. The other seats remain vacant. Paul assumes that Fran Jensen is in the hospital at Jenny's side.

In the centre of the room sits an impressive piece of furniture: an antique boardroom table made of dark mahogany. The foot-print of the table covers three-quarters of the office area, and as a result, everyone has to brush up against the table chairs as they usher themselves along to their assigned positions. At one end the court reporter adjusts his recording equipment, which includes a tightly compressed keyboard. Three microphones sit atop the table, their black wires trail past the court reporter's machine where they drop to the floor and attach to an audio tape deck.

Ben Stillwell eases his briefcase onto the table and sits in front of the bookcase. He dips his head toward Paul and invites him to sit beside him. He pours two glasses of water and sets one in front of his briefcase and passes the other to Paul. In the two chairs opposite them sit Bonnie Emerson and a young man who appears to be her assistant. Their area appears to be well-established territory bordered by piles of documents, folders, pens, writing tablets and coffee mugs. After a few minutes two other men attired in near-identical suits enter the room and close the door behind them. They sit at the end of the table nearest the door and trade whispers, a joke of some kind that results in their bemused snickering. One of them clicks open a briefcase and begins to sort through its contents.

"Perhaps we should get started," the court reporter announces after a few minutes. He looks directly at Paul. "For the benefit of newcomers—or newcomer, I should say—I'll make introductions. First, I'm Bruce Clanton, the court reporter during this examination for discovery." Clanton presses his lips together in a forced smile. One by one, he introduces the lawyers at the table. Bonnie Emerson's assistant is John Dunster. The lawyers next to the door represent the kayak manufacturer and an insurance company—Paul assumes the company covering Brad's kayaking school liability insurance. Clanton concludes his introduction with references to Brad Reedshaw and Jensen.

For the first time since he's entered the room, Paul allows himself to examine Jensen. He, too, is dressed in a suit but it cannot disguise his weary, exhausted pallor. He has shaved the scrap of beard that had cropped up over the past month, and the clean, bleached skin on his face reveals the old scar that cuts under his chin. When he feels Paul's eyes on him he curls his lips downward and glances away.

Bonnie Emerson is a petite, bespectacled, well-dressed woman with untinted grey hair. Nothing about her physical appearance suggests that she has legal training or experience. Rather, she is the sort of woman Paul has politely ignored while he pushes his grocery cart through the crowded aisles of Safeway: faceless, submissive, unattached. Now he suspects how dismissive he has been. He guesses that she is enormously cunning, inspired to win this legal fight because her client is an innocent victim of circumstance. She glances up at him through the thick lenses of her glasses and turns to Clanton and nods. "I'm ready," she announces in a voice that is slight, yet full of stamina.

Ben leans toward Paul. "All set?" he asks in a whisper.

Paul takes a deep breath. "I guess."

"Remember to stick to the facts and answer only what is asked of you. I'll interrupt if you're pressed to answer anything beyond the scope of the discovery; otherwise, they control the questioning."

Paul takes another deep breath. He can feel the pressure building around him.

Ben nods to Clanton, who then administers the oath to Paul.

"I affirm," Paul says and Clanton sets his Bible back on the table. Paul had planned this, to make an oath on the basis of his word alone, without reference to the Bible or his soul. If anything should go wrong, perhaps the ultimate spiritual consequences might be less severe.

Bonnie Emerson begins with a brief monologue, an overview of what she understands about the facts under review. She reveals that they have heard testimony from two physicians about Jenny's health and her prognosis. They have testimony from Reg and Fran Jensen, from Brad and Jake Peters. They have sworn affidavits from the children who were on the kayaking trip during which the accident had occurred. Now, they would like to hear Paul's version of the events of that day. "We are trying to uncover all the facts relevant to what happened," Bonnie says, "and what went wrong. Please tell us, from the time you arrived at the kayak school, how events unfolded."

"I'll try." Paul's voice is a mere whisper. He coughs into his fist and says with more weight: "To the best of my knowledge, that is."

Bonnie nods and turns a page in a folder. "What time of day was it when you arrived?"

"About 8:15."

"In the morning?"

Paul darts his eyes at her. Of course in the morning. "Yes."

"And what was the weather like at that time?"

"A typical mid-winter day. Overcast. Not raining, but clear enough to see across the bay."

"Could you see across the water to Discovery Island?"

"Yes." He pauses. He decides to pause whenever he needs a little breathing room. Emerson moves the questions at a brisk pace and already she's stuck him on one point of fact. "At least I think so. Later on it became very foggy."

"So you don't recall if you could see the island when you arrived at the beach?"

"No. I'm not sure."

Emerson turns another page in her folder.

Bonnie Emerson continues to work through her inventory of preliminary questions. How many kayaks were in the party the day of the accident? How many two-seaters, how many singles? How many people? Adults or children? Did everyone have life jackets? Did everyone wear them? Were all the kayak spray skirts deployed to ensure no one would be swamped? What time did they depart for Discovery Island? Who led the way and where was Jenny at this time? Where was Jenny at that time? At another time?

Paul carefully contemplates each query. Whenever he's not certain of a response, he makes it clear that he does not know. Cannot remember. Can only guess. As the interrogation progresses, he realizes there are dozens of factual details about the voyage he'd never considered before. It's impossible to answer them with certainty now.

After an hour it's clear that Emerson is ready to let Paul tell the story in his own words. Perhaps it's her strategy to keep him boxed into a corner, then let him run a few laps, then box him up again. Perhaps this is simply her courtroom style. All this is unknown and Paul realizes that he is speaking the part of an unscripted character, an improv amateur, playing opposite Emerson, an old hand whose well-rehearsed lines are inscribed on each page in her folder. "So tell us, Mr. Wakefield, what happened from the time you left Discovery Island until you reached the shore here in Victoria."

"I can't tell you all of that," Paul begins, "because I can't remember being fished out of the water or even getting back to shore." This is his bulwark position. His strength. While Emerson may have a prepared text for any eventuality, his defense is in what is left unsaid. What is now forgotten, or was never remembered.

"Please." Her voice is weary but determined. "Just try your best."

"All right." He takes a sip of water. "I was in the last kayak to leave the bay on Discovery. I was a little late getting back to the others. The kids were getting rowdy during lunch so I took a walk around the shore to a derelict homesteader's cabin. Brad Reedshaw told me I had half an hour, but no more. He was concerned about some bad weather coming in. I returned after twenty minutes to see everyone out in the bay ready to paddle home. I guess he got everyone ready a few minutes after I left on my walk. I suppose he figured trouble was coming sooner rather than later."

"Move to strike that from the record." The lawyer representing the insurance firm leans forward and makes a brisk motion with his forefinger. "The last statement is speculation."

"Just tell your side of the story," Ben says and nods to Bonnie.

"Sorry." Paul lifts his hands from the table and puts them in his lap. This is a warning, he thinks. Don't deviate from the facts. Remember: brevity is a virtue.

"Please continue."

"I could see a low, heavy bank of fog moving up from the Juan de Fuca Strait around the Oak Bay shore. I quickly shoved my gear into my kayak and paddled into the bay. As soon as I was on the water, Brad had us all paddling at a quick pace toward home." He stops to think a moment, takes another sip of water. They are coming to the episode with the sea lions. And drifting on the kelp beds. Or did that happen before they encountered the sea lions?

He decides to tell them about the sea lions first. He explains that because of the current and tides, they had to pass the north side of the Chain Islets or risk being swept into the Juan de Fuca Strait. This is where they came across the sea lions. He remembers the fury of the bull lion, its primal urge to drown them all. He describes the fear he felt and Brad's firm command of the boy who taunted the bull. He takes another drink of water and remembers his nightmare, the metoprolol-induced horror of the bull lion pulling him into the black heart of the ocean.

He moves on to sketch the short break they took floating above the kelp beds, the kayaks neatly rafted up, Brad passing a bag of trail mix—or was it granola?—from boat to boat while they examined the thick fog draped across the shore. Brad formulated a plan. He would lead them single file to the marina, taking a bearing on his deck compass. Everyone was to keep his bow on the stern of the boat ahead. Paul was to bring up the rear. He'd made a joke about that, one he could no longer remember.

"This may be more speculation," he adds, "but Brad had come up with a thoughtful, safe plan that everyone agreed to, including the Jensens." For the first time since he began talking, he glances at Reg Jensen, who sits with one hand pressed to his mouth, his eyes fixed on Paul.

"We were all singing," he continues, "*Row-row-row your boat.* Brad had us singing in rounds. It was good for morale and it ensured everyone stayed within ear-shot." Or did they sing *Ninety-nine bottles of beer on the wall?* The fact that he cannot remember makes him stall again.

"And then?"

"And then I realized we'd become separated from the others. Jenny was supposed to have kept us on the stern of the boat ahead of her. She told me she couldn't see it. I paddled beside her and realized she was right. We were separated."

Paul lifts his hand to his mouth and wipes his lips. This is where it starts. This is where memory and reality and truth and fiction merge and divide. This is where the fog absorbs everything. Yes, the fog is still present. It's the only factor that maintains an effect on them all.

"I called to Brad when I realized we'd been split. He called back. The Jensens called to us. They told Jenny to stay with me. I rafted

196

up with her and tried to determine where the rest of the party was."
He sips at his water and swallows just enough to moisten his throat.
"The fog was so thick at this point that I could barely make out the
front of my own kayak."

And that's when you heard the engine approach. Yes, he nods to
himself and speaks this thought aloud. "And that's when I heard the
engine approach. From the yacht that hit us. At first I didn't know
what it was. Then I could tell. Then I guess Brad and the others
heard it, too. They called to us again and again. You couldn't see it.
You couldn't even tell what direction it was coming from...."

"Then," he says after a moment, "then the rest happened very
quickly. The yacht was coming in very quickly, the engine revs were
still up. The next minute I could see a lamp sweeping the fog just
ahead of us. It was high up and I could tell it was a big boat bearing
straight down on us."

He stops, lifts his hands and drops them on the table. A gesture
of surrender. "Do you want me to go on?"

Bonnie Emerson looks at him and nods. "Yes."

He drinks a little more water and his eyes settle on the centre
of the table. "I could tell we were going to be hit. The boat would
strike Jenny's kayak first. I decided to pull her into my boat if I had
to. The next thing I knew we were dumped in the ocean."

Another pause. "From this point on, I'm not sure what happened. You have to understand how cold the water was." He looks
at Emerson, a plea for her to examine the obvious and see it for
herself: the ice in his blood, the moisture crystallizing on Jenny's
mouth.

But her face is expressionless, a dictum to go on.

"I remember coming up for air. I still had my paddle. I grabbed
the side of my kayak. I called for Jenny. I don't know if she responded. Then I remember grabbing her by the life jacket with my arm. I
... lost hold of the kayak. I grabbed it again. Then—"

He stops and covers his eyes with his hands. This is all he can
reveal. The unspoken truth is shrouded in the mist, lost and now
abandoned.

"Thank you, Mr. Wakefield." Bonnie Emerson sips her coffee and turns to a new page in her folder.

"You're welcome," Paul says and blinks with surprise to hear these words emerge from him. He leans back in the chair and runs his tongue over his lips. It's a relief to have finished this. To be done and over with it.

Emerson removes her eyeglasses and presses the plastic rim against her mouth as she contemplates how to continue. "Now you say you realized you became separated from the rest of the party after you started singing. Was it Jenny who alerted you to this?"

Paul thinks a moment. "I think so, yes."

"And just before you were dumped in the water you say you thought the boat coming at you would hit Jenny first."

"Yes."

"Did it?"

"I guess so. It must have."

"And once you were in the water you said you called to her."

"I'm sure I did." Paul looks at her. Now she's employing more focused questions. Tight, little probes intended to box him in again.

"But you don't know if she responded."

He shakes his head and looks at Ben. "I don't think so. I just reached out for her and my hand caught her life jacket. It was blind luck."

"Blind luck. And once you had her in hand, what happened?"

"I'd lost hold of the kayak. I had to pull us both back to the kayak."

Emerson leans forward and looks at Paul. "Now you just said you still had your paddle in one hand. I assume you held Jenny in the other. In all this cold water how did you manage to swim to the kayak and grab it with both hands occupied?"

Paul sinks into the back of his chair. She's very clever.

"Hmm?"

"I must have let go of the paddle." His voice is low, uncertain. "I don't know. Maybe at that point I dropped the paddle. Perhaps I braced her around the shoulders with the paddle still in my hand. It's just a guess. I really can't remember."

"Well, perhaps I can help you." She flips to another file and then turns a few pages. "We've heard from Mr. Reedshaw that when he pulled you out of the water you still had the kayak paddle braced under your left arm. You held the tow-ring of Jenny's life jacket in your right fist."

Paul had never heard this before. He nods his head. "I don't remember being pulled from the water at all. Whatever Brad Reedshaw saw, I can't speculate," he adds with a glance to Ben.

Bonnie Emerson lets this comment pass and turns the page before her. "So your hands were full and you don't know if Jenny responded to your calls. Do you recall if she did anything to save herself?"

"I don't know."

She leans forward and turns her head to Paul. "Did she do anything to save you?"

Paul pauses a moment. He knows what is coming next. "No. Nothing."

"Well, that's somewhat contrary to what we've heard earlier."

As she opens another folder and sorts through a few pages, Paul can feel his belly beginning to sink into itself.

"A short time after the accident, on February"—she searches for the exact date in her file—"the 28th, you met with Fran and Reg Jensen and Samuel Watson. Did you not tell them at that meeting that in fact Jenny had saved you from drowning?"

Paul forces himself to take another drink of water. "Yes," he says. "Yes, I did say that. But I was trying to make the Jensens feel better."

"So today you're saying that Jenny did not save you once you were in the water."

"Yes." His voice is firm.

"You were lying."

"I tried to relieve their pain. I tried to make them believe their daughter was a hero," he says in a trembling voice and he can feel himself falling into the ocean once again.


"I don't quite understand. Can you explain this for us?" Emerson presses the bridge of her glasses against her nose. Ben had prepared him for this, the one lie that he had to reveal: the episode in which he'd been blindly manipulated by the Jensens.

"Look, Reg Jensen came to my house. Uninvited, I might add. He told me what a sorry state Fran was in. I could see that he was struggling, too. He asked me to come to the hospital. Just to talk and explain what had happened when Jenny and I were cut off in the fog."

Paul glances at Reg with a look of disgust. "When I got there—to the hospital with my wife, who can verify this, by the way—the Jensens were with Sam Watson. The mood was terrible. I felt they were on a death watch over their daughter. I guess they still are," he says and immediately regrets this. Ben folds his hands on the table and Paul takes the gesture as a message: he's gone one step too far.

"I felt terrible watching them," he continues. "I decided to do the little I could. To tell them how brave their daughter was. How she'd grabbed my life jacket and towed me over to the boat. In fact, it was just the opposite." He looks at Emerson and explains, "What I told them was the exact opposite of what actually happened."

"So you lied then?"

He takes a deep breath. "I was trying to relieve their grief."

"Yes or no, Mr. Wakefield: did you lie to them?"

He turns his head to her and glances away. "Yes."

"Or are you lying now?"

Paul looks at Ben with an expression of disbelief. Ben nods to him: answer.

"No. No, I am not lying now."

"Because I wonder, Mr. Wakefield, if Jenny was at all conscious in the water with you."

Paul stops to think. "Is that a question?"

She levels her eyes at him. "Yes."

"I don't know. I was barely conscious myself."

"Well, then I do wonder about all of this, Mr. Wakefield. I wonder how Jenny Jensen was knocked into unconsciousness. How she was hit with a blow that made the impression on her temple like that from a narrow pole. That's the report we have from the medical examiner. He says"—again she sorts through her folders—" 'that the concussion was struck by a blunt object resembling a narrow pole or handle.' " Emerson waits a moment and then continues. "It strikes me that the concussion could have been delivered by a kayak paddle. They are about the same thickness in the shaft, aren't they, Mr. Wakefield?"

Paul draws another deep breath. "I don't know."

"About the same heft?"

"Look. I don't know where you think you're going with this. Consider the facts: we were struck by a yacht motoring through the fog without regard to smaller craft. The boat hit Jenny. Maybe in the chaos she hit herself with her own paddle. But I was not responsible. I tried to save her, for Godsakes!"

"Indeed," she says and turns another piece of paper. "That's what we're trying to determine."

There's a break in the tempo of the questioning. Emerson has launched a solid opening but Paul senses that she doesn't know how to follow through. She doesn't know how to tear open his memory to reveal the raw truth of what happened once he and Jenny were in the water. But she's not going to give up, that much is clear.

"All right, Mr. Wakefield," she says, tapping her folded glasses against her lip. "It's obvious that this experience was very traumatic for you. But I need to clarify certain details. Take us back, if you would, to your point of departure from Discovery Island."

Paul nods his head slightly, then looks at Ben. "I've already explained this several times," he whispers.

"It's standard examination procedure. Just keep it brief and factual," he says in a barely audible voice.

"From the time you realized everyone in the party—except you—was ready to paddle home. Did that make you panic?"

Paul looks at her and frowns. "No. It simply made me hurry along." He assumes that she is toying with him. His best response will be to ignore her deceptions and innuendos.

"All right. So you got your kayak back into the water. Take us along from there, if you will."

Paul draws a deep breath. "As I said, we made our way over to the Chain Islets. They were inhabited by maybe ten or fifteen sea lions. We took a few minutes to rest and observe them. Then we moved on to the kelp bed—"

"Excuse me, but wasn't there more that happened with the sea lions than a simple observation?"

Paul closes his eyes. He can see the male bull rushing toward him. In one move he could drown them all.

"Something about one of the boys?"

"Yes." Paul again describes the scene in which one of the teenagers taunts the sea lion. There is Brad's harsh reprimand, then they paddle over to the kelp bed. The kayaks are rafted up. The thick fog is drawn against the shore. They form a file and paddle towards shore. Brad has the lead and Paul brings up the rear. They are singing a song in rounds, but he cannot be sure which song it is. Then they realize they are alone. He recalls the action in every scene like a well-rehearsed script and then realizes he is no longer the amateur guest artist at the improv. He's the old hand now. This is his story and the more he speaks it aloud, the more each detail becomes concrete. And the more deeply his secret becomes buried.

After every fifth or sixth sentence, Emerson interrupts him to seek some clarification. She tries to pry open the smallest inconsistencies in order to probe his memory and breach his self-confidence. But he offers her so little room to manoeuvre. He has lived with this history and its fictions for too long. He has made sure the details snap together like a wall of Lego that Eliot builds and destroys a dozen times in a single afternoon.

Nothing in the reams of papers and folders that Bonnie Emerson continues to shuffle through provides her an advantage. For a fourth time she prods him through the final scene in the water. But Paul only uses the repetition to reinforce his position: once they were in the water, he could not tell if Jenny was conscious. He had to let go of the kayak to pull her toward the boat. That is the last thing he can remember. Each time he says this it's as if he is closing a book; there is no further denouement to satisfy her curiosity.

"One more thing," she says after a pause. "When you met the Jensens in the hospital on February 28th—was there a point when you realized it might have been a mistake to lie to them?"

Paul sits back, startled by this odd turn.

"Was there?" she asks again.

"I guess when my wife, Valerie, asked if Watson was a lawyer. He said he was an accountant but as we left the room he advised us to get a lawyer."

"Do you think that when you lied to them it compromised your testimony here—today?" She points to the centre of the desk with her folded glasses. He can tell she has exhausted her attack by returning to this small tactical error. An error made when he had no suspicion he would need tactics at all.

"I hope not," he replies and he fixes her with a wide-eyed look. "What I told them in the hospital was intended to relieve their grief. What I've told you today was intended to reveal the facts I know about this terrible accident. All of it was caused by a yacht that hit us and then somehow completely vanished. What I know is that no one in this room has responsibility for what happened to Jenny Jensen." His voice is strong and direct. He takes a deep breath and looks at Ben, who nods his head and pats Paul's knee.

Bonnie Emerson closes her folder and turns to Clanton. "That's all for today," she says. "But I may need to recall Mr. Wakefield at another time."

Clanton glances up from his keyboard and proclaims, "This examination for discovery is adjourned for the day. Counsellors, we'll reconvene, same time, same place next Thursday."

Paul watches the lawyers close their briefcases and prepare to depart. He shakes Ben's hand and leaves the room without glancing back at Reg Jensen or Brad Reedshaw. He checks his watch. He'd been interrogated for two and a half hours. What he needs now is a bathroom. Preferably an empty one.


When he enters the washroom he sees two men pressed against the urinals. They stand in silence, facing the ceramic wall tiles as Paul walks into a toilet stall reserved for the disabled. He closes the wide door to the stall and leans against the wall. His heart is driving. The two strangers exchange a few words about the wet spring weather and prepare to leave. Paul listens for the flush of water, leather shoes stepping over to the sink, the tight spray gushing from the taps, the fight to yank a scrap of towel from the paper dispensers. When the men are gone he hangs his jacket on the door hook, unbuckles his pants and squats on the toilet. He cannot believe that he is here. Intact. Once again, a survivor.

Overall, he thinks, the discovery hearing went well. He'd turned away every attempt to suggest his culpability. Yet Bonnie Emerson was clever and experienced. In the end, she abandoned the real issue and focussed on the lie he'd told the Jensens. That was odd. He openly confessed—yes or no, she demanded—and he said yes, he'd lied to them. So in the end, what was her purpose in revisiting his gaffe—his well-intended white lie?

Perhaps Bonnie Emerson had worked the same equations that Paul calculated over and over in the past weeks. The only hope for Jenny lay in seizing a fortune that would finance her care over the rest of her life. If Bonnie revealed that Jenny's injuries were the result of Paul's assault, she would lose access to the vast insurance funds intended for the child. She was no fool. None of them were at this point. Except, possibly, Reg Jensen. And he was more madman than fool.

Paul tries to urinate but cannot. His bowels are locked. He unravels several feet of toilet paper and winds it around his hand and dapples his face. His skin is clammy. His eyes are tired and he holds the tissue against his closed eyelids and listens to the hum in the room, the incessant buzzing in his ears. It may be that you will never hear silence again, he tells himself. He decides he should get out of the city for a day. Take the Volvo up the Malahat Drive, park somewhere and walk into the hills until he reaches a place where the only perceptible noise comes from the wind pulling on the fir boughs. There would be no silence, but at least the sound in the air would be clear. He hasn't heard anything clearly for months.

In the outer hallway, he can hear footsteps approaching, then the broad swing of the washroom door opening. The heavy padding of thick-heeled shoes thuds around the floor. There is a pause. He suspects that someone is scanning the gap beneath the toilet stall doors, looking for legs dangling from the toilets. Paul coughs once and shuffles his feet. He considers waiting until the stranger passes on. Then he realizes his respite here is over. He should go home now,

*The Good Lie*

have a glass of wine, cook a pasta dinner for Eliot and Valerie. There is cause for celebration.

He tosses the toilet paper into the bowl, zips his pants and presses the flush handle with his foot. When he opens the stall door he sees Reg Jensen leaning against the sink countertop. His expression is vacant, unknowable.

"That was quite the performance." Reg wraps two fingers over his lips as though he's smoking a cigarette. "I mean real showy. You didn't crack that whole time. You got more to you than I suspected."

Paul glances around the room, hoping someone will wander in. He stares uneasily at Reg. His suit does not fit him well. Although he's lost weight, his chest and arms still hold the bulk he's built up from years of cutting meat.

"Reg, come on … I don't want to talk about this." Paul takes a step toward the counter so that he can wash his hands. Reg keeps his feet locked in place, blocking access to the sink.

"Why? Do you think you've said all there is to say in there?" He jabs a fist in the direction of the hearing room. "Do you think there's nothing more I have to say?"

"I'm sure you've told them everything they need to hear. Look, can I get in there to wash my hands?"

Reg doesn't budge. "Oh no. I got a lot more to say. You know I didn't even start talking to the police you sent over to investigate me last week. I haven't told them what I think happened. I'm saving that for later. Same here in the court. I told them what I saw, but I haven't told them what I think. And you know what I think?"

Paul narrows his eyes. Bastard—I think you're going to move so I can wash my hands.

"I think the story you told Fran and me and Sam in the hospital was all true. I think Jenny did save you. I think she was fully conscious right up to the end." In one move he hoists his buttocks onto the counter, completely blocking access to the sink. "And the only way she lost consciousness was when you beat her with your paddle. That right?"

Paul's belly begins to rise through his chest. "You're crazy," he says and decides to forget about washing his hands.

"I think you were going under and panicked. That was the only good question that Emerson asked you. 'Did you panic?' "

Paul shudders and inches toward the door. As he steps backward, Jensen slides off the counter and moves forward.

"And you know how I know all this?" he asks and steadies himself in the middle of the room.

Paul considers what will happen if they fight. He is slightly taller than Jensen but probably ten kilos lighter. And Jensen's posture, his wiry frame, the cocky movement of his chin when he speaks—all of it suggests a street fighter teasing out a fatal first move from his victim. Paul decides to leave. To simply pull open the door and move out of the sphere of Jensen's madness.

"Because you're the same as me." He angles his thumbs to the lapels of his own suit jacket. "We're like twins. Except the exact opposite. We're connected by the same thread, except you're on one end and I'm on the other. I've lost my kid," he says with a gasp, "and you've still got yours."

"Reg, please. Don't talk like this," Paul says. He can see a line of white spittle on Jensen's lower lip. "It's terrible what happened to Jenny. But really it doesn't have anything to do with my son."

Jensen takes a deep breath and wipes his lip. He seems to regain some self-control and then in a steely voice he says, "It does now. By God, I know it does now."

Paul stares at him and realizes how unhinged Jensen has become. "Look. You stay away from him." His voice rises and he tightens his fists.

The bathroom door opens and Bruce Clanton, the court reporter, enters the room. He takes two paces toward the urinals and stops. His head turns from one man to the other and then he steps backward to the wall.

"We'll see," Reg continues and edges toward the door.

"You come near him, and Goddamnit, I'll kill you!" Paul screams and watches Reg Jensen step through the doorway.

Paul stands in the middle of the room and unclenches his fists. He sees his reflection in the mirror. His face is red, his chest is heaving.

"Are you all right?" Clanton dips his head. The expression on his face is of utter bewilderment.

"What you heard me say," Paul says punching a fist at the spot where Reg stood, "is not what really happened."

He washes his hands, wipes them dry on a wad of paper towel and leaves the room.


That evening Ben Stillwell calls on the telephone. After a brief conversation with Valerie, he asks to speak to Paul.

"It's past 9:30," he whispers to Valerie as she passes the phone to him.

"Maybe it's about Jensen," she replies with a look of urgency.

"Sorry I had to run off after the discovery this morning," Ben says, his voice thick and weary. He coughs to clear his throat. "Still, I thought you did very well." He sighs deeply and Paul is struck by the feeling that Ben has pushed himself to the point of exhaustion.

"It's good to hear you say that, because I have no idea how well I did. Emerson was relentless. That's about all I know for certain."

"True. But it's good she was so thorough. I doubt she'll recall you for more testimony. You left her no room for further examination." Ben pauses as though he's shifting gears. Paul can hear him turning pages on his desk "So, I've dug up some information about Jensen. At one time he was what the press often describe as *a person known to the police.*"

"What the hell does that mean?" Paul slumps into his chair.

"In this case, his temper seems to have gotten him into a few scrapes. But most of it was long ago—more than ten years ago, in fact. He was charged with assault, but found not guilty. He was also discharged early from the navy, but no mention of cause was attached to his discharge. There's no way of telling if he simply had chronic seasickness, or if his commanding officer let him go for cause but they agreed not to tarnish his record."

"Brad Reedshaw told me some of this. I guess Brad's uncle knew him. Anyhow, the assault charge was for pounding some kid into unconsciousness." Paul closes his eyes and rubs his free hand over his face. "I just think Jensen is dangerous. Can we not put some kind of restraining order in place?"

Ben sighs deeply as though he's already given this idea consideration and dismissed it. "There'd have to be evidence to support a restraining order. I understand the police have talked to him, but at this point there's not much anyone can do." He pauses again, then continues, "You know, in a lot of these cases, when the police do their interviews and remind everyone of their rights and responsibilities, that's all it takes to settle things down."

Paul blows a long stream of air though his lips. "I hope you're right," he says, but he doesn't believe it.

"I hope so, too. But whether I'm right or not is not the issue," he continues. "In terms of legal solutions, there's nothing we can do at this point."

Until it's too late, Paul thinks, but he doesn't say this aloud. "Okay," he concludes, sensing that Ben has determined there's no point in continuing the conversation and he really needs to get out of his office and back to his own family. "Thanks for checking everything out."

"You did well today," Ben reminds him. "Better than most. I'll call you after the counsellors' meeting next week. At that time I should know where we go from here."

Where we go from here, Paul murmurs to himself after they hang up. The lawyers are so sure of themselves. So certain they can set things along a path to salvation. But what do they really know about where we're headed? How can anyone control that?

# CHAPTER 12

EARLY THE NEXT MORNING JERRY SAMPSON STANDS AT PAUL'S FRONT DOOR AND RUBS THE STUBBLE ON HIS CHEEK WITH A HAND. Before he says a word, Paul can see the exhaustion in his body. The tension in his wiry frame has gone slack and the residual toughness from his career in the RCMP has vanished.

"I've got to take Bettina in," he says and dips his head towards his house next door.

"Come on in, Jerry." Paul gestures into the hallway. "Can I help you somehow?"

"No, I've got to take her up to the General. With the hospital workers threatening to strike, we could be there all day." Jerry shifts his weight at the front door, then makes a move to head back down the staircase.

Paul follows him onto the porch. "Hip bothering her again?"

"I don't know." Jerry purses his lips. It's clear he's worried something much worse has struck his wife.

"Is there something we can do to help?"

"Just keep an eye on things if you would."

"Of course."

"And in case I'm gone into the evening," he says, gripping the handrail as he eases down the steps to the lawn, "let Chester into the house and give him a cup of kibble."

Paul looks at the dog, who's taken to sunning himself on his front sidewalk whenever there's a break in the cloud cover. "Sure. I'll walk him, too, if you like."

Jerry lifts his hand to his forehead, makes a half salute and heads over to his car. When Jerry opens the door Paul can see Bettina buckled into the passenger seat, her neck slumped against the headrest.

Paul watches their car pull out of the driveway and up Transit Road. Does everyone have to end up like this? he asks himself. But he quickly forces the question out of his mind and walks into his house. He's been very successful in putting several key questions out of his mind in the past few days. But it's a process that has created a new set of worries.

After Valerie and Eliot are out the door, Paul decides to take Chester for an early walk to the Oak Bay village. His morning routine has altered since Dr. Biggs advised him not to drive the car. Instead of Paul dropping his son off at school, then enjoying a coffee with his wife at Starbucks, Valerie now drives Eliot to school on her own and lets their son out at the gate to the schoolyard. As he gathers with his friends next to the basketball hoops, she waits in the Volvo and watches him play for a few minutes until the bell rings them all into the building. After he's in his classroom, he waves to her from the classroom window. When Valerie's certain he's safely installed with Mrs. Becker, she drives up to her gallery and begins her work day. Back at home, Paul cleans the breakfast dishes and reads the paper, or if he's lucky, dozes for a half hour in his office chair.

But today, for the first time in weeks, the possibility of a shift—a change of tone—emerges. As Paul clips Chester's collar to the leash he realizes his family can now return to their former routine. Now that you're off the blood pressure meds, he tells himself, we can all go back to normal. In fact, they should have reverted to their old system a few days after the last effects of the medication had passed.

Yes, we'll change that tomorrow, he thinks, and leads the dog along Central Avenue toward Monterey School. It's an easy twenty-minute stroll along the leafy suburban streets, quiet and prosperous-looking with their mock-Tudor homes flanked by SUVs and BMWs.

When he arrives in the village, he ties Chester to a street lamppost and buys an espresso, then sits alone at a table on the avenue and sips his coffee under the Starbucks awning. Occasionally a neighbour or a school parent will walk by and he'll engage in light conversation, the sort of talk meant to protect everyone from the substance of his situation. Few people ask about his accident or Jenny's coma or the lawsuit. More often, people will inquire if he's feeling better. His response is always the same: "I've felt a lot worse." Everyone smiles at this with a sense of relief, a sense that if Paul can manage the trauma he's going through, perhaps their own difficulties can be successfully limited and contained.

Yet he knows his own anxiety has spiked again. After his coffee, he walks into the Pharmasave drug store and measures his blood pressure at the kiosk next to the pharmacist's station. It's a free service and on some days there is a line of two or three older men waiting their turn. But today the booth is empty and Paul sits at the meter and takes his reading: one forty-two over ninety. He writes this in a pocket notebook and compares it to the other figures he's recorded over the past month.

That's up again, but it's likely just the after-burn from his espresso, he thinks as he walks back to the avenue and unties Chester from the lamppost. The systolic rate is back where it was when he was wandering through the nightmares inspired by his medications. But there's no need to tell anyone. The new danger with Reg Jensen requires that he keep a clear head. If he's going to ensure his son's safety, he cannot ingest any drugs that will reduce his capacity to react.

He checks his watch and realizes he has fifteen minutes to get back to the school grounds before the ten-thirty recess break. Each day at this time he walks around the school fence watching his son play with the children, always on the lookout for Reg Jensen's Dodge 500. He follows the same routine during the lunch hour. Then at three o'clock he returns to the school and meets Eliot at the schoolyard gate. At least Chester is getting lots of exercise, he thinks. Which gives Jerry and Bettina Sampson one less problem to worry about.


As he steps off the curb and crosses Hampshire Road, he considers his latest deception. He has not told Valerie about his encounter with Jensen after the hearing. What if it becomes too much for her to bear? And yet … he realizes he must tell her. The rage inside Jensen is boiling and Paul is convinced that soon it will explode. The police, his lawyer, his attempts to reason with Reg—none of it has delayed the impending catastrophe. But what to do?

This nagging question surfaces in his mind with pressing regularity. It's the same old problem but with a new set of parameters. Just weeks ago he dreaded the approaching discovery hearing. Now that it has passed—and its dangers successfully avoided—a new fear has emerged to replace it. But unlike the legal procedures, this new anxiety is not set in time. It has no schedule of arrival and departure. Instead, it resides at a purely emotional level, in the darkness of Reg Jensen's doubtful sanity.

Despite his worry about what Jensen might actually do, Paul's most gnawing concern is the renewed battle with his old enemy: insomnia. It returned after his outburst with Jensen in the court reporter's washroom. Like the shift in his anxieties from the discovery hearing to Jensen's growing threats, the new pattern of sleep deprivation is similar to the old, worn groove—but with a fresh twist.

Sometime after eleven o'clock, he nods off in bed beside Valerie. But within an hour he's lying awake, buzzing with thoughts about his situation. The sound of Valerie's light, sleepy purr builds in his mind like a whirring engine. He turns on one side to block his ear against the pillow. Then the other. After an hour of grinding restlessness he pulls himself from the bed, tiptoes to his office and settles into his La-z-boy, props his feet on the ottoman and wraps his chest and legs in a blanket. In this position he might doze lightly for another thirty minutes or so. Then he realizes he has not been sleeping at all, but merely drifting in the sea of semi-consciousness. When the hope of finding real sleep dissolves he pulls himself from the chair and rubs his face.

A month ago, he would have spent the next few hours surfing the Internet, seeking clues about his legal case and medical concerns. But after several weeks he convinced himself there was nothing new to discover, that he'd exhausted all the on-line resources directly related to his condition.

With this new bout of insomnia he decides to change course and begin a nightly stint of reading. He hopes that if he can find something sufficiently challenging and dense it will occupy his mind and deplete his energy. He's decided on the philosophical writings of the Stoics. He found a few of their texts in the University of Victoria library and on the bus home from the campus he began to study them. In one night he read Seneca's letter on tranquility. During another, he devoured Epictetus's *The Manual*. Now he is immersing himself in the *Meditations* of the Roman emperor, Marcus Aurelius. This last book provides genuine comfort. It is a slight volume, but written with poetic intensity, and Paul knows the text requires at least a month of study. Aurelius maintained that the essence of life lay in aligning human nature with the nature of the universe. Because nature is indifferent and without desire, the secret to living is to eliminate desire and achieve an indifferent attitude toward circumstance. To achieve this you make choices. Even the slave had the freedom to choose personal dignity during life-long captivity. And the power to conform your attitude and behaviour to nature offered its own reward: an insight into the daemon.

This last point fascinates Paul; he has only a vague notion of what Aurelius meant by "daemon." The two dictionaries he kept at home provided no references for the word. One day he walked Chester to the local library and leafed through the *Compact Oxford English Dictionary*. Using a magnifying glass to examine the fine print, he found the following: "a supernatural being of a nature intermediate between gods and men; an inferior divinity, spirit, genius." More research led him to discover the Greek origins of the word and the altered interpretations that evolved over two thousand years. As Christianity superceded Greek and Roman mythic theology, the letter "a" was dropped from the spelling and the original meaning—an intermediary spirit between the gods and mankind—had been converted to its opposite: "demon."

Paul realized that Marcus Aurelius was describing a connection that joined him to some form of universal consciousness. He believed the one necessity of life was to contact and live in harmony with this natural intelligence—and to do it in the only dimension in which we have influence: the here and now. It reminded Paul of Jack Wise's description of the individual's connection to The Mind and that this link was the only durable aspect of reality; everything else was perpetual change. As he approached Eliot's school, Paul wondered what they would do in his situation. What would Marcus Aurelius and Jack Wise tell him?

He squats on the lawn outside the school yard and watches the children pour from the red brick building into the playground. Chester lies beside him, stretches his muzzle toward the tall grass along the fence and inhales the fresh scent of chlorophyll. The dog slips a rear leg over Paul's knee, a flirtation that he plays insistently until Paul lifts the paw into his palm and begins to stroke the black, callused pads under the dog's toes.

After a moment, he spies Eliot in a huddle with six other boys next to one of the basketball hoops. They're engaged in an intense discussion until one of them, James Parker, throws a hand in the air and releases a bag of confetti on the heads of his friends. This inspires a mad dash as all the other boys—including Eliot—chase James across the soccer field to the north side of the playground. Once they corner him, a rage of terrorism ensues. They poke and shove him until he trips over the leg of Daniel Benoit, who has snuck behind James to ensure his fall. For another few minutes they hound the boy with taunts and feigned kicks, then one by one the boys move off to other distractions until only James and Eliot are left on their own. As James climbs back onto his feet, the bell rings and the two children race back to the main doorway. James wins the footrace by several strides, margin enough to enable him to turn and celebrate his victory with a triumphant holler. His face beams with pleasure as he disappears into the building. Eliot follows two steps behind, not once suspecting his father's surveillance.

Paul feels a quiet delight in all this, in guarding his son's safety in a manner so distant and unobtrusive that it never exists in Eliot's mind. Now that's high-end parenting for you, he confides to himself. One-way quality time. He runs his thumb over Chester's paw, then tickles the thin line of white hairs protruding between his pads. The dog's leg jumps out of place, then after a minor hesitation, settles back into Paul's hand. Paul teases another band of hairs. Chester yanks his leg away and turns his head to examine Paul's face. The look in the dog's eyes is utterly mystified: why are you toying with me? Why are you unravelling this bond of love that I have granted you?

Paul stands and Chester immediately rises beside him and stretches his legs in preparation for their next journey.

"All right," Paul says. "Let's go visit Valerie at her gallery. I need to talk to her."

He rubs the dog around his scruff and considers the mute dilemma of all dogs. They exemplify the virtues of affection and loyalty but—so sadly—can articulate nothing of their intelligence. Chester looks into Paul's eyes with a disheartening self-awareness. If he could utter one sentence it would be: "Please understand: I am but a dog."


The walk to the Sky Light Gallery takes about forty minutes. The gallery is a single-storey, fifteen-hundred-square-foot building with a loft that Valerie has converted to a small office overlooking Oak Bay Avenue. Her shop is near an intersection known as The Junction, where the avenue cuts across Fort Street as it heads from downtown Victoria to Willows Beach and Cadboro Bay.

As Paul approaches the gallery he considers how fortunate Valerie is to have her father's support. Wally Burbank bought the building after Valerie told him her plan for the shop. She paid her father a dollar a year for rent. He maintained the building, paid the taxes and absorbed the renovation and decorating costs. Over the years he expected to triple his real estate investment. Ultimately, the property would be transferred to Valerie—along with all the other assets in Wally and Jeanine's estate.

A brass bell tinkles above the entryway as Paul enters the shop.

"Need a hand?" he asks as he closes the door. Valerie is fixing a display case on the far wall. Her left hand holds a staple gun and her right bears a long satin ribbon.

"Oh hi."

Paul is pleased with the gentle easiness in her voice. "We thought you might want some company."

"Does Chester want a cookie?"

Hearing his name, the dog strains at the leash and drags Paul next to his wife. She sets the gun and ribbon on the counter and digs a biscuit from a bowl next to the cash register. Paul's surprised to see she has a stock of dog biscuits in a glass cookie jar.

"This is routine?" he asks.

"Some clients have dogs," she says and kisses his cheek. "They get all worried that I don't want their pets in the shop. When I treat the dogs well, my clients know I'll treat them well, too. Besides, no dog has ever caused trouble. Especially when I give them a treat." She makes a hand signal for Chester to sit. His rump promptly drops to the carpet. She dispenses the cookie.

As Chester cracks the cookie between his teeth and the crumbs litter the floor, Paul wonders: who is training whom?


Valerie pours Paul a cup of coffee and they sit in two of the white wicker chairs that are set in a row between the long walls in the gallery. She's preparing for an exhibition of a new artist she's discovered, Koery Wente, a realist specializing in nudes, heavy-set men and women who usurp the space of the canvasses with their bulky sensuality.

Paul sips his coffee. "I walked past the school."

"Did you see Eliot?" Valerie turns in her chair and braces a knee against the chair arm.

"He was running around with Benoit's kid."

"Daniel?" Her lip curls. Two weeks go Eliot informed his parents that Daniel Benoit had stolen candy from Casey's corner store.

"Him and a bunch of other guys. They're all pretty good boys. You can tell by the way they fight."

"You can?" Valerie leans forward. She's never completely decoded the play style of boys. To her it appears to be nothing more than non-stop fighting and farting. To maintain the masculine mystique, Paul has assured her there's much more to it than that.

"Yeah. Once they get a guy down, it's all fakery. No one ever delivers a real punch."

"What about Martin Baker last month?" She's referring to a broken nose dispatched during a street hockey game.

"Maybe that got out of hand. An exception." Paul turns his chin to one side. He smiles. They both know he cannot defend this position much longer. The fact is a lot of boys would love to kill one another. Slowly. Methodically. Ritualistically.

"Anyway, Eliot's not like that. I watched him pal around with the kid everyone else was picking on. James Parker, that's who it was. Eliot was the one boy to stick with the runt of the litter."

Valerie sips her coffee and angles her knee toward Paul. He finds this sexy, an invitation to touch her. "He's such a good boy," she says and blows a stream of air over her coffee cup.

Paul nods and blows a stream of air over his coffee. He decides not to touch her leg. They look at one another, a two-second exchange that he interprets as a covert agreement to invoke this moment later tonight, in bed.


"Did you see Jensen?" she asks.

"No. I haven't seen him since the discovery hearing." He sets his mug on one of the wicker tables. This is the segue he's been waiting for; the opportunity to reveal his fears. "It's funny, though, because when I did see him last it wasn't pretty."

Valerie drops her knee.

"At the end of the discovery hearing, I mean."

There's a pause. "Go on," she says.

Paul stands and walks across the room. At the back of the gallery, Valerie maintains a small, revolving collection of Jack Wise calligraphies and the occasional mandala. They sell erratically, but over the years demand for his work has been steady. Valerie never met Jack, but she admires his mandalas. While she could use the space more profitably, she reserves the back-store display for Jack as a tribute to Paul's memory of the man—and for high-brow clients who are pleased to see his paintings still on display.

"You know what I've been thinking lately?" He stares at a small block print as he waits for her to respond.

"Okay, I'll bite: what?" She walks next to him and brushes a stray hair from her blouse.

"That I want to write a review of Jack's work. Something that will reveal his philosophy. I was thinking of calling it, 'Stoicism in the Work of Jack Wise.' "

Valerie wraps her arms across her chest. "You've never written art criticism before."

He tips his head, a minor concession to her point. "Not yet, maybe."

"And what do you know about Stoicism?"

"Hey, it's my new obsession. Seneca, Epictetus, Marcus Aurelius."

"Right. The *Meditations*." Valerie studies the weave in the carpet and shrugs her shoulders. "Well, I guess you've got the time right now."

Paul narrows his eyes. There's an edge of sarcasm in her voice. A hint that rather than waste his time with an intellectual dalliance, he should iron the laundry. "I find it comforting," he says in a low voice. When she says nothing, he decides to repeat this. "I find the Stoics quite ... soothing. Right now, I mean."

"I heard you," she says and walks in a tight circle, then turns to face her husband again. "Sorry, I didn't mean to put you off. But why this diversion all of a sudden? You were going to tell me what you found out about Jensen."

"I was until you got me off on this other—" He stops and rubs a hand over his eyes. What foolishness, he tells himself. Just get on with it and tell her what happened.


Paul leans against the counter and describes the scene in the bathroom following the discovery hearing. While he would like to provide an objective narrative, he finds himself dwelling on the despair in Jensen's face and the notion that it would lead to some disaster.

"I tried to calm him down," he says and draws his fingers over his eyes again. "But every time I tried to be rational or even empathetic about his daughter, it just widened the chasm between us."

"What did Ben say about this?" Valerie stands next to the cash register. They are about ten feet apart. A heavy whooshing sound fills the room as a city bus pulls away from the curb outside the door.

"He didn't see it." He takes a deep breath. "I didn't tell him, either."

"Did anybody see it?"

"Yeah. The court reporter. He came in at the end of it."

"Well ... that's good then, right?" Valerie loosens her shoulders. "What better witness could you want?"

Paul heaves his body away from the counter. He feels like he's pushing a boat away from its moorings at a dock and an extra shove is required to overcome the inertia. "Yes, except he came in at the end when I'd completely lost my temper. Right away I realized that I'd blurted out something really stupid."

"What did you say?" Valerie sits on the stool next to the cash register. Chester lies at her feet, glances up in hope another biscuit will come his way.

Paul shakes his head and paces toward the back of the gallery. "Something like: 'what you heard me say didn't actually happen.' "

Valerie shakes her head. "What do you mean?"

"What matters is what the court reporter thought I meant. He probably thinks that what I'd said in the discovery hearing is not what happened. That I'd lied under oath. That I committed perjury." He glares at her. "Do you get it?"

Valerie folds her hands together. "Paul ... maybe you're too close to this. Why would he assume what you said to Jensen in the bathroom would apply to your testimony in court?"

He swallows. His throat is dry and empty. "I don't know. It's just what I thought."

Valerie walks to the front of the store and gazes through the window. After a moment Paul follows and stands next to her.

"What really has to concern us," Valerie says, "is what Jensen might do."

"I know." Paul sighs deeply and looks at her. He wants to slip his arm over her shoulders and embrace her.

"I think maybe I should call Dad. He could get someone to watch Jensen. Discreetly." She glances at Paul and then away. She hasn't asked a favour of her father since he bought the gallery for her. Apart from the gallery, neither of her parents has dispensed any benefactions since she and Paul were married. "What do you think?"

He frowns a little. He wants to handle this alone, but he senses this trouble is too deep and wide—and without a concrete resolution in sight. "Maybe. I'd like to think about it. Or maybe try to get Ben Stillwell involved or the police—this time with some concrete action."

"Ben? You just talked to him last night." Her voice rises with exasperation. "And what have the police done for us so far? Nothing but make matters worse."

"I know." He shoves his hands into his pockets. "All right. Let's call Wally tomorrow. First thing in the morning after we get Eliot to school. I just want one more night for us to think it through. So we can ensure whatever happens won't come back at us."

Valerie shrugs and glances away. "All right, tomorrow for sure ... Hamlet," she adds with mock emphasis. Then her voice drops to a more serious tone when she says, "But there's another issue here we need to discuss."

"What?"

"Us."


"Let's sit down." She walks back to the wicker chairs.

Paul sits beside her and feels a wave of exhaustion roll up his chest into his head. The weariness washes through his muscles and tendons, then pools in his bones. He tries to smile but cannot. He can barely look at her.

"I need to be honest with you," she says and opens her palms on her lap. "I know since the accident you've been under a lot of stress. There's been the medication, the insomnia, Jensen's threats—all kinds of things."

And the impotence, he thinks, but he does not say this.

"Through it all I've felt this wall building up between us. It's like anytime something important happens you put up a new row of bricks."

"Like when?"

"Like right now. You knew about this latest threat from Jensen yesterday. Our child faces a new risk and you don't think enough of me to tell me about it."

Paul tilts his eyes to the ceiling. "I know," he confesses. "I just couldn't bring myself to tell you about it."

"Why not?"

"Because I couldn't bring myself to think about it." His belly feels hollow. "Because the fact is, I can't handle what's happening." A sense of surprise comes over him. That's absolutely right: he can't handle anything any more.

"Look." Valerie takes his hand into her own. "Eliot is the centre of our lives. In order to help us—all of us—I need to know what's going on. Do you hear me? It's like you don't trust me; like you're hiding something from me."

He pulls his hand from her fingers and wipes his mouth. She knows, he thinks. She knows everything that's happened. You just need to tell her—to confess—that you beat Jenny into unconsciousness and Valerie will offer you a reprieve.

"Are you hiding something?" She leans forward. "Paul, I need to know."

He stands, takes a step away and stares down at her. "You tell me. What about you? Are you hiding something from me?"

"What are you talking about?" A blank look of surprise crosses her face. "What do you mean?"

"I'm talking about the phone messages I've heard on the answering machine."

Her face pales and she leans back in the chair.

When he sees her retreat he continues: "I'm talking about Rory Stillwell. Remember his number? That's what he was asking. 'In case you've forgotten.' That's what he said. Well, have you forgotten?"

She exhales a long stream of air through her tightened lips and waves her hand as though further discussion is impossible.

"So tell me: why is open communication important for you and not for me?"

Her head shifts slightly, an almost imperceptible gesture.

"Tell me. Why for you and not for me?" His voice is hard but he doesn't care. He realizes now how deeply this wound has infected him.

"He's dying," she whispers.

"What?"

"I said he's dying. Of AIDS." She wraps her fingers over her mouth as if she cannot believe this news—as though she herself is hearing it said aloud for the first time. Then she narrows her eyes and continues. "Yeah, well ... my ex-boyfriend liked to screw around a lot. But you knew that, didn't you? I did tell you that, did I not?" Valerie's mood has changed. She stands and walks back to the cash. "And after what?—ten years?—after he ditched me, he returns to the scene. Apparently I was his greatest love." Valerie eyes Paul to ensure he can feel every word of this revelation. "Apparently, now that he lies dying and nothing else matters, the one thing he wants to do is confess his undying love for me."

"All right. Enough." Paul waves a hand in the air. "Ben told me he was ill, but I didn't know it was from AIDS."

"Mmm. I guess that's your point, isn't it." Her hand thumps onto the countertop. "But you know what? You know why I didn't tell you? Because you're right: you can't handle it. You've sunk so far into your inner world—this crazy dreamy morass you're in—that it's obvious to everyone you can't handle anything. At the one time Eliot and I really need you."

"Okay, Valerie. I can hear you. We can all hear you." Paul sweeps his arm around the room as if to introduce a gallery of spectators.

"So while we're on this, let me give you the full disclosure. Rory Stillwell is in the hospice. Over on Richmond Road, not ten blocks from here. I have gone to visit him four or five times. He just likes to talk. Sometimes I hold his hand, but that's all we do. Maybe for a half hour at a time. Like you, he can't handle much more than that."

Paul sits in the chair again and in a deliberate whisper, he asks, "What do you talk about?"

"This and that. The weather. My gallery. All the travel he's done."

Paul feels the tension in his chest easing. "You don't talk about your past together?"

"He likes to, but when I don't respond to it he just says he's sorry. And that he loved me. But from my point of view, we were never very good together." She turns her shoulder to one side, a gesture revealing a warmer mood. "Not like you and me."

"No?"

"I've told you that before. But you don't believe it, do you?"

"Yeah. I believe it." His voice is calm now. He presses two fingers to his temple. "Or maybe I don't. Hell, I don't know anything anymore."

Valerie wraps her arms together and gazes out the front window. "You know, envy is when you want what someone else has. And jealousy is when you want back what you've lost." She presses her lips together and steps toward him. "In either case, you really don't have cause for concern, Paul. At least not from me. Certainly not for envy. And not for jealousy either."


Paul walks home from the gallery without a sense of intention or purpose. By the time he reaches 565 Transit Road he is certain that Valerie is right. His ongoing obsessions have immobilized him. He has to wake up and become the man he was a few months ago. Above all, he has to embrace the fact that their life together with Eliot is the centre of his existence and nothing can be allowed to jeopardize their internal balance.

When he steps onto his front porch he realizes the time he's lost. It's just after two o'clock; he forgot to check on Eliot over the lunch hour. He swears to himself, unleashes the dog and begins to jog up his street to Central Avenue. Within a few minutes he reaches Oliver Street and turns onto the schoolyard. He yanks open the heavy wood door next to the school gym and as it slams behind him, he double-steps up the staircase to the third floor. When he reaches Mrs. Becker's room he stares through the open door.

"Where's Eliot?" he blurts out.

The students are hunched over their desks working in pairs. Many of them are holding scissors and glue sticks. Magazine clippings litter the floor. At the far end of the room, Mrs. Becker is hovering above two girls who turn their heads in unison toward him.

Paul paces over to the teacher. His face is red and broken with beads of sweat. "I said, where's Eliot?"

A look of recognition crosses Mrs. Becker's face. "He's fine," she says in an even voice. "No need to worry."

"I'm over here, Dad." Eliot emerges from the coatroom behind the teacher's desk.

Paul nods. He considers the spectacle he's created. His son's embarrassment.

Eliot stands beside him. He holds a *Canadian Geographic* magazine in his hand. "I was just getting this magazine from my back pack. I took it from your office at home," he says. "That's okay, isn't it?"

Paul nods once. "Of course." He smiles.

They look at one another a moment, then Eliot asks, "Want to see the project I'm working on with James?"

"Of course," he says again and in a breezy tone intended to reassure all the children, he adds, "That's why I'm here."

He settles in a chair next to the two boys and studies the poster project they are assembling on marine mammals. When his heart rate and breathing ease back to normal he begins to flip through the magazine. Maybe he can find a picture of a sea lion for them. He can tell James the story about the lions he saw when he was kayaking. And how, when you're up close to them, they can be pretty scary.

That night, like most nights, he reclines on his La-z-boy with a blanket wrapped over his legs and torso. He is calm. His left hand is pressed to his heart. His right hand, palm facing up, is transmitting spiritual energy—his daemon—back and forth from The Mind. This is the one way that he has discovered to achieve a deep peace without the hazards of medication or booze. Each night as he enters this state of awareness, he utters a silent prayer of thanks: "Thank you for revealing yourself to me." He does not know to whom the

prayer is addressed or what benefit it confers. It is a merely a statement of gratitude offered into the black of night.

This night, in particular, the pulse of his heart is visceral and its
heat radiates in his palm. His left hand settles on the flat flesh of his
chest and after several minutes they seem joined together. His palm
is millimetres from his heart. By adding a little pressure he finds that
he can slow the palpitations to a gentle idle. The process fascinates
him. He takes a long draft of air through his nostrils and sinks even
deeper into the cardiovascular lull. His heart rate drops again. Has
it dropped to twenty, even fifteen, beats a minute? Hard to tell in
this timeless, drifting state of being. Yet it may be possible to bring
this beating to a conclusion, simply by guiding the rhythm to a fatal
stall. Death by meditation; was it possible? He draws another long
breath and his heart quickens slightly. Each beat fills his palm and
when the pulse is completely fused to the sensations of his fingers
he realizes his hand has penetrated the wall of his chest. A moment
later he lifts his hand into the air. His eyes are closed. Yet he can see
his heart suspended above him, still pulsing, clean and bloodless, the
arteries and veins snipped free from his body.

He gazes at his life with complete indifference. He is nothing. A
speck in the passing breeze. All that remains is to admit this wisdom
into his being and accept the freedom it bestows. Yes, he thinks, it's
the one, true liberty. "Take my heart if you want it," he whispers,
"and then ... dissolve my soul. And pass whatever life is left in me
to the young girl I have broken."

# CHAPTER 13

THE NEXT MORNING PAUL STEPS ONTO THE FRONT PORCH OF 565 TRANSIT ROAD FEELING A MIX OF EMOTIONS. He and Valerie have agreed to drop Eliot off at Monterey School, then stop in the village for a coffee together. After sipping his espresso, chatting idly, leafing through the newspaper—he'll escort her to the gallery. The plan is self-satisfying, almost indulgent. It emerged at the end of an early-morning conversation in which they settled yesterday's argument in the gallery. Furthermore, they decided that Valerie should call her father to discuss Jensen's threats and ask for his opinion. Yet as they discussed the plan, sipping their orange juice at the breakfast nook before Eliot awoke, Paul's sense of renewed harmony was dissipated by his ongoing exhaustion. Last night's bout of insomnia—with its bleak epiphany—had taken its toll.

Now, as he walks down the staircase toward the car, a dull grogginess buffets his senses. He feels as if his range of perception has been reduced to a two-metre radius. No matter, since his only goal now is to start the Volvo and await Valerie and Eliot. You'll come to once you roll down the driveway, he assures himself and wipes a dry hand over his face.

Before he walks another step he sees Jerry Sampson standing at the bottom of the stairs. The dreary grimace on Jerry's face alerts Paul to the possibility of bad news.

"How's Bettina? Everything go okay yesterday?"

Jerry rolls his shoulders and frowns. "She's okay. Likely to spend another day or two in the hospital. Which she hates," he adds with a chuckle. "But listen," he continues and the dreary look returns, "have you seen Chester? I got home last night at eleven and there was no sign of the mutt."

A sinking feeling washes through Paul's belly. He was supposed to feed the dog and let him into the house. Instead, after he returned from the gallery he unleashed him and ran back to the school. It was the last time he thought about Chester. "I don't know," he says without suggesting alarm. "Let's check around your yard."

The two men walk into Jerry's back yard. There's no sign of the dog anywhere. A well-chewed bone lies abandoned in the bed of Bettina's untended rose garden. They enter the basement door and scan the concrete floor. Chester's brown sleeping mat is vacant except for balls of yellow hair gathered on the fringes.

"I don't know," Paul says again after a few moments. "Yesterday morning I walked him up to Valerie's gallery then brought him back here after lunch. Then—"

Paul stops when he hears a scream. The men gaze at one another. Then the scream becomes a siren, wailing with excruciating pain.

"That's Valerie," Paul says and darts through the door and across his yard to the Volvo. As he runs, Valerie's shrieking fills the air. He's never heard this sound from her before. A cry of utter terror.

His first thought is of Eliot. But when he sees his son standing at the car door, his loaded backpack still strapped to his shoulders, he feels an immediate relief, bends to embrace him and presses Eliot's face to his chest. Then he sees Valerie hunched on the driveway at the front of the Volvo. She's slumped over at an awkward angle. Was she trying to change the tire? He cannot see her left hand. Had the jack slipped free and the wheel collapsed on her?

Valerie struggles to breathe. Her cries have changed to choking sobs as she pulls herself away from the car, crawling backwards, both arms clawing at the loose gravel.

"What's wrong?" he says and tries to stabilize her shoulders.

Her eyes are dilated, vacant.

"What is it?"

Her choking subsides but she is unable to speak. She shakes her head and points to a paper bag lying next to the tire.

"Valerie, what is it?" he asks and eases her onto the lawn. The bag is waxed on the outside, but otherwise resembles an ordinary paper grocery bag. Something has been scrawled with a red marker on the front of the glossy paper. The top has been folded down, scrunched several times from repeated use.

"It was sitting on the hood of the car. Just look," Valerie whispers and coughs. Then she adds, "Eliot, get into the car."

The boy glances at his father. Paul nods and Eliot quietly climbs into the back of the Volvo and closes the door.

Paul takes a step toward the bag. This must be from Jensen, he thinks. This is his work, his madness at work. He nudges the bag with one foot and watches it flop onto its side. He bends to examine the writing, the dull red letters partially turned toward the driveway. He can see the letter N. He lifts the bag, feels its weight in his hand, then reads the one word printed in red crayon: NEXT?

"What the hell is this?" he asks and turns to Valerie. She is still on the ground, her eyes staring at nothing. Then, exasperated, he unrolls the top fold and peers inside.

At first he can't make sense of the bulky shadows in the bag. Four long sticks, broken cleanly at their tops. Not broken, but sawn through. And not sticks; they're more like short hatchet handles, covered with a thin layer of brushed upholstery. No, not upholstery, but hair, blond horsehair spattered with red dots. He touches the end of one of the handles with a fingertip. My God, it's bone, he thinks. He narrows his eyes and lifts one bone between his thumb and index finger. He pulls it two or three inches from the bag to examine it in the morning light. When he realizes the horror before him, he gasps. He is holding one of Chester's front legs, severed just below the shoulder.

"Oh Jesus," he cries and releases the dog's amputated leg. He rolls the wax bag shut, lays it on the ground and slumps against the car. His breathing comes in tight gasps. He sets his jaw. You're finally there, he tells himself. You're finally in the place you've dreaded so long. He can feel his body harden, all the hollowness in him is compressed and expelled.

"Valerie," he says and turns to her. "Get in the car."

She nods once and stands.

"Do you have your purse and credit cards? Some money?"

"Yes." The look of shock is gone from her face. "Yes, I've got everything."

"Drive straight to the ferry. Then to your parents' house." He lays his hand on her shoulder and squeezes it slightly, unsure of his grip. "Don't stop at the school. I'll phone in sick for Eliot. And don't call me, I'll call you later tonight."

"All right," she says. Her voice is steady now. She clips open her purse, rifles through a few items and closes it. "Yeah, I've got everything," she says again.

"All right." Paul opens the car door and dips his head toward Eliot. "Mom's taking you on a trip to Vancouver." Eliot glances away and then turns his eyes back to his father. "I know you don't know what this is about. Just do what Mom tells you, though, okay? It's important," he adds and gives him a single kiss on the forehead.

Valerie struggles to get her key into the ignition, but she's able to start the engine on the first crank. She smiles with mock pride that the car is idling properly; a minor triumph.

"I'll call you," he says and kisses her.

"What are you going to do?"

"I don't know." Paul presses his teeth together and scans the length of the street. "I just need to make everything safe again. I'll tell you when I figure it out."

"All right. I think I've got everything," she says for the last time and backs down the driveway.

Once they're gone Paul lifts the paper bag in both hands and examines the yard. There's no sign of Jerry Sampson or Reg Jensen. No cars on the street. No breeze, no heat in the air, no scent of disaster. He realizes that he didn't tell Valerie that he loves her. Or Eliot. But that was understood. It goes without saying; like so much else these days.

Paul stands at the kitchen counter and examines the waxed bag. It's from a butcher shop, he's certain of that. It's no leap of genius to conclude that it came from Jensen's meat store. A forensic expert could identify a match in minutes. Yes, the bag provided concrete evidence and he had to preserve it. Already he and Valerie had contaminated it somewhat, but from now on he intended to treat the bag like a clinical specimen. And then what?

He washes his hands and wipes them with a dishtowel. He decides to call the school and lie about Eliot's unannounced trip to Vancouver. He explains that Eliot's grandparents had planned a party for their fortieth anniversary. It would be a real smash; they'd rented a dozen hotel rooms in Whistler for friends and family. At the last minute Valerie decided to take Eliot along even though he'd miss some school. As he repeats the tale to the Monterey School secretary, he realizes how easy it is to pose a casual lie once you've committed perjury under oath. It's no more difficult than telling a passing acquaintance that you feel quite well when in fact you're suffering from high blood pressure and chronic insomnia. The overriding truth is that no one wants to know these small truths. Not the little nitty-gritty facts. The secretary does not want to know about the life-threatening dangers facing her students any more than the personal injury lawyers want to expose any details that might reduce a ten-million-dollar claim to less than 10 percent of its potential.

Paul returns to the counter and studies the bag. He could call the police. But would it solve anything? The last time the police were involved with Jensen it only served to feed his madness. Now his insanity had combined with his stupidity. Obviously he'd assumed that Chester was Paul's dog. He'd seen him walking the dog to school, probably seen Chester lying in the sun on Paul's lawn during one of his many stalking episodes. In fact, bringing the police in too early had partially created this bloody mess. "Look where it's led you," he says aloud. "The neighbours' dog mutilated and your wife and child run out of town." No, he has to do something more direct than call 9-1-1. He has to confront Jensen and bring this to an end. Yet despite his sense of urgency, he knows he's never done anything like this before. There's never been a need.

He decides to take one of Chester's limbs from the bag. This will be the evidence he'll present to Jensen, the concrete proof that now he has gone too far and has to back off before serious harm came to someone.

Paul continues his forensic approach and tugs on a pair of latex gloves that are lying over the end of the dish rack. He opens a drawer and pulls out a "super-size" zippered baggie, one of the many Valerie employs to seal blackberries before she stores them in the basement freezer. He opens the top of the pouch and sets it next to the waxed bag. Then he draws a deep breath and unrolls the top of the bag to expose the stumps of the four severed legs.

With the right tools an experienced butcher would take less than a minute to cut each limb. He wonders if Jensen used a band saw or a cleaver to make the amputations. Must be a saw; there's barely a chip or burr on any of the bones. Surely he must have killed the dog first. That would be essential. Even Jensen would possess that level of humanity.... Right?

He lifts one of the front legs in his hand and stuffs it into the baggie. He bends the wrist joint so that the dog's paw folds under the forelimb. The pads are lined with blond hair, the sensitive tufts he tickled to the dog's perplexed annoyance as they sat next to the schoolyard yesterday. Now the hair is flecked with blood and he shakes his head with dismay as he drags the plastic zipper across the top of the baggie.

He intends to preserve the three remaining legs as criminal evidence until the time arrives when he has to disclose everything to the police. But the timing is secondary. What counts is linking Jensen to this depravity. He folds the top of the waxed bag and pinches a clothes peg over the end. Carefully lifting the package with one hand, he walks down the staircase to the basement storage room and opens the freezer top. Fortunately, the freezer is only half full.

Later this fall Valerie will have it fully stocked once she's collected enough berries for her annual production of homemade jams and jellies. By then, they'll be well past this mess. In fact, she'll probably never know he'd stored Chester's remains on top of the organic fruits and wild blackberries.

He brushes aside the ice blocks stacked together in the wire rack and sets the bag face up, exposing the word 'NEXT?' scrawled in Jensen's awkward script. He stares at it a moment before closing the lid. The most disturbing part of this disaster is the question mark. How much better it would have been if Jensen had used a simple period.


Paul climbs aboard the number two bus in front of Casey's corner store and settles into one of the vacant seats opposite the side exit doors. He has packed Chester's leg at the bottom of his old backpack and covered it with a few books from his office desk, the collection of Stoic authors he'd borrowed from the library. The books are intended to disguise his cargo in case he has to open the bag for inspection.

His plan is to transfer to the number six bus on Yates Street and ride it to Jensen's Meats in Esquimalt. He intends to show up unannounced, present Jensen with Chester's amputated leg and tell him to back off or he'll press criminal charges. He'll be simple and direct and confront Jensen in his own style. All very quick and to the point—so quick that Jensen will only be able to absorb the impact after Paul departs. There will be no violence, not even a threat of it. That would play into Jensen's considerable physical strength. No, this will be Paul's gambit—his first move in the dubious game Jensen has been playing over the past month.

Yet his strategy is not a closed proposition. Quite the opposite; it is fluid and subject to change. That's unavoidable given the unknowns set before him. He doesn't know the shop hours or if Jensen works alone or with his wife or if he runs the butchery with hired help. On the other hand he knows the Jensens live behind the shop and that since the accident, when she's not at her daughter's side in the hospital, Fran Jensen has maintained a prayer vigil at her home with members of a regional church. These facts were reported in the papers after the news of Jenny's coma became a centrepiece of the local news columnists' sympathies.

As the bus pulls out of the stop it shudders uneasily along the road. He considers browsing through Marcus Aurelius' *Meditations* but decides against it. He wants to sit and think. Rather, to sit and not think. To centre himself in the present time and eliminate distractions. As the bus chugs through its various stops he wonders how he has arrived at this exact moment, seeking truce in a battle that has gone on far too long, with no weapon other than his desire for peace and amnesty.

When the number two bus stops at Richmond Road, Andy Betz climbs aboard and steps down the aisle toward Paul. "Paul ... I can't believe you're here. I was planning to call you today. Can I sit with you?" He makes a gesture with his head and Paul dutifully shunts over to the far side of the seat. Andy is, after all, his director and even this unexpected meeting calls for deference.

"Seriously," he continues and wedges his solid frame onto the bench, "I was thinking of you not five minutes ago." Andy straightens the lapel of his grey pin-stripped suit and adjusts the knot in his tie. He plumps a leather briefcase onto his lap and stitches his fingers together as though he's about to call a boardroom meeting to order. "Tell me. How are you?"

His tone suggests that Paul must not look well. "I've been worse, Andy," he says, suddenly aware of his attire. He too, used to wear a blazer and tie and tote a minimalist briefcase to work. Now he is wearing jeans, a T-shirt, an old GORE-TEX jacket and a pair of worn Nikes. He slips the backpack behind his legs and presses it under the seat frame. "Day off from the office?" he asks to shift their attention.

"Not really. I had to take the Taurus in for some repairs. Again," he says with exasperation. "Jess drove me back home in her car. So I thought I'd do some work on the outsourcing proposal before I went back to the office. Were we working on that before the accident?" He appears puzzled, unsure of where Paul's departure fit into the sequence of ever-shifting political projects. If ever there were a political football, he used to say (and say it often), it's public education.

"It'd just started," Paul says and glances out the window. He calculates they'll spend another ten minutes riding the bus together before he transfers to the number six. He would like to invent something to discuss, but the memory of his working life has faded; he can scarcely recall his colleagues' names.

Andy scratches at the thick skin of his forehead with a thumbnail and exhales a long draught of air. "I know last time we talked you were worried about the lawyers getting involved. Did any of that happen?"

A polite, back-door question—one Paul knows he must avoid. "The short answer is yes. Very much so. But Andy, my lawyer has told me I can't talk to anyone about it."

"Of course." He waves a hand dismissively. "I just needed to know if you'd gone down that road."

Paul looks at him and rolls his eyes. "It's not a road. It's a ten-lane freeway," he says, "with toll booths at both ends." Andy laughs at this and they both smile and glance at one another with fondness. They'd worked well together, not closely or as good friends, but they'd achieved some real successes.

Andy rubs his forehead again and says, "You know, I look forward to you coming back to the office."

Paul nods, a gesture of thanks.

"Not because we're short-staffed." He flashes a wink. "Or because we genuinely need someone who can write policy briefs—but because it would be good to work with you again."

Paul glances away. Andy is so genuine, so generous, that he feels embarrassed. "Thank you. I needed that," he adds.

"I'm not surprised." Andy flattens both hands on his briefcase. "When I divorced my first wife the whole mess ended up in court. And let me be blunt: I was the aggrieved party," he says with bitterness. "The one thing I learned is that to get through it in one piece, you have give something to yourself. Know what I mean? In my case, believe it or not, I took up singing." He smiles and examines Paul's eyes.

"Really?" It is hard to believe. Then again, Andy Betz is built like an operatic tenor. Thick, grounded, unshakeable. Notes would resonate through the earth, travel up his legs and emerge from the wide barrel of his chest.

"Don Gi-o-van-ni." He sings the five signature notes of Mozart's tragedy in a beautiful, hushed voice.

Paul smiles, unsure what to say. A compliment is in order, but it could sound gratuitous, even fawning.

"So my question is, are you giving anything to yourself?"

Paul thinks a moment. They have another five minutes until the conversation will expire. "I've been reading," he offers. "Reading quite a bit, in fact," he says with some confidence.

"What? Tell me."

"The Stoics. It may surprise you—I mean it surprised me—that I would start this elaborate study of the Greek and Roman Stoic philosophy. Three months ago I could not have named more than one of these guys—"

"So name one."

"Marcus Aurelius. You've probably heard of his *Meditations*, right?" He slips open the backpack, extracts the slim volume of prose and quickly jostles the other books to hide Chester's leg.

"The Roman emperor?" Andy takes the book in one hand and flicks through a dozen pages. "What's it about?"

Paul wonders how to respond. No one has asked him about his recent fascination. Like the rest of his inner life, it's been shrouded and unexposed. "The fundamentals come down to one word," he says. "*Autarky*. It's Greek, meaning self-sufficiency. Most people think Stoicism is about enduring personal suffering. But it has more to do with fulfilling your individual destiny. The Stoics hoped to provide their followers with the spiritual tools to thrive in the midst of an eternal void."

Andy exhales another long stream of air. "Sounds like existentialism ... with a ray of hope."

"A kind of theistic existentialism," he says with a corrective tone. "The latter Stoics, like Aurelius, found this link between human consciousness and the inherent intelligence of the universe." Paul waves a hand in the air in a broad circle. "Through the daemon, or the individual spirit, it's possible to actually harmonize yourself with Nature." He stops at this point, sensing that he has started to rave.

Andy forces a smile and shakes his head. "You really are into it. I had no idea."

As the bus rounds the corner onto Douglas Street, Paul remembers the uneasiness he felt when Jack Wise tried to explain the most arcane principles of The Mind to him. At the time, he didn't want to talk about it—or even hear about it. Now he'd like nothing more than to sit in Foo Hong's and slowly uncover the myriad mysteries in the universe. But Jack himself had long ago passed into The Mind and Paul didn't know anyone else who could plumb the depths of that conversation.

When he detects Andy Betz's hesitation he decides to say no more. "So ... if you're ever looking for a good read," he says taking the book from Andy, "keep this one in mind." He smiles and carefully places it in his backpack.

"I will."

"My stop," Paul says and stands.

Andy pulls himself from the bench to allow Paul to squeeze past him. "I mean it," Andy continues. "I'll read it for you. Then we can talk."

"I'd like that," he says and suspects he is reaching a turning point in his relationship with Andy, a move in a new direction. Perhaps to an intellectual friendship.

They shake hands and Paul lifts the backpack onto his shoulders and walks toward the exit bay. He glances back at Andy Betz who has turned his head to the window and stares through the glass.

Paul steps onto Yates Street and sees the number six bus waiting at the curb. He stops and decides to let it go without him. He'll catch the next bus. It'll give him time to think without any more distractions. To determine how he can bring a madman to reason.

Jensen's Meats is housed in a one-storey stucco building. The stucco exterior is a mossy green, the white trim on the door and windows is chipped and peeling. In the front window a metre-square sheet of waxed paper is taped to the glass. On it are written three words, one atop the other:

PRAY

FOR

JENNY

A driveway runs along the east side of the building and leads to a garage. Two cars sit parked in the driveway, an old Mini and Reg Jensen's Dodge 500. A tattered awning hangs suspended above a side door. Paul assumes this is the entrance to the Jensens' home. He decides to enter the meat shop first, since it would be better to visit with Jensen in a public place. If no one is in the shop, he'll wander down the driveway and knock on the door beneath the awning.

He pushes open the door to the meat shop and stands for a few seconds to assess his surroundings. There are no customers present, no sign of anyone working behind the glass meat cooler next to the cash register. Behind the cash is a knife rack and a walk-in refrigerated meat locker. The metal door is closed and bolted. Beside it is an open door leading to a back room. Through the doorway he can see a stainless steel meat saw. He hears a dull thumping in the back room, the sound of a butcher blade whacking sideways against a strip of meat. Tenderizing.

Paul walks to the cash register and peers into the back room. He catches the eye of a heavy-set man draped in a white coat. He has a hairnet pulled over the top of his head. It is not Reg Jensen.

"Yo," the man calls out. He sets his knife on the butcher block, wipes his hands on a rag and leans one shoulder on the doorsill. "I didn't hear you come in."

Paul studies his face. His build is similar to Jensen's. Maybe this is his brother. "I'm looking for Reg Jensen."

He frowns and turns his head. "You won't find him here," he says and steps up to the counter. "You can try the apartment." His head ticks in the direction of the driveway, then his chin nudges toward Paul. "You a friend?"

"We know one another," Paul says and runs both thumbs under

the backpack straps looped across his shoulders. "It's just down the driveway, right?"

The man narrows his eyes. "You're that guy, aren't you."

Paul glances away. He decides he doesn't need to say anything about who he is. "What guy?"

The man nods, sure now that Paul is the one. "The guy in the boat with Jenny."

"So it's that door under the awning," he says.

He nods again and wipes his hands flat against his butcher's coat. "Yeah."

"Thanks." As Paul turns and leaves the shop a shudder rolls through his chest. He didn't count on Jensen having family members on the scene. He expected a short meeting with just the two of them. He'd talk about Chester, about how Jensen had butchered Chester and now everything had to stop with that. None of this could go beyond what had already happened.


Paul knocks once at the side door. He can hear voices, then soft footsteps approaching him from inside the apartment. A woman opens the door and holds a hand above her eyes to screen the light streaming into the dark room.

"Yes?" she asks in a tentative voice and steps out of the light.

"Hello." Paul feels a sense of relief. This woman is thin-boned, almost frail. Certainly not a threat. "Is Reg Jensen here?"

Instead of answering, the woman walks across the room and eases her thighs against the back of a sofa. The curtains are pulled shut against the only two windows in the room. Three doors lead to other parts of the apartment. One opens to a compact kitchen littered with dirty dishes. The other two doors are shut. Opposite the sofa stands an oversized entertainment unit housing a stereo and TV. On the near wall hangs a crucifix with a bronze Jesus suspended from the crossbar. Next to the kitchen doorway a brown paper sheet duct-taped to the wall is inscribed with a handwritten message:

PRAY

FOR

JENNY

Two other women are sitting on the sofa. It's obvious they were engaged in an intense conversation when Paul knocked at the door and an air of expectation suspends them, as though they need to conclude whatever they were saying. As they look at Paul their sense of anticipation slowly fades.

"Hello, Paul," one of them says. She stands and brushes her hands against her jeans.

"Hello." He's startled. Everyone here seems to know him already. Nothing is beginning the way he hoped. Then again, what did he expect? He had no plan, simply the intention to set down this new limit on things.

"What brings you here?" She takes one step toward him but he does not recognize her. Her face is lean and lined with two creases running down both sides of her face. She takes a deep drag on a cigarette. "You don't know who I am, do you?"

Paul takes this as an invitation of sorts and he eases forward. Once he's in the room, his eyes adjust to the shadows. "I couldn't see in this light," he says.

"I guess." A thick cloud of smoke pours from her mouth. "Some things no one ever sees."

"Maybe." At last he can make out Jenny's mother. "You're Fran, right?"

"Let me guess why you've come here."

He shifts his weight. Could she know why he's come here, today, with Chester's amputated leg in the backpack?

She walks toward him and wraps the fingers of one hand around a strap on his backpack. "You've come here to pray, haven't you? You've come here to pray for Jenny with us."

Paul steps out of her reach and glances into the kitchen. There's no sign of Reg anywhere. He realizes now that the women have been praying for Jenny. The sense of anticipation he felt was their hope for an answer to their prayers.

"I would pray," he says. Then he adds, "In fact, I have prayed."

The woman sitting on the sofa smiles at him.

"I've felt your presence," Fran says and she takes another drag on her cigarette, then leans over and stubs it out in an ashtray.

"We all have." The frail woman who answered the door smiles, too. "Would you like to join us now?"

The cigarette smoke, the stagnant aroma from the kitchen and the suspended hope of the women blend in the air. He takes a deep breath and shakes his head. "I've come to see Reg. Is he home," he asks, "or ... out with Jenny?"

Fran sighs and looks away. Another plume of blue smoke escapes her nostrils. "I never know where he is." She waves a hand as if she's tired of smoking cigarettes and would like to give it up now that she's certain it offers no relief. "Is his car in the driveway?"

"The red Dodge?"

She walks back to the sofa. "Yeah, that's it," she says and sits down. "Look in the garage. If he's here, that's where you'll find him."

The second woman wraps an arm around Fran's shoulder and the frail girl leans over the side of the sofa and kisses her cheek. As Paul leaves the apartment they pick up their conversation in discreet whispers that he cannot decipher.


Reg Jensen eases open the garage door. When he sees Paul his head jerks back as if he's taken a light blow to the chin.

"What d'you want?" He wraps his hand around the edge of the half-open door.

"To talk."

"Already been enough of that. What's left to talk about?" He opens the door completely now and Paul can smell coffee on his breath. His beard is stubbled and his eyelashes are encrusted with small flakes. He's wearing an Arkansas Razorbacks T-shirt emblazoned with an image of a hog jumping through the triangle in the letter 'A.'

"Look. I'm not here to make trouble." Paul glances away. "But there's still things that have to be said."

Jensen thinks about this a moment, then motions for Paul to enter his domain. The door closes with a metallic clack as he steps into the two-bay garage. Hoisted onto woodblocks in the far bay sits a '50s-vintage Cadillac with swept-up tail fins. The wheels and rims have been removed and the hood is open. A rack of tools fills the far wall. At the other end of the room is a fridge, two-element stove and microwave oven. A sleeping bag lies on an army cot tucked below the only window in the building. An Arborite kitchen table with two facing chairs is covered by an open newspaper, three coffee cups, a plastic sugar bowl and matching creamer. Next to it sits a tattered green sofa, a Salvation Army giveaway that never made its final journey to the city dump.

"Well, well," Jensen says and saunters to the sofa. He eases onto the armrest and cocks his head. "Look what the dog dragged in."

"That's not funny," Paul says and turns to face Reg.

"What's not funny?"

You don't need to answer his questions, he tells himself. This is not about you anymore. This is about Jensen. About his madness and how it all has to stop. "You know, sometimes things can be made worse than they need to be." He takes a step toward the sofa.

Reg sneers. "Some might say that."

"But no matter how bad it gets, at some point it has to stop." Paul presses his lips together. "Somebody has to say enough is enough."

Jensen nods his head. "So what are you saying? You had enough?"

"You know that dog?" He pulls the backpack from his shoulders and sets it on the concrete floor. "That yellow Lab you've seen me with?"

Jensen sips his coffee and smirks. "Yeah. I've seen him. What'd you call him, anyway?"

"That wasn't even my dog. It belonged to the neighbour. A guy and his wife in their eighties."

He blows lightly over his coffee. "Too bad. I bet your son would've liked a dog a like that."

"You know where he got to?"

He shrugs.

"Do you know what happened to that dog?"

Jensen stands and walks in a tight circle. "Why are you asking all this shit? I mean, Christ, what the fuck did you come here for?"

Paul nods slightly. He opens the bag and reaches beneath the copy of *Meditations*, and pulls out the plastic baggie containing Chester's amputated leg. He holds the bag in the air, waves it toward Jensen and says, "This is what I'm here for." He tosses the bag onto the sofa. "You seem to have left this at my place."

Jensen walks away from the sofa to the stove. A coffee percolator sits on the element. He fills his cup then crosses his arms over his chest. Some of the coffee spills onto his shirt. "Christ," he mutters and dumps the mug onto the stovetop.

"You cut the legs off that dog." Paul walks a little closer. "And that's where this has to stop, Reg." He pauses while Reg wipes the spilled coffee from the razorback hog on his shirt. "You wrote 'NEXT?' on that bag with the dog's legs in it—but there won't be any *next*."

"I don't know what you're saying." He continues to brush one hand over the coffee stain on his shirt.

Paul shakes his head. Now he's going to start the denial. Now they're going to have to play that game. But it's all a ruse. All that Reg needs to understand is that the madness stops here. Call it denial, call it stupidity, call it death's avenging angel. Whatever he wants to call it doesn't matter, as long as he understands that it's over.

"I'm saying the game is over. With this dog—with what you *did* to the dog—it's finished. There's no more innings left to play."

Reg drops his hand from his shirt and looks at Paul. "I'll tell you something. Nothing finishes with anybody's dog. Everything starts—and finishes—with Jenny."

"You don't understand—"

"No! You don't understand." He paces out the tight arc of another circle. "But if you want to understand, then you sit and listen." He points to the sofa. "And if you've got something to say to me, then you're going to have to play it my way."

"What do you mean?"

"Sit down. And for two minutes—for a change—just shut up and listen."

Paul lifts Chester's leg from the sofa and sets it on the floor at his feet. He sits on one end, sinks into the flattened cushion, while Jensen slumps onto the armrest opposite him. For a moment, neither of them says a word. Then Jensen's face forms a deep frown and he begins to speak into the centre of the room without looking at Paul.

"Have you ever had to pick up the pieces of your life and start everything again—from scratch? I'm talking about starting from a place where ... you've just been broken." He lifts both hands in the air as if he were warming them above a campfire.

Paul thinks of the time when his parents died. When Michelle LaBaie had broken down and he pushed her out of his life. When he quit his job and realized that after decades living in Montreal he had no friends to turn to when he needed them. Still, he felt confident in himself. Ready to start again. "No," he whispers. "Never that bad."

Reg narrows his eyes and nods his head, satisfied with this answer, as though Paul is granting him a measure of respect. "Well. I'll tell you. Sometimes you can get some of it back. A few pieces here. Some there. I had two pieces thrown back at me. Fran and Jenny."

Paul closes his eyes. He doesn't want to hear this. To hear what is sure to come. But he knows he must listen, to let Reg purge whatever grief has seized his mind, at least until he can absorb the one message Paul has to deliver.

"First I got Fran. Then Jenny. From those two pieces I started to build a new life." He points to his world beyond the garage door. The butcher shop and apartment. Some free time and the prospect of rebuilding a '57 Caddy. Enough money to give his daughter kayaking lessons for her thirteenth birthday.

Paul gazes at the floor, at the bare concrete where Reg is addressing his confession.

"Then there was this accident"—he turns one of his hands to Paul, assigning the event to him—"and the loss of my daughter." He pauses and draws a breath. Paul almost interjects with some kind of rebuttal: that the girl is not yet lost, that there's real hope she'll be revived. But he abandons the thought when Reg brushes the back of his hand over his eyes and continues to speak. "But with her gone

244

... then I started to lose Fran." He tilts his head so that he can see Paul, see his reaction to this second loss.

Paul shakes his head. "I don't understand."

"Did you go in there?" he crooks a thumb toward the apartment.

"Yeah."

"Well?" His eyes widen with anger. "I lost her to Jesus Christ and two religious whores." He spits on the floor. A dot of spittle clings to his lip. He wipes it away, then sits on the sofa and turns toward Paul. "The thing with Jenny is I knew I'd lost her that first day. But with Fran it was slower. It took two or three weeks. Then this Monday I realized I can't even talk to her anymore. That's when I moved in here." He scowls and points a finger at the floor.

"What happened on Monday?"

Jensen sets his jaw and examines Paul's face. "You want to know?" The confessional tone is gone and a new mood has seized him.

Paul closes his eyes. "I'm just asking."

Jensen smiles, exposing a row of dull, even teeth. Paul realizes he's never seen Jensen smile before and wonders what it can mean now.

"Let's play a game," he says. "Something we used to play in my navy days. It's called Dead Eye."

Jensen leads him to the Arborite table and clears away the newspaper and coffee cups. "Sit here," he says and sets two shot glasses and a bottle of Captain Morgan dark rum on the centre of the table.

"What's this?" Paul stands next to the table and places one hand on the back of the chair.

"I told you. It's from when I was in the navy." He grins again and sits opposite Paul. He tips a hand toward Paul's chair, a slight, gentlemanly gesture.

"I don't know." Paul considers the idea of leaving, to say his piece one last time and get out. "I'm not much of a rum drinker."

"This is a navy game; you drink rum." He gestures to the chair again.

If you're going to make him understand you, Paul tells himself, then you'll have to humour him. Up to a point, that is. Just figure out what the turning point is and then move on. Paul sighs and sits in the chair. He leans forward and looks Jensen in the eyes. "All right. What do we do next?"

"You already got a quarter of the game down." He pours two shots of rum. "The next part is you want something. Then I give you something. Then we have a drink. Then we do it again. Only next time, I want something and you give me something. Then we have another drink." He tips his chin toward the bottle. The ragged scar jutting across his throat is visible under the stubble of his thin beard.

Paul frowns and says, "So it's a drinking game."

"It's called Dead Eye, because you got to look the other guy in the eye as you're wanting—and giving."

"What do you mean?"

"Let's start with your question."

"What question?"

"You asked me what happened on Monday. Now look me in the eye and ask me that again."

Paul shakes his head in confusion.

"Say 'What happened Monday?' "

"What happened Monday?"

"Look me in the eyes and say it."

Paul stares at him. He can feel an edge of anger building in his chest. "What happened Monday?"

Jensen nods: you finally got it. "On Monday, Fran sold the butcher shop." He narrows his eyes. "Right from under my fucking feet."

Paul sits back in the chair. "Without you knowing about it?"

"Uh-uh." He wags a finger in the air. "You're only allowed one question at a time. But since you're new to this, I'll allow it." He sets his jaw and continues, "Yeah, without me knowing. The shop was in her name. For legal reasons," he adds.

Paul glances away. Everything about Jensen seems gridlocked, impossible to navigate.

"You wanted, now you get," Jensen says and he holds Paul with his eyes. Then in one short jab, his fist delivers a stinging punch to Paul's shoulder. It comes in a flash and hits squarely on the joint between his humerus and scapula.

"Christ!" Paul jolts back in the chair. "What was that?"

"That was you getting." Jensen smiles narrowly. "Now we drink."

"The fuck we do!" Paul stands up and rubs the pain flaring across his shoulder. "You're crazy, Jensen."

"Drink," he says. "That'll fade away in a minute. Then it's your turn."

"Up yours," Paul snarls. "This is crazy."

"Is it?" Jensen shoots his draught of rum down his throat. "You come here with this cut-off dog leg and call me crazy. It's early innings, mate. I think you should ask yourself why you came here. Ask me your questions while we're still enjoying the friendly rounds."

Paul rubs his shoulder and draws a deep breath. The pain flares under his skin. "You know why I came here."

"If we're not still playing, mate, then you leave. Otherwise, sit down, drink your shot and let's finish our business."

"All right, you bastard. I do have a couple of questions for you." Paul sits in the chair. He downs the rum and looks Jensen in the eyes. "All right. Your turn."

Jensen leans forward. "When you were in the water with Jenny," he pauses as though he needs to adjust the question in his mind, "after you'd both dumped into the water, did she save you from drowning?"

Paul leans forward. He can feel the anger in his mouth now. "No," he says. "Like I said in court, it was the other way around."

Reg nods. He lifts his right hand to his left shoulder and rolls up the sleeve of his Arkansas Razorback T-shirt. His biceps are thick from years of cutting meat. He pours two more shots and sets his gaze on Paul's face.

Paul considers his next move. There's a chance that he'll break his hand hitting Jensen's arm. Besides, any advantage he can gain will be psychological, not physical. "Pass," he says and downs his shot of rum.

"Pass? Never seen anyone pass, before." Reg cocks his head and drinks his shot. "If the game goes long, mate, I don't think that's such a good strategy." He pours two more glasses.

"My turn?"

"Carry on."

"Did you cut the legs off my neighbour's dog?" His hand gestures toward the leg lying in the plastic bag on the floor.

"Point of clarification: that yellow Lab I seen you walking?"

"Yes."

He waits a few seconds. "Yeah. That was me."

Paul clenches his jaw against the anger rising through his body. He has just one more question to ask and he'll be done with this. He turns his right shoulder toward Jensen. "This side," he whispers.

Jensen waits until he can fix Paul's eyes with his own, then delivers a hard whack to his shoulder. Paul barely moves. "Drink," he says. "Pour another."

They drink and Jensen sets up another round.

"Why does the truth never taste this sweet?" Jensen leans forward as though this question has created an advantage for him.

Paul can feel the alcohol now, the buzz and the numbness that would enable some men to play this game to a deadly end. "Is that your question?"

"No." He leans forward in the chair. "Here's the question: When you were in the water, did you hit Jenny?"

This time Paul sets his eyes on Jensen. He's told this lie to himself so often that it has become the truth. He is no longer afraid of it. It holds no power over him any more. "No," he says evenly. "I did not hit Jenny." He waits for a moment then drinks his shot in one gulp.

Jensen curls his lips with bitterness. He wipes his face with one hand then exposes his shoulder to Paul.

"Pass," he says and shakes his head to brush off the too-sweet taste of the rum as it burns through his throat.

Jensen casts his eyes away. He downs his drink and pours another two. "In for another … round?" His voice wavers, a minor betrayal.

"Come closer," Paul says and wags a finger.

Jensen leans forward. Paul can smell the booze on him.

"Will you stop coming near my house and family?"

Jensen smiles again and leans back in his chair.

"Look at my eyes." Paul waves two fingers beneath his eyes. "Answer the question."

Jensen's lips squeeze together in a thin smile. "Yes. Of course. I promise," he says with a snort.

Paul shakes his head in disgust. They're both liars. "Deal me out," he says and turns his shot glass upside down. The rum splashes across the table onto the floor. Paul grabs his backpack and heads for the door. He leaves Chester's amputated leg for Jensen to deal with. Let it sit on his conscience—if he has one.

"Don't ever come near my wife or son again," he calls out as he pulls open the door. "You've been warned."

As he leaves the garage, he approaches the apartment under the torn awning and sees Fran Jensen waiting for him at the open doorway. She steps onto the walk, blocking his passage. She crosses her arms under her breasts, then drops her hands to her sides.

"I see you found him." Her voice carries no expectation that he should reply to this. When he says nothing, she continues. "I don't know what you hoped for but I've got one hope only. One hope—and that's for a miracle." She scans his face. "You've got to help us. You're the one person who can make this happen. You were there at the beginning; so you must be there at the end," she says. "You've got to pray with us. Tonight, every night until Jenny's better."

Her eyes are grey and bloodshot from tears and nicotine and worry. Paul cannot look at her. He hikes the pack onto his back and adjusts the straps.

"He's godless," Fran calls to him as he walks up the driveway to the street. "That man in there is godless and you shouldn't have let him touch you."

# CHAPTER 14

AUL STANDS AT THE TOP OF A WELL-MANICURED KNOLL ABOVE THE SEA
WALL ON THE NORTHWEST SIDE OF VICTORIA'S INNER HARBOUR. For
thousands of years, Songhees Point has served as a lookout to
observe sea-going vessels moving north or south through the inlet or
along the Juan de Fuca Strait into the Pacific Ocean. Paul slides the
backpack from his shoulders and settles on the bench overlooking
the shore. He feels tired and sore as he stretches his feet and props
his heels on the ground. He decides to study the activity on the waterfront: it's an exercise in distraction, an act of forced sanity.

On the south shore, just in front of the Parliament Buildings, the
*Coho*, a grey-and-white tub owned by Black Ball Ferries, backs out
of its berth and prepares to sail for the USA. Loaded with tourists, it
makes two or three round trips a day from Victoria to Port Angeles.
The words COHO, SEATTLE are imprinted in black letters across the
ferry's stern. Two Canadian flags ripple in the light breeze above
the wheelhouse, a single US flag is draped above the stern deck. Not
far away hangs the Black Ball standard, a black circle with white
trim on red background. It's the ugliest flag he's ever seen. As the

ship passes Songhees Point, Paul studies the narrow horizontal red stripe painted on the ship's hull just above the water line to see if any waves break above its demarcation. None do.

While the ship turns and sets its bow toward the harbour mouth and the open waters of Juan de Fuca Strait, a line of eight seaplanes rev their engines in the queue for takeoff clearance. Dodging about them are two motorized gondolas, each loaded with about ten tourists, punting toward the dock in front of The Empress Hotel. Scattered throughout the bay a dozen kayaks and another dozen millionaires' yachts jostle for position. It's a busy place—and in the chaos of motion Paul tries to find his bearings, some sense that his world has not gone adrift.

Both his shoulders ache from Reg Jensen's punches but he tries to ignore the dull throbbing and concentrate on his situation. Rather than wait for the bus, he walked to the harbour from Jensen's butcher shop, a half-hour-long journey he cannot remember now. The one thing that has become clear is that the danger has not passed. How he would love to let the hazards slip beneath him like the water skimming under the hull of the Black Ball ferry. Twice he'd taken passage on the *Coho*; once when he first entered Victoria on his return to Canada from his five-year tour around the world. Then again, when he and Valerie embarked on their month-long vacation to San Francisco.

The vacation was not about San Francisco. It was not about the gorgeous meandering highway scenes along the coastline from Port Angeles to the Golden Gate Bridge. Nor was it about the mountain hunting lodge they discovered on Quinault Lake, nor the Alaska king crab they cracked open next to their beach campfire north of the mouth of the Columbia River, nor the bottles of California Chablis they downed over the course of a week in the private cabin just outside Cannon Beach on the Oregon coast. All these places were merely passing scenes that enhanced their private love affair.

And private it was. After three weeks they reached a point that Paul considered a twin-ship, a foundation of erotic empathy that varied with intelligence, surprise, humour, mockery, tenderness and even wisdom. Valerie made love with forethought and abandon, with heat and calculating dispassion, with generosity and insistent demand. They were democratic and equal, yet completely enslaved to one another and they dedicated themselves to the bond that fused their unconscious worlds together. By the time they drove into San Francisco in Paul's newly purchased Toyota Corolla Valerie could turn her chin to one side or drop her voice a half tone and she would reveal the prospect of his desire. Paul, in turn, could touch her knee or the small of her back and she would confess that she was flooding with anticipation. For his part, Paul was besotted by her and she drove him far above the height of passion to a long plateau, a state of mind without mind, of thinking without thoughts—into a state of completion.

"That's what I feel. Completion," he told her as the car pulled up to the Sir Francis Drake Hotel. They'd arrived in the heart of downtown San Francisco, the nominal end-point of their tour, yet he had no sense that the trip was over. Nonetheless, he repeated the word, this word about a feeling he'd never experienced before. "Yes, that's it. Completion."

Valerie pressed her lips together as she thought about this. Over the past three days they'd started talking about what was happening between them. They tried to be very articulate about it but the conversations inevitably fell away from their feelings. The only cure for this failure was to make a running joke that revealed the impossibility of fixing in words what they'd discovered. "So you're telling me it's over?" She smiled a smile that revealed she knew they were not at all finished.

Paul laughed. "Yeah. Let's find the bus terminal and I'll drop you off right now."

"I'll drop you off." She narrowed her eyes and made a move for the steering wheel.

"All right. I'm kidding."

"You are?"

"Yes. You know I am."

"I don't think so. You must prove to me you are kidding. You must love me with laughter."

"Be careful, or I'll start to imitate comedians."

"You mean stand-ups?" Her voice turned hopeful.

"No, I mean Buster Keaton. And Charlie Chaplin."

"They're dead. How can they get it up?"

"Is this all we can think about now?" He looked into her green eyes with a plea for sympathy. "I start out with this transcendent, ethereal insight into the possibility of existential completion in the late twentieth century and you come back at me with this?"

"This what?"

"This.... " He stopped long enough to enjoy the expression on her face. "This delightful, salacious"—he leaned past the steering wheel to kiss her eyes, one then the other, then her mouth—"lustful, puckish, obsessive libido we have given birth to."

"Puckish libido?" She laughed again and kissed him back. "My God, it sounds like a monster."

"It is," he admitted. "And we must unleash it upon the world!"


They were late. They'd lingered in their motel room in Marin County and now it was three in the afternoon, a Friday, and Valerie had told her mother they would visit Alcatraz Island. "It's the one thing I promised her," she said and she tapped her watch as if hitting the glass crystal might set time back a few hours. "If we go see it right now, we don't have to worry about my mother for the rest of the weekend. And believe me, since you've never met my mother, you don't want to be worrying about her."

Paul didn't care about Alcatraz or Valerie's mother or anything other than Valerie. "All right," he said. "Stay here with the luggage. I'll check in so we don't lose our room. Then let's drive straight to the wharf, catch the ferry to the island, have dinner after the tour and come back here when we're ready."

It was a fine plan, but weighted with new complications. Paul checked into the Drake Hotel and they began the drive to Fisherman's Wharf. Within a few blocks they became confused by the steep hills, the odd street grid, the mounting rush hour traffic, and the near impossibility of finding a parking place.

"Over there." Valerie saw a spot a half block behind them on Powell Street. "Just behind that Cadillac."

Paul cranked the wheel and slowly backed the Toyota into the slot in one move. "Jeez, that Caddy took up a space and a half—but it's no trouble for the kid." He smiled with pride. "Come on. We're going to have to run to make the ferry. Remember where we are," he said and made a note of the nearby magazine and tobacco shop as he yanked open his door. He didn't care if they made the ferry today or not. He just wanted to run with her, to feel a sense of urgency about something other than sex. Valerie stepped onto the sidewalk, he locked the doors and they began a sprint down to the wharf.

They were the last people to board the boat, cheered on by a clot of tourists who saw them jogging toward them from the ticket booth. Once they caught their breath, they walked hand-in-hand to the bow as the launch eased out of its berth and turned toward Alcatraz Island. A fog bank was creeping in from the Pacific and it shrouded the water under the Golden Gate Bridge. Spooky, he thought. It was a word he repeated to himself once they docked on the island and the tour guide led them up the ramp, past the overgrown, abandoned gardens and through the prison gate. They toured the laundry facilities, the yard, the cell blocks, the gun galleries, the light-proof solitary confinement cells. Valerie held his arm as groups of five or six tourists were shunted into the individual cells. The tour guide slammed the barred doors in place and for less than a minute the parade of visitors could imagine what it might be like to stand alone in this bleak jail and hear that clank of steel slam in your face. To hear it every day for twenty or thirty years—until you died.

Yet the grim hopelessness of Alcatraz was dissipated by the tour guide who was able to transform the island into a colourful historical artifact. The patrons asked about the quality of the meals, which apparently was excellent and considered essential to prevent food riots. A few children dipped their heads into the open toilet bowls to relive the legendary "toilet talk" that served as the prisoners' voice line during the enforced evening silence. Nearly everyone wondered if any of the birds nesting on the shore were descendants of the Birdman's flock. As they walked down the ramp to the waiting ferry Valerie wrapped her hand around Paul's biceps. He could feel her breast riding against his sleeve. The Birdman never would have felt that, he said to himself, and he became saddened and frightened by the power of the prison system. The moments of comfort and intimacy that were stolen from all the men: that was the theft they suffered every day.

"I have a new sense of the word *criminal*," he told her as the boat pulled away from the dock and into the bay—back into their vacation.

"Yeah. And I have a new sense of Hell."


Their mood changed as they sat down for dinner. Valerie blamed their sense of despair on her mother and they spent an hour discussing her parents, whom Paul was due to meet when they drove back to Canada, to the Burbanks' home in Vancouver. The mood was improved by a bottle of Chablis, plates of grilled swordfish and salmon, a chocolate bag filled with creamy trifle, two rounds of espressos and lattes and twin snifters of the house brandy. They held hands and braced their knees together under the tablecloth at a corner table in a restaurant in the heart of Fisherman's Wharf, a restaurant whose name they would later forget.

It was not all they forgot. After the meal they strolled back to the car, or rather to the place where they thought they'd parked the car.

"Did we forget where we parked?"

"No. It was right here."

"So where is it?" Valerie looked around, her open hands swept the air.

Paul shook his head. He eyed the magazine and tobacco store. The door was ajar. The proprietor stood at the cash register tending to some paperwork. "This is odd," he said and turned where he stood, scanning the street to see if someone had moved the car up the road.

"Someone took our sad, abandoned car." Valerie's face had a look of mock-distress, a hint that this episode would add a new twist to their adventure. "And all our luggage," she added.

"It was right here." Paul pointed to a white BMW, its front tires neatly banked against the curb. The Cadillac that had hogged the space ahead was gone too. "I'm going to ask that guy in the store if he's seen the car."

Valerie waited on the street with her hands in her pockets and scuffed the toe of one shoe against the pavement in the direction of the BMW. A few minutes later Paul stepped back onto the sidewalk. "They towed the car," he said with disgust.

"What?"

"They towed the car." He showed her a slip of paper bearing a towing company name: LUCKY TOWING.

Valerie glanced around for no-parking signs. "What for?"

"Apparently it rolled into the car ahead of it. The Cadillac. I guess I forget to set the hand brake."

Valerie suppressed a grin. Her chin wobbled slightly but she held it in check.

"And apparently," Paul continued, "the Caddy belonged to the mayor."

"The mayor of San Francisco?"

"I guess." Paul shrugged and looked away. He could see Valerie trying to control her laughter. He felt absurd. In order to retrieve his car he knew he would be held to some official accounting. He would be required to display a certain amount of grovelling and humiliation. A certain amount of money, too.

"So our lonely Toyota knocked into the mayor's classic Caddy," Valerie said in a pronounced whisper. She might have been gossiping with her high-school girlfriends. "I sure hope the mayor's Caddy doesn't get pregnant."

"Oh, stop it."

"Come on. This is ridiculous—laugh!" She laughed and dug her fingers into his ribs and tickled him until he started laughing too.

"All right. Enough!" He wrapped his arm around her shoulders. She pressed her body next to his and danced him three or four steps across the sidewalk. After a moment he realized she was right, there was nothing he could do to change what had happened, and they started a leisurely walk back to The Drake. All he had was his credit card, a hotel reservation and Valerie. That would be enough.

They spent Sunday morning idling away the hours in a queen-size bed in The Sir Francis Drake Hotel, in a room refurbished to accentuate the glories of the hotel's opulence. There seemed something wonderful about the excesses of the 1920s, something more sensuous than the extravagance of the '80s with its narcissistic, fully invested self-satisfaction.

"They had gangsters then," Valerie said and she draped her hand on his chest. "But some of them were chivalrous. Bonnie and Clyde, for instance. Or was that in the '30s?"

"Right. Now they've got kids blowing one another way in their schools. That's what I mean. It was better then." Paul stopped himself from saying more. It occurred to him that they'd become more American in the past three weeks. In the years he travelled the world he discovered that genuine assimilation into most countries was impossible. In France, Italy, Greece one remained an outsider. Even England maintained a society of castes. As a result he found that he was always on the periphery, always passing through. But the US was exactly the opposite. American society was a vast, electronic assimilation machine. You simply tuned into it from anywhere on Earth. And when you visited the US, the American dream became visceral and seductive and absorbing. Things were different in Canada. Canadians possessed no national *über-kultur*, and pressure to conform to the racial patch-work could be politely ignored. Being in Canada allowed you to become more yourself. For many people that was the most difficult challenge: the absence of cultural context. That and surviving the climate.

"You know something? I'm ready to go home." He looked at her. She shifted her forearm between her breasts to cover her scar.

"Me too." She kissed his shoulder. "But what about the car?"

"We'll get it tomorrow. Just like they said."

"Like Lucky Lindy said." More word play. In the last week Paul discovered that Valerie liked to rattle off a alliterations, puns, nonsense syllables—all simply to please her own ears. "You think it will be that easy?" she asked more seriously.

Who knew? Paul had called Lucky Towing on Saturday morning. Within minutes it became clear that his case was complicated by the fact he had rolled into the *mayor's* Caddy. Furthermore, when his lordship had called for a tow, the hoist had locked the cars' bumpers together. In the ensuing tug-of-war, the Caddy's tail lights were smashed and the Toyota's bumper broke away. Therefore, there were damages to settle. Furthermore, Lucky had to be paid (one hundred and fifty dollars), plus the city's impounding fee (fifty dollars for every day the car sat on their lot). Unfortunately, except for his unpaid bill at Lucky's Towing, none of this could be resolved until Monday at the earliest. The news inspired Paul and Valerie to spend most of Saturday shopping for a change of clothes, toothbrushes, a shaving kit—and tickets to a local jazz club.

"I hope so. I'm almost ready to go."

"*Almost* ready?" She pulled the sheet to her shoulder and propped her chin in one palm. "You have unfinished business in the country of my mother?" Now she'd acquired a Brooklyn accent.

"Are you always this frivolous?"

"Hey, I haven't had a month's holiday since I was eighteen," she said defensively. Then her tone turned smoky and seductive: "Besides, I think I'm becoming obsessive-compulsive. I've got a bad case of ... erotomania. It's especially difficult to control," she added stroking his belly, "with a man so magnetically charming."

Paul smiled. In the past week she had said this a dozen different ways. They'd been on the road for twenty-five days and they hadn't experienced a moment of tension or compromise. Even the episode with his Toyota served to clarify their harmony. In the past twenty-five days he'd learned everything he needed to know about her. It was all good.

"There is one more thing I want to do," he said.

Her eyes widened and she lifted her head from the palm of her hand. "Uh-uh?"

"Are you going to read my mind to find out what it is?"

"No. You have to tell it to me."

"Don't you know it?"

"Yes, I know it. But you have to tell me."

He took a breath and they looked at one another. He wanted this moment to last a long time.

"You can't joke about this," she said and moved her face closer to him. "This is the one thing you can't joke about."

"All right. I'm serious." He nodded to confirm his solemn intention. "I think we should get married."

She looked away and then her eyes darted back and forth across his face. "That's close," she said.

"What do you mean, it's close?"

"What you just said is like a theoretical proposition: 'I think we should get married.' That's probably how Einstein proposed to his first wife—and, hell, *they* didn't last." She sat up on the mattress and pulled all the sheets around her. She made a little island of herself, wrapped in waves of bed sheets. "I mean, I think we should get married, too, but not as some kind of passing speculation."

Paul shook his head in surprise. He hadn't thought about how to do this. He knew he wanted to be with her. He was worried about what might become of him if he couldn't keep Valerie with him forever. He realized he wanted her to have his children, even though he had never imagined he would have children.

He stood up and faced the bed. She pulled an edge of a sheet to her mouth as she sat on her linen island and he stood naked facing her. He spread his arms and inflated his chest. "Valerie Jeanine Burbank," he said. "I, Paul Egan Wakefield, am totally, completely in love with you. I wish to have your hand in marriage. I want to have you and to hold you." He nodded and lowered his arms. "And I want you to have our babies. But I don't know what," he added, "what ... will happen to me if you say anything other than 'yes.' "

Her mouth dropped slightly as she studied him. Her eyelids closed and opened.

"Well?"

"I was just enjoying the moment," she said. "Come here." She dropped the sheets from her breasts and drew him to her. "Yes. Of course, it's yes," she said. "You know it's yes. After all, if we're going to unleash the product of our puckish libido on the world, it would never be as a bastard child."


They were so frivolous back then. Everything came easily: money, their careers, their home and marriage, their beautiful son. It was as if an invisible hand guided them from one privilege to another.

Perhaps they possessed a divine grace that emerged from their bond of love. Who could know this for certain? Yet certainly their marriage had transported them to an intangible, spiritual plateau that they understood to be one more gift.

As the number two bus ships him through the streets of south Oak Bay toward his empty home, Paul wonders about the gradual shift that had opened between them. Was it a breach of faith? No, that was overstating the tension. But there was trouble between them now, Paul thinks as he steps off the bus and walks through the growing dusk to 565 Transit Road. As he moves up the sidewalk to his porch he checks for lights in Jerry and Bettina Sampson's house. Nothing visible. Perhaps it's too early for them to click on the lamps. In any case, he doesn't want to inquire.

He unlocks his front door, pulls off his jacket and dumps his keys, wallet and loose change on the office desk. The answering machine light is blinking. There are two messages. He blows a stream of air between his lips and listens to the machine's digital monotone: "Message one, today, at 1:52 pm." The next sound is a breathless sigh, then the muffled clatter of a telephone hang-up. "Message two, today, at 3:16 pm." Again, the caller hesitates and hangs up. Paul rubs his bruised shoulders as he considers the possibilities. Was it Jensen? The police? Or perhaps his new friend, Andy Betz?

Anybody's guess, he decides, and wanders into the kitchen and scavenges for food. After a few minutes he prepares a tuna sandwich and settles in front of the TV to digest the six o'clock PBS evening news. For years he's preferred US to Canadian news. He takes perverse pleasure in identifying their national biases, their self-absorption, their righteousness—everything that makes the Yankee so detestable. Besides, unlike Canadian news broadcasts, theirs is seldom petty and boring. He once confessed his lowbrow approach to the news to Andy Betz, after Andy revealed that he considered the news media mere entertainment, a virtual coliseum perpetually renewed with narratives of death and sex. A difficult point to dispute, Paul thought. When you consider the millions of cameras around the world and the images they deliver every hour onto the screen, it makes the Romans look quite civilized.

After his meal Paul sets his sandwich plate on the table and walks down the basement steps to the freezer room. He lifts the top door to the freezer and peers inside. Only when he sees the paper bag containing Chester's three legs does he wonder what he is doing. He is confirming his situation, he decides. He is proving that what happened today is real and assessing where it could lead him. He lifts the bag, unrolls the paper and verifies that Chester's legs are indeed where they are supposed to be, in the bag marked 'NEXT?' Perhaps his curiosity is no different from the Roman fascination with public torture, or the current global hunger for news of famine, war, rape, disease. It was all about our desire to confirm what awaits us. To establish multiple possible fates and to affirm that each of them is accessible, that others have passed on to The Mind through such horror, and therefore, it is possible for each of us to endure a similar end.

Still, the living must turn away from such thoughts, must return to the demands of day-to-day life and somehow bring sanity and reason to the world. Paul rewraps the paper bag, closes the freezer, climbs the staircase and sits at his office desk. He feels well enough now to telephone Valerie. He can tell her that he saw Jensen, talked to him and his wife and told him the madness must end. He won't tell her about the game of Dead Eye. He lifts the collar of his T-shirt and examines the bruises on his shoulders. Eventually you'll have to explain these marks to her, he tells himself. But not yet.

Jeanine Burbank picks up the phone on the second ring. "Hello, Paul," she says, her tone guarded. "We've been waiting for your call. Is everything all right?"

"Yes. How about Valerie and Eliot?"

"They're here. Valerie's downstairs, but I've been teaching Eliot some new rhymes." He can hear her stirring something on the stovetop. In the background Eliot calls out to him.

"Can I speak to him?"

"Sure. Then I'll get Valerie for you."

Short and sweet, he thinks. He was anticipating an interrogation, cross-examination, charges of moral failure.

"Hi, Dad."

"How are you, son?"

"Good."

Eliot's in a detached mood. Paul realizes he'll have to work hard to draw him out but that maybe it's not worth the effort right now. Better just to reassure him that all's well; remind him of everyday things. "I saw the *Coho* pull out of the harbour today."

"You did?"

"Yeah, and you know what? There had to be fifteen seaplanes waiting to take off while that big old tub rounded the bend and got out of their way."

"I'd like to fly a seaplane."

"I know you would." Now that Paul has Eliot talking, he tries to create a sense of expectation. Of hope. "You know what I was thinking? I was thinking that when you get back home we could rent a plane for an hour. And we could fly over that island where I saw the sea lions. Just the two of us. Would you like that?"

"But Dad, you don't have a pilot's licence." Eliot's voice adopts a new tone. A hint of skepticism, of doubt in his father's ability to direct their world. That would be Jeanine's influence.

"Well, we'll hire a pilot to fly us out there in his plane."

"They do that?"

"Sure. All the time."

"Then that would be okay." An air of confidence has returned. "I like sea lions."

"You should see them out on that little island," he says. "What did you do today?"

"Granny taught me a new poem. Want to hear it?"

"Of course."

"It's called *Good, Better, Best.* " He pauses prior to the recital:

> Good, Better, Best
> Never take a rest
> Make your Good into Better, and
> Make your Better into Best.

Paul presses a thumb and forefinger against his eyes. "That's very clever," he says. "That's Granny for you, huh?"

The sound of another telephone coming on-line clicks through the handset. "It's me," Valerie says. "We made it over here."

"Bye, Dad."

"You gotta go?"

"Granny wants me to make dessert with her."

"All right. I love you."

"Love you too."

Eliot hangs up and Paul allows the brief silence to fill with these last few words.

"You all right?"

"Yes. Can you talk?"

"Mmm. I'm in the basement bedroom. I think I slept most of the afternoon." Her voice is distant, but not disaffected. He can tell she wants to test him, to see if he's resolved anything.

Paul shifts in his chair and imagines the basement guestroom. The queen bed, the ensuite bath, the sitting area overlooking the garden, Grouse Mountain in the distance.

"Did you see Jensen?" she continues.

"I went to his butcher shop. He's living in the garage at the back of the property."

"And you talked to him?"

"Yes." He weaves the telephone cord between his fingers. "But I don't know what good it will do," he confesses. "I really think he's lost it. He's not with Fran anymore. She's living behind the butcher shop. Two other women have taken over her life with this ongoing prayer vigil. Apparently they won't leave her side. That's partly what's driven him over the edge. That and the fact she sold the butcher shop from under his feet without telling him."

"Could you reason with him?"

"I spoke to him for about twenty minutes. But if you're asking did I talk him out of whatever he's doing? The answer's ... no."

"Do you think he's the one who hurt Chester?"

Paul nods his head and considers the poor, beautiful dog. "Yes," he sighs. "He told me he did it."

"Bastard," she says and in their separate places, they consider the horrible death the dog must have endured.

"You know, I was talking things over with Dad." Her voice drops a little, acquires a measure of certainty.

"What did he say?"

"He thinks we should hire someone to help us. He agrees that if we call the police again, it could just get worse. That's what happened last time. That's how Chester died."

For a moment Paul feels that Valerie is with him. She could be sitting on the sofa at his side, her hand pressed against his thigh, while they debate their inertia. He reconsiders why he cannot go to the police, and immediately recites the answer to himself: because your role in all this may emerge.

Neither of them wants to speculate how badly things could go wrong if they make a tactical error. Instead Paul decides that they must capitulate. That Wally should be consulted and his resources— whatever they are—be called upon. "Let me talk to him, then."

"I'll get him," she says and lays the phone down.

Paul waits for almost a minute. He can hear some whispering in the background, then Wally's resonant voice as he approaches the phone while concluding a conversation with his daughter.

"Here's what I propose." It's clear that Wally has given this some thought. Over the past ten minutes, Paul has revealed most of what he knows about Reg Jensen and briefly explained his encounter with him earlier in the day. "I've already been in touch with someone I've used before. His name is Frank Lowe. He's ex-police but he's been running a private investigation business on his own for ten or twelve years."

"Ex-police?" Paul can't imagine why Wally would need extra muscle for his pharmacy business. "So what do you expect him to do?"

"If you agree to this, then after we hang up, I'll call him. He told me he could meet you tomorrow evening. He'll come to your house." Wally's voice is warm and full. Paul conjures up the image of their last visit, when Wally spoke to him privately in the office and his massive body seemed to fill the space defined by the

---

doorframe. "You'll find he's pretty unobtrusive. Very quiet and calm about these things."

Paul nods and says, "All right." He can't think of anything to add. What can you say to the person hiring a PI to solve your problems? "Thanks," he says in a whisper and he realizes this was the same reply he offered when Wally revealed that he loved him.

"You can trust him," Wally says. His voice has a confidential tone. "I know this is a difficult time. That's why it's a good idea to bring in some professional help."

Paul can think of no response other than, "So when was it you had to hire Lowe?"

"Gee. Maybe a decade or so ago."

"What for?"

There's a pause. "You know, son, I'd rather not say."

A mixed message. Wally seldom refers to Paul as his "son"—yet he plants the word in the middle of this denial, this exclusion from inside knowledge.

"All right. So I'll see him tomorrow."

"Unless you hear otherwise." His voice rises to the formal tones of closure. "Oh, Valerie wants to say a little more."


"So how are you?" This time Valerie sounds affectionate, contrite. "I realized while you were talking to Daddy that I didn't even ask about you. Sorry."

Paul sits back in his chair and scans the office ceiling. "I don't know. Exhausted, I guess. Maybe that means I'll sleep well tonight." He thinks about how he feels, about his condition. "Remember your high school physics? There's this tension that builds up when you fill a test tube with water. The tube can hold more water than the actual volume of the test tube. There's this little arc of water sitting on top of the full tube. Did you study that in school?"

"Yeah, we studied that," she says. "It's called 'meniscus.'"

"That's right. Meniscus." Paul lifts his feet onto the desk and emits a long sigh from his lungs. "Well, that's how I feel. As though I'm containing more of the world than I can hold. It's like one more drop will.... " Paul wipes a hand over his eyes. He does not want to start crying. If he does, he's worried he'll have a complete breakdown.

"Paul, I'll be home soon. I'll leave Eliot here and come home tomorrow."

"No. It's better to wait until this guy Lowe does whatever he can. By the way, do you know who he is?"

"No idea. I didn't even know my father knew anyone like that."

"Well, let's see what he can do." A measure of self-control has returned. It's a mistake to talk about how he's feeling, though. He shouldn't do that any more.

"Okay, I want you to call me tomorrow, all right?"

"Yes." He sets his feet back on the carpet.

"I love you, sweetie."

"Yes. I know. And thank God you do," he says and hangs up the phone.


Paul sits in his office until the evening is thick with darkness. He imagines that now might be a good time to call the hospital. In the past, the simple process of dialling the phone and waiting for the head nurse to provide an update on Jenny's status offered a fleeting sense of hope. It opened a chance for Fate to intervene. But on those earlier occasions the hope was contained only in the pause between when he dialled the nursing station and the moment when she informed him there was no change. Sometimes this period of expectation would last a minute or even more. But on those days when the head nurse answered the phone herself, the feeling was so brief that it did not exist at all.

Sensing that this would be his situation tonight, he turns on a lamp and wanders the house, turning on a few lights as he ghosts through the hallways. He visits Eliot's room, the gallery, the family room, and then the storage room—where, after a brief debate, he decides not to examine the brown paper bag in the freezer. He settles in front of the TV and begins to click aimlessly through the channels. After an hour the exhaustion that has been building in his body becomes tangible and he realizes that a deep sleep is within reach. He checks all the door locks, clicks off the lights in the house, and enters his bedroom and the ensuite bathroom. There he pulls off his T-shirt and examines the bruising he has taken from Jensen. Both shoulders are ringed with deep purple welts. He rubs them with ibuprofen cream and prepares for bed.

As he lies alone on the mattress he considers his disaster. He cannot imagine a solution. His only salvation is to continue his communion with his daemon, to link himself with the emptiness beyond. He lies on his back and begins the nightly practice he has performed for several weeks now. His left palm settles on the skin above his heart, his right hand lies flat on the mattress, palm up. He studies the night sky through the half-moon window in the ceiling wall, then closes his eyes and recites his silent prayers to The Mind.

He waits until his pulse slips to an idling rhythm and his body loses sensory awareness of the sheets. He conjures an image of Jennifer Jensen, of the bruise across her temple. He imagines the hairline fracture in her skull and the orbit of her consciousness knocked off its centre, hovering a few degrees from its primary axis. He sets his attention there, in this mental space they share, until he feels he has fixed her mind into the track of his own consciousness. When the feeling of connection is constant, he focuses on the energetic transference rippling between them as his heart beats steadily—an engine spinning the psychic flow across this transcendent bridge. Perhaps this phase lasts two minutes, perhaps twenty. But when his concentration begins to falter and he feels the link to her fading, he makes a final effort to nudge her, to knock Jenny's lost world back into place. When finally she is gone—utterly disappeared from his intuitive perception—the tide of exhaustion washes through him in a single wave and he slips into an uninterrupted sleep that lasts seven hours.

# CHAPTER 15

A LITTLE AFTER 7:00 IN THE MORNING THE TELEPHONE RINGS AND ROUSES PAUL FROM HIS SLEEP. As he reaches for the bedside phone he rubs his eyelids with his free hand and utters a curse. Then he picks up the phone and with forced alertness, says, "Hello?"

The sound of light breathing enters his ear.

"Hello? Who is this?" He sits up and pushes his feet onto the carpet. "Listen, Reg, it really is time to put an end to this...."

He hears a light clicking noise, then nothing.

"Damn it." Paul looks at the phone in his hand and sets it back on the night table. Despite this nuisance, he feels restored. He glances behind the bedroom curtain at the bright sky and senses the warmth of the morning in his backyard. All right, this is the day, he tells himself. The day everything will be resolved.

Through his breakfast and morning coffee he begins to anticipate Frank Lowe's arrival. He's certain now that bringing in a pro is the best strategy. Someone who can settle this for everyone concerned. Someone with legal knowledge, experience and the substance required to demonstrate serious intention. Dead serious, he thinks. Make no mistake about it.

He takes the time to read at least one story from every page of the morning paper but later, as he folds it into the recycling blue box, a novel idea occurs to him: star-sixty-nine. He can simply punch in the code to retrieve the number of the last incoming telephone call. He's never used this service before—why would he need to?

He walks into the office, draws a pencil from the pen mug on his desk and dials *69.

A computer responds in a digitized female voice: "The last number that called your line was 250-602-2458. For one dollar I will dial that number for you now. Would you like me to dial it now?"

He copies the number onto a pad and hangs up the phone, then studies the last seven digits and tries to recall their connection to anyone he might know. It's fruitless. Most of Paul and Valerie's acquaintances are programmed into the speed dial. He can barely remember his old office number at the Ministry.

He takes his coffee mug and wanders into the dining room and gazes over his front lawn to the street. There are no cars visible on either side of Transit Road. No sign of Jerry or Bettina Sampson. The sun is in full flood on his grass and the pathway leading down to the road, the warm patches where Chester used to stretch out and snooze.

He's thought about telling the Sampsons what happened to the dog. It would relieve their ongoing anxiety, but on the other hand, send them into grieving for the poor, tortured animal. No, it's best to wait for Frank Lowe to unravel this mess, take the loose ends to the police, then go to Jerry and Bettina when the entire story—beginning to end—can be told in one sitting. At that point they'll understand the depths of Jensen's madness and realize what luckless business it meant for their dog.

He finishes his coffee and nods in agreement with this assessment, confirming that this is the best path to follow. To wait. But there is no need to wait on calling his anonymous prankster. That he can handle from here without delay.

He returns to the office telephone and sits at the desk. He has a pencil and a pad of paper ready to take notes. He decides it will give strength to any testimony that may follow if he can exactly quote Jensen's response. It might also be helpful to Lowe when he arrives later in the evening.

He dials the number; the call is answered on the first ring: "Victoria Hospice Society, how can I help you?"

Paul blinks and sits upright. "I'm sorry. Is this 370-8715?"

"Yes. This is the reception desk at the Victoria Hospice Society. Can I help you?"

Paul hesitates. He needs room to think ... Rory Stillwell. Valerie said she'd visited Rory in the hospice. "I have a question, I guess." He leans forward and underlines the telephone number three times. "If a patient in hospice makes a telephone call, does the call go through your line?"

"I don't know, sir. Probably—since all the rooms have local extensions that come off the 8715 number."

"Do you have Rory Stillwell's extension?"

"Rory Stillwell? Yes. It's the same as his room number, 113. Would you like me to connect you?... Oh—sorry, one of the staff says he's having his bed-bath right now. Can you call back in fifteen minutes?"

"Sure. Thanks." Paul jots 113 next to the number on the pad and hangs up the phone. He leans back in his chair and tilts his head to the ceiling. Rory Stillwell. Maybe every one of the previous telephone hang-ups have come from Rory alone. That would be better—not nearly as bad as hang-ups from Jensen. But how could he know for sure?

He waits until the lunch hour to enter the hospice. No one is at the front desk, so he wanders the hall and finds 113 just a few doors along the corridor. He stands at the doorway to determine if Rory is alone. The room is quiet. A drape is pulled over the window and filters the light into a dull, jaundiced hue. The scent of antisepsis fills his nose. Without detecting anyone, he can tell death is at hand.

He steps forward one pace. He can see the bed, the blanket pulled back so only a sheet covers the body beneath it.

"Rory?"

There is a slight motion, an adjustment of the hips. "Yes?"

"May I come in?" Paul walks to the foot of the bed. He can see Rory's head and shoulders. He is little more than a breathing skeleton. The shock of his pale, gaunt flesh turns Paul's face to one side. What the hell do you think you're doing here, he asks himself.

"Yes. Please come." Rory shifts on the bed and lifts his head to make out his visitor.

Paul steps closer and tries to smile. "Do you remember me? Paul Wakefield; Valerie's husband. We met once ... quite a few years ago."

Rory manages to settle on his back. He pulls the sheet up to his throat with one hand, then lays his forearm over his chest. His skin is spotted with purple bruises and sores, his face hollowed by disease. His eyes are opaque but able to focus. "You're the lucky one," he says as if they'd both made a bet in a high stakes poker game long ago.

"I guess." Paul braces his thighs against the top of the footboard. He nods his head in the affirmative. Yes, I am the lucky one.

"Is Valerie coming to visit today?"

"No. She had to go to Vancouver."

"With her son?"

Paul considers this a moment. Circumstance suggests he should not claim Eliot as his own. "Yes. Have you met him?"

"No. But she tells me a lot about him. He's very smart. And good looking, I imagine."

Paul nods again. "He gets that from her, I suppose."

Rory smiles a little, a yawn that exposes his gums and a few remaining teeth. Paul realizes that the disease has chipped pieces of life away from every part of his body. Likely the same decay has happened in his brain. There's no sense to be had here. Just a few memories, many of them probably distorted or broken, too.

"Listen. I'm sorry. I shouldn't have come here without calling. I should just leave."

"No." He lifts his forearm and curls a finger, a gesture of approach. "No, I slept most of the morning. Ben said he couldn't visit today," he wheezes. "I could use the company."

"All right."

"Sit here." His wrist ticks in the direction of the bedside chair. "That's where she sits when she comes."

Paul feels as though he's little more than Valerie's shadow. He sits in the chair.

"You could tell me what it's like," Rory says when Paul has settled.

"What it's like?"

"To have her love you."

Paul's first reaction is one of embarrassment. To articulate this intimacy to a stranger would be difficult enough, but to tell all to his old rival—it would be embarrassing for both of them. "I don't know," he says and glances at the array of medical equipment in the room. "I mean ... I really don't know what to tell you."

"When did you first know she loved you?" Rory's voice has a hollow quality to it, as though the AIDS has carved out an inner part of his speech. This question, so personal, is uttered with complete innocence, like a toddler trying to make sense of the mysteries in the world.

"I guess I knew at the same time she did. It was very early after we met."

Rory draws a stream of air through his lips. His chest rattles and he sputters with a light cough. "When was that?" he asks when his breathing clears.

"Almost ten years ago." Paul rolls his shoulders. The conversation seems so unlikely. And yet so harmless. Why shouldn't he tell Rory whatever he'd like to hear? The memory of what he says now will lie buried within a month.

"I met her a year earlier. During our graduation ceremony at the university. It was a beautiful day. We both agreed on that." He turns his head toward Paul. "Do you mind me telling you that?"

"No. No ... not at all."

Rory gestures with his wrist again, a request to continue his story.

Paul looks at him with a deepening sense of empathy. "We met late in the summer," he says, "at Open Space, the gallery down on

Fort Street. There was a new showing by some string artist—I don't remember who it was, he did these elaborate three-dimensional weavings that were quite good. And it was raining that day. You had a better day to meet her than me," he adds, a statement meant to give Rory an edge. A small gift.

Rory closes his eyes and waits for Paul to continue.

"I remember coming off the street, just soaking from the rain. I'd been in Victoria about three or four months before the rainy season started and so I didn't know I'd need a good jacket."

He stops to think about those days. He'd arrived in Victoria after so many years of wandering Europe and Greece, Africa and then the length and breadth of India. Ultimately he discovered that he could find no place to fit in—no place to live. He decided to return to Canada via Hong Kong and Los Angeles. From LA he made his way up the west coast to Port Angeles, then crossed the Juan de Fuca Strait into Canada. When he stepped off the *Coho* ferry into Victoria's inner harbour, a sense of belonging overcame him and he decided to try life in this beautiful port city, with its amusing imitations of England. He experienced a period of culture shock, but eventually found his footing, bought his condo in a renovated heritage house, and decided to start his personnel business with a résumé service. Within the first month Jack Wise responded to his ad in *Monday Magazine* and he began work on Jack's curriculum vitae. But his business was doomed. He had no contacts on Vancouver Island, no network to make the necessary business connections. Worse, he started to barter away his services—as he did with Jack, exchanging a signed mandala print and a woodblock impression for his hours of labour. Four months later he abandoned his home-based venture and found employment with the civil service. He was recruited to develop and manage the ministry professional development policies. It was work he liked and for the first time since his parents died, he felt an urge to succeed.

Rory shifts his weight slightly, opens his eyes and focuses his attention on an image—perhaps the image of Valerie—hovering in the air a metre above his chest.

Paul watches Rory's quiet reverie with a sense of dread and decides to continue. "She worked at Open Space as an intern. She was offering glasses of wine to the guests as they came into the room."

"She started volunteering there ... after she graduated," Rory whispers. "No one ever understood it. They didn't pay her ... but she worked day and night."

"Yes, I guess she did." Paul blinks and looks away. He realizes that Valerie never would have stayed with Rory if he couldn't grasp this fundamental part of her personality. He was never a rival for Valerie's affections. Not then, and certainly not now. Still, Paul would like to know if Rory's been calling their home, leaving the imprint of his vaporous breathing on their answering machine.

"By the way, Rory, I wanted to ask you something." He stops himself, then decides he must continue with this question. "I wanted to know if you've been calling our phone over the last month or so. You know, without leaving a message. Like this morning ... did you call this morning?"

Rory turns his head on the pillow and stares at a point past Paul's head. "I'm sorry. Was that a problem?"

"No. Just a mystery." He eases his back into the chair, surprised at the relief he feels. "You know how it is just to have these things cleared up."

"Then you can understand me, too. For the same reason." He clenches the sheet to his throat. "Tell me what you thought when you met her. It helps me remember what I must have felt."


Paul tries to set the context. He was dripping into the puddles welling under his feet when she approached him with a tray loaded with glasses of red and white wine. At first she didn't say a word. Neither did he. Perhaps they were both shocked, shocked by the sense of instant recognition that washed over them. It was a feeling of knowing and not knowing someone, of awakening a lost memory of a mutual past and future—and the confusion of all this was delivered in an instant. Valerie wavered and balanced the wine tray with her right hand. She opened her mouth slightly but did not smile. She blinked, then turned and walked back to the serving table. She set the tray on the tablecloth, held a hand to her chin and began whispering to a woman beside her. As she walked away from him, Paul observed every detail of her transit across the crowded room, watched the movement of her legs and arms and hips, absorbed the way her dress draped across her body.

Suddenly he felt defeated. He had no idea how to approach her now that she'd walked away. He needed an excuse, a reason, a good old-fashioned set-up that would bring them face-to-face. And then he would need to say something intelligent. Something insightful.

He found the washroom and did what he could to brush the water from his soaking shirt and pants. He daubed his hair with a paper towel and pressed it back along his scalp. When he returned to the reception he couldn't see her anywhere. He wandered the room. She'd vanished. Eventually he approached the woman who'd been whispering with Valerie.

"Hi," he said and tried to smile. "I was hoping to meet a friend of mine here tonight. I thought I saw her talking to you about ten minutes ago. When she set the wine tray down over there." He pointed to the serving area, now surrounded by guests cheerfully serving themselves.

"Oh?" The woman smiled broadly with a hint of amusement. "You mean Maxine?"

"Yes. Do you know where she's gone?"

"Gee, I think she was trying to find you, too. Let me have a look." She smiled like a beauty queen—her smile unflinching through every word she spoke. "What's your name?"

Paul turned his head away. How could he make this work without falling into an embarrassing charade? "Paul," he said. "Paul Wakefield."

"Let me have a look," she repeated and dipped through the crowd and disappeared.

Paul frowned and made his way to the wine table and poured himself a glass of red wine. When he turned around, Maxine and the beauty queen stood side by side.

"Found her!" she said, then added, "Oops. Gotta run."

Paul looked at Valerie and nodded slightly. The sense of familiarity tugged at him again. "Glass of wine?" he said and offered it to her. "I haven't touched it yet."

"Thank you." She took the glass and smiled. She was good at holding his eyes. "But I'm supposed to be serving the wine tonight."

"No, no—allow me." He turned and poured himself a glass then raised it to her in a toast. Their glasses clinked and he smiled, thinking he was over the first hurdle. "So, you're Maxine, right?"

She smirked and her head tipped backward with surprise. She glanced in the direction where her friend had disappeared. "And please—tell me you're not Rex."

"Uh ... no."

They frowned in mutual embarrassment and glanced away. The beauty queen's little ruse was out. How easy for her to deceive them.

"Good." Valerie pulled a strand of hair over her ear. "I don't really care for men named Rex."

"No. What about women named Maxine?"

"Horrible," she said and scanned their neighbours to ensure there were no legitimate Maxines eavesdropping on them. "They all have implants."

They began to laugh and he introduced himself to her and when she told him her name and shook his hand he realized it was going to work. He would see her again after tonight and if luck embraced them, the night after that, too. "Maybe we were Rex and Maxine in another life," he suggested.

"Maybe," she said doubtfully. "I'm sure we would have changed our names. To something more credible like ... Paul and Valerie."

They stayed at the Open Space party until the last guests had stumbled down the stairs and Valerie was left to shuffle trays of empty wine glasses onto the back counter and click off the lights. As she attended to the details of closing up, he whispered silently to himself over and over: Don't blow this. You do not want to blow this one.

"Can I take you home?" he asked. It was a very modest question, one she could refuse without entirely damaging the hope of securing a date.

"It's still pouring rain," she said. They stood on the doorstep watching the rain splash back into the air after it hit the pavement. "You don't have an umbrella, do you?"

"No." He was still damp from his dash through the streets a few hours earlier.

"A car?"

"Not yet." Then to counter any sense she might have that he was a man without means, he added, "I just bought a condo off Rockland. It's near Moss Street so I can walk almost everywhere."

Her head tipped to one side and she smiled. "How about if I walk you home, then. I go just a little past your place." She popped open her umbrella and marched up the street without waiting for his reply. He leaned under the edge of the umbrella, careful not to brush against her, yet careful to allow their shoulders to ride together the few times they shuffled past the late-night carousers.

As they walked along the streets he felt like a teenager, eager and bright with anticipation, but worried that his hopes would dissolve from some unwitting gaffe. He could smell the sap in the trees and he could smell the beautiful woman next to him. She talked about her plans to open an art gallery and was surprised—impressed—to hear that Paul had just finished working for Jack Wise. They strolled past the art galleries, antique shops and bars they would visit in the months ahead. In one of these restaurants, on the far side of the harbour, Valerie would reveal the secret about her childhood illness and the traumatic surgery that followed. When they reached Paul's condo (where in a few weeks they would stumble toward his bed, their hands awkwardly balancing brandy snifters, their bodies pressed together with undeniable urgency), they stood before the building entrance for another five minutes trying to sort out their next step. No, she didn't want him to walk her the six blocks to her apartment. And no, she wouldn't come up to his condo tonight.

"Not tonight?" he asked. "Then that means there may be an-other night."

"There might be." She glanced away as though she had to think carefully before she said anything more.

When the growing silence threatened to finish their affair before it could start, he said, "So what are you thinking?"

"What are you thinking?" She turned the question on him with a look of satisfaction.

"I'm thinking I would like to see you again."

She smiled and let her eyes settle on his face.

"That is … if you want to," he added. She was gazing at him.

He was surprised by what her eyes revealed. She was unhesitating, open, inviting, desirous, certain.

"Yes," she said. "I want to."

Then he saw something of himself in her. It was part of what he was and would become. He realized he was stepping into a new life and leaving the years of his wandering and isolation behind. He felt renewed and fresh and young and he decided to explore this new world, all of it, from the beginning to the end.

Rory's eyes are closed. Paul has no way of knowing how much of what he recited has been heard or absorbed. He sits quietly watching the man before him, thinking how odd it is that he should have told this personal tale to a stranger once intimate with his wife. Yet it seems perfectly natural. The same sort of honest disclosures are made by Catholics to anonymous priests every day. Confessions by the tens of thousands. He understands the relief it offers.

He considers this emotional release and realizes that he might find even more relief by disclosing the details of his crime to Rory. It wouldn't matter what he admitted to; in a few weeks—perhaps in just a few hours—Rory would be merged into The Mind. By confessing now, it would be like slipping his message into a bottle and casting it ahead of him into the unknown. That's what he needs, he realizes, a brief respite from the secret he's been clutching so closely. A confession would open his own destiny to a new variable. An element of chance. But what if Valerie spoke with Rory one last time—what if Rory revealed that Paul had assaulted Jenny Jensen? It would be an indictment from a dying man. Unprovable. Untenable.

The allure of disclosing his crime is now palpable and Paul rises from the chair and leans over Rory. He decides to rouse him by touching the flesh on his exposed shoulder. Wake him just enough to ensure what he has to say will be heard. To ensure his confession would be genuine and whatever redemption it conferred on him, tangible.

"Rory?" His index finger touches the dying man's collar bone. When their flesh is joined a shudder rolls through Paul, catching him by surprise.

Rory's eyelids flutter open briefly and then relax in two narrow slits of consciousness. "Yes?"

"I'm still here," Paul whispers. "I have something more to tell you."

Rory remains motionless. He takes a breath that rattles his chest and briefly disturbs his stillness.

"Something terrible happened a little while ago. There was a young girl with me in an accident. I hit her—by accident—and she hasn't woken up." This is a beginning. He is relieved to have this much out of his mouth and spoken aloud. He has confessed before to Valerie as she drifted into sleep, but she never acknowledged that she'd heard him. He's certain she had not.

Paul pulls the chair next to Rory's bed and leans toward him. He continues his tale until everything is spoken. When he finishes the story, he sits there and wonders if it could really be this simple. So easy to speak the truth and be redeemed.

"You the new volunteer?"

Paul turns his head toward the doorway. A lean man dressed in a collared shirt, vest and jeans gazes back at him with a look of hopeful expectation.

"No." Paul slumps in the chair and tries to conjure an answer. "I'm a friend of the family," he says. "Rory's brother is my lawyer. Ben Stillwell."

"I see. I'm Tom, the volunteer coordinator." He approaches Rory's bed with a look of concern. Rory's head is canted to one side and his eyes are closed. His breathing is steady but still rattling his lungs.

He must be sleeping, Paul tells himself. "Is he sleeping?"

Tom nods and smiles. "Apparently he hit a rough spot last night." He holds the palms of his hands over Rory's face in a light caressing movement that hovers a few centimetres above the cheekbones.

"What are you doing?"

"Reiki healing." He smiles again. "Just moving the energy into him, letting him absorb it and transfer it where he needs it most."

Paul studies this mute process and wonders how long Rory has to live. He considers asking this, but decides against it. Instead he asks, "What will it be like?"

"What's that?"

"When he dies. What will it be like?"

Tom lifts his hands from Rory's face and smiles again. He appears genuinely happy to be here. "It's always different," he says. "Like birth. There are thousands of us coming in and going out every day. But each passage is unique."

"That's true." Paul thinks of Eliot's birth, the wonderful climax to Valerie's day-long struggle to deliver their baby from her body. That moment, that fragment of time, would always stand as a singular particle of his memory. "So you think it's like a birth?"

"Something like that." He moves his hands above Rory's chest in an effort to calm his breathing. "There's one thing the same about them. No one ever remembers either coming or going." He smiles with a wide grin and continues his ministrations. "That way there's no worries, right. I just tell them to breathe in life and breathe out love."

As he watches the procedure Paul cannot quite fathom Tom's beatific aura. Is he smiling from amusement ... or enlightenment? It's a question that he uses to distract himself for the rest of the afternoon as he sits in his La-z-boy awaiting the arrival of Frank Lowe. Eventually he decides that in Tom's case, amusement and enlightenment are likely one and the same.

A little after 7:30 that evening Frank Lowe stands at Paul's front door and adjusts the collar of his jacket. He shakes Paul's hand and says, "I'm Frank Lowe. I think your father-in-law might have mentioned me to you."

"Yes. He did." Paul introduces himself and waves him into the hallway.

"Sorry I'm late. The 4:00 o'clock ferry was cancelled. Some kind of glitch with the prop or rudder." He waves a hand in frustration, pulls his jacket from his shoulders and drapes it over an arm. He quickly scans the hallway, the paintings on the wall, the doorways leading to the office, the kitchen, and dining room. He then turns back to Paul and they eye each other uneasily. "So, we've got some work to do," he says and clicks his tongue against the roof of his mouth.

Although he'd prepared himself to meet Frank, Paul can't think of anything to say. He leads him into the kitchen and they sit at the breakfast table. Frank passes him a business card, the most succinct Paul has ever seen. It bears Frank's name and a cell phone number, nothing more.

"I like to keep it to the point," he explains. "In my business, it's best if information flows one way only."

Towards you, Paul guesses and slips the card into his shirt pocket. "So what do we do?" he asks in a near whisper, then adds, "I've never done this kind of thing before."

Frank smiles, bemused by Paul's innocence. His smile dips at the corners of his lips like a card shark dealing poker cards to a novice. "It seems to surprise a lot of people, but what I mostly do is gather information," Frank says and leans forward. "And I need a lot of it from you. I've talked to Wally and Jeanine and your wife. I understand someone's been stalking you and your son. Reg Jensen. And that yesterday his game turned ... a little ugly."

Paul nods once and looks away.

Frank takes an audible breath. "You know, I just couldn't swallow that stuff they called coffee on the ferry coming over here."

"Yeah. Well ... let me fix some." Paul feels a tinge of embarrassment and scuttles to the stove to prepare the coffee filtering system. "You like mocha java?" he asks.

"Suits me fine," Frank says and his tongue clicks softly in his mouth.

Over the next forty minutes Paul reveals all he can about Reg Jensen. He's surprised at the ease of the narrative flow—completely different from his interrogation in the examination for discovery. This time Paul unravels the events as they occur in his memory. There are no contradictions to resolve, no ploys to trip him up with minor details. Furthermore, Frank Lowe is interested more in Jensen's recent behaviour than the accident and Jenny's medical condition. Each time Paul pauses, each time they stop to sip their coffees, Frank plants the down-dipping smile on his lips and records another note in a little coil-bound pad. When Paul nears the end of his narrative, the moment when he and Valerie discovered Chester's severed legs in the paper bag, he realizes he's provided an exemplary model of one-way information flow. How easy it is to tell all; and how powerful the inquisitor's discipline of silence.

"Then everything came to a head yesterday morning. When we found the neighbours' dog," Paul says and studies Frank's face. He seeks a sign of recognition, a hint that Frank has already been told the grisly details.

"You found the dog?"

"No. Just his legs, actually. In butcher's wrapper—a brown waxed paper bag."

Frank nods and puts his pad and pen aside. "Go on."

"I have them. Downstairs in the freezer." Paul points at the floor and Frank cocks his head to one side.

"Let's look at that a little later." There's an aspect to his expression suggesting this is exactly what he'd have done: preserve the evidence. "Tell me what happened yesterday after you found the dog's legs."

Paul concludes the story with the details of his visit to Jensen's Meats. He describes the prayer vigil with Fran and her two religious allies, the confrontation with Jensen in the garage, the game of Dead Eye, Jensen's confession to him. As if to prove the madness of yesterday's encounters, he pulls the collar of his T-shirt to one side and exposes a purple welt, now in full bloom on his left shoulder.

Frank Lowe gazes blankly at the bruise without comment. "Have you called the police?"

"We've had two go-rounds with them. Both times, things just became worse."

Frank runs a thumbnail along the length of his pen. "Did you see the remains of the dog anywhere?"

"Nowhere around here. And nothing at Jensen's place." Paul shrugs and with both hands wrapped around his mug, swills the dregs of his coffee around the bottom of the porcelain cup.

Frank nods and narrows his eyes as though he's well familiar with Paul's situation. The frustration, the exhaustion, the pain—all of these ingredients are present in the faces of people when they first call him for help. Now Frank's face, which reveals so little, hints at this moment of recognition. He leans forward in a manner that lifts Paul's eyes from the coffee cup. "All right," he says and smiles his patented, down-dipping smile. "I think I can help you with this."

Paul presses his lips together as he considers this statement. No one has said anything like this to him before, or said it with such confidence. It would be nice to believe Frank Lowe.

"Let's have a look at what you've got in the freezer."


Frank lifts one of the dog's limbs from the bag and holds it against the ceiling lamp. "You can rest assured the dog never felt a thing," he says. He's wearing surgical latex gloves, which he pulled from his back pocket and slipped over his fingers when Paul opened the freezer lid. He runs his thumb along the site of the amputation and studies it. "I spent two summers working in my uncle's butchery and I can tell you this is a professional cut. No burrs or abrasions. A live animal would have bucked like hell during the amputation."

Paul steps away from the freezer and leans against the doorway. It never occurred to him that Chester might have been alive while he was quartered. "That's good, then. Right?"

Frank ignores this question and examines the paper bag, dwells on the inscription written with a red marker: NEXT? "Sign of a wing-nut if I ever saw one," he mumbles and pulls a second limb from the bag. "Wait a minute. There's something's wrong here."

"What?"

"Where's the fourth leg?"

Paul realizes he omitted this part of his story to Lowe. "At Jensen's," he says and explains how he confronted him with one of Chester's legs. It was this piece of evidence that forced Jensen's confession and made his guilt undeniable.

"And made your visit there undeniable, too." Lowe clicks his tongue and tips his head to one side.

"What?"

"Over the years I've found that deniability is the one thing you want to preserve in any situation. In your case you want to be able to deny provocation. Leaving the dog's leg behind eliminates that option."

But the fourth limb is irrelevant, Paul thinks. There were witnesses to his visit: Fran and her two friends engaged in their seance. Even Andy Betz could be called in to confirm his trip to Esquimalt. But he doesn't protest. Frank Lowe is absolutely right; Paul has spent the best part of the past months perfecting criminal deniability, eliminating the traces of his assault against Jenny in every place but his own memory. This afternoon, with Rory, was the first time he'd lost his resolve.

"All right." Lowe slips the legs back into the bag and places it next to Valerie's frozen berries. "Let's see what we can find in Mr. Jensen's abattoir."

"Like what?" Paul steps through the door and clicks off the light.

"The dog's torso for starters." Frank Lowe pulls off the gloves with two brisk snaps from his wrists. "If we find that, I can get the police to lock him up. And if we lock him up we're likely to uncover a few other darlings in his little rat's nest."


"It must be ten years since I've been over to Victoria," Frank says as he tugs the plastic seal from an egg sandwich he'd purchased on the ferry. With one finger he pries the sandwich triangle from the packaging and bites into the white bread. "You get into a groove and tend to stay where you are. Even in my business," he adds in case Paul might be assuming there's a travel component to a PI career.

"What about when you were with the police?" Paul is sitting in the passenger seat of Frank Lowe's Ford Taurus. They are parked one door down from Jensen's Meats, on the opposite side of the street from the storefront, engaged in the most personal (yet still so very shallow) conversation that Frank has permitted. As Paul navigated the drive across town, Frank dropped his guard a centimetre or two, enough at least to reveal he has a life of his own. "Didn't police work get you out of town?"

"Occasionally." He swallows a bit of sandwich and pats the front of his wrist over his mouth. "But looking back on it, not more than once or twice a year."

"Were you with the RCMP?"

Frank shakes his head. "No. With Vancouver's finest. Homicide." He continues to work on his sandwich, diligently chews a length of crust.

"I don't travel much anymore either," Paul confesses when it's clear Frank isn't going to continue his autobiography. "Years ago, though, that's all I did. I spent almost five years on the road. Most of it in Africa and India."

"I heard about that." Frank rests his free hand on the steering wheel. He's rarely shifted his eyes away from the meat shop since they parked at the curb.

"You did?"

"From your wife. After your parents died and you and your girl-friend split ... " He stops himself as if he's revealed a little too much. "Like I said, I get as much information as I can about the case in hand."

Paul considers this as he stares out the window. He doesn't quite understand how his distant past is relevant to 'the case in hand,' but he realizes Frank Lowe found out much more than he needs to know. Paul stares at the meat shop, at the makeshift sign in the front window with its bleak message of hope:

PRAY

FOR

JENNY

They'd driven past the building twice and when Paul explained that Reg lived in the garage, Frank Lowe idled the car at the foot of the driveway and studied the premises for signs of activity. The Dodge 500 was parked next to the garage. The Mini he'd seen yesterday was not in sight. The path leading to the apartment door behind the butchery was cluttered with garbage from a can that had tipped over and been raided by crows or raccoons.

It's just after 9:00 o'clock and now that the evening dusk has enveloped them, they sit waiting for the house lights to come on. At least that's what Paul assumes—yet he feels more uncertain of what he's doing here now than he did the previous day when he barged in on Reg in his garage. Thinking back on it, he really had nothing more than a fantasy of how he would bring an end to Reg Jensen's cruel obsessions.

"Somebody's home," Frank says when a light from the back of the meat shop blinks on. He pulls a pair of micro-binoculars from the glove box and fits them to his eyes. "Did you go into the store yesterday?" He pushes the last corner of egg sandwich into his mouth and chews it slowly. The binoculars are wedged under his brow.

"For a few minutes." Paul leans forward. He can't make out any movement in the shop.

"Describe the layout."

He thinks a moment. "You go in and face a glassed-in counter full of meats. There's a cash register to one side. On the right, behind the cash, there's this long knife rack on the wall," he adds in order to provide a semblance of precise detail.

"Where's the meat locker?" Frank lowers his window a few centimetres to improve his vision. "You know, the refrigeration room."

"Behind the cash. Behind the meat counter to the left."

Frank Lowe sets the binoculars on his lap. "That's where the light's coming from," he says. He raises the window and slips the binoculars back into the glove box. "All right," he whispers, an affirmation meant only for himself. He pulls a cell phone from its belt clip and opens his coil pad, flicks a few pages and dials a number.

"Hello. Yes, I'm inquiring about my niece, Jenny Jensen. Can you connect me with her ward nurse?" There's a pause, then he continues. "I'm a relative of one of your patients, Jenny Jensen, and I called over from Vancouver earlier today to find out the best time to visit. I must have been speaking to the ward nurse on the morning shift, but I've forgotten the name.... " He let's this hang, waits for the name of the ward nurse to land in his lap. "That's it, Joel Howe. Anyway, Joel suggested I call ahead once I'm in town, and I'm—" Frank stops and begins to nod his head in rhythm to the response from the ward nurse. "Tomorrow. Nine to eleven. Or, one to three," he repeats. "Thanks."

He ends the connection and with barely a pause, flips to another page in his notebook and dials a new number. With each ring of the phone his tongue clicks lightly, moist puckers of impatience. After ten or more rings someone answers. "Hello?" he says with surprise. "Hello?" He eyes Paul, his face drawn down with a questioning look. "Yes, is Reg Jensen there, please.... Mr. Jensen, it's Joel Howe at the hospital. The ward nurse on Jenny's ward." He takes a shallow breath while Jensen responds. "Right. Listen, we have some news about Jenny. There's been a little motion in her left hand," he says with contained enthusiasm. "Yes. And the doctor thought it might help to have you here with her. If you could talk to her, it might help draw her further out." He waits a few seconds for the news to settle in. "Great. We'll see you in twenty minutes or so."

Frank Lowe closes the lid on his phone and clips it back onto his belt next to several other snap-case utilities. "Now we wait," he says and stares at the meat shop without a glance toward Paul.

Minutes later the red Dodge 500 backs out of the driveway and turns onto the street. Reg Jensen is visible behind the wheel as he tugs his jacket over his shoulder. Frank and Paul hunch next to the Taurus dashboard as Jensen drives past them.

Frank turns to Paul. "That him?"

"Yes. No question about it."

"He didn't take his wife with him."

"She could be there already. I've heard she spends almost every night at Jenny's side."

"You didn't tell me that. If I'd known that I would have told him to join her at the hospital. Now he might figure it out." Frank works his mouth into a frown. "You told me she was in some kind of prayer meeting. It sounded like a daily ritual."

"That was in the middle of the day," Paul says. There's a new tone—an attitude from Frank Lowe he hasn't noticed before. "I didn't say anything about it being a day-to-day thing." Paul casts his eyes across the street, away from the meat shop. Two teenage girls are walking a miniature poodle along the sidewalk. He watches them pass the Taurus and decides he doesn't like Frank Lowe. He doesn't like his manipulations and he doesn't like this insinuation that he's misled him.

Frank glances at his watch, waits a minute or two, then checks it again. "All right," he says and pulls something into his fist. "I want you to stay here. This is a two-way beeper." He opens his hand to reveal a black plastic device the size of a cigarette lighter. "It's made simple for a simple reason. You press this button and it beeps my connection." A light beeping noise sounds in another pocket. From it he extracts an identical beeper. He clicks the button on the second beeper and the sound terminates. "Now if I press my beeper, then you get an alert." He touches the small plastic tab and the first beeper sounds. He clicks it off and places it in Paul's hand. "Simple enough?" He tips his head to one side with a dismissive look that suggests even a moron could handle this toy.

Paul palms the beeper. "So what do I do with it?"

"You sit here. You watch." Frank Lowe holds two fingers to his eyes then points them at the meat shop. "You beep me on one condition only: if Jensen returns before I get back to the car. Got it?"

Paul nods.

"Try it," Frank says and stares at Paul's face until he clicks the beeper. Frank turns his off the moment it sounds. "All right. I don't know how long I'll be, so don't feel you have to come looking. All right?"

Paul shrugs off this last comment. At this point he can't imagine why anyone would come looking for Frank Lowe.

As Frank jogs across the street Paul realizes how fit he looks. He's a foot taller than Reg Jensen and his shoulders are like bulwarks set in place to turn back a flood. Even his jacket can't disguise the tight webs of muscle lining his chest and back. Yet he treads lightly, his feet dance across the sidewalk and up the rutted driveway to Jensen's garage. Paul watches him fidget with the garage door a moment, then in one move he slips it open and disappears inside.

Paul studies the garage expecting the lights to click on or the door to swing open and Frank to dash back to the car with Chester's lost limb hanging from one hand. But nothing happens. There are no shadows illuminated by a passing flashlight, no outbursts of panic, no scent of death in the air. After five minutes the low buzz in Paul's ears seems to fade. His sensation of emptiness turns awkward and the strange isolation he feels becomes an acid drip in his belly.

Then it occurs to him: you were under Frank Lowe's surveillance, too. The thought stuns him. What exactly had Frank said? That he knew Paul had travelled about for a few years. He'd pried this bit of information from Valerie. She told him about his parents' accident and that afterward he and his *girlfriend split*.... Frank Lowe stopped at that point. Stopped because he knew he'd said a few words too many. Paul never told Valerie about Michelle LaBaie, about her breakdown and their broken relationship. Never mentioned a word to her.

Paul turns his head from Jensen's Meats and stares at the apartment building on the opposite side of the road. A few trees stand beside the sidewalk in the middle of a narrow strip of grass. Now two other pieces of the puzzle lock into place: Wally had said he'd hired Frank Lowe about ten years ago, and Frank revealed he hadn't been to Victoria in a decade. All of this occurred around the same time Valerie and Paul announced their engagement. So ... when Wally realized his only child was about to marry, he hired Frank to conduct a background check on Paul. That would explain Wally's reticence to disclose why he'd hired Frank so many years ago. During his investigation, Frank had somehow dug up his past life with Michelle LaBaie. Had he spoken to her? If he did—what did she reveal?

As Paul considers these deceits, he notices the red Dodge 500 wheeling up the road and turning onto the lip of Jensen's driveway. He ducks under the dashboard, wondering if he's too late—if Jensen has seen him and will now storm over to the Taurus, pull him onto the road and gut him in a blind rage. He draws a deep breath and clicks the little button on the beeper. At the same time Jensen guns the throttle on the Dodge and it lunges up the driveway. A second later Paul's beeper sounds. He clicks it off and feels a sense of relief. Frank Lowe has been warned—but is it warning enough?

Paul lifts his eyes above the dash. He can't detect any changes in the scene, except now the Dodge is back in its place in the driveway. There is no sign of Jensen or Lowe. There are no lights illuminating the garage, the apartment or the meat shop. This absence of activity soon fills him with dread. The dread of stalking, of the hunter and his prey, the vulnerability of remaining where he sits.

Paul reverses the switch on the car's dome light and carefully opens the passenger door. He sets one foot on the curb, then the other. He kneels on the sidewalk without lifting his head above the frame of the car. He pinches the door closed and glances over his shoulders at the trees behind him, the shrubs nestled against the stucco apartment building, a row of garbage pails lining a low wood fence. The neighbourhood is silent, badly lit, hidden in shadows.

He steps back onto the lawn behind him and conceals his body behind a tree. He scans the meat shop and garage. Nothing. He glances at the two other maple trees along the sidewalk, and considers if they might offer a better vantage point and more protection. In the second he looks away, a single light in Jensen's apartment clicks on. He leans forward and listens. A moment later all the lights in the garage switch on in a single flash. The effect is palpable. The light floods across the road, onto the Taurus and against his tree. He pulls himself into the narrow shadow and clutches his fists.

With his head drawn back he tunes his ears for any noise that might offer a clue to Lowe's whereabouts. What if Frank runs back to the car, speeds away and leaves Paul behind? That seems quite likely now. With Jensen on the prowl, Frank can only be thinking about escape. He'd told Paul to stay put. It was dead simple, he'd said. But now you'd screwed that up, too. Moron.

When he hears a door slam, Paul edges his head past the tree trunk. Now the lights in the meat shop come up and he can see someone walk toward the meat counter and the cash register. There is a brief hesitation, then the man raises an arm above his head. Seconds later the butcher shop blinks into darkness. There is a pause followed by a terrible crashing noise, a scream and a gush of shattering glass as it sprays across the tile floor.

After sprinting across the road, Paul stands outside the meat shop at the front window, his head next to the sign that reads PRAY FOR JENNY. His breathing comes in hard, shallow bursts and he wonders what to do. He can make out nothing inside the store. He hears a sliding noise, like a mop swabbing wet glass on the floor. As he listens he can hear a low moaning and an angry mutter of barely audible curses. He waits a moment until the weight of the disaster inside the shop presses him to make a decision. He could run, but the instant this option arises, it sinks into impossibility. He knows he must call the police. Jensen has achieved some new level of destruction that he cannot face alone.

The instant he decides to call the police the beeper in his pocket sounds. The electric buzz startles him, deafens the strange sweeping noise in the shop, the raw muttering that bleeds through the darkness to the window. He pulls the beeper from his pocket and presses the button. A few seconds later the beeper sounds again. He presses the button firmly and again it buzzes back at him. He swears mutely at it and holds his finger on the small plastic knob to ensure its silence. He closes his eyes and tries to think what has gone wrong. He knows that if he releases his finger and the alarm sounds again that it can mean one thing only: Frank Lowe is inside and unable to save himself.

He lifts his finger from the button and it buzzes a last time. He stretches his arm over his head and pitches the beeper toward the Taurus where it clatters onto the asphalt and slides under the car. When he's sure he can no longer hear the thing, he nods with some satisfaction. He's done one thing right, he decides. It's like hitting a baseball with a bat, a physical act that mobilizes his body and pushes him forward to the front door to the store. Now that he's succeeded at this small thing, he leans on the glass door with confidence and feels it yielding to his weight as he steps into the butcher shop.

As he stands there the smell of meat fills his nose. He can still hear the sound of wet mopping and now the distinct voice of Jensen muttering in pain: "Fuck. Fuck. Fuck."

Paul sweeps a hand over the wall and when he finds the light switch he clicks it on. The fluorescent lamps hesitate, then sputter alive with their cold white light. Paul swings his head from the mess on the floor to the broken meat counter past the cash register and into the open door of the meat locker.

Frank Lowe lies on the floor in a pool of broken glass and crushed ice. He holds one hand to the flap of skin that has torn away from the bottom of his chin. Although his mouth wags in desperation as he tries to cry out a warning, he cannot speak. His free hand is gripping his beeper and his arm draws back and forth across the floor, swilling his own blood with shards of glass and ice and the slices of meat that have crashed to the floor from the broken meat counter. When he notices Paul standing above him, Frank's panic eases a little. His arm stops its compulsive sweeping and he points toward Jensen who stands doubled over next to the meat locker.

Paul steps into the middle of the room and stares at Jensen. He has stopped his rhythmic swearing and lifts his head to examine Paul. His eyes are exhausted and bloodshot. His face is drawn, his mouth open, fixed in a loose snarl from too many hours of drinking. "Fuck you," he cries and arches his back with a rabid energy. When his torso lifts above the broken frame of the meat counter, Paul sees he's been handcuffed by one wrist to a steel railing next to the cash register. In his other hand he holds a filleting knife. The narrow blade is smeared with wet blood.

When he sees the knife, Paul instinctively backs away, then bends down to Frank Lowe. He pulls his jacket off and fits a sleeve under Frank's chin to staunch the bleeding. Frank blinks and nods his head. His face reveals a sense of calm and he lifts his hand to point at Jensen again.

"I see him," Paul whispers. "You've got him locked up."

Frank blinks with tension and grips Paul's hand, forces it in the direction of the meat locker.

"Over there?"

Frank blinks again. Yes.

Paul eases towards the locker, careful to keep an eye on Jensen who is now braced against the cash register and the rail that holds his locked wrist, his body contorted with a mass of writhing emotions. With every step he takes toward the open locker, Paul's feet crush the glass and ice into the floor. He tiptoes forward, his balance uncertain as he leans against the open meat-locker door.

The cool air caresses his face and hands, his torso and chest. A refrigeration fan churns slowly at the top of the far wall. The frosted shelves are half-full with meat stacked in uneven blocks on the long metal shelves. Sides of beef hang suspended from steel hooks the length of his forearm. Then he recognizes what is hanging from the two hooks on the opposite wall. At first he can not quite make them out. Perhaps it's because he has never been this close to such depravity. Or perhaps it's the shock of seeing them here, in this cold place. Floating above him are the two women who kept the prayer vigil with Fran Jensen, the women who had conspired to sell the meat shop without Reg Jensen's consent. The palms of their hands are neatly pressed together, steepled in a posture of reverent prayer and wired in place so their fingers touch the top of their breastbones. He'd used piano wire, one- or two-metre-long strands of it to bind their bodies in these carefully articulated postures. It seemed that if Paul could clip the wires that held them in place, the two women might open their eyes and spread their wings and fly to their reward in heaven. But of course that was impossible now. They would never fly anywhere again. Sometime in the last day, sometime before they could take flight from Jensen's madness, they had been impaled through their necks upon separate meat hooks and now the grey steel tips protruded four or five centimetres from the centre of their throats.

# CHAPTER 16

THE LAST TIME THEY MET, JACK WISE GAVE PAUL A PRINT OF THE *RAINBOW MANDALA* AND THE ARTIST'S PROOF OF A WOODCUT HE CALLED *EARTH GODDESS WITH SPEECH SCROLLS*. In exchange, Paul delivered his final revision of Jack's nine-page *curriculum vitae*.

"Thank you," Jack said and he studied a few lines on each page, nodding his head in agreement with every phrase he read. "I really couldn't have done this on my own." The expression on his face was of genuine gratitude, as though he'd been favoured by a minor miracle.

Paul welcomed this generosity. In fact, the task of compiling Jack's artistic accomplishments became both inspirational and humbling. He discovered that as a young man Jack had apprenticed himself to an internal vision. After his initial success, he stumbled in this apprenticeship and then entered a period of artistic agnosticism and despair. Ultimately he renewed his efforts by unifying two apparently opposite worlds: the minute, disciplined squiggles of calligraphy and the mesmerizing form of the archetypal mandala. The radiant fusion that emerged was critically acclaimed as the rejuvenation of an ancient tradition in contemporary western art.

The greater triumph, however, lay in Jack's artistic tenacity, his simple, unrelenting belief that his life's purpose was to render the vision that presented itself to him through his brush strokes. He did not care much about money, nor even selling his work, for that matter. His conviction that the serendipitous forces that shaped his paintings also guided the fortunes of his physical life was unshake-able—even as his health began to fail. This was the manner in which Life governed the living, he said. It was so obvious. "For me, the only unanswered question," he said, "is why can't everyone see it?"

He unrolled the *Rainbow Mandala* on top of the corner table in Foo Hong's, as though he were just discovering the painting for the first time. It was a print (number 123 in a series of 375) produced on a sixty-centimetre-square sheet. His eyes darted back and forth across this brilliant microcosm, absorbing the precise intricacies of the calligraphy overlapping the concentric circles as they flowed to-ward the pink lotus at the mandala's heart. Then he sat upright and gazed at the aquamarine background, a flat sea on which the image floated, his fingers sweeping above the surface as he mused aloud: "This is the only mandala without an outer ring of fire. Normally the fire is there to purge and cleanse. But I don't know why this painting doesn't have one," he added and held his hand to his chin with a look of amused confusion.

Paul stared at the painting, marvelling that this gift would soon hang on a wall in his condo. He thought it was beautifully crafted, at once enormously complex in its detail, yet the epitome of sim-plicity in form. "What is this?" he asked, pointing to one of the four hexagrams that formed bridges leading to the pink lotus in the centre.

"The four gates to enlightenment," he said. "Each is a hexagram from the *I Ching*: the Creative, Fellowship with Men, Self-Possession and the Receptive. They all have multiple interpretations, but each one describes a route to enlightenment. Even the least likely path, through Fellowship with Men, can lead to nirvana. It's a bit like the European notion of the fool who stumbles into paradise."

"You think we can stumble into paradise?" After so much talk of

The Mind and destiny and disciplined consciousness, this last statement from Jack seemed out of sync.

"Why not?" he asked as his eyebrows rose on his forehead. "There's a huge element of luck in all of this." His hand swept through the room indicating the restaurant patrons, the pedestrians dodging traffic on the street outside, and all the world beyond. "The very fact we exist—Jack and Paul, here together, shaking hands good-bye," he said and reached out and shook Paul's hand with another smile, "it's all a piece of luck, don't you think? Luck and chance are simply the hammer-and-nails—the construction tools— of Fate."

Hammer-and-nails. They've been driven into him with short, flat punches, and as Paul listens to his answers to each of Sergeant Rick Manson's questions in his office at the Victoria Police Department, he realizes how deeply he's been wounded over the past months.

To begin with, Manson appears flummoxed by Chester's missing leg. The fact that Paul took it over to Jensen's astounds Manson and his face puckers with a look of incredulity. "Can you tell me why you did that?"

"Looking back," Paul confesses, "I don't understand it myself. It wasn't rational." He lifts his hands then lets them flop onto his lap.

"Sometimes people stop making sense," Manson says and presses the tip of his pen to his lips. "I guess in some cases it can go on for months."

Paul lets this pass. "So did anybody in your team find the remains of the dog?" he asks.

Manson shakes his head once. "You don't really want to think about what probably happened to that dog."

No, he doesn't want to think about that at all. Or anything else for that matter. But with Manson's prodding he can't stop thinking about what happened at Jensen's Meats a few hours earlier. Reliving the nightmare is unavoidable, he decides, and after he sets the context about Jensen stalking his son—and reminds Manson to check the police files about Jeanine's previous complaint—he relates the story from the time Frank Lowe arrived that evening. He describes everything up to the point where he entered the meat shop, then he stops. He realizes the events that followed are suspended somehow, lifted from his memory into a realm of speculation.

As he slumped against the doorframe to the cold storage locker—when he saw the women hanging from the meat hooks—he lurched backward as a knot of vomit shot up his throat and spewed onto the floor. He gagged and wiped his hand over his face and stumbled to where Frank Lowe lay on the ice and broken glass, his face now blanched and unmoving. Then it occurred to him: Frank is dying. The steady bleeding from his throat will drain away his life within minutes.

Paul pulled himself toward the cash register, grabbed the telephone and dialled 9-1-1. As he spoke to the responder he eyed Jensen cautiously. He was still doubled over, panting and whispering a long line of curses. Paul guessed that Frank started his surveillance in Reg Jensen's garage, then made his way into the apartment. From there he found an inside corridor leading into the meat shop. Moments after he discovered the murdered women, Reg caught him by surprise. They struggled until Frank clipped a handcuff to Reg's right wrist and the other cuff to a railing. Frank had managed to get in two or three solid blows and probably ruptured Jensen's kidney. Frank realized too late that the rail was in fact a knife rack—and too late to dodge Reg's uppercut with the filleting knife that opened a wide flap of skin above Frank's throat. The shock sent Frank crashing into the glass counter and onto the floor.

At least, that's what Paul imagined. And he could only guess at what he'd told the police when they arrived at the meat shop. He found himself squatting next to Frank, pressing his jacket sleeve against the open wound. He pointed lamely to the meat locker and one by one, the police and ambulance attendants glanced into the makeshift abattoir and turned away with a look of horror. Sergeant Manson had the good sense to fish the handcuff keys from a pouch on Frank's belt and unlock Jensen. Then he fit his own pair of cuffs around both Jensen's wrists and led him away from the shop.

Paul expected to bump into Jensen at the police station, but he hadn't seen him since he left the shop. Although he knows he'll have to confront him again at his trial, he swears to himself that he'll never look into his face again. It was too much to bear. But when he thinks deeply on it, sitting on the vinyl chair in Manson's office, he realizes his worst fear about meeting him again is that he might see part of himself—his own hammer-and-nails—in Reg Jensen's Fate.

In the hours that followed the fight in the meat shop, he was shunted through a bureaucratic gauntlet. It began at the crime scene with a few probes about why he was there and what had happened. When it dawned on Manson that Paul was a key witness to the double murder, he was driven to the police station and thoroughly interrogated. Recordings were made, notes taken, questions repeated three, then four times. Finally he was driven home, dropped off at his door a little after 3:00 in the morning.

His first call to Valerie is a rush of incoherent blathering that lasts less than a minute.

"What are you saying?" she asks after he blurts out a few details of the murder. She'd been asleep, of course, and unable to construct any sense from his outburst.

"That I need you to come home. With Eliot." He holds one hand to his eyes, pressing the lids shut. "Jensen killed two women. And maybe Frank Lowe, too. They've arrested him. But it's safe now," he adds. "Everything's safe," he says again, wanting to believe it.

"What?" Her voice is breathless, almost inaudible.

"Just come home," he cries and hangs up the phone. He can hold back no longer. "Come home!" he wails to himself and collapses on his bed and winds the bed sheets around his legs and arms and chest until he can no longer move. Then he buries his face in a pillow to muffle his crying until exhaustion—and sleep—overwhelm him.

The next morning Valerie and Eliot arrive a little before noon. When he first sees them, he's surprised by how fresh they look. How innocent.

Eliot runs up the steps and hugs his father around the waist. He presses his cheek against his belly and holds it there until Valerie stands beside them.

"Hello," she says. "I missed you." Her voice is tender. It makes a claim on him. When he wraps an arm over her shoulder she kisses him and he buries his face in her hair and inhales the aroma of her skin.

"Let's go inside," he says, and they wedge through the front door, his arms bound around his wife and son as they bump down the gallery into the kitchen. When Eliot begins to laugh he releases him and kisses Valerie.

"Eliot has something to tell you." She tilts her head to one side and pinches her lips together, waits for Eliot to pick up this cue. "Do you remember what you wanted to tell Dad?"

Paul looks at them both. "What?"

"Let's sit down." Valerie leads Eliot to the table and stands him beside her as she sits in the maple chair. "Eliot?" She slips an arm around his waist.

Paul sits and waits. Clearly some kind of confession has been extracted from the boy and now a second testimony has to be delivered.

"Do you remember the window," Eliot begins, "the one that was mysteriously broken?" He accentuates *mysteriously*, as if the mystery itself is greater than the cost of repair.

Valerie dips her head behind Eliot and winks at Paul. She smiles her lovely, consuming, generous smile.

"Yes. All three hundred and fifty-two dollars of it. Indeed, I do remember that window very dearly," he says wanting to string this out, this mood he detects among them. It makes him feel like a father again. Almost wholesome.

"So.... " He eyes his mother and when she nods, he continues, "The mystery is solved."

"It is?" Paul sinks his chin into one hand and props an elbow on the table. "Then there must be a tale to tell." He wants this to last. He wants Eliot to spin a very long story about a crow that dropped a rock through their window as it chased after a vagrant seagull. Or about a bear that threw an empty honey pot through the window in frustration. Although he can guess what is coming, he wants the suspense of it to last so he can taste the innocence of his child offering up his hard truth.

"James Parker did it," he says and pulls his lower lip over his teeth. "I was with him," he offers; an afterthought. "It was the baseball he got from the Seattle Mariners game last year. We were in the backyard and he threw me a pitch and I missed it." Now that the basic confession is out, Eliot seems quite willing to reveal all. "But he wouldn't let me keep the ball here to show you what had happened. 'Cause his dad would've killed him when he found out. It was the same ball his dad caught when Mark McGwire fouled it, then got him to sign it after the game. So that's why we put that big rock on the floor … so it looked like the rock had broken the window."

"Wow." Paul shakes his head with a look of amazement. "I didn't know his dad caught a foul from Mark McGwire," he says to deflect any further guilt that Eliot might suffer. He'd said enough; and Paul doesn't want to lead the conversation into the lies that had followed the original fabrication: That the Ratman had broken the window. That they'd seen him lurking around Transit Road after school.

"Yeah. He did." Eliot looks at his mother—who shrugs away his glance—and then back at his father. "I already told you his dad caught the ball."

"Really? Gee, tell me again." Indeed, he did know the story of Mark McGwire's foul ball. But the story was a good one and he wants the tale told again, full of fresh surprise and the intimate brush with celebrity. He needs to hear Eliot talk about his friend's triumph in a way that will make it his own. And he wants it to last a long, long time.

An hour later he receives a call from Andy Betz. Andy stumbles through his first few sentences, revealing that he'd heard about the double murder on the radio that morning and remembered that Reg Jensen was involved in the kayaking accident.

"It was his daughter, wasn't it?" Andy asks. "Isn't she still in the hospital?"

"Yes," Paul replies, hoping Andy will accept this response to both questions. "That's right."

"Did you hear what happened to him last night? What he did?"

For the first time Paul realizes he must prepare a public response, a formal position that will frame his role in this latest tragedy with Jensen. Andy is the first of many people who will ask him about the double murders and his part in the crime. "Yes," he says again. "Listen, Andy. I need to tell you something about this. But I need you to keep it to yourself. At least until you hear it from everyone else," he adds with a dull laugh, certain it will be impossible to contain the rumours. "I was there. Last night ... I was there."

Paul can hear a gasp on the line, a burst of air without words.

"I was the guy who called 9-1-1," he adds, as if this detail will authenticate his claim. He thinks a moment and then considers what his lawyer might tell him: say nothing. Tell no one. "But as you can imagine, Andy, I can't say anything while there's an investigation going on."

"From what I heard two hours ago the investigation is already wrapped up." Andy's voice lifts a little, as though he's pleased to provide some fresh information. Important information. "Apparently Jensen confessed to the whole thing. Both murders. It looks like he's headed to a slammer for the criminally insane."

Paul weighs what this might mean. The ropes knotted around him for so long are suddenly unravelling. He takes a deep breath and asks, "Are you sure he confessed?"

"During his arraignment this morning. It was on the noon hour news, my friend."

Paul stares through the window onto the empty street. A light rain falls on the asphalt. He'll have to call Ben Stillwell and find out what this means. Was it over? Was Paul now free of his on-going dread?

"I can't imagine anyone will let Reg Jensen out of his cell for a very, very long time," Andy continues. Paul envisions Andy hoisting his thick feet onto his desktop, relaxing into the attitude he adopts when he's certain about something. When he sees a clear path forward.

A week later, Paul meets with his lawyer. As always, Ben Stillwell communicates an air of preoccupation. Paul sits in the chair opposite the grand desk while his lawyer shifts a few folders next to his computer. "Let's see, let's see," he mumbles before settling on Paul's file. "So, a lot has changed," he says when he can bring his full attention to his client.

"Everything has changed," Paul says. He's never felt this kind of relief before, the heady sense of reprieve. "But you tell me. What are the legal implications of Jensen's confession—and of the new deal his wife has offered?"

Ben rolls his shoulders. "The implications of his confession to the murders are certain. I doubt we'll see him for another twenty years, maybe—the way things can go—you'll never see him again. Depends on how he does his time. What happens after that? Who knows.... " He frowns, a hint that on the other hand, Jensen could emerge from incarceration with unrelieved bitterness. "But regarding the civil suit, he's lost custody of his daughter. Fran Jensen now has sole parental discretion about how to proceed with the civil suit. Apparently she wants to settle out of court and—we have an offer." Ben opens the file and hands a new document to Paul.

Paul scans the pages before him, all of them filled with numbered and lettered clauses. "What does it mean?"

"Remember, the best outcome would have been to sever you from the case entirely." Ben smiles, a rarity, Paul realizes, and as soon as he thinks this, the smile fades. "What we have is our second-best-case scenario. The suit will be settled out of court and all clauses of the settlement will be sealed. No one can disclose the nature of the agreement, the assigned liabilities, or the amounts paid by individuals or corporations to the ongoing care of Jennifer Jensen. Your personal liability is limited to the amount covered by your insurance: one million dollars."

Paul leans back in his chair and brushes his fingers against his chin. It's all over. Finally, cleanly, totally over. "So ... that's it?"

"Apart from the details I have to work out with the other lawyers. If you accept what we work out, then you'll have to come in once more to sign it off. The last step is for the public trustee and guardian to approve the agreement. That's required in cases like this, for what the law refers to as infant settlements."

Paul gazes out the window. A dull rain washes over Broughton Street. "Ben ... I can't believe it. Really. I—"

"Trust me. Believe it." Ben leans forward and nods his head. "It's good news, isn't it?"

"Yes."

Ben nods his head again. "And I want to thank you, too."

"For what?"

"Rory told me you came to see him." He lets this hang in the air, then continues, "He felt relieved by whatever you told him."

"I don't know what I said…. " He feels a tinge of embarrassment, a realization that the brothers were never close and that to disclose Rory's obsessions with Valerie now would lessen Ben's esteem for his wayward brother.

"I don't know that it matters what you said. The fact you wanted to see him was enough."

Paul wonders if he should reveal that they'd only met once before, years ago when Rory returned from Europe to discover Valerie had married him. "Is he feeling all right?"

"He's still … with us." Ben closes the manila folder. "For a little longer, a least," he says and places the file on a pile next to his computer.

That evening, for the first time since the accident, Paul's family resumes a pattern of normalcy, a welcome return to a familiar ambiance in the Wakefield home. Eliot has settled into bed and while Paul stacks the pots and pans in the kitchen dish drainer, Valerie sits at the table leafing through art catalogues and making a few notes in the back of her daytimer. It's just after nine o'clock and Paul tunes the radio to CBC. The *Ideas* show is in mid-stride and he tries to grasp the thematic gist as the narrator cobbles together an argument based on interviews with disparate experts. There is some discussion about the nineteenth-century poet William Blake and a special guest who has a theory about Blake's visions, or rather—and perhaps this is the gist—his hallucinations.

"Did you ever study the art of William Blake?" Paul asks.

"A little." Valerie doesn't look up from her note-taking. "He's too romantic for my liking. And too pedantic."

Paul nudges the radio knob so the volume will distract Valerie.

In his second year at McGill he read some of Blake's poetry and liked what he could understand of it, and now he thinks Valerie ought to hear what the experts have to say. Maybe they will bring her around.

The discussion of William Blake on the radio shifts to an examination of near-death experiences, the similar visions encountered by scores of survivors who report that a deceased loved one came to escort them toward a radiant light in the heavens. Then a theory is offered by a dull voice from Harvard, a psycho-neurologist with a team of students who have completed a study of some kind proving these multiple, parallel near-death experiences can be explained by special neurons tripping off simultaneously and creating hallucinations of God's embrace.

"So what if it's *just* neurons?" Paul says to the radio. He turns to Valerie and continues, "Maybe that was God's plan. To give us all special neurons that fire off so we can see Him in our final seconds." It was one more example of science trying to outflank the soul without realizing that the ground on which the scientists laid their argument was simply a newly discovered tract of ancient spiritual firmament. That was what Jack would say, or something like that. He wished Jack had written down the essence of his rambling theories, distilled the core of his thinking, like Marcus Aurelius. Thank the gods that Marcus had discovered a key to it all, a way of coping—and left his guidebook behind.

"Can you answer the phone?" Valerie says without looking up. "And maybe switch to the jazz station."

Paul now hears the buzz of the phone, wondering how Valerie had heard it and he hadn't. He hits the preset radio button for KPLU and picks up the telephone handset.

"Hello?"

"Is that Paul Wakefield?" the voice is ephemeral, a whisper just called back from the dead.

"Yes?" Paul steps into the gallery, out of range from the radio's blasting trumpet, a wild Miles Davis solo.

"This is Fran Jensen." She pauses a moment, as if she's gathering strength to continue. "Do you have a minute?"

Paul agrees to meet Fran at the long-term care hospital that tends to Jenny's needs. Although she never articulates it, Paul understands that Fran needs some kind of closure and that he is both the first and last link in the chain that binds her to her daughter's side through the continuing watch. As far as he's concerned, visiting the girl means stepping backwards in time, back to where he'd been and—if things go badly—to be dragged under once again by some unforeseeable danger. .

He consults with Valerie and Ben Stillwell and gathers some assurance from both of them. Now that Reg is locked away, Valerie's sympathies for Fran emerge with guarded generosity. Fran has lost almost everything, she says. And the little she's been able to salvage is paid with the sacrifice of her best friends and husband. "Of course you can't do anything for her in any material way. But she's lost the father of her only child," Valerie adds and looks at Paul in a way that expresses the subtle bond between her and Fran.

Ben is more cautious, but he too can understand Fran's plea, and the need to respond to her desperation. "But you must not—can not—discuss anything to do with the settlement," he warns. He calls Fran Jensen's lawyer, Bonnie Emerson, who in turn advises her not to speak of the civil suit. Nor should Paul bring up the murders or Reg Jensen's incarceration; Fran is seeing a psychiatrist who's concerned about her stability. Ben even offers to accompany Paul, but after debating this possibility, Paul decides to proceed alone. When he considers all that has transpired, he realizes he wants to see Jenny for his own reasons. The image of her lying comatose, her life suspended a few days after her thirteenth birthday, draws him toward her. The impulse to visit her is odd—perhaps even depraved—and he mentions it to no one.

Just follow the ground rules, he reminds himself as he enters the ward where Jenny has been lodged. Everyone's sticking to the rules and it will be best to let Fran do most of the talking. After all, what do you have to say? He thinks of his secret—his lie—that was well buried now. It bears no marker, no cross; it is covered by the soil of the past where it slowly decays from memory into oblivion.

He enters her private room, B16, a pale green chamber in the middle of a long corridor with a south-facing window overlooking a scant stretch of lawn. A curtain is drawn in front of the bed and Paul stands at its near end, wondering what private communion might be engaged on the other side of the drape. He coughs lightly and hears the ruffle of someone stretching, as though rising from a long nap.

A hand eases the drape to one side and he sees Fran Jensen. Her face is drawn, her eyes as bloodshot as when he last saw her outside her apartment door. Paul tries to remember her as the proud mother of a feisty young girl, her short blond hair pinched under a baseball cap as she paddled toward Discovery Island. He remembers Fran's generous, easy manner as she passed the baggie of trail mix among the rafted kayaks as they rolled above the water on the matted seaweed before they passed into the fog bank. Her hair is matted now, layered in dirty, shellacked clumps over her ears, and her body moves with a brittle stoop as she pulls the drape open and leads the way to one of two chairs beside the hospital bed.

"This is where I usually sit," she says and pats the back of the chair with fond familiarity.

"Why don't you sit there, then." Paul tips his head to one side, a gesture of deference.

"No, today that's for you. I'll sit here," she says and drags the second chair beside him.

They sit down and Paul shifts slightly, just enough to move Fran Jensen from his line of sight. He examines Jenny cautiously, checks to ensure her breathing is steady and her face free of any scars. When he realizes that she is very much alive, a sense of surprise wells through him. She is an image of contrasts. On the one hand, her closed eyes have sunk into their sockets, her complexion is sallow and her cheeks are concave from her lingering weight loss. And yet she is perfectly groomed and preened: her hair washed and brushed, a cotton nightie buttoned just under her chin, the bedcovers pulled over her breasts and folded as though someone has just made up the bed with her in it. More surprising is the absence of medical devices surrounding her. There are the standard items, of course: an iv drip stands beside the night table. A heart monitor ticks silently above her, its wire leads tucked under the sheets where they are attached, he guesses, to her chest. He assumes there must also be a catheter, but he cannot see it. But there are no air pumps, no artificial life-support systems securing her tenuous grasp to life. Her face is clear and unmarked. Most strange is the manner in which her weight loss enhances her look of fragility, or rather, he decides, her delicate sensibility.

"It seems like she's sleeping," he says after a period of silence.

Fran nods with a look of sympathy. "To me she looks like a sugar plum fairy. Like she's napping between acts in a school play."

"Yes." Paul shifts in the chair again and glances at Fran.

"I've never seen it except on TV, but in *The Nutcracker*, there's little girl dancers who fall into a dream. That's how I think of her. She's fallen into a dream. All she has to do is wake up. Then she can go back to dancing again."

Paul presses his lips together and wonders about this possibility. Maybe it could happen that easily. Jenny's quietude seems so temporary; merely a nap, as her mother says. As he contemplates this, he notices the photographs above her bed, two amateur snapshots, one on each side of the steel headboard. He studies them a moment and realizes they are the two women impaled in the meat locker. They are Fran's murdered friends, her prayer vigil group, now suspended next to her daughter's sleeping form.

"They're angels, now," Fran whispers in anticipation of his question.

Paul's jaw hinges open as the image of their bodies hooked to the wall of the meat locker flashes through his mind. He would like to ask her what she knows of that terrible day. Of all the victims available to him, why had Reg killed them? And how had he managed this feat of madness without alerting Fran or the shopkeeper who purchased the meat shop from her a few days earlier?

"I don't know why he came back that night," she says, and Paul understands that she's continuing an ongoing conversation with herself, mulling over the same questions. "Or why he bound them up like angels. He never believed in anything like that."

He came back because he saw Frank Lowe's Taurus was parked on the street, Paul says to himself. He hesitated as he pulled out of the driveway and hesitated again when he returned. Somehow he guessed he was under surveillance. Perhaps he'd come back to the shop to clear away the evidence of his crime. Then he discovered

Frank Lowe in the store and realized he had to fight his way out of trouble. But Paul speaks none of this to Fran and when the growing silence becomes uncomfortable, he glances at her and says, "No, I guess he didn't."

"But I believe they're still praying for her now. They can pray for her constantly now because they have no need for sleep any more."

"Yes, I imagine they can now. Day and night." He draws a deep breath and presses a hand to his mouth. A feeling of nausea rises from his stomach and he swallows hard to force it back into his belly. He has to conclude this soon, find a discreet way to steer the conversation toward his exit.

"That's why I'm glad you agreed to come," she continues. "You were there when the accident happened. And I'm glad you're here now."

He looks at her with remorse. Her needs are so simple. To sit here, to maintain her vigil, to draw comfort from the one person who might understand her despair. How could he abandon her simple request? "You know, it's good for me to see her like this," he says and he drops his hand from his mouth. "I guess I needed to see that she wasn't ... broken."

"Oh, she's not broken." Fran smiles, pleased that someone else can see the bright hope in her daughter's condition. "She just needs to wake up. Tell me, will you pray for her?" She continues to smile and lifts her eyebrows in anticipation.

Paul straightens his back and nods in agreement. "Of course." Yes, he will pray for her, every night if he can. "Would you mind if I have a closer look at her face?"

Fran's head ticks to one side as her body is caught by a brief spasm. "Go ahead," she says. "That would be all right."

Paul walks along the bedside and stands above the girl. He leans over and studies the side of her cheek, the temple where he bashed the kayak paddle against her skull. "There's no bruising."

"No. That part has healed already."

Paul lifts his head from Jenny's face and turns to Fran. "I will pray for her. I promise." He fixes her in his eyes to assure her that he means this. "But before I can do that, I would like to have a minute alone with her. Just with the curtain drawn," he adds pointing to the drape along the bedside.

Fran considers this. "I'll just be here," she says and tugs at the drape, gathering it around the ceiling track with her stiff, angular motions.

When he is alone with the girl, Paul leans forward again, tilts his head down to her face. He can smell her skin, the odour of lavender soap still on her flesh. There is no trace of her injury at all. He leans closer until his forehead touches her hair and he kisses the small, flat line of the temple above her ear. "I'm sorry," he whispers. He presses his fingers to his mouth to stop himself from breaking down. "I am so very, very sorry."


As he waits in bed for Valerie to join him, Paul wonders about what Eliot has seen—and what remains invisible—of the events they have suffered through. He has seen much, of course, but never commented on any of it that didn't directly impact on him. There is the story of the Ratman following him from school. His lie about the broken window. The panic and escape to Wally and Jeanine's home in Vancouver. Apart from these episodes, Eliot has developed an impervious attitude, an understanding that he'll let the adults handle their troubles and he will deal with his own.

"He is such a good boy. He still cuddles right under my arm when we read," Valerie says as she closes their bedroom door. She's embarked on a new program to read her favourite childhood books to him, beginning with *Anne of Green Gables*.

"He's more than good." Paul turns his head and watches her undress before him. "I don't know what I'd do without him."

"Ssshh." She holds a finger to her lips. "Don't think about any of that." She quickly tugs off the rest of her clothes and slides under the sheets next to him. One of her hands rests on his hip and she presses her legs against his.

"You're very cuddly tonight." Paul smiles with an easy anticipation. He will have more good luck tonight.

"Yes, well ... I have a proposal I want to put to you." She smiles too and pulls an arm from under the covers so that her neck and shoulders are exposed and the top of her surgical scar is visible.

"A proposal? I thought we were already happily married."

"We are." She pushes this idea aside and fixes him in her eyes.

Something important is coming, he thinks. "All right. Speak."

"I want another baby." Her eyes do not waver and when he glances away she pulls his chin back toward her. "I really do. I want a girl. A Jessica."

He understands what this is about. If they're going to have another baby, it must be before her next surgery—and the life-long drug therapy that will follow. "So now's the time, is it?"

"Now's the time. This's the place. And you seem to be available." Her hand travels from his face to his belly.

"This seems to be a really well-developed proposal, is it not?" Paul decides to toy with this, tease her until she begs for him. "I mean within thirty seconds of climbing into bed—stark naked— you've got us toting around a new baby. A girl baby. A girl baby named Jessica. Do you have a box of diapers hidden in the basement? New colours picked out for the bedroom?"

"The colours will be eggplant and avocado. The curtains will be lacey sheers. And the daddy will change the diapers in the middle of every night."

"Oh he will, will he?"

"I think so." She caresses his hip and chest.

"Maybe, but I can't guarantee a girl."

"But you must." She touches him and settles her eyes on his face.

"All right." He winces as though the task ahead is daunting. "I'll try."

"You must try very hard." She holds him. "You see, I think you're well on your way already." She smiles. "Wow ... maybe we'll have twin girls."

"Maybe." He looks at her, their eyes open to one another, absorbing each other. It's their old way of beginning their mutual surrender. The way they love to love one another.

"Dad, are we really going to fly an airplane over those little islands?" Eliot points towards the Chain Islets. He is standing beside his father at the top of Anderson Hill Park. It is a clear day in late spring. In the distance the Chain Islets are lapped by a light surf and behind them Discovery Island sits undisturbed, lush and green.

"Next Saturday," Paul says and sits on the park bench. "I've got it all lined up with Captain Jack Riley."

"What if we crash?"

"We won't crash."

"How do you know that?"

"Jack Riley's airplane has a big engine," he says. "A very big Pratt and Whitney engine."

Eliot seems satisfied with this answer and turns his head toward the broom-filled meadow. "I'm going to look for sea lion bones, okay?"

"Okay. I'll just be sitting here." He watches Eliot make his way down the rocky path into the maze of yellow broom bushes. When the boy dips out of sight, he gazes across the water where a few months earlier the sea lions had challenged his approach in the kayak. Were they warning him, trying to drive him to safety? If he'd paddled to the left side of that rocky outcrop, he'd have been caught in a heavy tidal stream and dragged away from the other kayakers. Unable to fight against the currents, he would have been swept around Trial Island and into Shoal Bay. It would have been an easy ride, requiring only a few strokes to guide the boat around the hidden rocks. Twenty minutes later he could have beached his kayak at the foot of the sea wall, secured it to the railing and walked home to his wife and child. The tragedy that later befell Jenny Jensen and her parents and the murdered victims of Reg Jensen's insanity would have left him unscathed. It would have been one of those episodes in which you pitied the people you once knew, people entangled in a fate that brushed past you, while you went on with your life unscarred.

It was dumb, blind, outrageous luck. Hammer-and-nails. No wonder fortune has so many clichés attached to it, he thinks, and closes his eyes and feels the warmth of the sun on his skin. So many things had turned on the pivot of fortune.

And it was bad luck that Jerry and Bettina Sampson had lost Chester. Since the dog's limbs were amputated and left on the hood of the Volvo, no one had found the remains of his body. Paul joined them for drinks in their living room one evening and explained the little he knew of what had happened. Both Jerry and Bettina expressed their sympathies with an ease and grace that surprised him. Jerry offered him a third dose of brandy, but Paul refused on the grounds that he had to return to his job the following week and he wanted to keep his head clear.

About the same time a few good omens appeared, too. When he felt up to it, Paul telephoned Andy Betz and explained he was ready to return to his desk. Andy was very pleased. He'd picked up a copy of Marcus Aurelius' *Meditations* and although he hadn't read more than the first few pages, he believed "he might get to it when he needed it." He told Paul not to bring a lunch his first day back. "I imagine there might be some kind of welcome-back celebration over in the Empress Bengal Room," he said. "And neither of us would want to miss that."

In order to break the vicissitudes of luck—good and bad—Paul begins a nightly prayer ritual. It is the only means he can think of to re-establish his self-control: by applying his will to a single task. The impossibility of the task is unimportant; the essential thing is to achieve a focus of mind. Every night when he awakens next to Valerie, instead of wandering down to his office and settling into his La-z-boy, he lies on his back, presses one hand over his heart and extends the other next to his thigh, palm up. Each night, in the darkness lying beside his sleeping wife, he enters a communion with The Mind. When he settles there, in that realm which becomes more familiar to him with every visit, he waits until he can sense Jenny Jensen's temple gently pulsing beside him. He focusses on the image of her delicate face until he can feel a stream of energy flowing between them. He then directs his thoughts to the part of her that seems most distant and lost, holds his attention on her until he feels completely drained and slips into unconsciousness, too. The effect is so tangible that sometimes he awakens the next morning fully expecting a telephone call from Fran Jensen: *Our prayers have been answered. You must come to see Jenny right away.* And he knows he will go to her immediately, without hesitation or fear or remorse. When the call comes.

He never speaks of this to anyone. In a spiritually empty culture like our own, he muses, this kind of self-made communion is considered the threshold of madness. Even Valerie might suspect his sanity. Only the ancient and the dead would comprehend his ritual. And perhaps Fran Jensen. Amusing thought: his only ally left from their grand misadventure is the murderer's wife. She'd probably never read a book other than the Bible, never left Vancouver Island, never thought herself worthy of a marriage to anyone other than Reg Jensen. Yet she would understand his prayers. She'd pleaded for them.

After a moment, the light wind whispering over Anderson Hill settles into a hush that fills Paul's ears. He listens to the shush, confuses it with the ringing in his ears, and suspects that the steady buzz he hears is real. Maybe he has no hearing deficit after all. Perhaps he has simply tuned into a barely audible hum surrounding everyone at all times: the ubiquitous noise of the world brushing against the cosmic vacuum. The sound of the universe, spinning.

"I was thinking about the sea lions, Dad." Eliot has snuck up on him from behind the park bench, a clever approach he and his friends have practised over years of stalking one another on the hill.

"What's that?"

"What is it about sea lions that shows you they're smarter than humans?" His eyes widen slightly as he adds his favourite qualifying clause: "But it's something you can't see."

Paul lifts himself from the bench and steps a few paces along the path that leads back to their home. "Let me think. Their brains?"

"No. You can see their brains. Besides, their brains are supposed to be smaller than ours."

"You can't see their brains," he says to test Eliot's premise. "They're inside their skulls." He finds himself scanning the ground behind the bushes for any sign of Chester's brains; a bad habit he knows he must abandon.

"But you could see them if the skulls were opened up. It's supposed to be something nobody can see. Not ever." He wings a small stone over the hill into the corn-coloured broom.

"Nobody can ever see it? Yet it's supposed to show they're smarter than us. I give up." He's genuinely stumped.

"Sea lions never go to war with one another," Eliot says with satisfaction.

Paul smiles and settles his hands into his pockets. "I guess that makes them smarter, all right."

"Yeah. And if they don't do it, we can never see it."

The corollary, Paul says to himself, might be that if we can't see it, it never happened. He glances across the water to Discovery Island. There are no kayaks visible, no sea lions barking in the light breeze—nothing to suggest disturbance in the world. How sad to think that someday Eliot would learn that words and logical puzzles could not solve all the dilemmas that would confront him. But for now, it was lovely to believe such things. To believe that Chester was a few metres ahead—just out of sight—leading them down the trail.

He slips his arm over Eliot's shoulder and holds him back a little. "Let's take a long time to get home for lunch, okay? Let's have a *slow* race to see who can get there last."

"You mean the winner is the last one home?" Eliot asks, careful to clarify the ground rules.

"Exactly." Paul laughs under his breath. This will make for a good game.

They start along the path with half steps, and then quarter steps and soon they take no steps at all. They stand together, happy with this race in which the rules are backwards and the winner will be the loser. Happy to wait for one another and to let time pass with, or without them.

# AFTERWORD

ART OBLITERATES DEATH.

... Or so I believed for a while after I met Jack Wise. Because he lived the artist's life, Jack inspired such thoughts in people like me who were ready to accept that art has a special power in the world—that art could change things, perhaps even the cycle of life and death itself.

In 1981 he responded to an advertisement I'd placed in *Monday Magazine* for my sideline business venture, "The Last Word Professional Writing Service." I needed to earn some money and Jack needed someone to write his *curriculum vitae* to land a teaching job at David Thompson University in Nelson, BC.

My going rate for résumés at the time was fifty dollars, but when he showed me a few of the hundreds of paintings he'd completed over the previous decades I offered to trade my fee for some of his artwork. Whatever you think would be fair, I said to him. He smiled broadly and agreed. He liked this kind of barter: artistic goods for essential services.

We met three times, working together to construct his CV. On each occasion we discussed two of his favourite topics, art and Buddhism—and the special link he'd discovered between them. In my mind, I extrapolated what he said about yin and yang, to include life and death, with the hope that art could somehow modify the spin of it all. It was a very comforting idea.

Though I never encountered him again, I later heard that Jack got the teaching job which lasted a short while until David Thompson University was shut down by the government of the day. I still have two of his works: *Earth Goddess with Speech Scrolls* and *Rainbow Mandala*. I know I made the best of our bargain. I also know that was his intention.

Now, twenty-six years after I met Jack Wise, my belief about art obliterating death has softened, if not entirely melted away. Likewise, the portrait of Jack Wise in this novel is merely a shadow of the man himself. More precisely, it's an interpretation of a memory of an impression that I had of him some time ago. So dear reader, while his existence was real, and his art continues to inspire those of us who open our eyes to his work—as he appears in *The Good Lie*, he has been transformed into a character who guides our protagonist through the moral struggle of the narrative. Rather than change his name into an approximation (I've considered using "John Sage"), I prefer to keep his identity and presence alive as they were for me in 1981.

Realistic as that may seem, please bear in mind that this is a work of fiction, and—with the exception of Jack Wise—the names, characters, and incidents either are the product of the author's imagination or are used fictitiously; any resemblance to events or actual people, living or dead, is entirely coincidental.

— DFB, June, 2007

# ACKNOWLEDGEMENTS

I AM EXTREMELY GRATEFUL TO DR. DAVID ATTWELL FOR THE INFORMA-TION HE PROVIDED ABOUT SOME OF THE MEDICATIONS (AND THEIR SIDE EFFECTS) CURRENTLY USED TO TREAT HIGH BLOOD PRESSURE. I also wish to thank Aaron Gordon and April Katz for sharing their knowledge of personal injury law and the legal procedures related to an examination for discovery. Their insights exposed the complexities I had to address in order to tie the strands of my story together in a timely manner. While many—if not most—personal injury suits take three to five years to conclude, the case presented in this novel has been compressed in time to satisfy narrative efficiency. — DFB

For more information about
*The Good Lie* and D.F. Bailey
visit
www.thegoodlie.com.